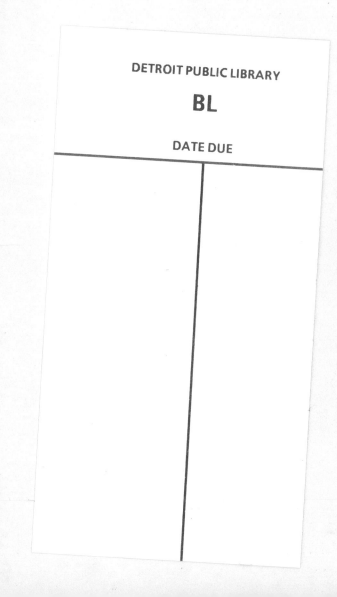

A Dream Journey

Also published by Horizon Press

ANOTHER WORLD
A WOMAN IN THE SKY

JAMES HANLEY

A Dream Journey

HORIZON PRESS
NEW YORK

C. 2

First published in the United States 1976
by Horizon Press

Copyright © 1976 by James Hanley

Library of Congress Catalog Card No. 76-17428

ISBN 0-8180-0623-4

In bomb punished WWII London, a failed
artist and his loyal wife wait on the
edge of existence, touching other's
lives only in sojourns in the air raid
shelter, until a small journey changes
all.

BL

Today

I

They both woke simultaneously when the light came, via a rationed sky, and the brick forest. The man immediately closed his eyes, but the woman stared up at the ceiling. They looked towards each other, the one from a single iron bedstead, the other from a settee. Neither spoke. And the light grew stronger. The man had drawn up his knees, and turned his face to the wall. The woman continued to stare upwards, penetratingly, as if she were intent on piercing the roof, and taking sight elsewhere than in this small, tight room. She lay stretched, inert, the hands listless on the bedclothes. They seemed more the hands of a man than of a woman, whereas those of the man were at once feminine, the fingers long and thin, though the thumbs seemed powerful. Unwrinkled, hairless. He did not stir. The woman's hands were rough, with short, thickened fingers, and carried an unhealthy discoloration. The man's hair was greying and thin, whereas that of the woman was abundant and had the look of foam. The man now turned on his back, glanced across at the woman, but said nothing, and she, after a few moments, got up and began to dress. Having done so she crossed to the window and looked out at the world. No change. She then left the room, and a few minutes later he heard the familiar kitchen sounds, and knew that she was doing the dutybound things. Once more he closed his eyes on the room in which he lay. He heard the door open, her feet across the uncarpeted floor, but his eyes remained closed.

"There," and the cup of tea was by his side.

He heard her sipping at her own, then sat up abruptly and picked up the cup. He too sipped. Their eyes met, but no words followed, an elected acceptance of the silence. The abrupt putting down of her cup broke it, and again she left the room, and he continued to sip his tea. He heard the noise on the landing, the creak of the stairs, so she would be four flights descending. Having finished his tea he put the cup on the floor, relaxed again, rested hands behind his head, and once more shut his eyes to the scene. Again a noise on the stairs, a kind of gentle thud on the landing, the door opening, shutting, steps across the room. Eyes closed, prone, stiff, he spoke.

"Post?"

"None."

"Newspaper," and she handed it to him, and he immediately flung this right across the room. She sat on the settee, her back to him, silence registered again, to be cut by knives. He heard her moving again, the door bang. The heavy tick of the clock hammered the air, and he opened his eyes and looked at it, and now knew it was eight o'clock. Another day. She heard him strike a match, give audible puffs at his cigarette, later got the strong whiff of tobacco in her nostrils. She sat on, stiff, unmoving.

"I wonder what will grow today?" she asked herself, and once more crossed to the window, looked out at the world. Same as yesterday, and the day before.

"I'm going out," so she at last spoke.

"Right."

"Shan't be long."

"Right. Where?"

"Where do you think?"

"Asking."

"Euston."

"Still a long way."

"I enjoy the bus ride," she said.

6

"Still a long way. Get anything round the corner."

"Anything you want?"

"Nothing."

A monosyllabic session, and their backs towards each other. Out of the corner of his eye he watched her rise, tall, and like himself slim, but the hair, unlike his own, seemed floating in air. She looked her age, but he did not look his fifty.

"Sure there's nothing?" she asked.

"Nothing."

The moment she left the room he got up and put on his dressing gown, then, like her, crossed to the window to look out and down at the world. He could hear her moving about in the kitchen, and he began an irritated pulling at the hem of the curtain. He turned, looked down the room, then went into the small room where he worked, stood hesitatingly in front of the easel and the covered canvas. She, hearing him go, returned to the bedroom. She wore a long black coat, a headsquare, and gloves. Sitting in front of the mirror she removed the headsquare, began studying her hair, leaned in and made a slow study of her features. Lazily, she tidied her hair, applied a little powder to her face, then readjusted the headsquare. When a scraping sound reached her ears she knew that another day had begun. She sat listening to this sound, and wondered about it, as she always did. The sound grew louder, and she drew even closer to the mirror, stared in at what stared out.

"That'll do," she thought, ran nervous fingers across her face. As she rose to collect her basket from the kitchen the routine calls of another day came to her.

"Will you be long, Lena?"

"Not long."

She gave a final glance into the mirror, a shopping day ritual, and he heard the loud bang of the door as she went to the kitchen. Going to Euston always made her remember last week, and the week before.

"Have you gone?"

7

"Not yet."

"Will you be seeing Gorley, expect you will . . ."

And she shouted back, "Then why ask?"

"Tell him I was pleased he liked the flowerpiece."

"I'll tell him."

"Good."

"Anything else?"

"No."

"Right," she said, the Euston butcher already clear in her mind, a tall, heavily built man, his blue apron fluttering in the breeze of his activities, fat, bloody Mr Gorley, sunk in his carcasses. She could hear his perpetual whistling, remembered his Friday morning smile. "Nice Mr Gorley," she thought, thinking of a small canvas hanging up in a Euston parlour. A butcher's weakness for colour that had ended up in free meat for a month. Thinking of this brought the first smile of the new day.

"How times have changed. Once, one could calculate, sell without a stutter. But not now."

"Have—you—gone?" he called from his room.

"Going."

"You won't be long?"

"Said I wouldn't."

He made no answer, and it did not matter, and as she passed the closed door of his room he caught the words from which he could never escape. "These bloody stairs," she said.

He heard her descend, counted the creaks on the stairs, and then forgot her. Picking up the small canvas he carried it to the window to catch the rationed light of the early morning. He did not hear her dragging steps, nor the loud closing of the front door. She had just *gone*, and he knew she would soon be back, as she always was, and he was glad of this. Always he listened for a key in the lock, echoing in the hall, and the long climb up four flights of stairs. And always he was at the door, ready, waiting, with the smile that pleased her, and she never forgot the slight sigh as he said, "Glad you're back," as though she had just returned

8

from a voyage round the world. He opened the door, went out, listened. She *had* gone. He then picked up the canvas, and returned to the bed-cum-sitting room, put it on the settee, went straight to the cupboard, took out the whisky bottle, swigged thirstily at this, and then sat back on the settee, the bottle swinging in his hand. He kept staring at the canvas in front of him. "Yes," he thought, and "yes," he said, loud into the silent room. He then bent over it, studying.

There were occasions when a sense of uncertainty angered him, frustrated him, and he cursed over his doubts, uncertain of the right answer, the right word, the resolving key.

"Sometimes," he said, taking yet another swig from the bottle, "sometimes I get a positive feeling that Lena hates me."

He put the bottle on the floor, and, unwashed, unshaved, he lay back. The broad forehead was encrusted with lines, a railway junction of flesh. A receding chin contrasted strongly with the positive, bold, upper features. The nose was long, and wide nostrils gave to it a negroid semblance. The eyes were almost hidden beneath the bushy brows, only one of which was now open, the left eye, and the sheer concentrated stare from this eye was in a sense assumptive, as though the right eye were fast asleep, or waywardly truant. He again picked up the canvas, bent over it, and the eye travelled up and down, and backwards and forwards, sensing, planning, wondering, exploring. The white dressing gown was wide open at the neck, beneath which one glimpsed a worn brown pullover, paint soddened, as were the blue denims he wore, and this was completed by paint-splashed brown carpet slippers. And in this moment there was nothing in the room save the flowers that he stared at, themselves lost in a fountain of light. If he had been asked the hour, or the day of the week, he would never have known, but he knew a moment when it was truly home.

"Yes," he said. "Good," he shouted, as though these flowers had suddenly begun to move, wave, suck in the light, the leaves so slightly stir. "Good." After a further swig at the whisky bottle he returned to his studio, and dropped it gently against the wall. He avoided looking at the covered up easel as he went to the window.

"The longer I stare through this bloody window, the less I seem to see."

With a loud "bugger it," he returned to the settee, and the bottle.

"God! Fancy me dreaming of Cruickshank after *all*—that—time," musing on it, and flowers and light a thousand miles away, *seeing* Cruickshank, feeling him *there*, and staring round this room as though it had reached some other dimension. "Good heavens," more surprised than alarmed with last night's vision. "And I never went to the funeral that day, no, sorry about that, horrible business," and again the bottle, and the hand shaky, clutching it with both hands, "but a lot of business was horrible around that time, yes indeed."

A human situation made futile by chance, thinking of it now, and momentarily lost, a cataclysmic night reaching everywhere and nowhere, and people wafted into oblivion when a floating mine came down.

"Cruickshank. Bastard never calls now, never even *writes*, we mightn't exist at all," taking another swig. "*Horrible*," the single word drawing him close, in this tight and tiny room, so he was absorbed in that time, and would not hear a door open or close, nor feet dragging up the stairs for the thousandth time. "I feel awful this morning, awful," and up came the bottle. There were also some bright, shining days, when he could remember them.

Lena made her way down, acutely conscious of the silence of the house. She was rarely seen leaving, rarely returning. It was like that at Chesil Place. She hurried across the hall, but paused for a moment at the front door, her fingers tentative at the knob, as though for some reason this might refuse to turn. Then she stepped into the street, deserted, and as silent as the house. Sometimes it seemed strange to her, remembering a time when nothing whatever was silent. "A time ago."

She listened to her own footsteps all the way to the bus stop, the same bus as last week, the same the next. A driver whom she knew by sight, a conductor who greeted her with a broad grin and a rumbustious "good morning". She found herself the only passenger awaiting it, and, unusual for that route, it actually arrived on time, pulling up with a harsh screeching of brakes.

"Morning."

"Good morning."

Climbing to the top deck, taking the same seat, right up front, glancing out at the world, then sat still, restless fingers kneading a basket, feeling for her purse. And sitting back, closing her eyes, beginning to dream, dreaming, and surfacing immediately the conductor cried, "Here we are, madam." Paying.

A top deck all to herself, liking it, feeling free, alone, really alone, after the closeness of another place. Her head swayed as the bus swayed, round this corner, round that.

"Nice," she said, "nice," after which the ritual, last Tuesday's, this, and the next to come. A pressure gone, time to think, to be herself. "I'll do the very same things," she told herself, "nice being ordinary."

Random thoughts shot up, echoed yesterday's situations, and now, locked in this bus, she was seeing again, and listening, hearing her own voice. "Try again, Clem," and remembering a muffled, and, she thought, a somewhat begrudging reply.

"Of *course* I will."

She had pressed, willing him to tread again the unsure, sometimes negative soil. And the way they had looked at each other, as if expecting an answer from air itself. She sat forward in her seat.

"What on earth did I say yesterday?"

At seven o'clock in the evening. She wondered about it, just as the bus turned a corner, swayed, made her grip the seat in front. Quite involuntarily she found herself talking to the empty top deck.

"Just one more row, nothing more," and a slow nodding of the head, and the bus tearing on. "Of course, it *was* at seven o'clock, just before supper. I recall looking at the clock that wanted winding." An end of the day quarrel, and silence, a blight unresolved. How did one resolve blight?

So she was miles from her seat, back in the room, looking at him stood in front of the gas fire, his shoulders slumped as though he were wilting under the moment, and what it held. She saw him crystal clear, staring at her, the mouth moving, as though searching for the words, trying to get them out. Getting them out, shyly, and barely heard.

"I'm sorry."

And I said, "So am I, Clem."

Acknowledging a wastage, a futile blow at the emptiness, and in her own throat words fighting to get out, wanting to rush at him, fling the words into his ear.

"A lifetime," I shouted.

"Christ," he said, and that was all.

The bus rolled on, and she was still its sole passenger. She listened to people boarding it, getting off, the lower deck must be popular this morning. "Awful," she thought, buried in the hour.

Going to him, putting her hands on his shoulders, and he glaring.

"Spent a whole bloody day on it, on *that*," and he picked up the canvas, and rushed from the room, flinging it to a wall, with the others, a pile. Slowly returning, suddenly holding her hand, trying to smile, and words grating at her, a dropped voice saying, "A whole day to get *where*?"

I understood. "Never mind," I replied.

"I *do* mind."

The stubbornness had irritated her, brought out the low scream.

"All right. I know, I know, I *know*."

Below, she could hear the conductor humming a tune, then fell to staring at her own fingers, feverishly clutching at the basket handle, the bus halting once again, and nobody getting off, on. They bound forward.

"Yes. And then we sat together on the settee, and said nothing, and the silence seemed right."

But she felt him here, *now*, too sudden, too close.

"Please," I said, and I was glad when he didn't answer me. Once, and I got a lightning sense of it, he looked at me, slowly raised his head until he was looking beyond me, and I exploded in his face.

"And don't tell me *again*," I shouted.

He sat very still, and there were no more words.

The brakes shrieked, and the bus pulled up violently, shot her back into the room again.

The things I did. Going to the gas fire, turning it off, and rushing from the room, and he called after me as I slammed the door, "Where are you rushing to, Lena?"

"Nowhere," which was a short voyage into the kitchen, and there I sat at the table, and thought of the whole day.

"Are you making tea, Lena?"

God! The shout made me jump, and I roared back at him. "*Yes.*"

"We've only just had tea."

"I'm making *more*," I called back, though I didn't, just got up and returned to the sitting room. And there he was, again stood in front of the unlighted fire, staring up and down the room, and the inevitable pose, a surge of yesterdays determining a physical gesture, and he remained there.

"Lena!"

When I looked up he was staring at the carpet strip.

"What?"

"I'm worried."

"What's new?"

"Been worried all day," he said, "I've never stopped thinking about it."

"About *what*? And please look at me when you're speaking, not at the damned carpet."

"The house," he said.

"What about the house?"

"Agent might yet sell. Everything's changed since those two old women passed out in Somerset, and the nephew catching it in the last raid didn't help much."

"Who told you that?"

"I heard. Could be only a rumour, but it doesn't stop me worrying."

"Don't keep staring at the *car*pet," I said. "Stare at *me*."

"The house is total, all there is, why shouldn't I worry?"

And then he actually looked at me.

"Leave tomorrow till it comes, Clem."

He joined me on the settee, seemed suddenly calmer, and looked at me quite shyly, saying, "Seems so long since I did anything worth while." And I thought, "Oh God! Not *that* ship again, the voyage is far too long."

Again the bus swayed, and again she held on to the seat. A man had come up, taken an opposite seat, but she did not notice him, still being in the room, back, *there*.

"Sometimes you astonish me, Lena," he said, and it was the first time he had used my name that day.

"Glad I do," I said. "Do you ever think of me voyaging up and down those bloody stairs?"

His hand holding my own made me regret saying it.

She sat up, glanced out of the window, and thought, "Nearly there. How I longed for an end to some of the stupid quarrels," and she remembered some that had been wordless.

"Here we are, lady," cried the conductor.

The warmth in the voice. And she stuttered her "thank you," got up, and once again felt for her purse, grabbed the basket, and made a swift descent of the stairs. Standing on the platform, back in the world, and close to one who knew the way he would go.

"Looks like rain, madam," the conductor said.

"Does rather," she replied, miles away, and she did not glance up at the sky.

"Bye."

"What a nice conductor," she thought, and gave him a

parting smile as the bus rolled away, lost itself in the distance.

She glanced up and down the long, dusty road, back in the world again, and thinking now of butcher and grocer. A tide breaking, watching people hurry by, coming out of shops, and sometimes very suddenly out of cars. No change in the pattern. And moving off, her step resolute, thinking of the things to be done. Periodically she halted, to stare into a shop window, and once she turned to look back, an expression of concern, as if she had got an echo of the scraping sound that broke the new day. And thought of the room where he worked, and the locked door, seeing him bent to his subject, wondering, hoping again.

"Ah well," followed by the softest sigh.

It was with a certain pleasure that she looked forward to seeing Mr Gorley, liking his bouncing "good morning," and the smile, the "Now, lady, and what can I do for you?"

The ordinariness of the moment, and the peace in it, and finally the smile as he saw her approaching, a waving of hands, and his teeth showing.

"Morning, Mr Gorley."

He fussed about her as though she were the biggest customer in the world.

"My husband's delighted you liked his little picture," she said.

His great bulk leaning over her, "Very pretty, madam, been thinking I might like another one, same size, make a pair, nice to look at on the wall when the sun's sulky."

So they both laughed, so she was far from the room, and the life in it. Gorley serving her, wearing out his smile, saying goodbye, waving. Watching her go, and Mrs Gorley peering through a slit in green curtains, then emerging, and saying, "That woman always looks tired to me, Alf, and she looks tired today."

"Been coming for years," he said.

"Still a long way to come for the bit of shopping she does."

"Used to live round here one time. Maybe she likes the bus ride. Funny, the things people like," he said.

"Still a long way," replied stubborn Mrs Gorley.

She vanished, and he returned to his carcasses. Lena went on her way.

The grocer's. Mason's. "That's changed," she thought, entering, and wondered if things would *ever* stop changing. Self-service, supermarket, help yourself, and at the other end someone just sat there waiting for your cash. She gathered up her few purchases and left, and finally pulled up at the same small café to which she had been coming for years. She took her usual seat by the window, and called for a small pot of tea.

"Cakes?"

"No, thank you."

Having served her, the proprietor promptly disappeared behind the spread pages of the *Sun*. Lena sipped her tea, glanced out at the world, then fell to studying the long narrow room in which she sat. She had been coming to this café for years, perhaps the one remaining relic of prewar days. It seemed incredible to her that in all the chaos of Euston Road, this single café should have withstood so many changes. Looking round she noticed that the table coverings, like the curtains, were of a French blue, and she was certain they were the same tables she had so often sat at down the years. She stared round the walls, a few changes, the pictures gone, but the usual big calendar hanging over the top table. No change in the ceiling, still discoloured. She took in its general shabbiness, which seemed only redeemed by the fact that the two long windows were clean. She glanced at the ample form on the chair at the end of the room. The proprietor was new, but then this place appeared to have a new owner at least twice a year. The sudden rustle of a newspaper disturbed her thoughts, and when she looked up she saw the tall, heavily built man coming in her direction, the newspaper dangling in his hand.

"Nice morning."

"Yes, isn't it?" Lena replied.

He bent over the table, and with some concern, said, "Making a fair mess of this road, madam."

"I did notice, but it's hardly changed, really. I used to live in this area. I never liked the Euston Road, ill-planned, too long, and it's noisy, dirty, in fact it's real shabby into the bargain," and concluded with a fleeting smile, "almost makes one feel we are back to normal again," and he quickly returned the smile.

She remembered so many excursions, up and down.

"But it's getting a real bash now, madam," the proprietor said, and looked towards the window. "Talk about the dust in the tea, madam. Yours all right?"

Lena nodded, renewed her sipping, and he returned to his post, and picked up yet another newspaper, and spread its pages, perhaps searching for *more* news, just in case.

She called down, "You've been altering things, Mr . . . ?"

"Sadham. Yes, madam, important thing today is to keep on one's toes."

"I suppose so," she replied, and he drowned in the world again.

She watched the traffic flow past, the people. "I mustn't forget," she told herself, remembering an occasion when, so lost in thought, she had gone out without paying, and took out her purse and put it on the table.

"The one day in the week when I really feel alone, quiet, peaceful. I do wish something nice would happen for Clem," but she knew this wish was purely routine, the barnacled phrase that popped out when you weren't thinking. She hoped the bus would be on time, even hoped for the same driver and conductor. "Strange," she thought, "Clem has never been in this café since the day I first met him here," and she saw him at the corner table, "must have been about twenty-five or six, and I was getting near forty. I remember his hair, abundant and fair. Looking back our meeting seems so casual now. We had some happy times, yes," fondling the memories in her mind. "We were the only two here. I never drop in here without remembering that, seems ages ago, really. He's changed in this past year, more touchy and irritable now, and as dependent as ever, leans on one. But he has worked, and he still does, and the patience . . . the *pat*—but I wish he'd go out, I really do. God! And the promises he makes, the *promises*."

A newspaper fell to the floor, a voice called, "More tea, madam?"

And she replied instantly, surprising herself, "Yes, please," and sat back, and waited. "I don't really want it," she told herself, "but it's nice sitting here, by myself," then, almost involuntarily cried out, covering her mouth at the same time, "and why not?"

"Thank you, Mr Sadham," she said, and he offered an even broader smile. He dispensed these, free, to good customers.

"Sure you want nothing with it, madam?"

"I'll try a cake."

"Certainly."

The doorbell rang, and a young man came in for cigarettes, and then vanished. "You're not very busy this morning," she called.

"It's up and down, madam, that's all. I sit and wait, good some days, some days no good at all, as though an interminable Lenten season had set in."

She watched the people go by, studied the faces, and thought, "What a delightful surprise if suddenly one came upon a known one."

"I'd better go," and she pushed away the plate with its uneaten cakes, finished her tea, and called to the proprietor. "Thank you."

"And thank you, madam," he said, and one more smile, adding, "you're quite a regular. You shop round here?"

"Always have."

She got up and moved to the door, he following, opening it. "Morning, madam."

"Good morning," Lena said, the bell rang, the door closed, and she went and stood on the kerb, it was better than being bumped into, pushed, but she caught the swirling wind and dust from a speedily passing bus.

"*What* a road."

She turned and walked towards the bus stop, and was quick to notice three big clocks, not one of which showed the same time. Time cut to shreds in the Euston Road, the world getting on. Progress. She found a small group of people already waiting for the bus, but stood a little apart from them. When it pulled up she was the last to board it, and was pleased when she found it had the same driver and conductor. A few people scattered about on the top deck, but her favourite seat was unoccupied, and she sat herself down.

"I seem to walk into that café almost automatically now," she thought. "Ah!" and again she examined the contents of basket and purse. All correct. She gripped hard at the basket handle until the knuckles whitened. In a split second, her spirits sank.

"No change at 19 Chesil Place. No. Clem would do the usual, open the door, wear the selfsame smile. Miles of days and smiles, almost a machine touch to the whole thing.

"Sometimes I've doubted that smile of his, almost too ready with it. And that sigh . . . that 'Glad you're back, Lena'," and laughed abruptly, to the surprise of the gentleman behind her, who sat forward, curiously.

She leaned forward in her seat, stared through the window, as she thought, "God! That awful day when his smile made me really angry, and I flung it at him, saying, 'What the *hell* are you smiling at?' He must have thought I'd taken leave of my senses. Yes, and I can hear him now, hear his, 'Because I'm always glad when you're back, Lena'.

"The expression on his face, the patent honesty of it, it quite touched me. Yes. I was sure then. It had root and meaning. Heavens. The very next moment, and how wilful it was, I said, 'I wonder what you'd do, Clem, if I didn't return, if one day, I *never* returned. Have you ever thought of that?'

19

"No. He hadn't, and I knew he hadn't. Poor Clem. Quite crestfallen. I can see him now, the way he walked to the window and just stood there, stiff and still, and when I called to him he didn't answer me, made no move. I went to him, took his hand and squeezed it. 'Only a joke, dear, that's all, just a joke. Wasn't meant.' He turned to look at me, quite bewilderedly, I thought."

"What made you say that, Lena?"

"*Forget* it."

"It's the first time you ever said anything like that to me," he said.

"*Sorry*. But I told you, dear. Forget it," my voice climbing into the air, "just a mood, Clem, a sudden feeling about things . . ."

"*What* things?"

"Doesn't mean a damned *thing*."

"*Sure?*"

"Yes," I said, "forget the bloody thing. Honest, Clem, honest," pressing it on him, cursing myself for ever having said it, and the look he gave me, the child coming out.

"I'm glad," he said, turned his back on me, got lost in the view from the window, almost as though I wasn't there at all.

"Don't take everything so seriously, Clem. I'll always come back."

"Does he cry 'glad' when the door opens?"

The bus pulled up at the corner of Chesil Road, but she did not get off, being quite lost in the occasion. The bus tore on. She closed her eyes, was lost again. The voice so sudden behind her made her jump.

"Sorry, madam," the conductor said, "but d'you know you've travelled all the way to the depot?"

"The depot?"

"That's right."

"Good Lord!" Lena said.

"That's where you are. Did you mean to?"

Staring about her, stammering it out, "Oh! Sorry. Never realized I'd gone past my stop. How silly of me . . ."

"Yes, madam," he said, and stood aside to let her pass. And the final stutter. "Thank you," Lena said.

He followed her down the stairs. "One going out in a few minutes. You'll soon be home."

"Must have been dreaming."

"Got everything, madam?" as though he were quite certain she had not.

"Yes, thanks."

"People do forget things."

"I must have dozed off," Lena said, and closed the incident with a forced laugh.

A wagging finger, followed by his "Ah" and "good morning".

His last observation was that it looked like rain, and she stood watching the bus disappear into the distance and again she did not glance up at the sky. She boarded another bus, took a seat near the platform.

"Fancy that," and then, as if alone, aloud into the lower deck. "Dreaming."

"Where to, madam?"

"Chesil Road."

"Ta."

A man sitting opposite gave Lena an odd look, and at that moment she heard a big clock striking noon. When the bus pulled up, she alighted, turned into Chesil Place. Home.

"Wonder how many thousand times I've walked up and down this street?" Slackening her pace she inspected the houses as she passed. She thought of changes, uncertainties, looked up at the once elegant houses, noted once more the broken windows and the peeling, blistered paint, the big gardens back and front, jungle, a house without a front door, and a pile of plaster at its entrance. "What a change," she thought, immediately pulled up, exclaiming, "Oh!" a returning pain, a sharp stab that made her at once lean heavily against some railings. The street empty save for a distantly approaching man, who, as he got nearer, increased his pace.

"Are you all right, madam?"

"Thank you, yes," she said, "I only live a few doors away," and he went on.

"Clem's probably right," she told herself, "the damned agent will get rid of the house. Yes, I am tired," and then went on, stopped at the front door.

"At last."

A short, stout woman came out as she entered.

"Morning, Mrs Grimpen."

"Morning. Not often I bump into you, dear. How is Mr Stevens?"

"Quite well."

"He doesn't go out much these days."

"Not much," and she passed the woman, and stood in the middle of the hall, the stout woman looking at her intently, remembering.

"Grimpy said he was here nearly a month before he realized there was anybody living at the top of the house. Queer people about these days."

She turned and opened the door, banged it, and went off, so shutting off the usual words with which Mrs Stevens began her climb to the top.

"These bloody stairs," she said.

"Hello, dear," she said, he opening the door, she pushing in. "I must sit down."

"You look all in, Lena," Clem said, "are you all right?" and relieved her of the basket, helped her off with her coat. "Come and sit down, dear."

He was all attention. "How's our patron?"

"I think he'll take another small flower piece," Lena said.

"Good, good," and he smiled, it filling the gap of a useless morning.

When he leaned close she realized he had been drinking, but made no mention of it.

"I'll get you a drink, dear, you look as if you could do with one."

Rather irritably she replied, "Don't *fuss*."

"There!" he said, handing her the glass, and he sat down beside her. "You seem to be lucky with our butcher."

"Seems mad about flowers," Lena said. "Said he'd like a twin for the parlour, and, to use his own words, 'nice to look at when the sun's sulky'."

"Good for Gorley," Clem said.

"Bumped into the caretaker's wife on my way in," she said.

"Is it important?"

She smiled then, "Not very," and noted his rather anxious look, dreaded him saying she looked tired. "I brought you a bottle, dear."

"Hurrah! Where?"

"In the basket. You wouldn't believe this, Clem, but I actually fell asleep on the bus coming back, travelled all the way to the damned depot."

"You *are* tired."

"I'm *not* . . . tired."

"Yes yes yes, all right."

"How did you get on?"

He clipped his words. "Oh, so so, on and off, and finally on. Only just left it."

"The whole place needs a good tidying up," Lena said.

"I was looking through some of the stuff in that room, Lena," he said.

"*That* room? Christ! I asked you to leave it alone, didn't I? Dead stuff, forget it." She leaned close, studied him, said quietly, "You are happy with what you're doing, dear?"

"I am."

"You wouldn't believe this, but I had tea in a café that perhaps you've forgotten long ago. I generally go in there when I've done the bit of shopping. Used to be called the Blue Bird, changed now, like everything else, it's called Trendy Spot now."

It did not seem to interest him, and it gave her a certain annoyance.

"You don't remember it?"

23

"So many cafés in that area, dear," Clem said.

She pressed her hand on his arm. "It's the same café where we first met years ago . . ."

"Good Lord!"

"I sat there a long time, just thinking about things. It was the thinking that tired me out, dear, fell asleep as soon as I boarded that bus. The conductor almost made it an occasion, poor man," and she smiled at him. "You're not worrying again, Clem, are you?"

"No."

"No need to shout, dear."

"Sorry."

"Good. Something will happen soon," Lena said. "I know it will, I *feel* it will," on which he embraced her, held her tight, saying into her ear, "You are good, Lena, by God you are, there's not many people would have stuck it out so long. It saddens me sometimes, even this morning. The years we've been together, the things we wanted to do, and didn't, the places we were going to go, and got nowhere . . ." so she knew at once that he had not had a good morning, meandering, doubting, always doubting.

"You must believe in yourself, dear," Lena said.

"I know."

He took her glass. "Another, dear?"

She noticed a weariness in his tone, and said abruptly, "Why not," and he went off to refill them.

"Empty, damn," and he picked up the basket and went off to the kitchen.

She lay back on the settee, reliving her morning, which he broke immediately, rushing back into the room with the bottle high in the air.

"He's cheering up," she thought.

They touched glasses, wished each other good health and fortune, he gave her a quick smile, and she cried, "Good luck, dear," and was pleased by the change in him, like a reminder of the old days.

"Clem?"

"What?"

"I wish sometimes you wouldn't say I look tired."

"An odd thought came into my head this morning, and I said to myself, 'I wish I could resurrect . . .' and another thing, last night I had a weird dream about my mother . . ."

"Don't . . ." she said.

He leaned closer to her, his voice dropped to tentative whisper, "It's true, I simply longed to get away from myself, wished I was someone else."

Her sudden laugh surprised him. "So long as you resurrect in a *pract*ical way, dear," and the look she gave him registered at once.

"You saw Whibley then?"

She threw it at him. "I did."

"Well?"

"One fifty and a few pence," Lena said.

"Oh hell."

"Oh hell," she replied.

"What does that mean?"

"What it says."

"He's probably done nothing all morning except sip from the bloody bottle," and when he cried, "Another, dear," she drew back, put the glass on the table. "Not for me, and you drink too much, dear."

He put away the bottle, picked up the glasses, and left the room.

"Said he was happy with what he was doing . . . I wonder . . . I've heard it all before," and the moment he entered the room she got up.

"Lunch," she said, but he caught her arm, said, "Come and look," and they went into the room where he worked. He flung the cloth from the easel, cried almost triumphantly, "There!"

She stood, motionless, stared at it.

"Go and *look*."

She looked, drew back, shaded her eyes, went forward again, drew further away.

"Well?"

"Something's not *there*," Lena said.

He exploded, "Not *there*. What the hell d'you mean by that, Lena?"

Turning away, she said slowly, "You are right, dear. I *am* tired. So why don't you just leave me *alone*, I want to be *quiet*," and then spelt it out for him. "*Qui*—et."

"I told you you looked done in when you came in, and you didn't like it one little bit."

She covered her face with one hand, "And I don't like it *now*."

"*What's* the matter, dear?"

She looked at him for so long he wondered if she would ever reply.

"I didn't feel too good going out this morning," Lena said.

"Why didn't you say, Lena? I'd have gone."

"You. You haven't left this bloody house in a whole *year*," and she pulled him down to the settee. "There are things I want to talk about, Clem."

"*Now?*"

Her sigh did not escape him, and she dragged her words. "No, not now, I said tomorrow . . ."

"What things?"

"*Tomorrow.*"

"Are you ill, dear?"

"And don't keep saying *that*."

"I'm *sorry*."

"I'm *tired*. Isn't that *enough*?"

"Then why not go and lie down," he said, "I'll see to things."

"What things?" she asked, and he hated her smile.

"Christ! You are angry about something today, and I wish to God I knew what it was."

"Don't," she said, and waved him away.

Nor could he hide the shock of the moment. This was something entirely new. She so rarely complained. "Suppose she is ill," he thought, desperately, "suppose . . . fell asleep on the bus, went past her stop. Extraordinary. Lena's so calm and collected, yes . . . poor Lena . . ." and the frantic call, "*Lena!*"

26

She closed her eyes, lay back.

"Shall I ask Beecham to come, dear?"

She slowly opened them, and he had to strain to catch her reply.

"Don't *fuss*. You've done your morning's work, and I've done mine, and now there's only the lunch," and as she rose he pushed her down again.

"I do understand," Clem said, and close to her ear, "I wouldn't know *what* to do without you, Lena, dear, and you *know* that."

She was pleased when he kissed her.

"Go and read your book," she said, "and remember, library day Friday."

"Nothing I can do?" he asked, the final appeal.

"Nothing."

He sat in the armchair, picked up the book. He heard the door close.

"Poor Lena," he muttered, and disappeared into the pages.

She sat at the table, making ready the meal, during which Lena talked to Lena. "A lifetime, really. I kept thinking about it all the morning, came to me so suddenly, this realization of what has passed us by. Poor Clem, he has tried, but so have *I*," and she stabbed the potato with the knife. "I gave it to him direct yesterday, quite shocked him, must have seemed like an ultimatum in his ears. Well, I've stood by him, believed in him. I've been sorry ever since I said that to him. For one awful moment I thought he was actually going to cry. I'd have hated that. There's a curious element of childishness in him that irritates me. And now he's changed, and that was sudden enough. Couldn't understand it."

She crossed to the stove, arranged the pans, lit the gas.

"Once, we actually used to read to each other. Not now. And I always looked forward to that, most often at night, and I was always glad he got so much out of books. Seemed to alter the whole rhythm of the day when he suddenly gave it up. Contagious, can't seem to settle to a book myself now," and lifted pan lids, and gave a final check on what was cooking. She went to the door, stood listening. Silence. He had got lost in the book. "And what was he thinking about, bent over his work this morning? Resurrecting?" She laughed. "Resurrecting indeed! Every morning when I wake, and look round that room, *our* room, *our* world, I find myself asking the same old question."

The sudden call made her jump.

"You all right, Lena?" he said, and she knew he was standing outside the door. "What's the matter?"

The warmth in his voice, the concern, touched her, and she called back, "Of course I'm all right, do go back to your book," and she heard him walk back to the sitting room. "He really does care for me," and the moment raised her spirit. "Just one of those bad days," she thought, as she turned down gas jets, took a final look into the pans, and went back to join him. He was still buried in the book, and did not even notice her come in, sit down.

"Clem!"

And she stiffened a little. *"Clem!"*

The book fell to the floor. "Yes, what is it?"

"I'm glad you got back to it," she said. "D'you remember the evenings I used to read to you, drawing kings and emperors and princes from the pages? Thank heavens for the Loeb library."

The book lay on his knee, he lazily turned its pages, as she continued. "And there was even a time when you used to read to me, dear. In bed at night. I loved that."

The smile made her feel that the morning was new again.

"You all right?"

She nodded, and he resumed his reading. Her eye made a slow exploration of the room, landed on two photographs that stood on the top of a small bureau, and she went across and picked them up, crossed to the window, and examined them, as though they were new only at this moment, never before seen. Strange. There they were, both of them. Clem smiled up at her from under a veritable bush of fair hair. She

28

looked at herself. "H'm!" and she put them down and returned to the settee. He closed the book with a loud snap, sat looking at her, and she watched the nervous fingers pulling at imaginary threads of the pullover. Perhaps he would say something, was making up his mind about it, perhaps determined to be resolute about things.

"D'you know what I was thinking about on that bus?"

"What?"

"The long time it's been since we went for a walk along the river. I thought of that little house we once had, I even remembered the colour of the curtains," and she stared hard at him, asking herself if he too, at this very moment, was trying to remember.

"It was just when the evenings were drawing in that I liked it best."

This sudden animation surprised him, and he joined her on the settee.

"How you *do* remember things, Lena," he said.

"It's good to remember," she said, and they held hands. "Let's have a drink, shall we?" and so induced in him his own animation, and it never failed on these occasions. "After which, there's one last practical thing," and he called from the cupboard, "What?" and she called back even louder, "Lunch."

He followed her into the kitchen and sat down.

"I'll have another look at that thing after lunch, Lena," he said.

Stood at the stove, she flung the reply over her shoulder.

"Yes, do that, Clem, after all I may be wrong. I often am," turning suddenly, smiling at him, "and who knows it better than you, dear."

"You may be *right*," he said.

"It just hit me, the once," Lena said, and came forward to serve him.

"Um! Smells good," he said.

"How grey Clem's gone," she thought, darting fugitive glances at him as he ate, "how worn."

He looked up, said, "I heard you this morning, dear."

"Heard me. Heard me what?"

"Cursing the stairs for the thousandth time. The bloody grind of it is not lost on me, dear. I count them, too, loud in my head."

"If you really like what you were working on this morning, then I'll climb them another thousand times. More?"

"Thanks."

"Clem?"

"Yes, dear?"

She stretched a hand across the table, said, "Take my hand, dear," and he took it. "Promise," she said.

"*Promise?*"

"That you will make up your mind, come out soon with me, I'd like that."

"All right."

"*Promise.*"

"I promise," he said, and held her hand. "Still looks terribly tired," he told himself, and not without dread, "and old, too. Old."

They resumed the lunch.

"Some new people in this house," she said.

"Oh yes?"

"Remember that MP that used to be here, I'm not sure he didn't come in just after the war. Extraordinary name he had . . ."

"Name?" and he was groping, on another tack, a momentary bewilderment.

"Grease. George Grease. He's gone. And there's two young men lower down. Bumped into one of them the other day. You'd have laughed, dear, *I* never saw anything like it, a tall, slim young man, he was wearing the brightest purple suit I've ever seen . . ."

"Oh yes?" and he was still trying to contact. "Who's he?"

"He had on a pink shirt, but it was tieless, and I can see him now as he said 'good morning', it was like a sharp cut from a razor blade, and all the way up the stairs he kept tossing his fair mane over very delicate shoulders . . ."

"You are becoming observant," he remarked, as he pushed away his plate.

"Coffee?"

"Please."

The moment he drew a hand across his forehead, she cried, "Damn! You've forgotten the pills, and I did *ask* you to *take* them, Clem."

"I just forgot," he said.

On which she rushed from the kitchen, to return with two tablets, and said aggressively, "Take them *now*."

"There's no need to blow your top about it," Clem said, and made a grimace.

"I worry about you."

"Don't."

"And don't you talk *rubbish*."

"Sorry."

"And for Christ's sake stop being sorry."

"I don't want any coffee," he said.

"Tea?"

He didn't appear to know, and she was now half way across the table.

"It's that damned room again, isn't it? Knew it the moment you opened the door to me, knew at once, we've had this before, and sometimes I think the whole thing's getting a bit stale. I know you inside out, dear. Why don't you get rid of the lot of it, *forget* it all? You've said so yourself countless times. There's always tomorrow, another try."

"Sometimes I wish I was as sensible as you," he said, sat back, took out a cigarette and lit it, sent smoke everywhere.

"That's enough."

She began clearing the table. "Rent day tomorrow."

"God, yes, the rent. What a damned nuisance, I mean, well, I mean since those old ladies passed out in the country. I hate you having to go all the way to Wells Street with it, you have enough to do, Lena. I'll make out the cheque."

He helped her to clear the remaining things from the table.

"I really am worried about the present position, Lena. This business of never knowing when, might be out in the street any old time. So much easier when Miss Benson was alive and Mr Grimpen downstairs came every week and collected the rents, and sent it direct to Somerset."

"Lots of things were easy yesterday," Lena said. "But today is to*day*, and tomorrow's to*morrow*, and the world's way up on its toes, and you daren't forget one single thing. I shan't ask you if you'd like to take it along to Wells Street yourself. Outing might do you good, you *never* go out."

"Not *that* again, please, Lena."

"Then I'll shut up," Lena said, and left the kitchen, on which he sat down again, bit into his cigarette.

"Just another day, no more. The way we get on each other's nerves lately, yes, even *now*, after all that time. Perhaps I should, really. Damn it, no, I hate going anywhere these days, anywhere. God! I hate everything I touch, and one time I was so *certain*, perhaps I'm as tired as she is, perhaps . . ."

The door burst open, and Lena said, "Just come back for my coffee."

"Come here, Lena," motioning her to his chair, and she came with a pronounced "Well?"

"Shall we both go and have another look at it?" he asked.

"*Well?*" he said, a mood vanishing, smiling again, "together," he said.

"If you like."

"Let's," and she followed him into the workroom.

"I must tidy up this place, Clem."

He stood at the easel, waited for her.

"Well?"

She took one look at the canvas, turned to him, "You are right," she said, "but you always are."

"Good."

"I'm going to lie down now," she said, and left him stood at the easel, and at the door she turned, and there he was, as usual, his nose almost buried in the canvas. "He does try," she told herself, and closed the door.

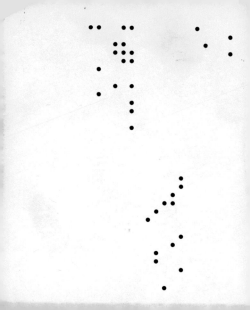

In the sitting-cum-bedroom she sat down at the bureau, opened and shut drawers, fiddled with the array of papers in front of her, then closed the top, and opened the bottom drawer. From this she took a large foolscap ledger, and carried it to the settee. Making herself comfortable, she opened the ledger, and began to read.

January 15th. Got up at half past seven, woke him, and gave him what he always waits for. The usual looks, the same words. After the morning tea I left him, and went to the kitchen to arrange his breakfast. Went and got ready for the leap into Euston. That's what it is, a leap to get out, *away*, from him, the room, the whole bloody house. What the hell is he working on? What will he do with it? When will it finish? I sit here listening to his movements in the next room, scraping things, dropping things, opening a window, shutting it, everything registers, and I don't know when I'll hear the door open, and him come out. God! I have an absolute dread of this ritual, and I wonder how he's got on, how certain he is, is he happy with it, yes, and yes and yes, those damned words again, "end", "finish", "satisfied", "happy". Only once have I asked him about progress, about how he *feels* about what's growing on that canvas, and he said nothing, not one single word. Sat on the bed a whole hour, a silence between us, perhaps we were both dreading to speak, and I would never say "how's it going, dear?" No, never again. He looks at me, and the very expression on his face tells me that he expects me to ask the dread question all over again. If only he'd break out, say it, say something, *any*thing, he's happy with it or he *isn't*, he hates it, and will kick it to pieces. I've never seen such a change in a person since he lost that big canvas in the raid, never. I never want to see it again, that awful look when I told him, had to. The bloody word "gone" must have rung like a deep bell inside him, and I can see the whole damned thing all over again, he sort of fell back on that bench, in the bloody stinking shelter. And he'd come back

33

from doing such a marvellous thing, and there he was, inert, hollow-eyed, just staring up at the roof of the cellar. Five long minutes it was, and I remember every second of it. Yes, that is it, the root and the cause, the break and the division. Those *moments*. I'll never understand how I managed at last to get the words out, and it was like there was nothing important any more, to him, to me, but at last I said them. "Come along, dear." He came, and I remember a little finger stealing almost shyly into my hand. And we went up together. It was like climbing Everest.

She shut the book, suddenly opened it again, bent low to the pages, turning them backwards and forwards. A name shot up, held, and she covered this page with her outspread fingers, as though to shut it from sight, yet at the same time muttering it. It danced beneath her fingers, it shot up again. She began to read, and suddenly realized that the page carried no date.

"Cruickshank. That bastard. Never forgive him, never. Stripped Clem to the bone that day, how many years ago is that? Does it matter, yes, by God it does, still does, and he's never forgotten the incident. How he hated those nudes. 'Ugly,' he cried, 'ugly,' the stupid man, as if the whole world was collapsing under his very conventional feet. *Why?* Because Clem has spread right across five canvases a whole day in an old woman's life. Never seen that man since. Vanished."

She shut the book, threw it to the floor, lay back, thinking, "Still there, and I'll bet that's what he was looking at this morning, yes, the minute I banged the street door he must have gone in, sat amongst the bones. He'll never sell them, ever." So thinking of them she was back in the St Pancras time, and the nudes clear in front of her.

Extraordinary, he was actually out with me, walking down a dreary road behind the station. Seems ages ago. The way we came upon her, sudden, like a surprise, an old woman leaning to the wall, bent under the biggest basket I've ever seen, a basket loaded, that bent low her shoulders. I remember the feeling of great strain in the hand that held it, and stared at her, she back to us, as she held close to this wall, perhaps resting. The world rushing by, not noticing. Clem stopped dead the moment he saw her, turned to me, said, "Look! Look at *that*, Lena," and I did.

Tallish, heavily built, and ripe in her sixties. I remember the short red coat she was wearing, and the hat that seemed too young for her. And as we stood watching she let the basket fall to the ground, and we heard her exclaim, "Oh!" At *last*. Clem rushed across to her, asked her if she was all right, and it was only then that she turned to face us. Such a face. Engraved with its age, and the extreme of exhaustion, the quite unexpected smile, a threadlike voice saying, "Yes, thank you." Clem began pulling on my arm, whispering, "Marvellous, it's marvellous, I *must*" . . . and he did, and out came the notebook, and he stood there rapidly sketching.

"You can't, dear," I said, and his reply was like a shot in my ear.

"I *can*."

I just stood there, transfixed, since a small crowd had begun to gather, and I had a sudden vision of a policeman turning up to complete the group. Clem was quite oblivious to it all. He closed the book, put it back in his pocket, went across to the old woman, and the group stood there, heard him say, "Let me help you, madam," on which he picked up the heavy basket. "Which way?" he asked, and the woman staring at him, a little bewildered by this attention, the group gradually breaking up, going their ways. I called, "Clem!"

"Come *here*, Lena," he shouted back.

I spoke for the first time to the old woman. "Good morning," but she did not answer me. I heard Clem say, "I'll see you home, madam, this is far too heavy for you."

"It's all right," she said, and made to take the basket from him. "I can manage."

"Where do you live?"

And then she rooted to the ground, lowered her eyes, bewildered at this sudden confrontation by a complete stranger, at whom she now looked with an expression pregnant with suspicion. Clem was both calm and casual.

"Let me carry it for you, madam, you're exhausted."

"I'm not exhausted, and you leave me *alone*."

He dropped the basket, we watched her pick it up, the sheer weight of it forced down her shoulders, so that her head was almost resting on her breast. I whispered in Clem's ear, "This is ridiculous, just let her go, she's a beast of burden that just doesn't know."

We watched her go, though not before she had dropped a curt "thank you", in Clem's direction. A beast of burden on a bright morning, poor old thing, see her now, dragging along, pushed and shoved about by those whom the world was telling to hurry up, isolated, pulling her way home, *pushed* along. I don't know how long we stood there, but at last we ourselves moved off, Clem's arm in my own, so that I was immediately aware of an inner excitement, and then he stopped dead. "Look at her," he said, and I did, and she was almost at the end of this road. "I wish," he said, "I . . . she's marvellous, and the exhaustion, total, never seen anything like that before," and he pulled out the notebook, opened it and held it in front of my face. "Wish she'd let me, wonder if she comes into this road every day, like to be behind her. Even better if she sat, I'd just *love* to get that down, a whole language of exhaustion there, if . . . if", stuttering it, suddenly halting in his step, moving on again, "Don't you *see*?" he said.

"Sit?"

"Love it."

"You had better forget it, dear," I said, and turned him slowly round, saying, "Let's get back, shall we?"

He looked at me, said, "You *amaze* me, can't you *see*?"

"What are you telling me, Clem?"

"I'm telling you that I'm fascinated, and I'd like her to sit for me."

"No!"

"Yes."

"Forget it," I said.

"I shan't," and it was emphatic enough, final enough. The whole occasion had drowned him, and when he added that he would come back tomorrow, watch for her, follow her, I knew that one single old woman with a heavy basket had made his morning.

"I think she was rather angry with you, Clem," I said.

"Bit of a shock, bewildered," he said, "and I think the people that grouped about us simply scared her stiff. I'm sure that if I'd been alone, I would have managed it. Damn the people," and the look he gave me then, I thought he might damn me, too.

"Please let's go home, dear."

He took out the notebook again, held it in the air, patted it, gave me a smile, which perhaps was the right seal for a very unusual morning.

She sat up, listened. There was no sound from the other room. "I shan't disturb him," and she got up, picked up the ledger and went back to the bureau, opened the bottom drawer, and buried the ledger under a mass of papers, sketches, discarded notes, old photographs, invitations and cancellations, a chaos of yesterday's ghosts. The closing of the heavy drawer she found something of an effort, and dragging to her feet was reminded of a duty to herself. She must go and see Dr Beecham this week. Going to the window, she opened it still wider, and stood there listening to London's distant roar. She knew the exact moment when the light would go. And she was now conscious of a silence in the flat, and went to the door, stood listening, knowing the ritual once the light had gone. Something flung down in *that* room, a banging door, and then she'd hear his shuffling steps, his coming in, and going directly to his chair, not looking at her, after which it was cigarette after cigarette, and the monotonous indulgence of smoking. It was a moment when nothing whatever appeared to link them, as though he carried back from his room the very aura and feel of it. So back to the window, and she stood there and watched the lights coming on over the city. An end to the day.

"He won't take that rent to Wells Street tomorrow," she told herself. No, she would take it, she always did, and again reminded herself that Dr Beecham must be visited, thinking of a crude reminder half way down Chesil Place this morning. She supposed the evening would be as other evenings, he buried in a book, she listening to music on the radio.

"I'm far more worried about the house position than he is." And then he came in, and as was expected immediately curled up in the armchair, to begin the cigarette orgy. He hadn't even noticed her at the window, her back to him, and only her slight cough reminded him that she was there. She talked to him over her shoulder.

"Through now?"

"Yes," he said, and made to rise, but immediately sat down again. "Why stand there, dear?"

"I like watching the lights coming up."

"You told me you were going to lie down, Lena, I *asked* you to."

"I did, and I read for a while, and then I went to the bureau to look for something, and only seemed to notice how horribly untidy it is, but the whole flat is. I'll have to do something about it," and she turned and looked at him, but he had no comment to make about that.

"The rubbish we seem to collect," Lena said.

"Rubbish?"

"*Rubbish.*"

"Come and sit down," he said, and she joined him on the settee, to which he suddenly transferred himself. "Cigarette?"

"Might as well. Thanks."

"Drink?"

"If you like," and she had expected this, his eye fixed on the cupboard.

"Course I'd like," he said.

The bottle came out, the glasses, but no salute and no wish came out of them. She noted one shaky hand, and the cigarette burning away in the other.

"I always enjoy this part of the day, Lena, I really do."

"I'm glad, dear."

There was an anxious note in his voice when he asked her if she really was intent on seeing Beecham.

"Of course. Tomorrow," she said, adding after a long pause, "and I suppose I might as well take the rent to the agents, since I know you won't."

"I'll make out the cheque," he said. "By the way, I've been wondering if the Ollensen people might be interested in what I'm on at the moment." He helped himself to another whisky, but she waved away his offer of another.

"What about Ollensen's?" she said.

"Told you."

Her lips parted, but only air came out, and she looked at him, incredulously, which prompted his abrupt "Yes?"

"Dead. You're behind the times."

"*Dead?*"

"Closed down a year ago, and they're not the only ones, bit of a famine in patrons at the moment. You *are* behind the times, dear."

"Honest?"

"Don't you read the papers that we buy?"

"Slipped up on that," he said.

"But I told you myself a while ago. Sometimes I think you don't listen to a word I say."

"Oh hell!" and "damn" he said, as he held up the bottle to the light, and found it empty.

"The other one will be in your room," she said, the gentle reminder.

"I often think of that exhibition at Ollensen's," he said.

And she snapped back, "And nothing would ever make me forget it. Your lucky day, ever since which one has had to *count* them."

"The people one knew then, but not now, vanished, the lot of them."

He rushed out of the room to get the other bottle.

"The old complaint," she thought, and it disgusted her, and she knew he knew, and then he came in with the bottle. "*No*," she said, to the proffered drink. "Enough's enough."

"As you wish," and he filled his own glass, went back to his chair, sat back, spread legs, seemed thoroughly relaxed, sipped enjoyably at his whisky.

She got up, saying, "Ollensen's wasn't the only trout in the stream," took the bottle from him, and returned it to the cupboard.

"As you wish," he said, and out came another cigarette.

"That's your trouble, dear, and it costs money," and she stood over him, emphasized the fact.

"You're quite right, I am weak."

"What contacts you lost remains your own damned fault, and I always thought you bloody cool with the MOI people Others couldn't afford to be."

"I didn't believe in it."

"And *you're* telling *me*," Lena replied, and the sarcasm was not lost on him.

"Christ! You have changed, Lena, I can think of a time when you were behind me."

"Changed. *Me?* For God's sake, it's you that's changed, Clem. I've never changed, never, always been behind you, *always*, though curiously enough this very morning I found myself wishing I *had*."

"*Lena!*"

"You sound shocked, dear," she said.

She was struck by his changed expression, even his tone of voice, in which she sensed a sudden dread.

"You wouldn't walk out on me, Lena, would you, *would* you?"

"I told you. I wouldn't walk out on anybody, so you're lucky, and please don't look at me like that when I'm talking to you."

She avoided his hand, seemed to be seeing him now as if for the first time. The new position, the way he looked up at her, a helplessness there.

"A weakness I despise," she told herself, drew away from him. "And do think about what I said, Clem."

He followed her across the room, but she was fully in motion, an aimless pacing of the room, up and down, and he behind her.

"I know now," he said.

"What do you know?"

"Felt it all morning, and I haven't stopped thinking about it. The way you spoke passing my door, the way you tore down those stairs, and that damned front door, it sounded like a gunshot," and he grabbed her arm. "Lena! Are you beginning to hate me?"

She swung round on him. "Don't be so bloody silly," she said.

"I *mean* it."

"Don't, and whatever you may think to the contrary, you're wrong. And we mustn't keep following each other around like a couple of lunatics. Do come and sit down. I'll make the supper shortly."

They sat down.

"And there's nothing very new about this, is there?" she said, and watched him light his ninth cigarette. "Had it over and over again, can't we . . ." and her hand on his knee. "Smile, dear."

He smiled. "If you asked me how I felt *now*, I couldn't explain it."

"Don't."

But he did, and was determined to say it. "I forget nothing. The things I wanted to do, and can't, *can't* . . ."

"You're working again, that's all that counts, and I'm happy about it. It's just a bad patch you're going through. You're beginning to distrust yourself. *Don't*. It's fatal."

"A big patch . . . and you never tell me how *you* feel," he said.

"Me? I'm simply aching to sink into a little normality, and you'd never know how much I enjoy those bus rides into Euston. Makes my day, and even talking to oneself makes a nice change."

"D'you know what I'd like?"

"What?"

"Somebody to surprise us by calling, somebody actually saying 'hello'."

She burst out laughing, saying, "It may happen, never know your luck. I'll make the supper," and she left him sitting there, and he shouted after her, "Yes, good."

She turned at the door, wagged a finger. "And leave that bloody cupboard alone, too. All right?"

He nodded gravely and she closed the door on him. But immediately he followed her out, stood in the kitchen doorway, watched her fuss at the stove.

"Is it to be tea or coffee, dear?" she asked.

"Whatever you like," he replied, and sensed a certain indifference in her very casualness. He leaned heavily against the door. She tossed potatoes in a pan.

"Extraordinary," he said, "I mean the way Cruickshank turned up. I even wondered whether a contact might be worth while."

She had crossed to the table, a pile of cutlery in her hand, and this now crashed to the floor.

"What's the matter?" and he was on his knees, gathering it up.

"After what happened?" And when he got to his feet, "You'd *crawl*?"

She gripped his arms, glared at him, spelt it out. "He told me that those studies of the old woman with the baskets were positively ugly."

"He said *that*?"

She waved him away, saying, "I'm like the elephant," and resumed laying the table. When she looked up he had gone. "Silly man."

Returning to the stove she drowned the incident in a clatter of pans.

"There are better things to dream about than that," she thought, and went to the door, called him.

"Ready."

"In a minute," he called back, and then she knew where he was.

He was standing at the easel, looking at monstrous clouds tearing across a canvas six foot by eight, a towering mountain, a sea sick green. "*Bugger* it."

Staring at the lie. "Christ. Cover it up. Leave it alone."

The shout made him jump, reached him as threat.

"Supper. *Supper!*"

"*Coming.*"

"It's no bloody good, *I'm* not . . ."

"Are you *coming*?"

And the frantic shout. "Said I was, didn't I?"

Covering it up, angry, undecided, wanting to look once more, turning his back on it, flinging himself out of the room, into the kitchen, slumping in the chair, and the usual, "Sorry."

Being served, and she silent, sat opposite, avoiding each other's glances, she concentrating on the changeless supper, soup, bread.

The words crept silently into the air. "Some Mozart on the radio, Lena." There was no reply, and he added, "I thought I'd get Burton on Friday."

She looked up. "Burton, Friday", what's he talking about?

"Must I *kneel* again?" he asked.

"Do get on with your supper, dear," she replied, and he heard the vicious scrape of her spoon in the bowl. "Don't you *like* it?"

"Of course."

"Then for God's sake, eat it."

2

"Tea or coffee?"

"Tea, please."

Pouring it, handing it to him, she exclaimed in a quiet, gentle voice, "You look as though you were on your way to confession, dear," but there was no answer, and no smile, and he said nothing, because there was nothing to say. He sipped leisurely at his tea, always avoiding her glance, though he noticed her own stiffened fingers gripping the cup so close to her lips, but she did not drink, but sat there looking at him, and eventually he lowered his head, made one or two noisy sups, and put the cup down, to be followed by the eternal cigarette. She knew the moment he was going to speak, and said very abruptly, "Don't, Clem," and got up and left the kitchen. He sat on, heard an opening door. "I never say the right thing, never. What the hell's wrong with me today?"

She, stretched out on the settee, heard him go out, and he never left a room without violently banging the door after him, heard him opening another door, this closing, and a key turning in the lock. Lying there, she contained the fury that she felt. And a name rankled in her mind, congealed there.

"I wish I could vanish as simply as that," she thought, sensed and saw him now, in the locked room, probably sat on the floor, staring it out, all of it. Waiting for an answer, "Always waiting for an answer," Lena said, closed her eyes, began talking to herself.

"Weeks and weeks of it. Watching him come in, crossing the room, sitting in his chair, not a word spoken, and I daren't ask. I'm speechless myself, not daring to. It'll never be finished, whatever the hell it is, it'll never be finished. Perhaps we're in for another session, another saga. Sometimes I've watched him at work, knowing he hated every minute of it. And thinking of the right words, a way round, a way *in*. Poor Clem.

"Close your eyes, Lena," she said aloud in the silent room, "*close* them," and she did, covered her face. "All those days, those *years*, and in spite of everything we're still together, locked together, terribly close, we *know*, understood from the very beginning. Liking each other in a moment, loving each other. Liking what he did, what he wants to do, rising with him, falling with him, and waiting with him. God! The waiting that's been stretched and stretched, yes, and the nice moments that sometimes halted it. And here I am, still here, *with* him, yes and I regret nothing, nothing. And the warmth of him just *being* there, sharing everything, all through that bloody war. He's never been the same since he lost that painting. Just by looking at it, living with it, one knew it was ultimate with him, nothing else mattered at that time, only that one thing, dreamed about, laboured over, believed in. Gone in a flash, yes, and I've never stopped telling myself it was that, that *one* work."

Her hands fell to her lap, and she felt the shock of the light against her eyelids. "How long will he be there? I can't settle to anything until he comes out."

She got up and went to the cupboard and opened it, inspected what she called his "sustenance chamber", counted the bottles, more empty than full, an anchor of sorts which she hoped would only be temporary. "I'm wearied of saying to him, 'That's enough, dear,' I'm kidding myself, it'll never be enough, perhaps I should let him drown in it, perhaps I . . ." and closed the cupboard. Noticing the time she went and switched on the radio, but a sudden cascade of atmospherics made her switch off again. She picked it up, put it on the floor by the settee, and settled herself down. "Fifteen minutes," she thought, and waited for Mozart. A sudden loud movement from his room did not arouse any curiosity. She lay back, shielding her eyes from the light, listened to the tick of the clock. Switching on again a man cried in a loud voice, "Hello there!" And again she switched it off. When an announcer said, "The Prague," she got up and switched the light off. The sudden darkness spelt a kind of security, an immediate oasis. She relaxed, stretched out, listened. But not for long. An interloper was suddenly there, before she realized it.

"Cruickshank," she thought, "he'd actually go and see that man again. Crawling," Lena thought, and it brought him nearer still. He was standing beside her, smiling, talking. She saw him real, stood at the bottom of a small gallery, stuffy and overheated, locked away between two tight little streets. And at the other end of this room, Clem, alone, looking up, hands in pockets, a few people passing by. Once only he turned to look down the room, saw Lena there, saw Cruickshank standing close. A dapper little man, goatee beard, fitted beautifully into a shining blue suit, and she remembered that, and the horrible suede shoes he was wearing.

"Two years, isn't it?" he asked.

"About that," Lena said, turning away from him, watching Clem again, hoping he would turn, catch her eye, come up, sever an unwanted meeting.

"How old is he?"

"Two years older than when you last met," I said, "and he was good even then," absorbing his long, questioning look for which she had the answer direct. And she refused the proffered cigarette, heard the slick click of the case, watched him put it back in his pocket.

"I'm forty," Lena said.

"*Indeed*! You don't look it, if I may say so, Mrs Stevens."

"We were never married," she said.

"Ah! Sorry, my dear, may I call you Lena?"

"Do," and she fixed him with a tense look. "You didn't like what you saw, Mr Cruickshank, I noticed it as I came in . . ."

"But I do," he said, and promptly took her arm, "there,

46

over there, that small one," pointing, hurrying on, dragging her after him, "there!"

"Do you, *really*?" exclaimed Lena, at once disarmed.

"Those eyes have followed me round the room ever since I came in. I hope it's successful."

"Thank you."

"Mr Stevens . . ." stuttering, "Clement, isn't it, he seems a rather shy man to me. And he's not London, either," and she promptly shook her head.

"Provinces?"

"If Warwickshire's a province, yes."

"But you're London," he said, and gave her an expansive smile.

"Kent, but that's a very long way away now. I'm Euston, and getting used to it."

"Yes, I do like it," Cruickshank said, and there seemed such sincerity behind the utterance she had an instant hope that he might buy it.

"And the model?"

"Bermondsey girl," Lena said, "hasn't an aitch in her head, poor child."

His smile was velvet, as he said quietly, "You sound a bit of a snob to me, *Mrs* Stevens."

Lena gave a sudden laugh, saying, "It's one way of hunting for my name, Mr Cruickshank, but it's strictly copyright. I think I can see Clem signalling down there."

"Do come and have a drink, Lena," Cruickshank said, carefully manoeuvring her through a plunging, talkative group. "What'll it be?"

"I like whisky myself."

"Good," and he stood on his toes, pressed forward, caught an eye, ordered and got the drinks, then again guided her across the room to the only two empty chairs stood against a wholly bare wall. They sat down.

"Well, here's how and everything, and the best of luck," and he raised his glass, looked up at her, and smiled. After which he mused a little, watching her finger running round the glass, watching her first sip, then drink solid.

47

"Looks more than forty," he thought, "quite plain into the bargain, but fine eyes, yes," and turning to her, and another free smile.

"Quite a group here now," he said, indulged in pointing movements which she ignored, her eyes darting to one side of the room, and then the other. Where was Clem?

And then she saw him standing at the table, talking to the receptionist, nervously fingering catalogues, picking them up, dropping them down, and finally smiling and going away, moving slowly towards the drinks.

"Clem!" and at once she deserted Cruickshank, who now began to relax, and sat back, and indulged in the usual ritual of watching for *faces*.

"There you are," Clem said, took her arm, and they rushed across to the counter. "You've got one," he said.

"I'd like another, dear," she replied, shyly, turned, saw Cruickshank engaged in excited conversation with an elderly, very colourfully dressed lady in her sixties. She wondered who she might be.

"Let's get clear of this lot, Lena," Clem said, and pulled her into a vacant corner.

She smiled up at him. "Happy, Clem?"

His returning smile was all the answer she required.

"That Cruickshank man likes the *Shadows*," she said, nervous fingers clutching at his free arm. "I was glad. I was talking to him."

"I noticed that."

"Wouldn't it be marvellous if it sold," Lena said, and then drowned in immediate shock and bewilderment when he replied, incisively, "Not selling, dear."

"*Why!*"

"Don't want to," Clem said.

"The others might not, dear," her voice at once aggressive, a hurt still there. "Oh, but I am happy, Clem, really I am. It's wonderful, it is really."

He leaned in, kissed her, saying, "*That* is better than any sale, dear."

She squeezed his arm as he said, "At last, a place to sit

down, Come on." And they were islanded. Nobody had spoken to him, just the receptionist. He whispered in Lena's ear, "Might as well not have been here at all. Still it's there, it's done, I've come, I've seen it. I'll just cross my fingers," and at that moment Cruickshank passed by with the elegant lady.

"What was *he* talking about?"

"He was a bit curious, and I was a good clam," she said, and they both laughed. "Asked where you came from, how old you were, asked if *Mrs* Stevens was enjoying the show. I gave him the lot, surprised him, he lives in Kensington."

"How nice."

"Paints miniatures and collects matchboxes."

"Really?"

"Really. Shall we have a look see ourselves, dear."

"When it's quieter," Clem said, staring around the room.

A small group chatting by the entrance, a very elderly man sitting at the top of the room, two giggling girls studying a landscape.

"Have another, Lena, you deserve it."

"Do I? Of course I do. Yes, *please*."

Watching him go, thinking of his so direct "No", remembering the Cruickshank curiosity. She studied his slow return with two glasses, and was immediately happy again, and she was glad. "He deserves it," she thought, "yes, by God, he does."

"Comfy?"

"Fine," she looked longingly at him. "I am glad, Clem, I am, I *am*," and a fierce whisper in his ear, all in a breath, "I'd like to shout hurrah at the top of my voice."

"Shout, Lena," Clem said, but she only laughed, spilt a little whisky on her coat, and he fussily wiped it, all the time smiling, and knew it was *their* day.

The room was yet dark, and Mozart had vanished beyond his own frontier, but the interloper was closer still, and she could hear him breathing. Another time coming up, and the ice with it. Another gallery, a mixed show, and Cruickshank there, a reminder, a confusing question mark.

"*Well!*" he bellowed, in an echoing gallery. "Here we are."

"Here we are," she said, flat, feeling flat, a little sad, a little angry that Clem had not come.

"Shall we?"

So again they had wandered down the length of the wall. Flowers and landscapes.

"Isn't he coming?"

"No. He isn't," she replied, definite, final.

"Sorry," the head raised, the head well back, surveying the ceiling, "one or two things I liked," he continued, "*that*," and walking on, "oh, and *this*. Yes," and he rooted before the still life, fumbling in his pocket, "damn it, I thought I'd a catalogue, blast," after which he met Lena's smile as she said, "It's fifteen guineas, Mr Cruickshank."

He stood back a little, surveyed her. "My name's *Ivor*," he said.

"Welsh and Scotch," she said.

To her amazement he said, very pronouncedly, "I'll take it Lena."

And to herself, and hiding an inner excitement, "God! He's actually bought something," then heaving it out, overwhelming him with, "Oh I *am* glad, Mr Cruickshank, Clem'll be so pleased, I can't get back to him quickly enough, I—"

A pressure on her arm, enough to hurt. "Ivor, Lena," he said. "*I*—vor."

"Ivor," Lena said, and followed him to the reception desk.

Darkness heightened the silence of the room. She switched off the radio.

"I haven't heard a single note of it," she told herself, feeling him still there, groping, finding out, making her remember. "Wonder what happened to him, must be seventy at least, strange little man. But still a bastard," she said aloud, another occasion hovering, being suddenly *there*.

Cruickshank. "Stood between us both. How the hell could I forget *that*?" she thought, looking directly at him, at Clem, at what stood before them, and the pronto question.

"What is it?" Cruickshank asked.

"Remember him looking at me, as though I would have the answer, sticking my neck out for *him*.

"What d'you think it is?" asked Clem.

"Asking *you*?"

"Why? It's *there*."

"A church?"

"Could be."

"No . . . of course not, it's a cathedral, damn it, it *is*," and after a pause, "Is it in the air, or on the ground? And the *blackness* everywhere," continued Cruickshank, "the . . . and the miniature explosion, what's that? And the door's closed, is it not?"

"Not quite," Clem said.

Lena's musing continued—I can see him now, bent right down, rocking on his heels, leaning in to it, to find out, and Clem behind him, saying, "*Well?*" Then Cruickshank dropping, seeming distant, and a further observation.

"And the doors are almost shut, so why the hand sticking out?"

"Big question," and Clem grinning.

"I enjoyed that," she thought.

"What does it *mean*?"

"Could be the Archbishop of Canterbury trying to get out," Clem said.

"Not funny at all," Cruickshank said.

Lena opened her eyes to the darkness, closed them again, thinking, "Perhaps it wasn't." And then she heard a door open and close, heard the voice say, "Hello. Why all this darkness?" he asked, and switched on the light.

"Oh!" Lena said, "there you are," and sat up, he standing over her.

"Enjoy the music. What was it?"

"The Prague," Lena said.

"Nice."

He went to his chair, sat down, lit a cigarette, flung her the packet, from which she took one. "Thanks ... I thought you said you were tone deaf," she said, like an accusation.

"Not a criminal offence," Clem said.

"And what have you been doing? Grovelling in the past?"

"I've gone through everything, Lena," he said, suddenly jumped up, sat beside her, and like an ultimatum, "I can't find the Bermondsey girl."

"The Bermondsey girl?"

"There's only one," he said. "Certain it was there, Lena," and his voice rising, the tempo increasing, "and the mere fact that it *wasn't* made me desperately anxious to find it. Not there! I never wanted to sell that, Lena, you *know* that."

Her irritation was quite lost on him. "Of course I *know*," she said.

"*Well?*"

"Search me. A good many things were lost at that time."

"It's a real mystery," he replied, and walked straight to the cupboard, flung open the door. "I feel sad about it, I really do."

She gave her cigarette a big puff, but made no reply.

"Like one?" he asked.

"Depends, dear."

Which made him hold up the bottle, which he put back, and rushed off to the other room, returning with his quarter-full bottle, saying, "Good. Good."

The glass he gave her dangled in her hand, and he returned to his chair. "I won't tell," she thought, and the thought itself resolved her, then inadvertently between her teeth, dropping her voice, "the bitch!"

"What's that?"

"Nothing," and she held high the glass, then wished him good luck.

She wondered how long the bottle would last, and she really *must* empty that cupboard! An awful sight!

And the question right out of the blue. "Why this sudden interest in it?"

"Because it isn't *there*!"

"You needn't take my head off," she snapped back at him, and then drawled with indifference, "all kinds of things were happening around that time."

"Such as . . . ?"

It sealed up her irritation. "Things got *lost*."

"All right. Why so excited, Lena? I know they did."

She stubbed out the cigarette, crossed the room, stood over him, and measured her reply. "And people actually *died*."

"*What* a day."

"Nearly ended, dear, and there'll be another one tomorrow. I thought you'd dropped off to sleep in there," she said, pointing.

He leaned forward, stressed. "Hadn't. I just went through everything, I mean every bloody thing, and that picture should have been there."

"It's getting late."

"That damned rent," he said, and went to the bureau and sat down. "I'll just make out that cheque."

"Do that."

She went and stood behind him, a hand on his shoulder, watching him write, a shaky hand scrawling, and "There!"

"Right. I'll see to it first thing in the morning. Now come and sit down." She took his arm, pulled him along.

"What about?"

"You know I hardly heard a note of that music, surprised myself really, I was thinking of you, seeing you stuck in there. I'll bet you were sat on the floor, staring it in the face.

And he had been, sat, his back to a cold wall, the light finding all, the line of canvases staring back at him, remembering, mapping known journeys, days good and bad, and from time to time stubbing a cigarette into an already overflowing ash tray, a mess of ash at his feet, and the bottle handy. Lowering his eyes, tracing patterns on a paint-riddled floor, getting up, walking the length of the room, sitting down again.

"Sometimes I think she hates this damned room, and everything in it. I'm beginning to hate it myself. What the hell's happening to me, I can't move, and where in hell has that canvas gone, where?" leaping to his feet delving again, picking things up, putting them down again, a wave of frustration washing into the room, kneeling, turning them round and round, and a sudden leap of delight. "No! . . ." carrying it to the lamp, "yes, of *course*," letting it drop from his hand, "but *where is that* . . ." He picked up the bottle, then, half way to the door, let it fall from his hand, stopped dead. "A bloody mystery. And if I hadn't decided to go through that stuff I'd never have found out. Blast!"

His hand on the knob, turning it, standing in the tiny passage, listening. Odd.

"So silent, thought she was listening in," moving in the darkness, calling "Hello", opening the door, filling the room with light, seeing her stretched out on the settee.

"Thought you were listening to that concert. Lena."

She eyed him. "I was, And you?"

"Wandering through the junk."

"It's a bad habit," she said.

"What now?"

"Feeling sorry for yourself," Lena replied.

He flung himself down, saying, "Don't *chase* it."

"I shan't."

"I'm bloody mad about that picture."

"I *know* that," she replied, and it sounded to him like a sudden pain. A quick scowl in her direction, and the inevitable cigarette, the lifebelt. "You *always* seem to bloody *know*," he said.

"I just couldn't concentrate," Lena said, "unusual with me, but in the end it was the darkness that got me, and I enjoyed it."

"You're not even listening to what I say."

"I never stop listening."

There was a long pause, and then she sat erect, concentrated on the moment, looked at him, and said, very casually, "I can't ever stop listening, dear, since I seem never to be anywhere but *here*, and I've been here a long time. And strange to say, I've been thinking of nothing else but that, lying in the dark. I did picture you in *there*, grovelling as usual."

He came slowly to his feet, the cigarette fell from his hand, and for a moment he appeared to wilt, the shoulders slumped, and he picked up the cigarette, growled, "*Well?*"

"And d'you know what I really thought?"

The change in him was immediate, he joined her, stuttering, "What?"

"I felt I'd like to walk through that door, and down the stairs, and open the door, and walk right out, and down the longest longest road I could find, and if it just went on and on and on I shouldn't mind in the least. And I thought, too, how well trained I had become over the years."

"*Lena!*"

"I doubt very much if you'd even remember the first time we ever met."

A strangulated whisper broke from him. "What *is* this, dear?"

"I took an immediate liking to you, and I remember the time, the day, and the hall. And the more I admired what you were doing the more I grew to like you. That's how it was, so we got closer and closer, and I *knew* we would be together, and we were."

He hardly realized how heavily she was leaning against him.

"And in the end we couldn't do without each other. You know what I brought with me, and I actually loved you, Clem. Even now I can't fathom what it was, but it was *something* about you, about *us*, and it sealed up everything at once. Not once did I interfere with you, and you did what you wanted to do. You had the key of the door, and you went off from time to time, but always you came back, because I was bound to be *here*. There were times when you came back with nothing but the ashes of things, and I never once referred to them. All that mattered was that you'd returned, so here we are now, after *all* that time. We've shared everything, we've lost things, and we've found things. I was happy when you were working, sad when you were not.

We tried the lot, and we had the lot. We've wished together, wondered together, waited together, we . . ."

"Some things just rooted in my system, Lena," he said, and felt unable to meet the penetrating glance she gave him. "The *silence* . . ."

"There's one rooted in mine *now*, dear, and we'd better nail it to the ground. It's been in my mind all day."

And he was eager, anxious, a hand on her knee. "*What?*" he asked.

"This *house*."

"Christ, yes."

"I'll see what I can find out at Wells Street tomorrow," she said.

"*I'll* go."

"You won't, and you know you won't. I'll cross my fingers in the morning. I couldn't help noticing this morning, odd that it was the first time, but this house has got really shabby, uncared for, and when first we came here it was beautiful, remember? Fancy two middled-aged spinsters living in a *whole* house, Clem."

He could only emit a slight sigh, and still he could not look at her, shame and frustration fought within him.

"*Look* at me, dear," she said.

"I remember that day, Lena, yes, I *do*. There was something both charming and eccentric about Miss Benson and Miss Cleate. Yes, it was a lovely house."

"You should see that splendid staircase now, dear. Of course you might never see it, since you've got out of the habit of going up and down, *haven't* you? I get some queer looks from the caretaker's wife. They always ask after you, but there's a kind of groping, icy curiosity behind the enquiry. Grimpen's collecting days are over now, and they're in the same boat as we are, not knowing the hour when they might get the order of the boot."

"Where the hell would we go, dear?" he asked.

She took his face between her hands, looked steadily at him, made as if to speak, but didn't, and thought, "I always wanted to say, 'Mother knows best'."

"I'm going to bed, Lena."

"And so am I. It's been a long day, Clem."

They stood facing each other. He held her hands, said gently, "I'll never cease to admire your patience, dear, never."

Suddenly she pulled away from him, saying, "I'm going to bed."

In an almost dreamlike voice, he replied, "Yes, of course. It is late."

He went and sat on his bed, watched her start to make up her own on the settee.

"Just look at the time," Lena said, but he didn't.

She lay there, waiting for him to switch out the light.

"And don't just *sit* there," she said.

He slowly undressed. "Good night."

"Good night."

His quick smile was lost on her. "Thank God," she thought.

The darkness shut them out, and she knew that this day had really come to an end.

3

"A Mrs Stevens," the receptionist said, and Dr Beecham said abruptly, "Fifteen minutes," and she went out, and he bent over a mass of papers, and got lost in them.

"Fifteen minutes, Mrs Stevens," the receptionist said, and the woman seated by the door said, "Thank you," and returned to her minute study of this small, modest, sparsely furnished waiting room. The walls were pea green, and there was a big calendar hanging directly over her head. Five chairs, and a single bench with a cushioned top. A small table littered with the usual kind of literature that did nothing save pass the patient's time. The brown carpet was much worn. A high-ceilinged room, and one big window, which looked out on a high wall. A clock on the wall said eleven fifteen. It had been a fair walk, and she had been glad to sit down. She had already called at the Wells Street office, and paid in her rent, and she had been up very early, dressing, and stealing out of the room without disturbing Clem, and her last recollection of him was seeing him quietly snoring. In the kitchen she had made herself a quick cup of tea sat and drank it, after which she crept on tiptoe to the room where he worked, quietly closed the door, and begun a study of what was lying heaped against the wall. Some fifteen paintings, and she had examined every one. And this seemed to her to be total, with nothing to add, since nothing seemed to have been growing, and it had been like this for quite some time. Having carefully studied the paintings she had removed the cloth from the easel, and begun a slow examination of what he was at present working on. Her first glance was distrustful, and she knew she didn't like it, and what wasn't "there" the other morning, wasn't there now.

She had stood back, gone forward, walked to the end of the room, and walked slowly back again, her eye darting and resourceful, searching, asking questions.

"I don't like it."

Kneeling down again, she had gone through the pile by the wall for the second time, then returned to the easel. It prompted the questions.

"What's wrong with it? With him? What is the *matter*?"

She knew the answer, spoke it aloud in the quiet room. "It's the same thing again and again," and she could only think of the hours, the energy, and it saddened her. Here, at this very moment, even the despised Cruickshank might have been a help. What on earth had happened to Clem during these last few months? Plodding. Plodding where? For what? "There's an answer to everything," she thought, and buoyed herself up with this casual observation. She thought of him lying back there, still snoring, and waking automatically at the usual time. But he'd know where she'd gone, one more job for Lena. Lena who was always around, always *there* when she was wanted. Worried about the future. But wasn't she? Where was *he* travelling, but where indeed was she?

Contesting with these questions she was wholly unaware that the door had opened, that the receptionist was standing in front of her, and quietly saying, "Dr Beecham will see you now, Mrs Stevens," herself struck by the violent jack-in-the-box jerk the woman had made, who now got to her feet and stuttered it out.

"Oh, yes. Sorry. Thank you, which way?"

With the ghost of a smile the receptionist said, "This way, madam," and Lena followed her into the consulting room. And there he was, waiting.

He made a quick, bouncing movement towards her, hand outstretched.

"There you are. How are you, Mrs Stevens? Ten years, isn't it?"

"Nine, to be exact," Lena replied.

"Sorry to have kept you waiting," Beecham said, "but it

was worth it. I'm free for the next half hour. Come and sit down. How is Mr Stevens?"

She lowered her eyes, momentarily wilting under the spontaneous salvo, and then sat down, and he sat opposite, fell to studying her.

The Stevens had been on his list for years. Looking at her now, he was struck by the change in her. She looked tired, and he didn't like her pallor. "Nice to see you after such a long time."

"I see you've still got the lemon tree," she said, having noticed it on the wall as she came in.

"Yes, still there. Clem, isn't it, what's he doing now?"

She killed curiosity with a single blow. "Still at it," Lena said.

"Glad to hear it. Well now, down to business," Beecham said. "What is it?"

"I've been quite well for the last two years, doctor, but one morning last week I was pulled up in my tracks by a sharp pain. It worried me somewhat . . ."

"It's not—"

"Not that," Lena said. "Lately I've felt very tired, and since I had to call somewhere nearby I thought I'd give you a ring."

"Another five minutes and you'd have missed me altogether. And otherwise you've been quite well since that operation?"

"Yes, doctor."

"Right, if you'll just undress," he said, and pointed to the small screen. Behind which she started to remove her blouse, and it made her remember the last occasion on which she had stood there, the time, the situation. Beecham sat on the couch swinging his legs, watched the screen, waited. He thought she looked more than sixty as she emerged from behind the screen.

"Good!" he said.

The examination was thorough, during which he was made highly aware of her nervous condition, and certain parts of the body reacted violently to the touch. And he understood the satisfaction that emerged with her big sigh when it was over, after which she vanished once more behind the screen. She could hear him shuffling papers, heard a bell ring, and a door open, heard him say quietly to the receptionist, "Miss Jessom, would you bring in some tea, please," heard the door close, and she stood trembling for a moment, then finally emerged and returned to the chair. She was conscious of his attention, sensed an interest beyond that of her health. It surprised her when he offered her a cigarette, which she accepted, and more so when he himself took one out, and lighted them both.

He said, in a rather jolly way, "A lot of water under the bridge, Mrs Stevens, since those embankment days. That was a tiny little place you had down there, still remember it, and wouldn't have minded having it myself."

And her first smile as she replied, "That's ages ago, doctor."

He then heaved out his own sigh, as he said, "Yes. Indeed it is. Tell me, is Clem still working? What's been happening?"

"You've really forgotten, doctor. We left the embankment cottage long ago, we went to Chesil Place. You once called there."

"Of course," he said, and then the receptionist came in with the tea.

"Are you sure I'm not holding you up?" she asked.

"Thank you, Miss Jessom, you can go now."

The door closed, and he said loudly as he leaned over the tray, "Sugar?"

"Thank you. No sugar."

"A cake? They're very small," he said.

"No. Nice tea," she said.

"The last time I saw you I got the impression that you were planning to head out of London altogether."

"We did go back to his home, a small Warwickshire village, but we only stayed a few months. After his mother died during one of the big Midlands raids he decided to leave, and he's never been back since. That is all finished now. I felt quite sad about it, being something of a simple-lifer myself. I made little of the decision, since the only important thing was that he should go on working. But I miss it very much, the peace and quiet of it all. Still surprises me, he's country lad all over, but he never quite got over the loss of his mother, and the circumstances were rather dreadful, a floating mine removed the small row of houses, and everybody in them. There wasn't even a funeral. In the end I was glad when he got back to town."

"I'm sorry to hear about that, Mrs Stevens. Very depressing."

"I'd love to be back there now," Lena said, "and I keep thinking about it almost to the point of distraction. But it's no use. He's in a groove, and I'm in a groove, and we've both accepted the fact."

He leaned back in his chair, took a long look at her.

"You need a holiday," he said, "a real break."

"I'd never mention such a thing, and I know he wouldn't budge, he's glued to London once and for all."

"Builders in a small way," you said, "his people I mean?"

"Yes. And what little money was left him he drank away."

Dr Beecham sat up, came erect. "I never knew that," he said.

"It was a real shock to me, doctor, and I couldn't even describe its effect on me. But I'm weak, I let it happen, and it just went on and on."

"Does he still suffer from those awful headaches he used to have?"

"He was never a *strong* man, doctor."

She watched him as his glance suddenly wandered away from her, noting his fugitive glance round the room, and a final stare up at the ceiling.

"If I'm ever your way I might look you up," Dr Beecham said. "I'm not much in the art line, but I might take a look at what he's doing now. I remember one exhibition he had years ago."

And the leaden reply. "So do I," she said. "I remember the last occasion you said that," she offered him a smile.

"*Did* I?"

"If you do look us up, doctor," Lena said, tentatively, nervously, "I . . ." and then he glanced at his watch, and she half rose, saying, "I mustn't keep you," but he sat on, was suddenly relaxed, and said positively, "Yes?"

"He doesn't go out at all now, and the past two months have been very trying. Hardly anybody calls, and the few friends he once had appear to have dropped out of the scene for good," and with voice climbing, she continued, "If you could persuade him to get away for a while, doctor, I *do* want that, even on his own. I shouldn't mind. I watch him disappearing into the workroom morning after morning, and most extraordinary thing of all he's taken to locking the door, it was like being shut out, it shocked me. I sit in the other room, watching the clock, watching the hands move, listening to silence. I dread the moment when the door will open, and him coming in. I daren't speak, even ask a question. Sometimes he scarcely gives me a glance. I mightn't be there at all. I never know what he's doing, or whether he's happy with it, and I don't know what he aims for, what he wants, what would *satisfy* him. I just lose myself altogether in books, and I do love reading, my one escape these days."

She stood facing him now, and he noted the nervous fingers that clutched her bag. "Pathetic," he thought.

"A pity there were no children," Dr Beecham said, "might have made the difference."

The harshness of her reply quite surprised him.

"I'm as barren as rock, doctor. But I have something to mother now," and her changed expression as she said this he found even more surprising. He could only think of a conventional answer, and said, "I'm sorry."

"He went off with other women from time to time, but in the end he always returned to mother," and he sensed a sourness there. The defence mechanism, the way out. "I'm sorry about that," he said again.

"I *must* go," Lena said, not wanting to, longing to continue, to talk into miles.

"How old is Mr Stevens?" he asked.

"Fifty-five, nearly fifty-six," she said.

Curiosity could travel no further, and she walked quickly towards the door, and Beecham with her.

"Nice to have met you again, Mrs Stevens," he said, "and I hope things improve for you both," and suddenly put a hand on her shoulder, saying, "I'm more worried about you than I am about your husband. You *must* get away, even on your own. You look tired, you need the break, we all need one from time to time."

"I'm happy if he is, and I don't mind waiting," and she took the proffered hand, and summed up all resolution as she added, "I still believe in him."

"Goodbye."

"Goodbye, doctor," Lena said, rather stiffly, being quick to note the sheer professionalism of that "goodbye".

The first effect of being out in the open street was feeling a kind of nakedness, as she stood there, looking right and left, her feet anchored to ground, afraid to move off. An aimlessness of direction, the instant realization of where she was, and the time on the big clock hanging over her head, Clem resurrected, seen, thought of, and then she turned sharply and walked briskly to the bus stop.

"Glad I went, glad I know, know what he *knew*, relief, really. Nice of him about the tea, I always liked him. So helpful to me that time, more friend than doctor, but he doesn't really understand, and it doesn't matter now."

Staring into a shop window, waiting for the bus, and now wanting to get back, to be in, to be *there*. "Yes, back home," she told herself, a slave again to the ritual of the day. "I expect he looked after himself," and saw the open cupboard, and the bottle emerging, the big swig, and he'd be well lost in his private world, the endless landscape choked with its own dark corners into any one of which he could hide. The whisky and the boredom, the bloody knife out when the brush got drunk, drunk as he got, pointless and stupid. And that scraping and scraping and *scraping*, the day's opening machinery. She still stared into the window, the contents of which she now saw as through a kind of mist. Islanded on the pavement she yet felt shadowed by Beecham, by the man who spoke to her at the office in Wells Street. Even found herself listening again.

"It's hard to say, madam," Jensen said, "we haven't yet turned the corner, difficulties everywhere, and the overheads don't diminish, and they don't vanish either. We hope we'll turn the corner soon."

She had listened to this in a daze, even wondered what kind of corner the man before her might turn.

"The market rises and falls, madam," and she uttered the words like a parrot, "the market rises and falls."

"Everybody will be notified in good time, and the usual order for possession will be obtained . . ."

"The rent's risen three times in a single year," Lena said.

"That we fully explained to Mr Grimpen, and I have no doubt he informed you. He never forgets things like that," Jensen said.

He peered steadily at Lena through his spectacles, and exclaimed abruptly, "You *are* Mrs Stevens of 14 Chesil Place?"

She said she was, on which he pushed back his chair, crossed legs, looked up at her, twiddled fingers in his lap.

"That's about it, madam," he said. "Naturally, we're sorry about the whole thing, circumstances were quite plainly beyond us, and we do realize the position of the tenants. But we have to bear in mind the perilous condition of the properties after the war. Be unsafe to allow them to stand much longer, and then again—" but Lena had already left the office and he talked only into the empty air.

People had bumped into her on two occasions, and she was deaf to the observations, still rooted at the shop window. She looked round, but there was no bus in sight. She walked on to the next stop, the thoughts chasing.

"I suppose I could go back to teaching, there is a shortage

of them," so blindly groped her way into another "situation". What to do *now*? And the Beecham ultimatum. "Must get away, Mrs Stevens, a break, yes, even alone."

"Where?" She thought it all sounded so simple. "Glad I went."

She boarded the bus, found a seat up front, composed herself, and didn't hear the conductor's zing of his ticket punch, and did not even see him standing there, suddenly saying, "Where *to*, madam?"

She wanted to cry, "Anywhere," as she fumbled madly at her purse.

"Chesil Road."

The banging of a door, and the echoes in the hall, the loud creaks on a perilous staircase, and slowly going up and up. A hand on the knob, turning it, thinking of the faithful sentinel behind the door, seeing the smile, hearing the soft sigh.

"He'll be glad *again*," she thought.

He wasn't at the door, there was no smile, and the grinding words were absent. He was sitting in the armchair, the morning paper spread out on his knee. Her first glance was towards the cupboard, her second to his feet, but this time the bottle wasn't there. He hadn't even risen when she entered.

"Hello," Clem said, and sat down again.

She did not reply, but turned away and slowly removed her outdoor things and hung them behind the door. After which she went to the settee and sat down, subjected him to a long, penetrating look, and waited for the words. They came.

"What did he say?"

"What did who say, dear?"

"Dr Beecham of course."

She flung the words at him. "He said I needed a break, dear."

"Oh!"

"*Yes.*"

"You paid in the rent?"

"*Yes.*"

"Anything wrong?" and she had expected this.

"Nothing."

Her aloofness irritated him. "Isn't there anything to say, Lena, dear?"

The "dear" grated on her. "Surely that's for you to say," she replied. "Don't you think so? I *have* been out *again*. And now I'm back. I just thought you might have some news for me, Clem. A nice change."

"News?" and he leaned forward in his chair, scattered the newspaper.

"There's nearly always a message from your den, dear," she said.

He got up, stood before her. "What's wrong, Lena?"

"What's right?"

"Don't tell me." He dropped to the settee. "You've had bad news, what is it? The bloody house. I expect so."

"I've no news."

"What did Beecham *say*?"

"I told you. Mentioned a break, he calls it a holiday."

"Didn't that agent say *anything*?"

"He gave me a receipt for the rent, dear, and I pointed out to him that it had risen three times in a year . . ."

"Three times. Is that right, Lena?"

"I do sometimes tell you things, dear. Mr Jensen didn't like the reminder but he had ready the excuses," and she removed the hand that now covered her own.

"Why can't you say something, Lena, and I'm not drunk, and I haven't been living in the cupboard."

She made him wait for the curt answer. "I'm glad," she said.

He nursed a rising anger, sat heavily on a growing irritation. He had never seen Lena like this. "What in hell has happened?" he asked himself. And aloud, "What has *happened*?"

"Nothing happening on the inside, dear," Lena said,

"and I've been pondering on things that might happen *outside* . . ."

"What the hell are you being sphinx-like about, dear?"

"I've been ruminating," Lena said, "that's all. Ruminating."

"It's you that's changing, Lena," he said, "yes, *you*, not me."

"Don't make me scream, Clem."

"*Scream?*"

"I was thinking about going back to teaching," she said.

"Now? At your age?"

"At my age. They say there's a shortage. I got the impression this morning in that agent's office that the future of tenants was very far from his mind. It leaves the position shaky, and all the way home I was chasing the situation. When? Where to? This morning whilst you were snoring, I went into your room and took a good look at everything . . ."

"You . . ."

"And the impression I got was that you needed a break yourself, dear, yes, you ought to get away somewhere, do you the world of good. Just forget what's in there. It made me sad, just standing there, looking at it. After all, it *is* work, and I know it's important to you. But you have your own blind moments, and it would be a help if sometimes you realized this. It's like trying to do a complicated sum in addition, half way up the figures begin to topple."

She realized his mounting anger, and met it head on.

"The fact is it's the same old thing over and over again. What inspires you, the walls, the ceiling?"

"I did nothing this morning, not a single bloody thing. You're right, dear, and I even doubt myself. I spent an hour going through telephone directories . . ."

"With no phone?"

"I was looking up old names," he said.

"They're all dead," she continued. "If they're not, then they probably assumed your death long ago. And I'm still disgusted at your idea of looking up this man Cruickshank. I've a longer memory than you, dear. Yes, I even remember that last exhibition of yours. It was I that collected the few laughs, and I made certain you wouldn't hear one of them. You *are* good, and if I didn't think that I wouldn't stay here another single minute. And this awful bloody ennui that's settled on you," she continued, and at the same time took his hand, "I've had my own empty moments, but I eventually floated up safely on your own exhilaration. Something's happened to you in these past months, I've seen it, felt it inside me. Do you know, it now seems absolutely incredible to me that once upon a time we haunted every gallery in London. And here we are now, *nailed* into this narrow, mean, shabby sort of life."

She stopped suddenly, and realized for the first time her own bitterness, saw this reflected in the expression on his face, and drew him close.

"You did have wonderful moments, dear, and I shared and remember them."

"I *hate* myself," he said, and turned away from her. "I really loathe myself."

"Don't *say* that."

"Christ! I *do*."

"We've been happy together, Clem, and for a long time. The things that were simple then are not so now, and I often long for a little quietness, a little peace. Last night I dreamt that I was sitting quite alone on a tiny beach, and it was so peaceful, it *must* have been a beach in Wales. D'you remember Wales, Clem? I just sat there, at the sea's edge, counting waves. I could have gone on counting them forever. I really could. I hated the moment when I woke up. How different things were then, how simple, how satisfied one was. I've often wanted to *claw* those moments back again."

He heard the deep sigh, was conscious of this tight embracement, yet he could not look directly at her, but turned his head slightly, and remained silent.

"If I ever thought you'd leave me, Lena, I'd end it."

Clutching at straws, asking himself the question, "Would I? Would I, really?"

She freed herself and went to the cupboard, stood with her back to him, fiddled with the doorknob.

"For the first time in my life I think a drink would do me far more good than you, and I'm going to have one now." She turned, holding the bottle high in the air. "A quarter full," she said," and it's brought you some costly answers, hasn't it, dear? Even now I know you wouldn't say no," and she held out the bottle to him. When she smiled, he knew he'd never be able to express the relief it brought him.

"Let me," and he took the bottle and put it on the table, then took out the two unwashed glasses.

"There, Lena."

She held the glass to her lips, and he noticed she did not drink.

"Please," he said, and watched her drink it.

"You've a strange, mercurial nature, dear," she said.

"What's that?"

"Just thinking out loud, it's not important."

"Do come and sit down," he said.

"The rent might just as easily have been posted," Lena said, "and it took me out of my way. Never mind, it's done now."

"If only one *knew*."

"I'm sure the faithful Mr Grimpen downstairs will be the first to bring us the news."

"Sooner the better."

She lay back. "Are you hungry?"

"Not very."

"I can still hear those waves murmuring in my head," she said.

She began to feel more relaxed, she had even enjoyed the whisky, but she would not tell him that. A sudden interest in what he was wearing made her sit up, and say, "By the way, Clem, I wish to God you'd tidy yourself up, I'm *sick* of seeing you going about like that."

"I'll have a bath and change," he said.

"And I must tidy up this flat, it looks terrible."

"Talking for the sake of talking," he thought, and was glad of it, and dreaded a silence.

"Fancy dreaming of that little place in Wales," he said, "can't remember where it was. Yes, we did do Wales on three occasions, a time ago. It wouldn't be Duffryn?"

"The sea was there, and I was there, and the name is less important than the fact that I was actually there," and abruptly, "Wasn't it Aberdovey, dear?"

"Lena!—You must be the most patient person I've ever known."

"Lucky you! I never really wanted this at all," Lena went on. "Even in the short time we were at Alton, can you remember *that*? I never wanted to come back. Remember the orchard at Deeney? I wonder if you do."

"If something worthwhile turned up, I might even think about it, Lena."

"I often wish for something nice to happen, dear, I'm *always* wishing it."

"You make me feel ashamed, Lena, I've been pigheaded, downright stupid. I've even felt sad about it."

"If something unexpected turns up, would you leave London altogether?"

"I'd think about it, dear," he said.

"And that's what's wrong with some of the things you do, that thing you've got on the easel now, dear. You think too much about what you do. Something's got congealed in the paint," and she noted the frown, and added quickly, "well, never mind. Mr Gorley loved that little one you gave him. It was good. And that *Lilac-tree*, Clem, why can't you do something with it? Would you like me to take it along somewhere? Galleries everywhere today."

"It's the longest sermon I've ever listened to," Clem said, and gave a curious little laugh.

"They're much longer in the Kirk."

He subjected her to the longest stare she had ever experienced, and when he exclaimed passionately, "You are good, Lena, you *are* good," the enthusiasm was unmistake-able, yet she registered it at no point.

"This is good," she said, waving the glass in the air. "I actually enjoyed it."

"You're not still angry about what I said about Cruick-shank?"

"If you want to find him, then find him. But what could he do? I ask you? Why, he must be an old man now, and was he all that important?"

"He knew people, Lena, that's what's important."

"Probably dead by now. Must be turned seventy, surely. Hardly in the scene as they say."

"I was lucky with that small show at the Olfan."

"Miles away, ages ago, you seem to forget we've lived a lifetime since. Nine years, think of it, *nine*. People forget, besides which, the whole situation is altered now. There's even a rat race on, dear. To quote the old song, 'Everybody's doing it now'."

"You know *everything*, don't you?"

"And that's enough," Lena said.

"Perhaps it is. Sorry, Lena."

"It actually *is*," she replied, and dragging her words, measured them out, her finger prodding his knee as she went on, "There are occasions when I actually travel about, dear. My weekly jaunt to Euston, the only place I now remember with any pleasure . . ."

"I thought it was the little place with the blue curtains on the embankment."

She wasn't listening, and she said quietly, "Take it," and he took the glass and put it on the floor beside him. "I leave you in peace," she said.

"You must be damned glad to see the back of me," he said.

She ignored this. "Moving about on my little occasions I have noticed that for every bookshop in London there's at least five art shops. Something quite new to me. Surprise you, too, if you ever break out." She leaned in close, put a hand under his chin, lifted his face. "The day I hear that

72

door banging after you, will be more real to me than those Welsh waves. Oh Christ! Here I am, at it again. I'll make some lunch."

"Can I help?"

"Why not?"

When he linked arms with her into the kitchen, she thought, "The child coming out again."

They stood close together at the table.

"What'll it be?"

Laughing, she said, "There's so much of everything, it's difficult to make a choice," and they sat down together. "Oh! There's the last of Gorley's beef."

"Gorley, Gorley? Why, of course, seems a decent old chap," he said.

And Lena said, "A decent young chap, dear."

"Look at me," he said.

"I am looking at you."

It saddened her when he replied, "It's not too late, Lena."

"That ship is home, and tied up. Cut some bread, dear."

She sat there, watching him. "He's clumsy, he's loaded with nerves, he's hating himself, he's ashamed, he doesn't know what to do, what to say, he wants to dig the words out, he can't.—No butter for me, dear," she said.

"Soup?"

"You like soup," she said.

"We had soup yesterday, Lena."

She went to the stove, turned the gas under the pan, and lightly threw it off. "Just another way of saying how things are at the moment, dear."

"All *right*."

"Good. Then that's finished. Just like old times."

They ate in silence, and she avoided his glances.

"Everything all right, dear?"

"Fine."

"I'm glad."

He hurried through the meal, then got up and left her, and she sat on, wanting and not wanting the meal in front of her, and pondering. Had she said too much? Too little?

"I could call him an infuriating bastard, but I won't."

She heard a door open and close, knew where he was. Tidied up, she went back into the living room. The first thing that caught her eye was the small bureau in the corner. It toppled with its contents, it threw out challenges. "I must tidy the damned thing up."

She sat down, looked at the pile of papers in front of her, at the crammed drawers that would not shut. Burn the lot. Burn everything. She concentrated, nothing escaped, she glimpsed, she read carefully, she bundled and flung to the wastepaper basket, she cleared the drawers. Pushing back her chair, she concentrated on one long drawer stuffed with old newspapers, old news, old history, worn out and forgotten days.

"The way it just piles up," tearing out newspapers, pressing them into an already loaded basket. "There!"

This sudden action had induced in her a wish to clear everything, and she went out and returned with a brush and shovel and dusters, and began a tidying of the room. Dusting a shelf, she would pause, some object catching her eye, a photograph, a small vase, an ornamental jug, and she held them in her hand, fondling, liking them, living occasions, glances that took wing and carried her miles from the room. She was totally unaware of the silence that surrounded her the moment she paused.

"Living in there," she thought. She was still on her knees when he came in.

"Can I help?"

"It's done now. What a load of rubbish," she said.

"Grows and grows."

"Go and open that window, Clem."

He sent it up with a crash.

"Nice. Fresh air."

"We've had these curtains a long time," he said, fingering them.

"Haven't we? I must do something about it."

74

He carried out the heavy wastepaper basket. It was the first time she had ever seen him do anything to help in the flat, and at the door he called back, "Anything else?"

"No. You might throw me a cigarette if you have one," and the packet came flying through the air. "Thanks."

She was standing at the window, smoking contentedly, when he came in, and she didn't hear him as he crept up behind, felt a hand on her arm.

"That was sudden," he said.

"What was sudden?"

"That," he emphasized, and waving a hand embraced the whole room.

"I've been neglecting things lately."

"Certainly made a change."

"Still can't believe I've done it," Lena said. "A match."

"You've gone quite pale, dear," Clem said, noticing it for the first time as the light revealed it.

"I'm all right."

"Wish you'd come clean about Beecham," he said.

"Leave it alone."

He left her and sat in his own chair. "Why don't you lie down, Lena? I wish you would. It worries me."

"D'you mind?" Lena said, and drew the curtains, then went to the settee and lay down.

"I'm not reading," he said.

He saw her cover her face with an open hand. He moved restlessly in the chair. "She *is* tired, I know when she is, seen it before. I wish to God she'd say something. The way she turned on me when she came back. I could tell at once. I hate myself for the useless bastard I am. Lena's done it all, every bloody thing. Never a complaint. No. Nothing but those silent, silent wishes of hers. The way she talked. I'm sure she would have burst into tears if she'd gone on any longer, absolutely loaded when she came in. Christ! I must try, I must, I must."

He sat up. Was she asleep? He tiptoed across to her. She lay flat and stretched, inert. "Poor, dear Lena."

He wanted to kneel down, to kiss her, he wanted to shout

75

his thanks aloud. But all he could do, and all there was to do in this moment, was to creep quietly across the room, go out, and close the door silently behind him.

"Let her sleep, *sleep*."

He tiptoed to his room, opened the door, but did not go in, just remained there. No change. A covered easel, and that work rooted all along the wall, two empty bottles, a chair, the carpet strip, the paint-sodden floor. He quietly closed the door and went into the bathroom, bathed and shaved, and changed, then walked along to the kitchen, and sat there for some time. Negations clawed at him, and he could still see her inert on the settee, the light in the room now softened by the drawn curtains. His inertia overwhelmed him, morning after morning struck at him like blows, wearing hours out, doubting what he touched, what he looked at, killing the morning, crawling back into the living room, cursing himself, stealing glances at Lena, wondering what she would say. The same as yesterday, the day before. And the answers, the pauses, the evasions, and she just sitting there, waiting. He remembered them all.

"All right," I said.

"Yes, I *am*," I said.

And it wasn't, and he was not. Weeks and weeks of it. Waste. Waste. The morning eating away the afternoon. And she still there, sitting, sewing, pretending to, a baleful glance his way, and buried beneath it her simple wish. A book in her hand, pretending to read, the radio on, pretending to listen. The reminder that was always brutal. "A little fresh air would do you good," she'd say. The promises shot through with the lies in them. "I will, really, Lena, I will," dreading to say it, saying it, cringing inside himself, in this terrible inertia. Weeks of it, months of it. Nothing happening, no move. The silences, the wordless quarrels.

"The patience she's shown. Poor Lena."

"I'll try, dear," I said, "I'll try again," and I didn't, I'd lost something, couldn't get hold of it, couldn't find it.

"Christ! I said I would. Didn't I say I *would*?"

And he writhed where he sat, knew he writhed, wanted to get up, to rush out, into another room. Those voyages from room to room, pointless.

"I hate myself."

Gripping the table, staring at it, at everything, here, where sometimes she sat, and he saw her sitting. He went to the window, wa'ched the light begin to go.

"I wish . . ."

Seeing her of an evening time, stood at the window, stiff, silent, looking out, looking down.

"I've sometimes stood there myself. I once said to her, 'The more I look out, the less I see.' "

"You've made so many promises, Clem."

Smashing the moment, searching for the answer, getting the wrong one, and the bile with it.

"It's very strange, Lena, but never a bloody letter reaches this house. You'd imagine everybody had died. You feel left out, ignored."

"I've sometimes wished that Father Christmas would ring us up," she said. Locked up, hemmed in, tied together, wanting to get up, to go, out, right out, anywhere.

"The way she looked at me just now, the lips so tight, refusing to speak, I felt lousy, lousy, such a searching look it was. And I wondered if she was just crying quietly inside herself. So often she's plain right, and how I loathe myself when I find out. Perhaps I have taken her for a ride, perhaps we should have gone back that time," and he told himself "yes" and "yes", he had had it in his mind. "You make a decision, you actually *want* to, then at the last damn minute you stall, hanging on again, the parrot repeating itself. 'No hold on, something may happen', the bloody see-sawing back and forth. She would have been happy up there, I know she would."

Squirming where he sat, knowing he squirmed, and a sudden feeling of wanting to be sick, rushing across to the basin, just standing there, and nothing happening. Leaving the kitchen, he stood for a moment in the dark corridor, one flat hand pressing against the wall. He tiptoed to the living

77

room door, stood there for a while. Should he go in? "Make up your bloody mind, Stevens," he told himself, and moved again. "I can't sit in *there*, not now," and went into the bathroom, stood looking at himself in the mirror. Later, he was to surprise himself.

4

Mr Grimpen was even more surprised, for he stood sentinel at the top of the basement steps, peering across the now darkening hall, heard footsteps descending, slow, uncertain footsteps, and when he looked up he saw Stevens coming down, a man pausing at every other step, as though still uncertain of what he would do. And it was only as he got nearer that the caretaker finally realized who it was.

"I'll be damned. Actually coming downstairs, actually on his way *out*."

When had the world last seen him? Up there so long one could assume he had just died. So slowly down the stairs, and Grimpen still watching, and still unbelieving. Looking at his watch, as the man halted again, then came on. Calculating movements, leaning against the wall, turning round, looking back.

"Well!" exclaimed Grimpen, "well!"

He stepped quickly into the hall and went forward to meet the man as he reached the bottom of the stairs.

"Evening," he said, having a good look, being certain. "Evening, Mr Stevens." Watching Stevens stiffening there, holding the hard, questioning stare, noticing the nervous fingers pulling at the flap of his jacket pocket. Stevens made no reply, walked straight past Grimpen as though he weren't there, and Grimpen turned sharply and watched him go slowly to the door.

"I'll be damned. Passed me as if I weren't even there, *looking* at him. The *pig*."

He closed his own eyes in utter disbelief, and when he opened them again it was to see the front door opening, and

79

now being quietly drawn to. A slight creak, and later a soft thud as Stevens descended into the street.

"What a surprise."

He hurried down the steps, burst in the door. "Cis!" and there she was.

"What, dear?"

He went in, shut the door, sat down at the table. "You wouldn't believe it," he said.

"Something wrong?"

"No, dear. Just got a surprise. You wouldn't believe this, but that chap Stevens from up top has just gone out. At this time of the evening."

"No!"

"Yes. I was just standing there wondering if I mightn't nip across to the Horse and Groom for half an hour, when I heard this noise on the stairs, and when I looked up it was him. The way he came down, like he wasn't certain, and he looked back up twice, and I thought he was going to go upstairs again, but he came on down. I crossed the hall and bid him good evening. It was Stevens. Talk about surprise, Cis."

"Well, I never," she said.

"I said 'Evening, Mr Stevens', but he never answered, just walked right past me as if I didn't exist. Think of that. Not a bloody word out of him, and I've never heard that front door close so quietly. I really hated the man, passing me like that."

"How odd, Grimpy. Perhaps something's happened."

"Perhaps," Grimpen replied, still sulking over the insult. "Know when I last saw that bloke actually going out? Last March. Think of that. Last *March*."

She lightened the atmosphere with a smile.

"Well, Grimpy, he'll have to be careful, won't he, might get himself lost."

"Who the hell does he think he is?"

"No accounting for people, dear, you ought to know that."

And Grimpen growled, and said, "Perhaps I should. Perhaps a glass or two will wipe it away."

"Grimpy," and she put a hand on his arm.

"What?"

"I'd rather you didn't go out, dear, what I mean is it would be nicer if you brought in a bottle or two, it's so nice and snug here, besides which you hold up that counter too long when you go over there."

"Right then. I'll get set," and she handed him his coat and cap.

"Don't be long," she said.

"The surprise of it," she thought, and heaped more coal on the fire, drew the curtains closer, drew in the two chairs. "Would have given me a fright if he'd bumped into me like that."

She heard the front door open and close, the feet on the steps. "Good."

Before the fire, snug and private, and over the stout, the Grimpens talked of other people. He thought a real fug would be nice, and got up and closed the window.

"I was thinking just now, Grimpy, how much things have altered since the war, even people themselves seem to have changed somehow. Poor Miss Benson, and that Miss Cleate, such nice, quiet, dignified sort of people they were, Grimpy."

"I never think of anything else when I go up and down those stairs," he replied, "that awful crack right down the wall, whole house is got real shabby, never be the same again. Pity, but there it is."

"Strange the way they passed on, so close on one another, Grimpy."

"Ah!"

"When d'you think they might do the dirty on us," she asked.

Grimpen hesitated, not liking this sudden confrontation with a hard fact.

"Could be any time, Cis. A great pity her property ended up that way. If only her nephew hadn't taken it in the last raid we had."

"Ah! Poor Larry," she said, "such a nice young man," and she heaved a sigh.

"Devil's luck, Cis."

He refilled her glass, his own. Suddenly he filled the room with a loud laugh.

"What on earth are you laughing at, dear?"

He lay back, started to fill his pipe, and remarked casually that he had just remembered one summer afternoon in London when Miss Benson and Miss Cleate had rushed off to Paris without their hats. She said he would laugh at anything, and he responded by exclaiming, "Ha", and then lighting his pipe.

"Yes, things have changed," she said.

"You just said that, Cis," and took a noisy sip of his stout. "How lucky those two ladies really were, Cis, stank of oof."

"So did Miss Benson's father, dear."

"A lovely house this used to be, and they used the whole of it, now it's just a kind of lodging-house. I sometimes wondered why Miss Benson never got married, Grimpy, with all that money, too."

"I used to think sometimes, Cis, that God almighty had been a bit sparing with what he put into their heads."

"Maybe. But they always kept their eye on the cash, spite of what you say."

"Ah! As to her marrying, well, I suppose she just wasn't anybody's fruit."

"Could be."

"Always thought their greatest weakness was too much love for anything on four legs. Ah well. Miss Benson knew when there was loyalty around. Turn twice in her grave if she saw this house now."

He gripped her knee, patted it, saying, "Well, Cis, there's one thing, you were real good while I was away at Hitler's bloody war. It's the split difference," and he gave her a big smile.

"Grimpy?"

"What?"

"D'you think Pomfrey might be able to get you that job over at those new Rainbow Flats—Victoria, isn't it?"

"That's right. Don't see why not, dear, though I'll have to

keep my fingers crossed about it, everything's razor-edged these days, all these people coming back after the war. But it was him that first mentioned it."

And she now patted his knee, saying, "I do hope it comes off, Grimpy. I'll pray for it."

"Course you will, since you pray for so many things."

"Funny to think that there's only us left now, and the two up top. D'you think they're hard up, Grimpy? She always seems to wear the same blue coat, and the same hat."

"Able to afford a bottle of whisky a week," Grimpen said, "and at a price you could call nasty."

"You think they'll be able to sell this house, dear?"

"Demolish the house, sell the land, that's today's showery, dear. *Land*. Bricks and mortar's just rubbish now. Well, look around London. Hundreds and hundreds of houses, nobody in them. What a mess. Don't talk to me about things changing. Makes me think of when that lot got in in '45, remember, knocked Winnie out, the talk, the shouting, the sheer *guff*, the things they were going to do, you'd imagine they'd got in carrying the rainbow behind them. Ah! They're all the bloody same, Cis."

She, miles away, sat up quickly, saying, "Who dear?"

"Pol—it—i—cians," he said.

Mrs Grimpen sat up, stretched her arms, gave a big yawn. "Wonder where Stevens was off to, Grimpy?"

"Couldn't care less."

"Tea, dear?"

"Nice."

She went off to the kitchen, and Grimpen leaned forward and spat into the fire. "Damn Stevens."

She had not heard Clem go out, nor in this moment did it seem to matter, as she got up and switched on the light again, crossed to the window, drew back the curtains, and a strong incoming breeze lifted her hair. She watched the small green mirror begin to shake on the wall.

"I wonder when I last looked into it?" she asked herself, and returned to the settee. She sat fully erect, somewhat tense with the feelings that had stolen in upon her, feelings which, at this moment, she could not fully comprehend. She seemed to be looking at this room as for the first time, the small tight room, the wandering eye taking in everything. The shape and size of it, the height of the ceiling, the walls, even the floor itself, with its long carpet strip of fading colour. The eye moved slowly from object to object. And the room, and the things in it stared back at her. Her eye lingered on the small oak bureau which she had recently cleaned out, the useless things, the rubbish of yesterday. The meaningless things locked in the too tight drawers. From object to object, the noticed and the unnoticed, silent witnesses of the life lived in this so confining room. She went to the bureau, sat down at the desk. She took down three photographs and fell to studying them. With a slight sigh she picked one up, studied it closely beneath the light. There they were again, the two of them, so long ago, new to each other, on the threshold of their own dreams.

"Fancy. Just fancy that," she said aloud into the room, and as with the room, so she seemed to be looking at Clem as though for the first time. Picking up another, one of his mother, a reminder of a few happy days they had once spent with her up at Alton. She closed her eyes, slowly savoured the moments. The happy, restful days, she felt them now, deeply remembered. Another day and another time. A strong earthy smell seemed to envelop her as she sat there, the photograph now dangling in her hand. The indolent days, and a sudden realization of the orchard where they had wandered, and sat, and roamed about. Clem and she sat under a great ash. That Clem had not appeared to enjoy it seemed of no importance now, as she enjoyed it all, the peace of it, a lavishness of landscape, the eye drowning in it all, making so real a recent escape from the brick forest, and that slit of sky that always looked mean when seen from the window of the sitting room. How silent he had been, conveying no delight of any kind, a seeming unawareness of sight and sound and smell, in that small haven that had sheltered them both for too short a time. Looking up at a sudden flight of birds, that passed over his head with the inconsequence of flies.

"How extraordinary," Lena said, again loud into the quiet room. "I loved it all, hated to go."

He had been blind to the scene, communicated nothing, and she remembered too, how the name of the commonest flower hardly ever fell from his lips. Just sitting there, silent.

How odd it had seemed, and even odder now, looked back upon, deeply recalled. It couldn't be that he had actually hated it all. And yet she pondered on this. "I asked him if he had enjoyed the day."

"Of *course* I did," the voice hot in her ear, Clem being emphatic, even protest in his voice, but the words had no ring now, leaden, hollow.

The photograph fell from her hand, which now moved about in the four tiny drawers, as though there might yet be some forgotten fragment, something she hadn't rendered as rubbish to the basket. Pushing back her chair, opening the two big bottom drawers, staring into the so recently ransacked desk. And there lay the pen and the ink, covered in dust and the new writing pad that had never been opened. She tried to remember when last he had sat there, read anything, written anything.

"We seem scarcely conscious of our own isolation," she thought, as though she had suddenly opened the door on the iron ritual of their days, his hopes, his promises, her patience, her support, losing oneself in books, in music, in yesterday, in silences. Something merciless in his withdrawal, and she becoming almost as blind as he to an insidious, penetrating boredom.

"I can't believe it's lasted so long, I can't believe that he is going to fail, I can't, I can't," as she began a voyage twenty years long. And she got up and violently switched off the light, lay down again, lost herself in the darkness. She was wholly unaware of the time, deaf to the tick of the clock, as she sank deeper and deeper into her memories of what had been; and before she had quite realized it a salvo of words in her ear, flung aggressively, vituperative, loaded with bile.

She covered her face with her hands, pressed fingers to her ears, but she could not stop Flo talking, a room now dense with Flo, with yesterday and the day before.

"God!" she thought, "fancy remembering her *now*."

"You must be *mad*," Flo said, "just walking off like that with a man, because you liked his work. You don't even know, him, dropping everything for *that*," the accentuated word like a knife tearing into distance, a light shining in Olney, a cottage looming up, *Whitestone*, an unbelievable calm.

"I thought you were happy there, it *was* our home."

Lena teaching, Lena guiding, children at her feet, days with peace in them. And the bomb that exploded, the hot breath of Flo too close for comfort. "So we sold the place, our home, and you got your money, and I got mine. And he drank it, as he drank his own. I only set eyes on him once, and I always thought he was a creep."

The room seemed drowned in light in an instant, and the cupboard wide, the bottles there. Loud into the room, as though she were quite alone, she said slowly, "One of us is becoming useless to the other."

Flo towering over her, Flo adamant, Flo final. "A *creep*," she said.

Limp words coming up, forcing them out. She remembered that, too.

"And I said to her, 'I believe in Clem, I shall stay with Clem'."

Flo's laugh only horrified her, and suddenly she felt she wanted to cry. And thought of her sister now, the last word and the last look, a feeling of being hurled from this room, against her own will, and finding herself in yet another darkness, and the wind like knives tearing at them both. Their feet cold on the concrete ground, an endless platform, the cavernous station, ceaseless hurrying of feet, the air rocked in shouts, an east wind in their faces. And Lena bewildered, Lena reaching out, groping, gripping her sister's hand, and saying mumblingly, "I just can't believe you're going, dear," and Flo quickly turning away, as though the slave of an instantaneous disgust. Lena resolute, saying for the sixth time, "I won't leave Clem, I'll never leave him," which made Flo move at last, turn slowly and face her, wanting to cry, wanting to shout "Waste!" wanting to shout "Don't" and something in her iron nature refusing to give, to listen, to accept. A sudden and uncomfortable silence as they looked deep into each other's eyes, and then the almost plaintive voice of Lena, which seemed at distance, the gentle words, and Flo leaning close to her, trying to understand.

"I hope you'll be happy, Flo," Lena said, and seeing the tear drop, knew she could add nothing to that, and the wish as powerful as a wave. "I hope you will, dear, I mean that."

"I can't believe it," Flo said, "I can't."

"What's that?"

"Nothing."

The hand reaching out in the darkness, feeling for another, and Lena's abrupt, heaved "I *wish* . . ."

"*Don't.*"

Then normal in a moment, "You'll write, Flo."

"I'll write," she said, an instant prisoner of her sister's violent embrace, a frenzied holding on, as if aware of the desert that would soon lie between them.

"I know you think I'm a fool, dear," Lena said.

"You *are.*"

"But I'm happy in spite of it, I really am. I love Clem, and I believe in him."

"Taking credit for your blindness," Flo said.

"I feel sad, *sad.*"

"Don't cry, Lena, don't."

Her face hidden behind a spread of handkerchief, and Flo's fierce whisper, "There! Did you hear that, I must go now, I must *go,*" and Lena deaf, Lena turning round and round, losing her sister's hand, searching again, gripping it with both her own, and stuttering, "I still can't believe it, dear, it's so strange, me here, you going, a world away, a whole world away . . ."

And lips to lips, and a last pressure of hands.

"Try and be happy, Lena," Flo said.

A lift of the spirit, in spite of. "Of course I will, dear," Lena said. "I'll walk with you right to the entrance gate," putting an arm through Flo's, a slow walk from darkness to light, through the barrage of shouts, and calls, and names lingering in the air, itself urgent with the occasion. Flo the last one through, a final desperate urge to pull her sister back, a longing to shout, "Don't, don't go, Flo, don't leave me now."

"Goodbye, Lena," Flo said. "I'll write, I'll remember," trying to loosen her sister's fierce hold on her hand, then warm in her ear, "I'm as much a slave as you, dear, but a happy one."

Laughing together, and Flo hurrying quickly away, turning to wave, the wave returned, the slam of a gate, the final shout, Flo distancing, Flo lost, standing there, listening to the last fading footsteps, following them into the distance, the sudden roar of a plane replacing it. And, quite without realizing it, finally clear of the cavernous building, standing staring down at her own feet, still listening to a roar in the sky, looking up quickly to meet the oncoming bus, and muttering to herself as she boarded it, "Flo *gone*. I can't believe it."

Restless where she lay, in the darkness, turning and turning, no longer aware of the silence that sealed the room. One hand tightly gripped the back of the settee, as though she was afraid she might be torn clear of it, her mind rocking with situation after situation, hours resurrected, and names as heavy as feet treading round and round. Another voyage, her whole body giving a shudder as she remembered the voyage of flesh, short, disastrous, and at last she could hold back no longer, and hid her face behind spread fingers, as if in this instant a whole world was looking in, and cried, and turned over to bury her face in the cushion, a surge of feeling she could no longer control. The white coat, the stiff child, a word in the air.

"*Sorry.*"

The ghost voice, and the real one following after, a

warmth of arms in the loaded evening. Clem there, sure, certain, his arms encircling, bearing her up, stroking her hair, her hands. Looking at him, glad he was there, saying it pathetically against his wet mouth. "Clem!" There. With her, in the room full of chattering sounds and the too loud tapping of feet, a whiteness everywhere, and in a far corner, holding each other up, accepting a fact.

"Clem," she said, smothering it in the cushion, turning over, facing the darkness again, and he was still there, an opening and closing of eyes and Clem gone, and then his name again, weak in the air, "Clem."

Falling asleep, exhausted, drained, a light fading, a single footstep up a long narrow room, waking with a start, and he was still there, quietly sat, and very still, looking at her, and after a while, quietly smiling as he pressed her hand. The whisper in her ear, and a fresh embrace.

"You never told them your age," he said. "A near thing."

Remembering the words that never left her tongue.

"If you lived to be a hundred, dear, you'd never know how I feel.".

"The way he helped me that time, the way he *worked*," a cold moment forgotten. "We grew closer still," she thought, dragged the repeated words, "we were closer still."

But that, like Flo, was already deserts away.

"Poor Flo. She never did write. How often I wished she had."

She longed for an utter stillness, a cessation of movement, a drowning of names, an obliteration of this voyaging to and fro, a room filling with ghosts, a sudden longing for sleep. It was only now that she became aware of the ticking of the clock, that even as she listened, seemed to grow louder in her ears. She came erect in a moment, cried out, "Where am I?"

She half staggered from the settee, groped her way to the wall, felt for the switch, pressed it. "How long have I been lying here?"

She stood there, her finger on the switch, and looking around her realized that nothing had changed, and it was still the same room. "How long have I been asleep? *Was* I asleep? I was dreaming, that's it, dreaming." And everything stared back at her, there was no change. She made a sudden rush to the window and threw it open, she felt herself smothering, and put her head out. A strong incoming breeze lifted her hair, and then a slight rattling sound, and when she looked saw that the small green oval mirror was shaking on the wall. She went straight to it, looked in. When last had she stood like that, watching herself peep out, and she withstood the immediate shock of it. Yes, she had changed, and leaning forward touched the glass with her lips, as she muttered to herself, "I am old. Yes, I am. And so is he." The fresh air poured through the window, and the facts with it. She thought of the things she would say when Clem came in, and she thought of the things she would not.

5

The first thing that Stevens did when he closed the door behind him, was to walk to the kerb and stand there. The noise deafened him, and then he rushed back to the door, walked a few paces, and leaned to the wall. He raised both hands in the air, as though stroking it. Yes, he was out. "I've actually done it, I'm out," he said.

He was acutely conscious of the incessant roar of the traffic, the passing of hundreds of feet, a continuous procession of glaring headlights biting into the distance. He paced up and down, always keeping close to the protecting wall. And he couldn't believe that he had left the house. He hurried towards the road, stopped dead on the corner, looked back.

"Where?" he asked himself, "where?"

He hardly noticed the people he bumped into, or they him, and was deaf to one or two angry observations. The lights that struck ever deeper into the darkness fascinated him. He turned another corner, increased his pace, without knowing where or in which direction his steps were taking him.

"Walk," he thought, "walk," he said aloud.

Head down, unseeing, blind to the lights.

"I am right. I know I am. I couldn't have said, 'Come along, Lena, let's go'," telling himself that where Lena was at this very moment was right, and he thought of her lying there in the darkness.

"She *is* ill. I'm sure she is. God! She looked exhausted when she came back this morning. I saw it. And what did Beecham say to her, what happened? She hasn't said a word. She's worried about that bloody *house*, but so am I," and the words in his throat that refused to come clear. "Suppose we do have to go. *Where?*"

Crossing another road, turning another corner. He looked up at the sky, at last was conscious of a distant London hum.

"Yes. We seem to have been living in that room for ages, even the bricks know us, and where the hell am I going *now?*"

A lamp in the distance, and beneath it a bench, and sitting down.

"What's been happening to us?"

Tearing at the cigarette packet, lighting up, a great puff and a sigh, leaning back to the wall, the cars coming on and on, the lights flashing, but he could no longer hear the sound of hurrying feet.

Leaning forward, staring down at his hands, flinging a cigarette into the air. "Done nothing for weeks, nothing."

And what was worse, Lena there, Lena *knowing*, close, all the time, living with it, accepting it; and bolt upright again, restless, lighting yet another cigarette, blind to the passers-by, digging deeper into himself.

"Horrified me when she said it, couldn't believe it, like an ultimatum, didn't want to hear," and the words bobbing up that would never lie down. "What would I do if one morning she never came back?"

No answer. He could only think of her loyalty, the things she had done for him, even supplying the smiles. "Yes, and watching me work, *try*ing to, working again, and the silences in between." He got a curious satisfaction from a sudden deep draw on his cigarette.

"I'd never leave her, never, she's been marvellous," and the very thought gave him a lift of the spirit, and, head down, he went on mumbling to himself, then surprised a passing man when he jumped to his feet, exclaiming in a near shout, "I wish to God I . . ." And dropping heavily to the bench again, he did not notice the man halt suddenly, turn, and look back at him.

Getting up, turning yet another corner, walking into a road, across it, entering a tiny street, stopping dead, staring at the short row of cottage-type houses, saying to himself, "It is, it must be," meandering down, and nearing the bottom suddenly seeing a church, the long embankment wall, rushing across the road, leaning on it, looking at the river.

"Good Lord!"

A chilliness in the air and he didn't feel it, but was now conscious of the loud rustling of leaves, seeing his own shadow ten foot long, turning away, recrossing the road, back to the small street, ambling down, first on one side, and then the other, staring at these houses, lights behind curtains. How dark it was, how shut away this small street. He stood outside a house, saw a blue door, a big brass knocker.

"What the hell am I doing here?"

And somebody else, throwing wide a door, and Stevens drowned in light, and a man emerging to the street, asking the same question, a tall man in a dressing gown, pulling the door behind him, his face a white blob in the darkness. And the hurled questions that shocked Stevens, drawing himself up, staring at this man.

"What the hell are you staring at? Want to buy the bloody house, rent it, set fire to it? You've been standing there nearly fifteen minutes just staring at it. What the hell d'you want?"

Getting closer, pressing his bulk against Stevens.

"Oh!" and Clem jerked it out, and a loud, stuttered, "I'm so sorry."

"Should damned well think so," the man said, and the door slammed in his face, so that he did not see Stevens begin to run, and not stop running until he was clear of the street.

Standing on the corner, hammering it out, "Yes, of course, it was, it *is*. God, fancy my bumping into a place where we once used to live."

Leaning against a lamp post, watched buses hurl by, the headlights moving on and on, the very air churned by noise.

"I can't believe that we were ever there, I really can't,"

and the first smile. "Damn!" flinging the empty packet into the air. "I'd better get back."

How long had he been out? He didn't know. The lights from a pub attracted him and he crossed over, but made no move to enter, unable to make up his mind, and then going on again, and walking, and walking and walking.

"Where the hell am I?" he thought.

Another pub at the bottom of the road, and on immediate impulse he went in, walked quickly to the counter and asked for a whisky, then quickly to an unoccupied corner table and he was glad to sit down. A distant clock chimed, and he looked across at the clock over the counter. An hour. He had been out one hour.

"Seem to have walked everywhere tonight."

There were only three people in the bar, and he was glad of that, and as he took his first swig of whisky hoped that he would be left alone. But nobody would notice him, there was nothing specially attractive about this tall, middle-aged man, overcoated, and a hat drawn down over his forehead. The questions came; he seemed to see them as on iron legs, walking round and round this table. The licensee gave him a single glance and then forgot him.

"Is Lena really ill? Is it too late for me? How can I begin *again*, where? And what use is that bloody stuff that I keep staring at, day after day, and putting another bloody canvas up, and doing nothing but stare at it? What the hell's the matter with me?"

He finished off his drink, crossed to the counter for another one.

"Wild night," the licensee said, but Stevens so remorselessly wrapped up in himself didn't even hear, paid for the drink, emitted a clipped "Thank you" and went back to the table. More questions, moving round and round.

"I know she's worried as hell about this house business. But Christ, aren't I? If only it could be cleared up. But when, how? Where would we go? We look at each other, all of a sudden *knowing*, the eye spells the question and the answer never comes. And now dependent on a butcher in

Euston. Nobody calls now, nobody writes, and we look at each other knowing we're both wondering and bewildered in the same moment." Sitting up, closing his eyes, and hoping they would vanish, which, at this moment were so real to him that he could yet hear them travelling around this table, this snug corner table, half in and half out of the garish lights of the room. "And I look terrible, too," he said to himself, regretting that fugitive glance in the big mirror as he came into the pub. Raising his glass, staring into it, slowly sipping the whisky, and one hand on the table suddenly clenched, as if, after the questions the mea culpa's were on parade.

"I should have told her I was going out. I hope she's asleep, I hope she hasn't gone to look for me. Yes, I should have told her. What the hell's big and secret about going for a walk. She would have come, I know she would, but I didn't want that, and she looks awfully tired, and I'm still scared about what that man Beecham said." Finishing the drink, wondering if he should have another, darting a glance at the clock, and catching the stare of the man behind the counter, a silence heightened by the fact that the last man had now gone. Half rising, sitting down again. "I'd better get back, yes, I'll go now," getting up, walking slowly to the counter, searching his pockets, pulling out the money, asking if he could have a bottle of whisky to take out.

"Certainly, sir."

Getting it, paying for it, saying casually, "Low on customers this evening."

"Never our good night, sir," the licensee said, "the telly nails them down."

"Of course," Stevens said, and pocketed the whisky.

"Wind seems to have dropped, sir."

"Yes, hasn't it," he replied, and he couldn't remember ever having heard it. He paused at the door, turned, smiled, called out, "Well, good night."

"Good night, sir." The licensee, locking the door after him, thought, "An odd lot."

Stevens was still standing outside the door. "Ah well,"

and he started off home. His feet moved forward, but his mind travelled backward, and of a sudden a name had shot into his mind, something right out of a forgotten distance.

"Cruickshank," he said, at first to himself, and then aloud, as he hurried down the now deserted road. Cruickshank. Popping up like that, after all that time, how long, and he knew he daren't put the question. Cruickshank. There. Beside him, coming all that way, smashing years down, and Stevens remembering. "He did me a kindness. The way Lena turned on me when I mentioned his name the other evening. 'Crawling,' she said."

"*Crawling?*" he asked himself, "he once bought two pictures of mine, perhaps she's forgotten," and the dampers that followed, hearing them, and noticing an angry expression on her face. "Years ago, an old man now, what the hell are you clutching at, Clem?"

"Yes. What am I clutching at, now, after all this time, kidding myself? God, I'm bloody good at that, yes you are, Stevens, you suck it all up, all in. That's what she said. I was sorry I ever breathed his name."

Suddenly halting, looking carefully round, saying to himself, "He's so close, can almost see the man," and saw him and walked all the way to where he sat.

"A really lovely day that," the fledgling's first day out, watching the tiny man, bent over a large table, his pince-nez skimming the surface of one page after another, a cheroot dangling from his lips, and this was real to Stevens, as he remembered that it never stayed lit, and was finally dropped into the ash tray. "I can see him now, and I waited and waited and waited, just for him to look up, say something. Which he did, at long last, and how I longed, and at the same time dreaded the words that would come."

So this was more real than pub, and the light over his head more real than the sound of feet scraping as they went to and fro between counter and table. Wanting to breathe a question, hesitating, wanting to blurt it out at once, "Yes, Mr Cruickshank?"

The eyes as bright as beads behind the glasses, sitting up, sitting back, looking at him. "I wondered if he'd ever speak. I remember that day," Cruickshank staring up at the ceiling, fingers of one hand running through his hair. "I wondered how old he was, older than me, looked it." And then he said loudly, heavily, dragging it, plunging the word into the room.

"Well!" he said.

I leaned forward, my heart in my mouth, how my hands sweated as I waited, didn't know what to do with them, then hid them deep in my pockets. And waiting, waiting.

"Have you had lessons, Mr Stevens?"

"A few," I said, and I felt scared then, I really did.

The promptness of his reply. Stevens remembered that, vividly.

"And you need more and more," Cruickshank said. "Draughtsmanship not good, Mr Stevens."

The surprise was wonderful, lifted me right into the air, and he came closer to me, "I do like your blues and whites," he said. "Your favourite colours?"

"I like black, too, Mr Cruickshank."

"Do you?"

And stuttering it out, "But I like *all* colours, sir," I said. And then I plunged. "I put everything into the nudes," I said.

And a too prompt reply, an inevitable summing up. "Ugly," he said. "Ugly."

"It shook me, it really did. I even felt like hitting him, I was so mad. I loved my bent and battered old woman, and I *still* do."

Leaning against a low wall, feeling the surprise, the shock of it.

"Are you all right, sir?"

And Stevens jumping at the sound, staring up at the officer, spitting it out. "I'm fine, officer, thank you."

A torch in his face. "I just wondered why you stood here so long, sir. Good night."

Heavy feet into the distance, watching him go, and

Stevens even began to count the steps until they faded into distance.

Cruickshank again, lighting another cheroot, more words in the air.

"Most kind of you to bother, sir," I said.

"Promise there," he said, and I felt at least ten foot high, really did.

Moving on, talking to himself, vaguely, dreamlike, loving the words that rang in his ears, in this long dark road, and only the echo of his own footsteps. Listening to them, repeating them.

"I like your whites and blues, Mr Stevens."

"I wanted to laugh out loud, take his hands, shake them, I was so happy."

Another clock striking, turning another corner, and loaded with another time.

"He even liked my still life, the fruit, he said, 'It'll disintegrate at any moment, young man,' and I said, 'I'm glad of that, sir, *glad*.' "

"I've a small gallery myself, Mr Stevens," he said, "nothing to shout about of course, but still a gallery. Perhaps you'll drop in on me some time."

"Of course, sir. Thank you."

"Where do you live?"

I told him. "Yes, and I'm still *there*," and suddenly he began to run.

Stood at a bus stop, and a dark figure emerging from a doorway.

"Last one's gone five minutes ago," the inspector said, and vanished into the dark again.

Running, and thinking of Lena, hearing her say, "Dr Beecham thinks I need a break, dear, a real break," and Beecham leaping out, confronting him. "Damned good mind to go and see him myself. Poor Lena."

Bumping into a girl, catching a big smile, the teeth showing.

"No," shouting it, pushing her away, moving on, she behind him, gripping his coat, saying, "bugger you then."

"Where am I now?" he asked himself, and then he recognized a known landmark. Chesil Place. And how badly lighted it was now, a lost street; beginning to run again, blind to the long row of once elegant houses, dark, and scarcely a light showing. "She'll wonder where I've gone, she . . . thinking of her sitting alone in 'that damned room'."

He pulled up, began searching for the key, in one pocket, then in all, cursing himself for having forgotten it. "What in hell did I do with it?" glaring at the closed door, hating to knock, knocking, waiting. Even as he heard the heavy steps across the hall, he knew, and angrily so, what had happened to the key. "I threw it at her weeks ago," just as the door opened, and he saw Grimpen standing there, exclaiming rather angrily, "And who are you?"

He stepped into the hall, Grimpen backing away, saying, "The name's Stevens, and I live in the top flat," passing Grimpen by, not looking at him, and the caretaker replying even more angrily, "Oh! You are, are you? Then it's bloody late, isn't it?"

He watched Grimpen cross the hall again, plod down stone steps, heard the door open and close, then stood at the bottom of the stairs, noticing for the first time the badly lighted hall and landings, and a rude echo of dilapidation on its way as he heard the first loud creak on a broken stair. Quietly up to the first flight, and then the second, in a now soundless house, passing closed door after closed door, reaching the top, tiptoeing to his own door, standing in the darkness feeling for the doorknob, turning it, creeping into the room flooded with light, and not expecting this, then seeing Lena sat in his chair, facing the door. He closed the door, stood looking at her. After which a late lie, as she said rather coldly, "There you are, Clem."

"Here I am," and he removed his coat and hat and hung it behind the door.

Her burst of laughter shocked him, and he turned quickly, hurried down the room.

"I heard you creeping out, dear, and I heard you creeping

99

back," then got up and met him face to face, and now wearing an incomprehensible smile, as she continued, "You haven't really been out into the world, have you? Surely not. Did you actually see people out there, dear?"

"You were asleep when I left, Lena," he said, and advanced down the room.

She was relieved when he didn't add that he was sorry. The hand on his arm brought assurance.

"What happened?"

Only then did she notice that he was wearing a suit, that he had bathed and shaved. He sat down, and she followed him, and her long steady look unnerved him for a moment. The words crept out.

"Are you all right, dear?" he asked.

"Of course I'm all right. And you?"

"Should've said, really, but I wanted to be really alone, dear. So I just had a bath and changed and went out, just like that," flicking finger and thumb.

She seemed on the point of smiling, and then did not.

"I can't believe it," she said, gripped the arms of the chair, bent over him. "You actually saw people. *Well!*"

"I walked and walked and walked, even went into a pub, had a drink. I brought something back."

She noticed a sudden flush, knew what he meant, and she remained motionless.

"Thought you'd have gone to bed," he said.

"As you see I didn't."

"You're not angry, Lena?"

"Why should I be angry. About what?"

"Hammered on the door."

"I heard you, dear."

"Searched for the damned key, couldn't find it, and Grimpen finally got up and opened the door, could hear him growling like an old bull behind it. I thought he was bloody impudent, into the bargain."

"Wouldn't you be, woken up at this time of the night? You know the Grimpens are early bedders, or you ought to."

"Glad to see the back of him. Then coming up the stairs I suddenly knew about the absent key, remembered what had happened . . ."

"Where was it, Clem?"

"Too ashamed to say, Lena," and she knew he was, and looked it.

"You threw it at me, dear, and I picked it off the floor, and after a while it didn't seem to matter very much, and I forgot all about it," getting up, and adding abruptly, "I'm going to make tea, dear, like some?"

"Please."

She turned as she reached the door, faced him.

"I've been thinking about such a lot of things this evening, Clem."

"Oh?" and he came half out of the chair.

"I thought something might be coming to an end, dear."

"Can I help?"

"*No.*"

And left him there, curiosity tearing at him. "Something's happened, I know, could tell as soon as I saw her when I came in just now. I wonder what?"

Later, she came in with the tray, put it on the settee and served him. "Would you like something to eat, Clem? You didn't have much supper."

"No thanks. Just the tea, Lena," and she watched his shaking hand as he gulped at the tea.

"What d'you mean, something's coming to an end? You make it sound like a mystery."

"Which it isn't. It's a bloody hard fact, dear," and then he spilt tea on his clothes, and she added quickly, "Clumsy."

"You appear to have spent the entire evening thinking, Lena. Can I get wise on it?"

She made him wait for the answer, noting his final gulp at the tea, then letting the saucer fall, dropping the cup, and a hand in his pocket, and she knew the infernal cigarette would emerge at any moment.

"I had a visitor."

He jumped to his feet. "A visitor?" then sat beside her. "Who?"

"The lady from the basement, dear."

"Mrs *Grimpen*?"

And just audible, she replied, "Yes."

"What did she want, Lena?"

"Nothing, really. She brought some news, that's all, and she didn't stay long, there seemed no reason to do so. I stood at the top of the stairs, watching her go down. How those stairs creak now."

The casualness was like bile. "Well! What *was* it, dear?"

"We must be out of here by November 10th," she said. "More tea?"

"*No*," he covered his face with his hands, spluttered through his fingers. "Christ! Wish I'd never gone out."

Her sporadic bursts of laughter made him feel uncomfortable, as she added vigorously, "And I wish I hadn't stayed *in*. Quite a change for you to receive a bit of news, I'm always on the receiving end. All the same, I'm glad that at last you decided in favour of fresh air."

As she rose he drew away from her, and she wondered why.

"You . . . you haven't been drinking, Lena, have you?"

Her loud "Yes" shocked him. She had had one or two, and now she was going to have another, and the smile that followed he found more disturbing. He had never seen her like this.

"Been cupboard exploring," she said, "found nearly half a bottle there, and I know you've brought something back, Clem. I could tell at once. I'm not *drunk*."

He half ran to the cupboard and threw open the doors, surveyed the contents, as he thought furiously, "What in hell's *wrong*?" bewildered and still a little frightened by the outburst.

"Must get rid of this damned stuff," he growled.

"You *must*," and she sat back, studying his approach with a bottle in one hand and two glasses in the other. "I should wash those glasses, dear."

He turned at the door, and his reply came wrapped in a sulk.

"You're not always like this, Lena," he said.

"And I'm not always like *that*, either," she snapped back, and knew she'd shocked him.

He found her staring into space when he came back with the washed glasses. He found it difficult to make up his mind, should he just stand there, should he sit down. He sat, and tendering a drink said quietly, "It's late, dear."

"I'm not tired."

She supped noisily at the whisky, his own remained in his hand, and she noticed it shaking. "Perhaps he's asking himself how he should cope with a new situation," and holding her glass aloft, asked, "Aren't you having it then?"

"Of *course*."

The expression on his face highly amused her.

"Then come closer, dear, you make me feel uncomfortable sitting like that. I slept and woke on at least five occasions, and I even noticed the clock as I put the light on on each occasion," she said, leaning hard against him. "Dreamland dealt me a rare portion this evening. Seem to have dreamed about everybody, and the last person ever was Flo."

"Flo!"

"*Flo.*"

"You have had a time," he said, but she wasn't even listening as she continued, quietly, casually, "Expect you'll remember her, sister of mine, gone now, poor thing, she never wrote, after all," hurt in the voice, "said she *would*. Perhaps we were strangers all the time. Just occurred to me, Clem. She never liked you, dear, told me first time she didn't, and I'd never tell you what she said . . ."

"Don't," he said, noticing the suddenly parted lips, the loose hanging mouth.

"I wouldn't tell you, dear."

"All right, all *right*."

She tossed off the drink, pushed the glass roughly into his hand.

"Come *on*," she said.

"There."

"How begrudging he is," she thought. "You're angry with me, aren't you, just because I found out for myself what it is that makes you like the stuff. And remember I always managed to bring you a bottle when I went out for my ration of fresh air. Don't be angry with me, you have no bloody right to be, dear. Tell you something, I didn't like what Flo said, and I never liked her very much after that."

"What the hell *did* she say?"

"You'd love to know that, dear, wouldn't you, yes, you really would," and concluded with a loud titter.

He exploded in her face. "*Tell* me."

He jumped to his feet, but she pulled him down again. "*Please*," she said.

"There's always a place I can go," he said, and tore himself free, strode across the room, and she rose, followed clumsily after him, taunting.

"Yes, of course. You can always go in there, study your life's work. Then bloody go," and she caught the tail of the jacket he was wearing. "But I'd like to come, too, dear, can I come?"

The moment she kissed him he knew she was drunk. He put a finger under her chin. "I'm not angry, Lena," he said. "I've never been angry with you."

"Why should you be? After all, we've been together for so long, Clem, and as I'm sure you know, I've always stood by you, helped whenever I could," and her weight pressed him against the half open door. "You must remember those times when I was happy, Clem, when you were *working*. And you were happy, too, I never forget nice things, never. And I . . ."

He freed himself, propelled her through the door, caught her as she was about to fall, saying, "Right. You want to see the stuff, then Christ, come and see it," and dragged her after him, kicked open the door of the workroom, switched on the light. "Okay. There it is, the whole damned lot of it. Sit there," and he forced her to the floor, where she sprawled, then leaned back against the wall. He tripped over her leg, himself fell, swore, came erect, then stood looking down at her.

"Bring the bottle," she said.

She heard him go out, closed her eyes, waited. "An infuriating bastard when he wants to be," she told herself, and almost without her realizing it, he was back, now sat beside her, the bottle between his knees, an empty glass sticking out of his pocket. Automatically she pushed out the glass, and said, with a slight stammer, "Here it is. *Again*."

He hesitated, took a long look at her, the head bent right back, the long arm, the dangling hand, the glass perilously held between two fingers. It was the merest whisper, but she heard it.

"Are you all *right*, Lena?"

"I'm fine. How are you?"

The glasses were refilled. He turned sharply as she gave vent to another titter and under his breath, exclaimed, "My, God!"

"What's *that*?"

"Nothing, nothing at all."

But it was, for looking at her now, her whole appearance saddened him. She seemed suddenly inert, seemingly unaware that he was actually sat beside her. His slight sigh went unheard, and he could only realize how ugly the moment had made her. He felt a sudden shame, and turned his head away, even as her heavy arm came round his neck, and she pulled him to her.

"I'm not . . . drunk," and the stare was brazen.

"Shall we look at the lifework?" he asked, but the words were leaden, and she did not hear them.

"But I'm happy, Clem, I'm . . . ha—ppy."

"Are we?"

'We'll look at everything, dear," she said, "I mean everything."

His shout seemed to shake the very room. "*Right*."

It was some relief when he finally came erect, and he felt he had been freed as from chains.

"You're not drinking," she said.

"I am," and he again refilled the glass. "There. See it. Look at it," the words climbed, the voice suddenly emasculated, and he held the glass close to her eyes. "*See?*"

Closing her eyes again, she avoided his single glance that spelt out a sudden disgust.

"Exhibit *one*," he said acidly, and stepped over her, ignored the abrupt giggle, got clear, bent over a large canvas, turned it round.

"There! Look at it. *Look* at the bloody thing."

She managed to drag herself to her feet, and he held her steady.

"No need to fall over the bloody thing. *There!*"

"C—Clem?"

And she got the roar direct in her ear. "*What?*"

"What . . . is . . . it?"

He did not answer, stood watching her as she stared at the canvas, and he noticed a slight glaze in the eye, a vacant, almost stupid expression upon her face, and then the dead weight of her against him, the glass falling to the floor, as she heaved it out, "D'you . . . d'you . . . think . . ."

"Not even thinking."

"Give me my *glass.*"

He bent down and returned it to her.

"*Please*," she said.

His hand enveloped the glass. "D'you really think you should?"

"Be—because . . . you . . . think . . . I *shouldn't*?"

Overfilling her glass he could no longer conceal his anger. "*Damn* you."

"Why . . . should you have it *all*?"

He put down his glass, caught her by the shoulders, held her close, and exclaimed angrily, "You're not even looking at the bloody thing."

"I *am.*"

He pushed her violently forward, and her face almost skimmed the surface of the painting. "*There!*"

But the moment she dribbled he pulled her violently back,

and hissed in her ear, "This is a bloody farce," steadied her hand, pushed the glass to her lips. "Drink it, Christ, *drink* it," held back her head, watched it dribble down her chin.

"The first time, the first time I ever saw Lena drunk," he murmured, just as she dropped the glass for the second time.

He sat her down again, and when he joined her she fell half across him, felt a wet mouth at his ear.

"Clem!"

"Well?" and he flung his answer ceilingwards.

"You're . . . I mean . . . you're not . . ."

"I'm *not*."

"Don't know what I was going to say."

"I *do*."

"Clem?"

"*Well?*"

"Perhaps it's . . ."

"I'm *not* . . . *ang*ry," he said.

"Shouldn't have . . ."

"*Know*. It's a bloody farce."

"Take my *hand* . . . can't you," she said.

She now lay fully across him, and he put an arm round her, saying, "Listen."

"What?"

And the instant gentleness that she didn't even notice. "I know how you feel, dear."

"*Do* you?"

"You're not yourself, Lena, I understand that, the whole bloody thing," he said, and then she felt his hand, stroking her hair.

"I *am* myself. Who are *you*?"

It came slowly, whispered, "I thought you said you wanted to see my life's work," he said, with heavy sarcasm.

"I do," she said, struggling to rise, but he held her down.

"You can't even *see* the damned stuff."

She tore herself free, stood up, staggered across the room, and turned a canvas round. And then bent over it, and the loud shouts.

"Hair flying away from the head, look at the *eyes*, you

hammered her face, the *chin*, no neck, collapsed tits, a mean backside and that figure of eight dance down to her feet, I've seen these bloody feet . . . *splayed*, look at the nails . . . uncut . . . claws . . . clinging on to all she is."

She turned and faced him. Then quietly, more controlled, "I really thought that was the beginning, I did, I *did*, at bloody last, but no . . . it wasn't . . . was it . . . was it? The strokes are marvellous," she said, "ruthless, that's *it*."

The room was suddenly silent, he looking up at her, she staring down.

"That all?"

She came to him, slid to his side, again leaned heavily to him, and her mouth half open stuttered, "You disrupted the whole damned thing. *Feel*ing. Dangerous as explosives . . ." putting a hand under his chin, spelling it out again, "Good, said it was, the rest's . . ."

He pushed himself clear, glad to be free of the weight, lay back against the wall, picked up the bottle, from which he now took a great swig, and then he held it high in the air.

A sudden belch shocked him, and the bottle hit the floor with a thud. He had never seen her in such a state. A fuzz was slowly creeping across her mind, and she was no longer listening.

But he droned on.

"My name's Clem, dear, and yours is Lena . . . *Lena*. We've been together a long time, a *long* time. If you left me, I'd fall down. But so would *you*. Come on, Lena, let's get out of here, *please*, come along," and again he was stroking her hair, again aware of her strong breath. "In the morning we'll talk about everything."

It was only then that he realized she had fallen asleep, her breathing heavier, more spasmodic. He turned away, looked across at the work she could no longer see. He took a final swig at the bottle, wondering about what had come to an end. He got to his knees, took a final look at her, saw that one hand was pawing the wall behind her, crept to the door, and returned to the living room. He made up the bed on the settee, then went back, picked her up and carried her back, lay her down, went back once more and switched off the light in the workroom. He undressed, and put her to bed. The mere fact that he had switched off that other light, that she was now flat and stretched and inert, induced in him an enormous relief. Something was actually *over*, the end of a situation that was no farce. As he began to undress he heard a movement and hurried to her. She had turned her face to the wall. "Poor old dear," he thought, and went back to his own bed, finished undressing, slipped across and put out the light. He covered his head with the sheet, lay still, and he tried to understand it all.

"Horrible. Horrible."

He listened to the laboured breathing, the periodic snort. Then he turned over on his face, talked into the pillow.

"Beecham. I must *see* him. There is something wrong with her," then turned over and over, fact after fact in tow. "Have to go, must find somewhere, where? Perhaps something will turn up . . . will . . . won't . . . She's right, needs a break, must get away, where? If we could start all over again."

The thought of seeing Beecham, of finding out, afforded him a temporary balm.

"Must see him, yes, in the morning, *must*," at which point thought stopped, the facts receded, dragged words into the distance. He pulled away the sheet, sat up, listening again, imagined he heard a thud. "She's fallen off," and he ran across, knelt there, looked at her, the face a white splash in darkness, then crept back, hid himself again, pulling at the sheet, and the words all over again, unable to be free.

"If only she knew how I despised myself, sitting in that damned room with her. The quiet, savage determination with which she drank and *drank*. Why did I ever go out? What did I find, get? Nothing. Suppose she wakes up, it starts all over again. I felt a pig. She's been so loyal. 'Who are *you*?' she said. 'All that damned stuff in the cupboard,' she said. 'All that lot,' I said, and I never realized there were so many bottles standing there. The complaint, the sour voice. 'I used to get sick,' she said, 'just looking at them, and

I carried some of them down the bloody *stairs*.' Stairs. Just like a whip at my ear."

A sudden movement on the settee and he was back again, listening to the now deep snores. Words on the way back, what she said yesterday, the day before.

"Suppose that one morning I never came back," she said.

Back to the bed, hoping to sleep, diving again, back into his own life, their first days, the singular happiness.

"So sad, the lot of it, even told me what her sister said, what did she say. Wish she'd never opened her mouth. It got me. How I wish . . . What *grew*? Hiding something. What *did* Beecham *say*? Must see him."

Later, his snores joined her own. A gust of wind fluttered the curtains, filled the room. And the thud that finally woke him. Picking her up, saying, "There, there. I'm here, it's all right, dear, *here*."

"What time is it?"

"Doesn't matter."

"It *does*."

6

The abrupt silence that followed embarrassed him. He moved down the settee. "I'm sorry about last night, dear," he said.

"I was drunk."

"So was I."

"Where do we go from here?" she asked, and felt the hand on her arm.

"We could leave London."

"Go *where*?"

"Anywhere, out of it."

"I've got so used to this place," she said, "I think I'll miss it."

"Matter of having to," he said.

"How practical you are."

"November 10th, you said."

"I did. When you came through that door last night and I looked at you, it'll amuse you, Clem, but I thought of yet another opus, and even the title. *Old Man Coming Home*," and he didn't like the light laugh that followed.

"I know how old I am, dear."

"So do I. I'm older than you."

"Where does this lead?"

"Wherever you like, dear," she replied.

He gripped both arms, and said with great emphasis, "Last night was horrible. And I've never seen you look so angry, and you had a bloody right to be."

"But you didn't mind my getting drunk?" she said, took his hand, gave it a squeeze. "I don't often get drunk, Clem. But I enjoyed it, and I wasn't even angry. I *mean* that."

"Really?"

"Yes, dear."

"Dead honest?"

"Dead honest."

He kissed her, saying "The relief, the relief," and then the voice that was uncertain, "I'm wondering what I could collect on the shares, Lena."

"How thoughtful of your mother, dear. I'd have bought some myself one time, but then I gave you what money I had. I didn't mind, not in the least, I remember saying to myself, 'He will do something, I *know* he will'."

Her whole expression had changed, and she noticed the quick lowering of his head, a shot gone home, and she sealed this as she added, "You've shown promise for years, Clem, that's why I stood by you."

"I've never known anybody like you, Lena," he said.

"And I've never known anyone like *you*, dear," she replied.

"The way you said that, it could mean anything."

"I suppose it could. I didn't really need to look at all that stuff last night, I know it by heart, I've seen them in my sleep, seen them when I woke up, when *you* were asleep, counted them over and over again. Inside I'm simply loaded with seas, and roads, and churches, and flowers, and crooked houses, and nude old women, I've had the bloody lot. 'Think of it,' I said to myself, 'twenty years, and nothing happening, nothing, *nothing*'."

It left him speechless, he could only sit there, still holding her hand, ashamed again, hating himself, and the eternal question round and round his brain. "Is she *ill*? *How* ill?"

"Tell me what Beecham *said*, Lena."

"I told you. Weren't you listening?"

"What did he *say*? It's not . . . I mean . . . it's not that . . ."

"No. Not that. Definitely not that. How relieved I was, you'll never know. But if you want to know what he said, I'll tell you again, he said I need a break, he said I looked worn out. Will that do?"

"I'm not indifferent, I *am* aware, yes, I have neglected you, thought of nothing except myself, I'm a selfish bastard, I'm—"

"Stop kidding yourself."

"Listen, dear," he said.

"Stop kidding *me*."

And then for the first time he shouted in her face. "Lash *away*."

"It's too late, Clem."

For a moment she thought he'd break down, actually cry.

"I've spent the most agonizing bloody year," he said, "and I've said nothing, bottled it up. I mistrust myself."

"Crawl to Cruickshank, if he's still standing on two feet. You seem to like him, you mentioned him only yesterday. *See* him. He might tell you who you are, because I don't know, you've changed, Clem, changed. Perhaps you promised too much."

"Take it to the end," he said, "go on, keep at it, it's your day, dear, your bloody day."

"My God!" she thought, "I've never seen him so bitter. But it's not ended, not finished, not yet."

And it wasn't.

"I know it's a long time ago, but it's what we're talking about. That first exhibition he gave you, you paid for the damned lot of it," then lightly, casually, "you never told me at the time. I wondered why."

"Yes, that's right."

"I thought you trusted me," she said.

"I do, I do, I should have told you at the time."

Her sudden smile intrigued him, and she ran a hand through his hair. "You've gone completely grey, dear," and after a pause, "I thought he was generous at the time. I mean buying that little picture of yours, forgotten what it was. Was I delighted when it happened? I *was*. Something happening for you."

"I'll get rid of the bloody stuff," he said.

"Do that. I often thought it a great pity that you, with your great enthusiasm for painting, had so little interest in other directions. I doubt very much if you'd ever read a book until you met me."

She saw a fist tighten, the knuckles whiten, wondered if he would hit her.

"*Lash* away," he replied, and pocketed his fist.

She went across to the window, opened it wide, put her head out, was glad of a slight breeze, felt it in her hair.

Hearing the sudden movement she called "Don't, Clem," and heard the settee creak when he sat down again. He felt it inside himself, dreaded it there, an instant flash, and then he said it very slowly to himself, "She's going to leave me, leave me." And he was there, behind her, before she realized it. Turning she saw the partly open mouth, the lips moving and nothing coming out.

"*Say* it," he said.

"Say what?"

He felt her stiffen as he pushed her back against the window. "*Say* it."

"The bloody dreams I've had tossed into my ears all these years," she said, and when he tried to turn her round she held on even more firmly to the sill. "It was my day right enough, walking out of one simple life into another."

"I said *say* it, Lena," and he forced her to turn and look at him.

Her almost indulgent smile bewildered him, but it met only the melancholy expression that had never changed, and she was quick to notice this.

"Are you going to leave me, Lena?"

Slowly she shook her head, and her smile vanished. "He really does love me," she told herself, "this strange, irritating, obsessed man, this silent, secretive person. He so depends on me."

She pushed clear of him and went and sat down at the now ransacked bureau, sat very still, her folded arms on the open desk. He remained staring out of the window, then suddenly she exclaimed "Oh", and he swung round, came slowly down, stood by her, looking at her bare arms, her hands, which had always seemed to him like those of a peasant. He thought this silence would never end, and quietly returned to the window, on which she looked up, got a clear back view of him. This back view, this very physical gesture she found touching, thinking, "A back view is always a weaker view."

Her voice trailed across the room.

"Nothing ever mattered to me, Clem, except you, and the work you tried to do. We mustn't quarrel any more, we really mustn't. In the end there's only us, just the two of us, and we belong to each other. Sometimes I get the feeling that we're locked in, seem unable to see beyond ourselves. Sometimes indeed I find myself asking the question. What's it all about? For what?"

"We do understand each other, Lena, we do."

"We're *old*," she said.

"You said that."

"But we're still real."

"The whole two days has been bloody horrible," he said. "Whatever I said, I just say, forget it, let's forgive each other," and she got up and went to him, as though she were now searching for the warmth that still held them so close.

"Let's go out, Lena," he said, "let's go. *Now*."

She piloted him back to the settee, saying, "Tomorrow, dear, we'll go out and see what the shares will bring, and after that we *must* make plans to get away."

"Yes. We will, Lena, we will."

A momentary change, and a suddenly flat voice saying, "Two exhibitions, ten private sales, a deal of barter, the sum total."

"Yes."

"I still like your old woman studies best of all, Clem."

And a suddenly formal voice, as if he had just received a free bottle of whisky.

"Thank you," he said.

"We must eat."

"Of course," and they went off to the kitchen together, and he sat down. He lay back in the chair, lit a cigarette, tried to relax, to forget. He watched her fuss about the meal, followed her from table to stove to cupboard.

"Who d'you think I bumped into the other morning, Clem?"

"Who?"

"That Robinson man that used to have the flat below us during the war. Remember him?"

"Robinson, Robinson . . . Rob . . ."

"The young RAF man. Remember his pretty wife, that awful crying child?"

"Yes, of course. Well, I'll be damned, just fancy bumping into him. So many people have scattered since that time one just imagined they'd all had it."

"Works on the turnstiles at Wembley now, dear. Gone almost bald, and what's left is quite white. No more than forty and looks seventy now."

"I certainly remember the poor child. His wife had a very good head, but there was nothing inside it. I once said to Robinson I'd like to do a sketch of her, and he looked positively angry about it, perhaps he thought I wanted to get her into bed. So that's what he's doing now. Poor devil. When you think of what people like that did in those really dangerous years of 1940. Makes you think. Where'd you see him then?"

"Walking in the Euston Road. You'd never recognize that road now, dear, all altered, but then everything has, and there's a different look in people's eyes, almost a new language operating. You hear people complaining about the shabbiness of everything."

She was busy at the stove, but he was thinking only of a young man high in the skies during a hot August and September, his pretty, doll-like wife, the pathetic, ever crying child. He joined her at the stove, watched things cooking, ran his hand down her arm, saying, "I was a bit of a fusspot in those days, dear, you remember?"

"I remember. It's almost ready now," she said, and he returned to the table and sat down.

"He asked after you, dear?"

But he was miles away at this moment, was lost, and blurted out, "Who?"

"Mr *Robinson*," she said.

For the first time in two whole days he actually laughed. The ice was beginning to melt.

"A strange time indeed, and nothing seemed permanent, nothing."

He concentrated on eating, enjoying his meal.

"All over now," he said, and "do *eat*, dear."

"Somehow, I'll still hate going from here, Clem, so sudden."

"*Don't.*"

"It always seemed so safe here, a real little world of our own."

"Nothing's safe, and there's not a thing you can be certain about, either."

"Let's not talk about it any more, Clem."

"Okay by me." He banged his fork on the table, she looked up, sensed what was coming.

"I really must, dear, I really must."

"And bring me one, too."

"I'll shift those empties this evening," he said, and she caught his shy glance as he slipped out of the kitchen.

"He's really harmless, perhaps I went too far."

Lost in speculation, she didn't notice his return, that he was standing there, glass in hand, saying, "There, Lena, do you good."

She pushed it away. "I don't want it now. You have it. I know you like the stuff. And you will empty the damned cupboard? *Yes?*"

"*Said* I will."

The eye again, fixed on the glass, the shaking hand. The cupboard. It depressed her. Whenever she opened it she expected an accusing voice to speak from it, someone saying, "Waste, waste." Root and meaning still held. She looked at him again, and there was the answer. An empty glass, the other hand raised, still shaking.

"I still can't believe it," Lena said.

"D'you remember the Fraser pair, Lena?"

"No, I *don't* remember the Fraser pair," she replied, not wanting to.

"*Really* lost people," Clem said, and she wasn't listening, only reflecting. Voyages up and down stairs, endless noise and tumult, crouching in a cellar, people hidden there, hand clutching hand, and the pressure, the pressure, eyes wide and ears alert for a known sound. A strange time, a beginning and end, no centre. And then the releasing sound, the voyage *up*. Waiting again for a voyage *down*. Days too short, and nights too long. She could see it, feel it all, at this very moment, seated at this table, watching his hands, and sitting up with a jerk the moment he spoke.

"Can't believe what, dear?"

"That we actually have to *go*."

"It's not the end."

"Christ! You're always saying that. If you don't empty the cupboard, I'll do it *myself*."

"Please, Lena, *please*."

And unaware of how far away she was, in the other time, the senseless time. The things one hoped for then, the *things*.

"Don't suppose you ever give it a thought," Lena said.

"What?"

"The time the future stopped dead, and everything mattered and then of a sudden it didn't."

"That!"

"That."

"Never think about the bloody war," he said, "don't want to, whole thing's a bad dream."

"Dream! *Dream?* It's real to me, *real*. This door opening and us going down, to join the mouses as that man Robinson used to say. Think of it, Clem. Remember the night it rained glass?"

"*Glass?*"

This was glass raining, this was raining glass.

Yesterday

7

It was anybody's time, it was everybody's, and it was six p.m., striking from the same clock at the perennial height, and heard by nobody, the chimes drowned in a deluge of sound, and it was raining, raining glass. It was only after this ceased, and the wind had passed, that the lone sailor fell, was sick, in the desert of air.

"Goddam! Get me out of this, get me out," he shouted, and the voice in his ear quieter, more casual, saying, "Stand up."

And he could not stand up.

"Stand *up*!"

The sailor struggled, and the crunching sounds came up, and the little man beside him began to pull, savagely, in desperation, still crying in his ear, "I said stand up."

"It's ice," the sailor said, "Christ, it's ice, get me out of this," so he fell again, and hands became feelers, pawing glass.

The little man's helmet had fallen over his nose, and he cursed the man, and the moment.

"I know ice, always something moving under ice. I *know*."

"Glass! You crazy bastard."

The cheap raincoat dripped water, and then he managed to tilt back the infuriating helmet. Afterwards he cursed the man under his hand.

"Stand bloody up," he said again, then, half bent, arms encircling the sailor, he began to pull, pull hard.

"Damn and blast you, sailor. You're *drunk*."

The sailor sprawled, and the moon appeared from behind a sheaf of cloud, but the little man came erect, conscious of his cold neck against the wet collar of the raincoat. He, too, was conscious of a black, moving shape that suddenly vanished when the moon was lost again. He bent down again, began to pull, and weight was dead weight.

"Leave me *alone*," the sailor shouted.

"What the *hell* d'you want? First you ask me to get you out of this, and now you say leave you alone. Shaking like a jelly you were. God! Wish I could leave you alone, and you could stand about all night on the bloody ice if you wanted to. Course that's just what I can't do. So come *on*, pull yourself together, get up. Being alone don't count any more. Nobody can be alone any more. See? Don't know who the hell you are, where you come from, but you just can't lie there. Come on now. Be a good chap, pull yourself together. We all lose our bearings from time to time, course we do. But I'm not going to stand over you all night. So up you come."

And he shouted again, "Up, *up*," heaving, feeling a little breathless, and again the helmet fell across his nose, and he hated it. "Blast you!"

" 'S'ice I tell you."

"All *right*. It's ice, and you're on a whole bloody shining sea of it. And watch out for that iceberg, just a degree to port, mate. Careful."

Desperate, he kicked the sailor, and then began to drag him across the sea of glass. A door was merely a vague shape in his mind as yet, but he felt he was moving towards one, and he knew he would throw this sailor behind it. He was filled with resolution, and nothing else mattered except getting one fool behind a door. "Dead drunk."

Suddenly the sailor struggled to his feet, cried again, "Christ! Get me out of this," and then he felt the hiss in his ear.

"I'm getting you out. Half a minute. I'm going to get behind you and push. Keep your feet, sailor."

He pushed hard, and as he pushed repeated, "This is *not*

ice. There are no icebergs, no rocks or reefs. You've had more than a skinful, and I wouldn't blame you, but don't start spelling it out for me. I reckon you'll stop listing after a good night's sleep. Good luck if you get it."

"Hate it, hate it," the sailor said, began to blubber. "Time is it?"

"Listen," and they both listened to the quarter hour strike from a nearby clock.

They went on, slithering and sliding, pausing and leaping forward, and all the way across the wide road the little man cursed the sailor, pressed hands even more determinedly into the small of his back. They stopped dead, the sailor's head began to loll, as though determining port and starboard.

"Christ, *move*."

The sailor's arms were suddenly outspread, and his overcoat flapped like a bellying sail, and from time to time he lost himself in incoherent mumblings, so they dragged on, halted, groped again, and he shouted at the top of his voice, "Where *am* I?"

The voice was sepulchral. "Nearly there, sailor, nearly *there*."

A black door seemed clearer in his mind. If he put out a hand he thought he would touch it.

"Get him behind it, and then he can do just what the hell he likes." His responsibility was finished, and it was goodbye to a man stood in the middle of a road crying, "Ice."

"Really drunk," he thought. "Thought he was in the Arctic ocean, I guess."

"Here we are," he cried, not seeing the door, yet knowing it was there. "You'll be okay now, sailor," he said reassuringly, even gently, "yes, you'll be all right now," and he released his hold on the sailor. Bending down he picked up a large sheet of glass, held it to the sailor's face. "See. *Not* ice. Glass. If you weren't so bleary-eyed, and could see closer you'd see this piece of glass was coloured, and that there was a head on it. So how the hell could it be ice? My guess is you've been having a bloody good time somewhere. Wouldn't blame you. Come on now," pushing again, pulling again. "Once in there you can lie flat and sleep it off. Okay when the light comes, and we're all waiting for it."

He shone the torch, and the door shone back at him.

"*Go* on. In you get," right into a sailor's ear, still dragging his way over icefields, glassy, transparent seas, bergs floating by, and boulders falling.

He gave the door a kick and it fell flat on its face. They walked in over it.

"There! Now you see what I mean, the door, the *door*, flat, no keys required, and you'll never be alone any more, sailor, told you that, nobody will. You're in. Got a match? No? Here," pushing a box into the sailor's hand. "You'll be okay now. Good night."

The door was propped up again, and the man had gone, and he did not hear the slow, crunching steps that gradually died into the distance. The sailor struck a match that immediately went out. He struck a second, and it trembled in his big, clumsy fingers. It burned.

"Hell!"

He dropped the match, covered his face with his hands, began mumbling through his fingers, "Where in hell's name am I?" turning round and round, staring into blackness, slowly surfacing from a dream area.

The next match remained alight, and holding it high he found himself in the long hall, and at the end of it a green door facing him. The high cream-coloured walls exuded damp, there was much broken plaster. He heard a tiny pattering sound, felt the draught at his feet. He bent down and felt the cold of stone, and later a carpet that ran the length of the hall. He dragged his hand to and fro across the flags. Cold. Another match yielded further secrets. The carpet was brown, and on the wall to his left a great damp patch where once a hatstand had stood. He turned and looked at the propped-up door, turned again and stared up the long spiral staircase. The match went out.

"Damn it."

The next was lucky, and then for the first time he noticed

a man at the top of the stairs, his hands gripping the rail, an eye staring down at him. The match flickered out, and he called again, "Aye, aye! Anybody there? Hello there!" and with a sudden fury began striking match after match. The box fell to the floor. He knelt down and groped about for it, suddenly sprawled, turned over on his back, crying even more loudly, "Aye bloody aye!"

At which moment the man on the stairs began to come slowly down, and his shaky hand never let go its hold on the rail. He called out in a thin, cracked voice, "That you, Mr Jones?" and waited for the answer. "That you, Mr Jones?"

There was no reply, and he came on, and on the bottom stair halted, breathing heavily, saying, "Ah! ah!" and furiously listening, but only an echo came to his ear. He staggered down the hall, went on his knees and began searching for the box of matches, and found it, and jumped at the sound it made. The struck match revealed to him the man lying flat on his back.

"Who are you?" he asked, sharply, nervously, "who are *you*?"

The loud laugh shocked him. "I'm me. Who in hell are you? Hello there, somebody. Bugger me, hello there."

"Who *are* you?"

The struck match showed him a tall, thin man, long face and long nose, with thinning fair hair. He was flat on his back, the mouth half open, the eyes opening and closing like shutters on what he saw, the sea of ice in a fast gathering darkness, and the desert of air that was colder than cold. "Aye aye there," he cried, stretched his legs, laughed, broke wind, and suddenly began to sing.

The front door fell in, and the old man cried out, "That you, Mr Jones?"

"Yes. It's me. Anything wrong?"

"I'm glad, glad," the old man said, and watched Mr Jones prop up the door.

"That's it," Mr Jones said, turned sharply, "what's the matter?"

"Somebody in."

The Jones torch suddenly swept down the hall. He saw the sailor.

"Hello hello . . . "

"Hello yourself."

"How'd you get in here?" and the torch shone full in the other's face.

"Mr Jones!"

"*Well?*"

"You all right then, Mr Jones?" stammered the old man, and moved quickly towards him.

"Sure I'm all right. How the hell did this chap get in here, Mr Fraser?"

"He was just *there*."

"And you can't stay here," Mr Jones said, took the old man's arm, led him to the foot of the stairs. "Up you go, Mr Fraser," and after a short pause, exclaimed, "Christ! I'm *tired*."

"You're very good," Mr Fraser said, "you are indeed. Mrs Fraser says so, too."

"Come along now, up you go."

When the old man moved, he moved; now stood over the prone man.

"Deado! *And* drunk. Who the hell is he?"

"Oh!" shouted Mr Fraser, hung desperately to the stair rail, "oh damn!"

Jones rushed at him, "I've told you more than once to watch the fifth stair up, Mr Fraser. Be careful now," and he followed the old man up, stair by stair.

"Listen!"

They both listened, the hall seemed suddenly drowned in loud sailor snores.

"Move, Mr Fraser, *move*."

A door on the first floor opened and closed, a telephone ring shot through the house, the sound of a piano was distant, and a woman violently coughing was very near.

"That thing drives me stark staring," growled Jones, "I'll pull the bloody thing out altogether one of these days." It went on ringing. "Easy there, careful, Mr Fraser," Jones said, as they reached the next floor.

"Always ringing that bell, Mr Jones, and nobody ever seems to answer it."

"Here we are," Jones said, "safe and sound. You'll be all right now. But remember what I said about that *stair*."

"Yes, Mr Jones. Thank you. But it's not me, no, it's her. Her all the time. Something's happened to our door, Mr Jones, she—"

Laughing loudly, Mr Jones said, "Oh that, we all know about it. We'll soon fix the door, don't worry. Here you are. The front door's right off its bloody hinges. There. In you go," and his torch flooded the Fraser entrance.

"I'm not talking about the front door," Mr Fraser said, "I'm talking about this," and then the torch was shining full in his face.

"Please," Jones said, "you're home. Do go *in*. I've lots to do."

"Told you, it's not me, it's Emily, Mr Jones."

"Indeed! Emily, Emily," stuttered Jones, half laughing, and staring down at the upturned face, at the terrified eyes almost hidden beneath bushy brows, the thin form lost in the folds of an outsize dressing gown, the trembling mouth, something funny, a joke, "Who's Emily?"

Almost coldly the old man replied, "My wife. You know it is. You forgot."

"Hell yes, sorry, Mr Fraser, I've been a bit confused half the night myself, so much happening, so quickly, can't remember a damned thing. *Well?*"

"It's her, Mr Jones," and a sudden break in the old man's voice startled the warden, the words tumbling out, confused, mumbling something about a door that wouldn't open, and wouldn't shut. "She's frightened," and the doorknob rattled in the old man's hand.

"What the hell's wrong? Afraid of what? What's the matter with your door?" asked Jones, and then he turned out the torch, on which the old man leaned closer to him.

"Last night," Mr Fraser said, "we were asleep, then we

heard terrible noises, woke us up. Door like you see it now, won't open properly, won't *shut*, getting on Emily's nerves, Mr Jones."

"But—"

And almost in anguish Mr Fraser cried, "Won't shut, look, look!"

"Keep *cool*, Mr Fraser," Jones said, "I'll fix it for you. But not now, not *now*," and he pushed and tugged at the door that would not budge.

"Damn and blast the bloody thing," he cried, gave it a kick, crying, "damn, damn!"

"No, no. Don't do that, Mr Jones. The noise, she can't stand much more of it. If *only* it would shut, can't sleep thinking about it."

"Get in, Mr Fraser," Jones said, pushed him in, "you'll get your death of cold standing there. Go on now," and he pushed. They were in the room.

"Emily, switch on the light please."

She flooded the room with light, sat up in bed, cried, "Thank goodness you've come, Mr Jones."

"I've been telling him about our door, Emily," Mr Fraser said, and to Jones, "Do sit down, Mr Jones, you don't mind?"

Jones sat gingerly on a cane chair and said that he didn't mind.

"Good, good. Thank you."

"Mind if I smoke?"

"Do."

He threw back the helmet and a riot of black curly hair shot free. He lit a cigarette, puffed wildly, he felt ill at ease, and he wondered why. It seemed odd. "I'm not always as irritable as this," he told himself, then, looking at Mrs Fraser he realized at once. There was something about the woman, the way she stared at him, now, at this moment, as he sat stiffly in the chair; and then she cried out, "I can't *sleep*."

He got up, approached the bed, leaned down, said quietly, "Don't worry. Tomorrow, have a look at it tomorrow, Mrs Fraser. Now I must go. I've been up all night, and my wife is waiting for me. Till tomorrow then," and he made for the door, and Mr Fraser trailing at his heels, and Emily shouting after them, "Fix the door, fix the *door*."

"Please, Mr Jones," Mr Fraser said.

"Now look here. You're upset, you both are, so are other people. It's been a real nasty evening, *bloody*," and something was impelling him to add, "and that's not all," but the words remained lifeless on his tongue. "Go back to bed, everything will be all right tomorrow. Good *night*."

"You don't under*stand*."

"The man in the hall, the sailor, is that what she's afraid of?"

"No," and the shout from the old man was quite unexpected. "It's the *door*."

"Then damn the bloody door," shouted Jones, direct into the old man's face. "I'm bloody tired, all in. See you in the morning."

Fraser blubbered. "It's Emily, poor dear," but Mr Jones had gone, taking two flights of stairs at a rush. "Poor old devils," he thought, and treaded much plaster on the next floor, and rushed for the door that opened like magic, and the smiling girl was there, arms out, welcoming.

"Oh Richard!" she cried. "Darling!"

"Hello, dear," he said, holding her tight. "You all right?" smothering her with kisses, "well, here I am, back again, safe and sound."

"Glad," she said, "glad," and hugged him, and cried out, "God, I *am* glad."

"There there!"

"I've something nice and hot and ready, darling," she said, and they went in and closed the door.

He slumped into a chair, spread legs, threw back his head, closed eyes. He slept whilst she fussed about, setting a table, stirring something violently in a pan, peeping from behind the kitchen door, looking at him, the blackened face, the lines under the eyes, the absolute inertness.

"Poor dear!"

She stood over him, listened to his deep breathing, touched the slack mouth with her finger, sat on the arm of his chair, stroked his hair, kept staring at him, and finally kissing him, and jumping to her feet as she heard the kettle, and rushing off to the small kitchen.

"Wake up, darling," she said, and he opened his eyes, and there she was, stood smiling, and the tray in her hand. "Do wake up, Richard."

She put down the tray, stood over him again, "*Richard!* Ready, darling."

"Oh yes," he said, with shocked surprise, yawned, stretched himself, and finally sat up.

She gave him tea, a hot stew, bread and butter, and he began to eat. And as he ate, slowly, almost casually, he stared hard at the girl in front of him, as though it were by some miracle she was there, enveloping her in his long, endearing look. A word now would spoil everything. There was something about his wife, the red, wavy hair, the pale face, and the eyes whose colour he could never really define. He liked the clearness of them, like that of water. How calm the hands lying folded in her lap. Then suddenly he cried, "You're not eating," and the spell was broken, but her smile touched him, and he thought, "Sometimes Gwyn is as calm as the lake itself."

"Gwyn?"

"What, darling?"

"It's so nice sitting down," he said.

"Do *eat*," she said.

"Sit here," Richard said, "here, *close*," and she sat.

"*God!* I'm glad you're back," and she leaned over and caressed the back of his red and roughened neck. "You *do* look tired. Best lie down when you're finished. I won't talk, won't ask silly questions. More tea?"

"He made a nice mess here last night," Richard said, so quietly that she sat up, strained for the words. "Did you go down to the shelter?"

"Of course. But I didn't stay long, darling, and came back. Feel safer here. I even did little things, too. Down there, just sitting, waiting, listening, worrying, everything seemed meaningless. I was glad to come up again," then suddenly she was crying.

He took her in his arms. "Never mind, Gwyn, darling. Next week I may have a different shift altogether. Everything's so chaotic at the moment," and then his mouth filled with her hair, and her whole body shook in his hold, but her sobs relieved him. If she hadn't cried he would have been afraid. He held her tighter still. "*Darl*ing," a great tenderness upthrusting, enfolding her.

"Richard!" she said, "the *relief*."

Like children, they were suddenly, easily asleep.

The kettle on the gas jet spluttered, rattled its lid, and the fire in the living room drenched with its heat. Somewhere a mouse pattered about behind the wainscotting. Flies buzzed around the light bulb, the light glared down on them. Jones snored, and she seemed scarcely breathing. The tropical birds on the wallpaper, perched and poised, seemed ready to burst into song, and the background of deep foliage shimmered in the heat of the room. It suggested Africa, a curve of the torrid zone. The man's snores grew louder, and once the girl shuddered violently in his arms. He murmured in his sleep, into the mass of her hair, whilst in the flat above footsteps endlessly paced the floor, and once again the telephone below began ringing through the house. But the two sleepers in the chair were secure, beyond staggering worlds, over a frontier in time.

"What's *that*?" she cried in dream.

It woke him, he was erect in a flash. "What's the matter?"

So they were awake, and his hand on her forehead felt sweat.

"Christ! The *heat*," he said, jumped up and flung open the window. He left her comfortable in the armchair. "That blasted gas fire," he said.

"All *right*, dear, go to sleep . . ."

"The kettle, Richard, the kettle," the sounds of which rattled fathoms in her mind.

"I'll switch off."

The burned hole in the kettle disgusted him, and he banged it down angrily on the stove. "Blast!"

"What woke you, Richard?"

"*That*," he said curtly, a finger pointing towards the kitchen.

"What, darling?"

He lost control, shouted, "*That*."

"Listen," Gwyn said.

They listened.

Somebody was talking outside their door, so they remained very still, listening.

"I tell you again, he *won't* see you," a woman's voice exclaimed, that was tired, exaggerated. "Why wait?"

"But he knows me. I was astonished when I heard he had started working again," a younger voice replied.

"He has never *stopped* working," the words sharp, direct, and they carried with them the air of an ultimatum.

"Just listen," Richard said.

"I am."

"But why outside our bloody door?"

"That damned fool above," Gwyn said, "just listen to it, the feet never stop, murdering steps up and down, up and down."

Richard laughed, said he wondered where the person aimed to get to with all that walking. "I wonder where he—"

"Ssh!" Gwyn said, a hand on his arm, and then the voice outside was louder still.

"How many times do I have to tell you that he won't see *anybody*?" and the voice rose higher, a sort of blind desperation behind it, "I tell you he won't," at which point Richard flung open the door.

"All right, all *right*, but find some other place to talk. Thank *you*." And as the young and the older woman turned away, the man called quietly, "Wait. Listen. People want to sleep. I've been out all day and half the night. There's lots of room downstairs, talk there," pointing towards the landing, the darkness, the void. And he stared at the women. He knew one, and not the other. He knew the painter's wife, but this girl, he had never seen her before. Young as Gwyn was, pretty as Gwyn was, but had not her calm, a single look told him that. The light from the doorway fell upon her, and she seemed disarmed, helpless under it. And then he glanced at the other. A tall, thin woman nearing fifty, he supposed, with a man's overcoat draped about her shoulders, a mass of greying hair drawn severely back from the forehead, so heightening a natural severity of expression, and in the pale, almost masculine features, two burning eyes. He saw the largish hands holding the coat to her.

"Well then?" he said, irritably, "aren't you going? In this flat, we want to bloody sleep. Good*bye*," and slammed the door in their faces. And when the knock came he opened it, and she was there, but the younger woman had gone. She walked up, confronted him.

"Have we disturbed you? Have we ever given you, or anybody in this house, one minute's trouble? Has *he*? Have we ever opened our mouths, we who are surrounded by people who never keep their own shut? Do we talk? Do we make gestures, do we throw up our arms, do we shout?" So the words streamed out, feverish, tumbling from the tongue. "What trouble have we ever given you, I ask you *that*, Mr Jones?"

And he stammered back in a tired voice, "Yes yes, I know, I understand, I . . ." and then his eye caught the sight of her mouth, he could not avoid it, continued staring, then stammered it out, "I mean . . . well . . ."

"Don't presume," the woman replied. "You understand nothing."

It only reminded Jones that he was tired, tired to the bone and the nerve's sharp edge, tired now, and shouted it, "*Go away. Please.*"

Gwyn was beside him, clutching his arm. "Do come *in*, Richard. Never mind Mrs Stevens," and a sudden wave of anger sent the words flying after the slowly departing woman. "Some people want to sleep, even if you don't."

Arms about each other they stood listening to the words that floated on the stairs.

"I said he *won't* see you," Mrs Stevens said. "Never sees anybody when he's working."

"I'll bloody see him," the younger woman shouted, and followed it up with a loud giggle. "There's that bloody phone ringing again," she cried, "somebody should do something about it."

"Get out of my way," Mrs Stevens said.

"There!" Gwyn said, "they've gone now. Thank heavens for that," but they did not move, just stood there listening to the slowly descending footsteps. A door banged loudly through the hall.

"Wasn't anything important, was it, darling?"

They went in and she closed the door quietly behind him. She saw him slump heavily to the chair, was more conscious of his extreme tiredness, the drawn features spelt it out for her. He looked up at her.

"Those two women seem to have met before. I think the younger one used to model for Stevens. It's bad enough listening to those damned feet upstairs," and he jerked a finger ceilingwards.

"Come on, Richard. *Bed.*"

She knew he was furious, but met his anger with a smile.

"Get me a drink," he said.

They sat close together, glass in hand, in the now silent room.

"Forgot all about that damned inventory for Renton."

"Never mind, darling," soothing.

"Got to mind. He must have particulars of everybody in the house, Gwyn."

"Yes, dear, of course."

"Put it out," he said, and she got up and switched off the gas fire.

"Odd," she remarked, "although it's hot in here I feel sort of shivery."

"Please," he said, paused, then added quickly, "Hope it's not the last of it."

He sat watching her refill the glass, mused as he waited.

"Extraordinary," he thought, "only six months ago I was travelling in chemicals, drugs, and now . . ."

"Here we are, darling."

"Thought they'd *never* go last night," he said.

"But they did, darling," ran her fingers through his hair. "It's over."

"For the present," he said, sharply, correcting.

"I do *know*, dear."

But he said nothing, being suddenly miles away from her, moving busily from one Welsh valley to another.

"Let's go to bed," she said.

He did not answer, did not look at her, suddenly finished his drink.

"That's the answer," Richard said, and she said, "Then come on," and only at this moment did he seem aware of her own exhaustion.

He followed her into the bedroom, slumped in a chair, seemed uncertain about going to bed, became suddenly talkative.

"Funny, Gwyn, I was just thinking of those two lucky old bitches pushing off in their smart car, all the way to Somerset."

His remark surprised her, and she said sharply, "They *are* people, dear."

"Probably more mercy under the Somerset clouds," he said.

He watched her undress, climb in. "You must *sleep*," she said.

He followed her, but did not undress, and switched out the light. They both listened, this now being the thing to do, in the new kind of lived nights. He addressed the ceiling.

"There's the Frasers, the Stevens, the Robinsons, and there's Warden and missus. That correct?"

"Try and sleep, darling," she said, "take what you can, *while* you can, they came back three times yesterday."

His sharp laugh split the silence. "Telling me something, dear?"

She smoothed his forehead. "*Please*. You'll be snoring in a tick."

But he did not, and continued to stare into the darkness, long after he knew she was deep asleep. Suddenly he half sat up, stiffened, and exclaimed under his breath. "Christ! That sailor. Forgotten about him. Must do something. The silly swine."

He slipped silently from the bed, stubbed his toe, exclaimed, "Damn!" put on his hat and overcoat and left the room. He passed a flat where the radio screeched, noticed a light splash from under another door, and hurried down, his mind suddenly full of the lost sailor. He thought of him in terms of physical gestures. Bound to a mast, open-mouthed on a fo'c's'le head, flat on his back in an open boat, and the face all shock and smother after the torpedo's tear into the house of steel that was his home. Something pulled him up sharply. He stood listening, fingering the torch in his pocket, withdrew it, switched it on, and there facing him at another door, a woman.

"Good God! It's old Mrs Fraser. Damned fools. Them and their bloody door."

He remained close to the wall, suddenly switched out the light, listened to his own heavy breathing, thought of Gwyn, last night, now, and tomorrow to come. "I must get by," and he veered away from the wall, overbalanced in his caution, dropped the torch, clawed empty air, almost fell, and then the woman spoke to him.

"Mr Jones!"

"Bugger it. I'm nailed *again*."

"It won't *shut*," Mrs Fraser said, her very tone of voice accusatory.

Richard remained quite still, musing.

"Don't mind Fraser himself, both a bit barmy, really. What the hell can I say, do? Hang me for a damned fool. And hang that bloody sailor."

Their eyes met.

"Damn! What can I say to her *this* time? There's a war on, perhaps."

And he groped for the words that would not come.

"I'll try and slip past the old dear."

Was that her bone shining on the doorknob? Sometimes she prayed out loud. Was she now praying silently? And then he was past, beyond her, who stood almost sentinel-like in the darkness, her very gesture seemed grown from a moment, a memory, a terror, seeing nothing, lost in darkness. "Poor old dear! Oh hell," he cried in his mind, feeling a sudden relief, a slackening tension, a balm over nerve. He went on. Cold draughts of air struck at him, and gave him a feeling of emptiness. So stair by stair, slowly descending. The telephone bell had ceased to ring, and the singing sailor was silent. No song. No snores. He was standing in the hall, still listening.

"I say," he called, the words trembled out, and others fluttered about in his mind, wild birds, like pigeons seeking home. "I say there!"

The echo returned to him as from a void. He was moving again, searching in his pocket for matches, the torch would be searched for later. He found and struck one on the damp wall, the light blinked in damper air. He looked down. Nothing there. Perhaps the man had gone. Yes, the black front door was stood up, he must have gone. And wondered where, for no reason at all beyond fugitive curiosity. Why had he gone? All this way down for nothing. "Damn and blast him," he shouted. Defeated, he made his way back upstairs, bent and feeling on each landing for the torch. Mrs Fraser might still be there, one with the petrified wood, and light would shine from under a door behind which an airman lived with his ecstatic smile, whose nervous fingers lay always at the switch of his radio set, a vain endeavour to get the music that he wanted, from a station that he would never reach. He liked it South American, and he liked it hot. Richard found the torch, then passed the Robinsons' door, behind which there was nothing save a violent humming of a tune that never finally broke into song. "Twenty-four hours' leave. Poor bastard. You can't blame him."

He could pass these things, cease to think about them.

Nor would he think of that woman who kept her mouth shut, her body lost in the folds of an overcoat. He wouldn't think, and he wouldn't be angry any more. Something in him had cooled, a pecking and scratching at the surface of his mind, ceased. He entered his flat as silently as he had left it. He felt his way across the kitchen, touched the foot of the bed. So he lay again, and she did not move, was lost in the sleep that was welcoming. Turning to her, he bent low, but did not speak. Gwyn was well away, in dreamland.

"That silly old woman," he thought, and wondered if she was still stood outside her door, patiently waiting for the miracle hand that would heal the door that would neither open nor close.

"Christ, I'm tired," he muttered, and lay back, yawned, sank deeper into the bed. Later snore met snore.

A sudden wave of noise from above did not disturb them. Somebody was pushing a bed or chair across a floor.

The woman in the overcoat had pushed a big horsehair sofa right to the other end of the room. She stood erect, looking up and down, surveying; her chest was hurting her a little, and she wondered now if the effort had been worth it. She supposed it had.

"There now," she said, "there."

A room with a high ceiling, and a riot of canvases about, the walls smothering, and some behind grey curtains, against the wall just inside the door. Everything was dusty, even the battered typewriter that stood on a rickety card table. The Stevens couple had lately moved in. From where nobody had ever found out; secret, private. An enormous grate, and a glimmer of fire within, at any moment it might vanish. There was a distant smell of something frying. One large canvas hung over the fireplace. Stood some way from the fire yet another couch, its green leather rubbed a dirty brown, a strip of carpet in front of it, shockingly bright. The horsehair sofa stood stiff and prim, the fading couch sprawled. There was sat at the far end of the carpet strip, a tom-cat. At the right hand side of the fire a man sat in a cane chair, a cigarette dangling from his mouth, at which he puffed distractedly.

"Is that any better, dear?" she asked, which made the figure in the chair move, make to get up, then promptly sit down again.

"I suppose it'll do," he said.

"Do *say*. Be definite. Will it do?"

"Yes, dear. That's fine." He drew his chair nearer the fire. "No letters?" He spat out the cigarette, and lit another.

"No letters. Do you want your gruel?"

"Later on."

She walked to the end of the room, disappeared behind red curtains, emerging later wearing a green dressing gown. She sat down at the card table and glanced at some letters and cards that lay there. A circular about the miraculous properties of water came soundlessly out of a long buff envelope. She picked up a card, gilt-edged, beautifully white. She liked the clean look of it, but it had a cold feel, a granite touch. She read an invitation to a one man show at the Goupil gallery, and another printed postcard advised her as to the best method of exterminating rats and mice. There was a bill for gas, and a courteous note from a Mr Bilsom, the grocer, the gentle reminder.

"Damn!" and she tossed the lot into a heap.

"What a lot of effort," she thought, studying the pile. She rocked the table with the violence of her movement, and went down the room, sat opposite the man.

"Light's been lousy today," he said, very quietly, not looking at her, and not thinking of the light.

"I know, dear," she said, consoling. "Do say when you want the gruel."

The word "gruel" appeared to induce some life into the cat; it began to stretch, scratched at the carpet, finally washed its face.

"Thought I heard somebody knocking here a few minutes ago," he said, then mumbling the words, "somebody enquiring . . . something . . ."

"Knocked at the wrong door," Mrs Stevens said, and had

only to close her eyes for a moment to get the clear view. A short young woman with a mass of red hair, petite, though some distance from chic. Saw her under a dim light, heard her saying, "I hear he's working again. He knows me, Clem does." The picture vanished when he spoke.

"What time is this Dr Beecham coming?"

"Didn't say," she replied, casually, turned her head, and her eye covered the room. "Yes, it does look better now," she said.

"The things light can do," he said, got up, and went to her. "I worry about you, Lena," took her face between his hands, kissed her, "I do worry."

"Wish you wouldn't."

"Somebody must have answered the bell downstairs."

"Expect so. Can't keep the gruel much longer, dear," she said.

He lit yet another cigarette, lay back, thinking, "Not always dear, not always Clem, not Stevens, and not Mr, not darling, just 'you'. Do *you* want your gruel? There are no letters for *you*." The smile came and vanished again.

"Any news?"

"No. The people that own this house are still away; they say they'll stay up in Somerset for some time, perhaps for the duration. The RAF chap's on a leave. Noisy pig, and very noisy yesterday, must have drawn blood somewhere. They're very excited, I heard his wife singing."

She jumped as though struck. "I'll get your gruel."

"Good," he said, watched her go, followed her with his eyes, saw her tall and erect, like a man, powerful, definite.

"Lena," he said, softly, "Lena."

He could hear her pottering about in the tiny kitchen, and when a smell of something burning came to his nostrils he thought, "Those sausages again," as though the cooking of them might be a criminal offence. He got up and walked the length of the room and back again, stood still, covered his face, stared through his fingers. He focused on the height and depth of the room, on the grey curtains drawn across the window, the carpet at his feet. He went to the window and looked out. Same view. The forest of brick, and the sky rationed. He lifted and felt the blackout material, dropped it, turned away as he heard her approach. "She *is* good."

A white bowl in one hand, a silver spoon in the other.

"Here, and do eat it. It'll do you good. I *want* you to eat it."

They sat down, close, she watched him eat.

"Have you ever thought of Gough?" she asked, and it seemed too sudden, too abrupt.

He put down the bowl, stared at her. "Gough?"

"Gough."

"Doesn't write," he said, "doesn't write letters any more," returned to his gruel.

"How do you know that?"

"Know, that's all. Feel it."

"What about Cruickshank?"

"Wouldn't understand at all," he replied.

"There!" she cried, "that's him."

"Who?"

"Dr Beecham."

"Oh," and he went on sipping at the hot gruel, suddenly glanced at the clock, at Lena.

"He can't come in the day," she said, "he's far too busy."

The spoon clattered to the floor. "I forgot that," he said. "Yes yes . . . I . . ."

"What'll I do?" he asked, confused, pushing away his gruel.

"Wait in the kitchen until he's gone," Lena said, "I *told* you he'd be coming. And do eat that gruel." She gently pushed him to the door.

"I've switched on the electric, shan't be long," closed the door, and hurried to answer the continued knocking.

"Good evening," Dr Beecham said, tall, red-faced, jolly, beaming with health, sleek-haired and strongly smelling of soap. He walked right in. "The best time I can manage, Mrs Stevens," slumped into a chair. "Quite a job in this blackout, I can tell you, and there seems to be so many other things to attend to," following this up with a vigorous rubbing of the hands. "Right then. Get yourself ready," he said and jumped to his feet. She was ready in an instant, the chest exposed. "Right!"

He stood looking at her, a finger at his mouth, said, "H'm! Ah . . . yes, I see. Oh dear," and after a pause, "Well now?"

She seemed hardly aware of the chest tapping, the feel of groping fingers.

"You'll have to go away for a few days, Mrs Stevens. Not a difficult matter, really. How old are you?"

She merely smiled. "How old do I look, doctor?"

"Not difficult at all. But it'll have to be removed. Yes. Safest. I'll make the necessary arrangements."

"No."

"But you must . . ."

"No arrangements can be made at present," Lena said, and the words stumbled out, heavy clumsy words, she imagined herself at the bottom of a high stairway that must be climbed. "I can't leave him."

"But surely he can manage, and it's the day of extremes," irritable, protesting, "surely . . ."

"How would you know that?" she asked, her eyes fixed on his clean, white hands. "It'll have to wait. He can't be left, doctor, besides, the pain isn't half as bad as it was."

She sat down in Clem's chair. "I'd never leave him, *never*," a ruthlessness, a finality in her attitude.

"It's in your interests. It's vital. Something could be arranged for *him*."

"You mean my husband," Lena said sharply, correcting him, stung by his casualness. "His name is Clement Stevens."

"I do know that, Mrs Stevens," he said. "Indeed I recall hearing it years ago."

"So did he. That's his name, and he's my husband."

He folded arms, suddenly put them behind his back, then clasped them, rocked on his heels. "I came a long way to see you," he said.

"I know. And it was most kind of you, doctor. Thank you."

She looked him direct in the eye. "He's worried, has an

idea something is wrong. It was to stop him from worrying. Something *is* wrong, I know that, but I daren't go away at present. Perhaps I could arrange for some daily treatment . . . yes?"

"Can I see him?"

"No. I don't want that. *Please*. He's in the kitchen, and I can't keep him waiting there. So sorry. I'll come and see you at the surgery."

"You have the address, of course. Daytime preferably, the nights are pulling heavily at present, Mrs Stevens."

"Let me see you out, doctor."

He gave her his first smile, shook his head, picked up his hat, and made for the door. She followed him out. Suddenly he felt his arm clutched, and the voice low in his ear.

"Of course he knows what it is," she said, "he's too clever not to, but he thinks it could be cancer of the heart."

"The heart? What a curious idea to have. Never been known. Ah ha. People do tend to go to extremes, jump off at tangents, rather silly. But you must have the breast removed, Mrs Stevens."

He shook hands with her, wished her a good evening, found his own way out. She listened to his steps on the stairs, and when they died away she closed the door, called out, "He's gone now. You can come out, Clem."

He shuffled out, and the expression on his face became puzzling to her. They stood together by the fire.

"I didn't eat it after all, Lena," he said, "didn't feel hungry."

She picked up the bowl, thinking, "The way he came out of the kitchen, handed me the bowl, just like a child." She went in and out of the kitchen.

"Go and lie down," she said. "Better still, go to bed. You've been working most of the day, you're dead tired, I know it." She took his hands, said gently, "Go to bed."

"What about you?"

"I'll follow soon. I've a letter that I *must* write. Is there anything you want?" and she put her arm round him, after which a momentary silence.

"What did Beecham say?"

"Who . . . *oh!*" and the note of surprise in the voice seemed wholly genuine. She was worlds away, but pulled back quickly, blurting out. "Of *course*, the doctor. Didn't say anything very definite. Have to see him one day next week. At the surgery. I think I'll be able to manage an afternoon."

"Was that all?" and his words dragged.

She was laughing, laughing in his face, saying, "And he didn't agree at all with your mad theory, called it nonsense."

He stood watching her, the laughs having bewildered him, there was something absurd yet irresponsible about the laughing.

"Why *shouldn't* a disease be new?" he asked.

She slowly shook her head, measured the words. "No such thing, Clem. He said the operation would be simple, no fuss, very ordinary, he said."

"Operation?"

"Some time, but not at the moment. I fixed that all right. Come along now," she said, putting a hand through his arm. "Do come *along*."

They went into the bedroom, sat down on the bed, looked at each other but remained silent. She saw tiredness in him, saw worry, so forgot her own.

Suddenly she blurted out, "Euston was better."

"Better than *this*?"

"Better than this. Those bloody stairs," she said, savagely, and he knew she hated them, all four flights.

He squeezed her hand, offered a weak smile. "Better than nothing," suddenly rushed out of the room saying, "must have another look at it," and she followed after him.

"It's good," she said.

" 'Tisn't."

"What's wrong with it?" irritably.

He leaned into the canvas, suddenly leaned back, studied it.

"The colour must bleed," he said, "*bleed*."

She patted his shoulder, said gently, "It's still good. Now

do go to bed," and he liked the warmth of her voice, but not the words.

"I must get that letter off," she said, gave him a push. "Go to *bed*."

He turned at the door, seemed uncertain as to whether to go in or out. "Lena!"

"What, dear?"

So she was close again, warm, encouraging.

"I believe in you. Isn't that enough?"

"You're right, you're almost always right," he said, and closed the door after him.

She shuffled down to the card table, sat down, looked round the room, and knew all over again that Euston had been better than this.

"Lena!"

"I'm here. I'm writing a letter to Flo, I shan't be long."

She took a sheet of paper and an envelope, concentrated, began to write:

"Dear Flo,
         I got your letter and am glad to know all is well with you," paused, then continued, "how awful about the little dog. I've been trying to make up my mind about asking you if you could, if you would be able to . . ." and then the pen was in the air again, and she was thinking of the country, *all* that green, a garden, a lawn, a field; would ink reach that far, count against all that green . . . "able to get down to London for one afternoon, a matter of about two hours perhaps, certainly not more than three at the most . . ." paused once more, thinking "Explanations, explanations" . . . "just to be with Clem whilst I'm at the hospital," and the pen moved, words flowed to the paper, but she didn't see them, wasn't thinking about them, only about a little dog. "What *rot*!"

And she hurled the pen to the end of the room. She jumped to her feet, the ink bottle fell, the sheet of paper swished towards the fire, its edges suddenly curling under the heat.

"I'm so sorry about your dog, your little dog," began laughing, and so suddenly crying, "little dog, little dog . . . oh God!"

She switched off the fire, collected her coat and hat from behind the door, put them on, then noticed her slippers, and crept to the bedroom to get her shoes. A night-light burned in a corner. She looked at the bed, but couldn't see him. The blanket was drawn right up, his head covered.

"Are you asleep?"

Receiving no answer she tiptoed from the room, closed the door silently behind her.

"I'm sure he'll sleep. Those pills are good," she thought.

Her resolution strengthened, her spirit lightened. She noticed the light under the Robinsons' door as she passed, and the music within was no longer strange to her. She noticed Mrs Fraser stood in the doorway of her flat, heard snoring from within.

"Evening, Mrs Fraser," she said, but the old woman did not hear her, and did not see her, she being too closely wrapped up in the mystery of her own front door. She felt herself being drawn downstairs by the two words that went circling round her mind. "Get out! Get *out*!" Mrs Fraser might stand there for all eternity, but she must go out.

Feeling the cold air she drew the coat more tightly about her. She stood at the door. "Was that a light?" She was certain she had seen it. Somebody had opened and quickly closed a door in the house. She wondered how long Clem would sleep, where she might walk at ten o'clock at night, whether they would be over again. The wind blew about her feet. She heard the pattering sound. "Still raining."

She wished it would stop, and then she saw the light again. It flashed out behind her, and she heard a man's voice calling out, "Aye aye there, somebody."

She turned quickly. "Of course nothing matters very much now, *reely*," a woman's voice.

"Hello there! Hell bloody lo."

She heard giggles behind her, and walked slowly back

down the now dark hall. Surely she knew that voice, surely
. . . and then once again the light flooded out. The door was
wide open. Lena drew close to the wall, held her breath. A
young woman had appeared in the doorway, and now she
knew.

"Of course. Came to see Clem. Said she knew him. Ten
years ago. I wonder. Yes, of *course*." How stupid of her not
to recognize the Bermondsey voice, and the whine in it. "A
silly little bitch."

She stood just away from the door, staring into the big
room. A man was sprawled in an armchair, a gas fire blazing
up at him. There was a table with a green cloth on it, a full
bottle of whisky, and an empty one, and two glasses touched
stem to stem. And then she saw her, face to face, a young
woman staring out, her shoulders hunched, her hands
clasped.

"I don't see anybody," she cried, began giggling again.
"You must be drunk," and she laughed outright.

The woman outside remained perfectly still. Yes. This
was a former model, from Bermondsey. Come to see him,
heard he had started working again. "Bloody insult. He's
never stopped working."

That red hair, that face, the cheap finery, the powerful
scent, the purse-like little mouth, the snub nose. She felt
glad she had locked the door behind her. She jerked violently
when the man kicked at the gas fire as he stretched his legs
even further, and began to sing.

"Come on, lady. Come in. Have a drink," his every movement clumsy, the table shook, one of the bottles fell, started
to roll across the now uncarpeted floor.

"Come on in, Cis, and shut that goddamed *door*," the
sailor shouted, gave an abrupt belch and then slid lower into
the chair. He picked up the nearest available bottle, guzzled
noisily. "Come *on*, Cis." He turned round in the chair, and
started to laugh again.

Lena for the first time saw him, the big face with its heavy
stubble, the discoloured teeth, and the hand that was raised
in the air to beat time to the music he heard faintly from the

flat upstairs. He hummed an unnameable tune. "Jese! Where in hell you got to, Cis?"

She walked into the light, confronted the model, noted a great tear in the white blouse she wore. She was faced by a broad grin, a low chuckle that turned to shaky titter.

"Hello," Cis said, and in the same moment the sailor rose, and staggered towards the door, the bottle still in his hand.

He seemed unable to distinguish the one from the other.

"Why, hello there, Cis, there you are. Good show. I bin calling you, sure. Come on in. Lovely stuff back there, *free*, think of that."

He then staggered back into the room, spread arms and gripped the mantelpiece, stared up at the big canvas hanging above, and indulged in a stream of gibberish nobody could understand. The two women remained silent, surveying each other.

"He won't see you," Lena said.

A loud titter echoed in the hall. "No. I'll see him. That's the difference," and followed this up with a giggle.

"You're *drunk*."

And the sailor bellowed, "Shut that goddam door."

Lena stiffened where she stood. Words formed in her mind, crowded the tongue, she opened her mouth to speak, but the words froze. The younger woman only smiled at her, and in the same moment felt the big hand on her shoulder, the spluttering sailor was close again.

"Thought you'd gone, Cis. You're not, that's fine. Come on in, lady. You're good, sure, I told you that," and the arm round her, and Lena now glaring at them both.

The sailor got too close, and Cis fended him off, her fingers on the stubble, and pushing, pushing.

"Hope you're expecting nothing, lady," the sailor said, "nothing, I mean nothing, all there is. Come on, Cis, you're fine," and he dragged her back into the room, just before the drunken eye got another focus. "Good night," he shouted, "good bloody night," and turned his back on the woman at the door.

Who now saw, not the sailor, and not the young woman

under his arm, but only the room that was long, high-ceilinged, and her eye took in the paintings on the wall, the wallpaper, the lighting, the furniture, the fireplace, and the bottles everywhere, and the cupboard doors flying and more bottles within. She noticed the big carpet rolled up and heavy against the wall by the door. Her eye took in the splendour and the chaos of the room. The French windows opened out on to a garden that she imagined would go on and on, for ever and ever. "Beautiful," seeing it all, studying it all. Much bigger than the box where Clem lay, and better than the slate forest and the rationed sky. She was so caught up in this that she was hardly aware of the young woman walking so slowly towards the door, and did not notice when this itself was suddenly banged in her face. She remained rooted and lost in the darkness. She wanted to be sick, and dared not. She thought of Clem, tormented herself. Was he asleep? "Yes, I'm sure he is," strengthening her resolution, "yes, those pills really *are* good. I must get *out*."

She turned quickly and walked to the door, hingeless, and carefully worked her way past it, and then felt the night air on her face. "Out," she said. "How good the air is," and at last was stood in the long, dark, and now deserted street. She stood for a moment, looking up and down, and always listening. She mused.

"There was a time when we both went out together. Yes. Nice to remember." But everything had changed, the day, the meaning, the very sound, the shape of streets, everything. It was another time.

"Always the same time every night, about eleven," and always towards the embankment, so peaceful, so quiet, and only the odd night voice that cried into the wilderness. Seeing the wall, and the man that leaned on it, and listening, as they used to do, to the living water flowing past. "If only he would come out, just once, it would be the link to the days that were nicer, had shape and meaning. Yes. If only," and almost without realizing it she was walking down this street, staring at the ground she walked over, her hands deep in the pockets of her coat, and a rush of images across her mind, the days coming back, slowly but surely, remembering the things they did, and the words that were spoken. Footsteps rang in her ears, shadow after shadow passed her by and she did not notice, aware only of the fact that she was on her way to a known place.

"I once sat there a whole morning watching him working on that elm. Just opposite where we lived," and saw it again, the small house, and the blue door, and the curtains that seemed never to be drawn against the light. "Strange. That was when we first came here, from that place," from some place, from any place, long ceased to matter, this was new and was real to her, getting the shape and the feel of the days that had been good. And at the end of the street she paused, uncertain in a moment of the direction, as though a whole city had changed in a single night, and heard in the distance the rumbling in the sky, a dog barking, and a car tearing past down the road, at the edge of which she now stood, wondering, still listening, still thinking of Clem, asleep or awake, of the sudden flight down the stairs, the longing to be out, away, free. Another car shot by, and a lone walker muttered, "Good night," and automatically she said "Good night," without even imagining how good that night might be.

She thought of Clem again, his stubbornness, his blindness, the way he withdrew, so easily got lost in his work, you could not always reach, even the level of air was different, so tight, so determined, and the thing to be done as close to him as to his own skin.

"I admire him. I always did."

Walking again, and darkness as balm, hiding a man flat on his back, that lived at the very tip-top of a house that was sometimes haven, and sometimes prison. She thought of other doors, other lives, hidden, perhaps mysterious. And of the new time, tense in its moments, bewildering, aimless, uncertain, frozen dreams, the plans under foot.

"I never thought . . ." and didn't, her sudden violent moment stopping it in its tracks, and walking and walking, gulping night air, and getting the river smell that drew nearer and nearer. Known ground. And listening, always listening. "I'll cross here," she said, and crossed. A man bumped into her and said he was sorry, and added that it might rain, and at once she gave a little laugh and asked, "Why?" and then he had gone round a corner that was dark, and as dark as the next would be. She stood against a row of shops, stared up at the sky, staring hard, intense, as if perhaps this sky might drop the answer.

"How long?"

And the voice in her ear said, "It's only just begun."

If only he'd done what she asked, gone to see Craven. And what was wrong with going to Scotland, and what was wrong in going to Newcastle? Others had done it, why not Clem? Because he was working on something, because he was nailed to an easel, because he was involved, and drowned in the thing that had to be done. Because he wouldn't listen, and she knew now that he would never listen. She crossed another road, knew this at once, many times walked. Strange. It seemed ages since she had stood here, since they had both stood together, in the time that was normal. If she walked five hundred yards she would come to a green bench, and she would sit down on it, and begin to remember the things that were old. So she counted the days and the nights that they had not gone out together, seeing things, sharing things. A sudden thought became an icicle.

"Perhaps he'll never go out," she thought. "Doesn't want to, doesn't *care*. But I do, I always will, and when I go out, I always come back. He knows that, too. He knows that I give and give and give."

She found the bench and sat on it, cursed herself for this sudden assault of self-pity, and only thought of the man with the brush, and the pain in his head. "Poor Clem. I believe in him. Always will."

She got up and walked on a little further, and she was quite alone. She leaned against the wall, leaned over, caught a single dark glint on water, watched a river flow by. "I'm glad I came out. I had to, *had* to," even as she felt herself carried back to a top room, was stood close to the man in the bed, and saying, "I'm sure you'll sleep, Clem."

Across the river she heard voices, hailing each other, watched a fussy little tug ride past. "The air is good," telling herself again that she had to do it. How quiet all of a sudden, not a sound, only that of water that she knew just went on and on and on, so reaching invisible sea. She moved away, returning to the bench, sat down, folded her hands in her lap, and closed her eyes. She was one with it all, the darkness and the silence. She did not hear the approaching footsteps, notice the tall bulky form that now stood over her, nor the voice that was no more than whisper. "You all right, madam?" which made her jump and cry. "Oh! I was just resting, officer," she said, and got up, and gave him a smile. "I'm going now."

"And that's what I call sense, madam," the policeman said, returning her smile, and stood watching her go until the darkness swallowed her up.

8

"Oh," she said, stumbling against him, "I'm sorry."

She wasn't really; you had to say something when you were frightened. She was moving, past him, past something she had not expected, her mind full of the woman that had said no, wondering who she was, and then the big hand came, the hard squeeze, the heavy breathing, and a stronger smell. Drunk. A drunken man.

"Hel*lo* there," the sailor cried, "hell bloody lo, your voice sounds like that of—" a big hiccough, "like", stuttering it, "like an old friend of mine. Sure. That's it, lady. An old *friend*. Ha bloody ha."

In the darkness she thought only of frogs, could feel him staggering to his feet, and conscious of a shivering cold in herself, only to hear him shout in her face, "Christ! It's cold here, lady, let's get in some place, sure. Help me up, help me—" and was suddenly on his knees. "Help me *up*."

"Come *on* then." Her hands grabbed, began to pull, she caught the sleeve of the coat. "Come on now," and then she felt the weight. "Don't be bloody silly, man, get up I said."

"Goddam this dark," he said.

"I'm helping you up," she said, not thinking of him any more, but only of one that she had come to see, it was really he that she was helping up, Clem, her friend. "Fancy him working again. I *will* see him." When he pulled suddenly, she staggered, knew where she was.

"Do get yourself up off the bloody floor," she shouted. "Damned fool." And then he was conscious of a hand's softness. At last. He had a purchase. What next?

"Must have been asleep," he growled, "some bastard's playing a joke on me, this goddam dark, where am I? And where in hell are my *matches*?" The voice thundered in the hall, followed by the violent breaking of wind. "Who in hell are you, lady?"

He was laughing in her face. "Of *course*. Recognized your voice, lady, that of an old pal. God, I bin longing for a pal for a long time. Sure."

She couldn't see his face, though she smelt his breath, and then she laughed into it. In the darkness she imagined it. A fear had gone. Who was this man? What was he like? Dead drunk. Asleep on the floor of a dark house. She felt the serge of his coat, and now the top of his head. He had no hat.

"Where's your hat?"

"Aye aye," he said.

"Your *hat*," she shouted.

"I dunno. Where in hell's them matches? Had them," hiccoughed, said, "excuse me, lady. How you doin'?"

She laughed. "You're funny," she said.

"Sure. My damned matches, where *are* they?"

"*I* haven't got them."

He bent down, knelt, began groping about. "Ah! Here we are, lady. Goodo."

He struck one, held it aloft. She didn't speak, and the one she stared at certainly wasn't Clem Stevens. She had come to see *him*. Not this one, and seeing he wore a big blue jersey, thought, "Sailor. Course. He's a sailor blew in. From where?"

The match went out.

"Where in hell am I?"

"You're in a house, leastways used to be one, all flats now. You were stretched out just inside the front door. Nearly fell over you."

He struck another match, and then he towered over her, and she was conscious of this, and the sheer weight of him. He went on striking match after match.

"Should be a light somewhere," she said, "here, gi'me those matches."

She struck one, flooded the hall, crossed to the opposite wall, and switched on the light. So he came up to her, close again, his hands on her shoulders, looking into her eyes, and saying nothing. He stared about him.

"Where's *this*?" directly in her face, an ultimatum.

The weight of his arms tired her. "Please," she said, lifted them clear. She then noticed some dried blood on his chin. Must have fallen, perhaps he'd been fighting, shouted at him, "This is *Chel*sea."

"Goddam. Where in hell's Plaistow, lady?"

She thought, "We can't stand here—a long way from here, sailor."

A voice tore down the stairs, struck them.

"Put that bloody light out will you. Go on. Put it *out*."

"Who's that?"

"*Put . . . it . . . out*."

She ran to the switch; they were in darkness again.

"Expecting them again," she said, "that's it. Christ, I thought they'd *gone*."

"What's the *matter*?" he asked.

"Expecting them over again, got to get in somewhere," she said.

"What the hell."

"I'd better go, I'll go," she thought, "go now," and then, "No. I *won't*. Came to see Clem. I'll see him. Yes, I *will*."

She was pulling on his arm, shaking him. "We can't stand *here*."

"Jese, lady, you're great, you're swell," and for the first time he began to laugh, and continued laughing. "Hell's bells, how'd I get in here?"

She wasn't listening, something tightened in her, tormented, and then the words as tumbrils. "God! They're expecting them *back*," wondering if they really would, and thinking of Clem Stevens, about the woman with him, about Plaistow. Name of a place. Where *was* Plaistow? Now? This very minute," and thinking of a place to go, to sit, to be quiet, and she burst out furiously with, "Can't stand here all bloody *night*."

The fog in his mind was slowly clearing, he belched again, struck yet one more match, saw her staring towards the stairway. "Some damned place," he said, *"who'll* be over, I said who, lady?"

He felt her fingers at his mouth. "Ssh! People are trying to sleep," and then the whisper, the fear, the fact. *"They'll* be," she said.

He roared. "Who's they?"

"God. You *are* drunk. Who's lucky? How the hell did you land in here?"

He was leaning over again, heavy again, "Who in hell's they, lady?"

She pushed him away, but he followed her up the hall.

"And don't you follow me," she cried. She was angry, and a haze in her mind. What *was* all this? And why didn't she just *go*? Standing here, talking to some drunken fool. Curiosity suddenly exhausted itself.

"H'm! I can see *him* any bloody time I want to. Course. I'll go," and then she seemed close to the tall woman in the overcoat, and this flapped at her, became a question mark in her mind, and even heard quite clearly in her ear the words that the woman had spoken.

"But *can* you?"

And then she was by the front door, heard the pouring rain.

"Oh no!"

The world listened, and so did she. Would they come again? Twice in one night? She wondered, she doubted, she dreaded the very thought of it, she thought only in terms of sound. "Oh God, I hope not." And the single heavy footfall right behind her did not tell her that now she might never go.

"Come on, Cis, let's go places, let's do something, you're fine, lady, you're goodo. Come on," and linked her arm, held her tight, felt the hands tearing at his coat, and she, sensing his strong breath, drew back.

She screeched in the darkness. "Leave me *alone*."

It made him laugh.

"Gi'me those matches, gi'me them. You playing a joke on a feller, lady? Aye aye there, talking to you, lady—playing a joke on me like that bastard that pushed me into this place, gi'me those bloody matches," but the box was already in his hand, and then he struck one. "I'm a sailorman, Cis—said your name was Cis—okay by me, lady, you're fine, you're cute, sure, and warm with it. Ha ha. You think I'm drunk, and I ain't. Just scared, scared as you, lady, how it is when you can't see what's scaring. Needn't be scared of me, lovey," and he gave forth a final hiccough.

"I'm not scared of you," she said.

"That's fine. Sure. Recognized your voice right away."

The speech was no longer thick, words had shape, a fog was clearing fast. Striking another match, he held it high, saw the big green door, left her, walked up to it, knocked, then hammered. "Open up there." He rattled the knob, he thumped the wood with his fist. "Hello there! Anybody in?" Only then did he notice a small plaque to the right of the door, reading. Miss Benson. Miss Cleate. He began a vicious rattling of the knob. He thought of the young woman behind him. She looked fine. She had red hair. Way she fell over him in the dark. Falling. Where from? Laughing in his face, telling him they might be over again. Who in hell were they? Yes, who in Christ's name was that lot? Cupping hands he sang out, "Hello there. Hello someone."

She heard the rattling knob, then heard a foot against the door. And then in a sudden quietness she was aware that he was humming a tune. "I'll go," she thought, "I must go."

The crash that followed frightened her.

"Show a bloody leg there," he shouted, and burst in the door, struck a match, then called back, "It's a room, Cis, it's a *room*."

But she heard only the pouring rain, and a late bus tearing down a windy road. And sounds that were distant, and high up, and thinking of Clem, here in this very house, way up at the top. Working again, after all that silence. And the woman with him. She could not forget her.

The man from Plaistow had switched on the light, and now came rushing from the room, finding her, throwing an arm round her waist, so she was at last moving when he moved, back to the big lighted room.

"That's fine," he said. "Sure, I knew you weren't scared of a sailorman. Here we are. Jese! You're great, lady. Let's have a drink, yes?" They were at the door, in the room, and he kicked the door shut, against the dark hall, against Miss Benson and Miss Cleate, airing views in Somerset. "There we are, Cis. In. *Somewhere*. At last. Just look at the stuff those dames left for us. Gee!"

He was behind her, gently pushing her towards a chair, who seemed unaware of being pushed, unaware of a sailor, intently studying the room, and everything in it.

"Fine," he said, and grabbed another chair, sat opposite her. "Hello," he said, and the smile was free. "'Lo, Cis."

"Hello," she said. "Nice to sit down."

"Sure."

He got up, knelt at the cupboard, she heard the movement of bottles.

"Still got this," he said, whipping the flask from his pocket. "Bugger me, Jack! Am I lucky?"

"Surprised it didn't smash when you fell down," she said.

"Smash. What didn't smash?"

"The flask," she screeched, suddenly lost in a dream that was green. Green curtains, an oak table with a green tablecloth, a bookcase full of books with green bindings, a green jug on the mantelpiece, a big green vase on a shelf, only the air lacked colour.

"Everything's bloody green," she shouted. He was back in the chair, the flask dangling loose in his hands, and for the first time she was studying him. The big head, big hands, the long legs, the big feet. Thin, sandy hair, rapidly receding, the long face. The nose amused her. She noted the heavy slack mouth, and the eyes, so wide apart, which she thought were grey, and they seemed divorced from all this hugeness, this strength. They were so calm, she thought, "*Too* calm!" They were in the wrong kind of face. She watched him pour neat whisky into two tumblers. The glasses tinkled.

"Here we go," he said, and handed her a glass. "Skin off your nose, Cis." The hand high in the air, trembling, and she hoped he wouldn't drop it. "Drink her up, Cis," he said, and finished his own.

"Oh God," she said, spat, "awful. Can't drink this without *water*."

"Hell, no. Should've got water, lady, sorry," and a fugitive hiccough was bravely held back, then he banged down his glass and rushed from the room, returning almost immediately with a small jug.

She laughed. "Good heavens! Another jug. It's *green*."

"Eh?"

"Nothing," she said, the voice flat in a moment, and slowly sipped at her drink.

"Jese! You're good, Cis," he said, leaned across, patted her knee. "Sure."

"Am I? You're drunk, sailor, you've had far too much."

"Sure," he said, "a sailorman don't get drunk by proxy, lady," grinning.

"By *what*?"

"*Proxy*, lady."

"Oh!"

"*Sure*."

He leaned forward again, began a slow patting of her other knee.

"Know what proxy is, lady?", and she both felt and saw the smile that came.

She studied his teeth, a few green teeth, a broken one, and a glitter of gold. She thought there was something warm, endearing, about that sudden smile. Feeling the warmth of it, and yet a little afraid of it. A big hand was suddenly running through her hair.

"By God, lady, you got some hair, *real*."

She said nothing, felt the fingers roaming up and down, and as he stroked he carefully noted her features. The snub nose in the small face, a mole under her chin, the big eyes and the small mouth, the white throat and the well-developed bosom, the long black coat that hid something white. Then he got up quietly, and switched on the gas fire. After which he sat on the table, dangling his legs.

"Have another, Cis—'tis Cis, isn't it, said it was—sure, it's Cis. Okay."

Her glass slid to the rug, the whisky ran across the floor.

"Ah!" he growled, "you gone and spilled it all," came closer still, looked into her eyes, blurted out, "You seen a ghost, lady?"

She didn't hear a word, hadn't noticed the falling tumbler, hadn't noticed his smile, she thinking only in terms of sounds. She imagined she heard them now, near and distant, faint and thunderous. She jerked herself erect, stared up at him, remained motionless.

He knelt, he took her hands. "What's the matter, lady? Goddam it. Your coat, it's singeing, Cis," and dragged her to her feet, removed the coat. "That's it, lady. Two's company, you're tight, too," grinning again, and this time he heard the words.

"They're back again," she said, and then he knew she was really afraid.

He held her tight. "Who's back again?"

"Those bastards," she said.

"Christ who, Cis? Give them a *name*."

The voice dropped, and she said slowly, hushing it, "*They* are."

"No, no . . ."

"I can *hear* them."

"Christ almighty! What you want, lady, is another drink. Sure. *I* know."

She watched him leaning over the table, clumsy in his movements, and then he came back, generous with whisky, miserly with water. "*Drink*." She drank.

"You're a good kid," he said, "sure you are," a hand on an arm, a hand on a breast.

"I'm not drunk," she said, slobbered a little, "I'm no . . ."

He sat again, was very close, laughing, stroking arm and breast.

"Glad you turned up, Cis, sure, you're real dandy." Saying it. *Again*.

She pushed him clear, shouted at the top of her voice, "I'm *not* . . . *drunk*."

She drew away from him, saying, "I'm not, I'm *not*, I heard them, and you didn't, and the bastards are coming back."

He got himself another drink, took a bottle from the cupboard, set it on the table, then leaned sharply over the bottle, mumbling, as though he were praying. "Seem to be quarrelling or something, lady, what for? Don't be scared of me, I'm just a common sailorman, Cis. 'Tis your name, isn't it, I mean Cis. *Cis*."

Her quietness surprised him, an instant calm there, and he straining for the words that fell from her lips.

"I'm not quarrelling," she said, and after a pause, "I think I just imagined those noises," and pointed skywards, and she felt poised, suddenly without fear. "I'm not *drunk*, said I'm not," protesting.

"Then goddam it, get drunk, lady. I got more. Sure. Trust a sailorman."

She was hesitant again, awkward. She wasn't certain, didn't know. "Suppose the people that live here come back. Suppose somebody else comes in . . ."

The real belly laugh shook her. "That'd be fine, Cis. I'd say hello there, and we'd all have a drink. See?"

She sipped from the glass, kept an eye on him, and thought, "He's awkward in this place. Doesn't belong, should be in Plaistow."

"Suppose you lost your way coming from somewhere. *Where?*" she said. "I lost my way, too. Easy to get lost these nights, know all about it. Came a long way to see somebody, friend of mine, thought he'd just died, came on a train, then walked, rained most of the bloody time. It's *still* raining. I was just going back to where I come from and I stumbled over you." She put down the glass, folded hands in her lap, and she still watched him. "Who the hell *are* you, anyhow?"

"Jese! Told you, lady. Just a sailorman. Lost my way. God's truth, but some feller pulled me clear of the ice, and here I am, and am I all *in*? I was scared stiff."

"The ice?"

"Sure . . . the bloody ice, Cis," and she saw him shudder. "Hate it, Cis."

The strain told, so she said, nervously, "God, you are drunk."

"Ugh!" he exclaimed, half rose, flung his glass against the fireplace. It filled her with horror.

"What's the matter? I said what's the . . ." crouching in the chair, like the sounds she dreaded were now back, flooding, downpouring sound. "They're over again, they're *back*."

She was astonished when suddenly he knelt down, and said, "Don't laugh at me, lady, don't laugh."

"I'm not *laughing* . . ."

"I said it. He got me off the *ice*. A crawling guy with a helmet on his nose. See him now. Said to me you'll never be alone again, sailor, never, for ever and ever."

"I'm not laughing at you, I'm *not*."

The big hands trembled, pawed air, looked for a purchase, she wondered where they would land. And she wanted to get up, to fly, to forget him, to forget the man she came to see, to forget a green dream. She flung herself out of the chair, crying, "Let me go, let me *go*," struggling to go, to forget.

"Half a mo, lady—half a mo, I said. No, no, don't. Don't go, Cis, don't leave me, please don't go on me," and clung to her, his weight against her weight, his fingers crawling up and down her arms. "No, lady, not yet." She felt the fingers, the hands, "I'm not scared, Cis, no, but ice, Christ, that's different, lady, sure . . ." and the final stammer. "Don't you be scared, lady, no, you don't. 'S'orl right, said it."

She spelt it out for him, quietly, calmly. "I am not scared."

"Course not, and I wouldn't scare you, lady, said I wouldn't, so come on now," another glass at her mouth, "drink it, drink up, you're fine."

"Listen," she cried, and broke free, running towards the door, but he was behind her, caught her, held her very tight, shook her, saying, "I'd never scare you, Cis. *Never*. You're all right. Come along, dearie."

He took her back, made her sit down. "There there!" and for the first time noticed the great tear in a white blouse, a bare nipple.

"Jese!" he said, lowered his head, stared at the floor. "Ah!" he said, "ah!" gently, the warmth coming up. "That's it. You're okay now, lady."

He sat opposite her but did not look at her, his eyes suddenly roaming the big room, the walls, the furniture, the bright colours of things, the odd shapes, the glass case with the shining crockery, the books on shelves, the carpet, a door that was green on the outside, white on the inside. He was speaking so softly that she did not at first realize that he was close again, staring into her eyes, and back on the rack again, justifying, and telling her who he was.

"Thought this was a bloody ship, sure, honest to God, thought she was a ship and she ain't. It's no ship. It's a room and somebody used to live here, ain't dumb, Cis, know some things, course I do."

He leaned close again. "Still trying to work out who that guy was pushed me in here. What in hell's place is this, I said. I live at Plaistow, lady. My name's Johns."

"I'm Downes, Celia Downes," she said.

"Hello, Celia," he said, "why hello there. Shake."

She shook, and he held on to it, light, small, soft, lost in his own.

" 'Scuse my paw, Celia," surprising her with a sudden flush of shyness.

"I'm sure you're all right," she said.

"Got a queer name, lady, Ephraim."

"You *what*?"

"Ephraim Johns," he said, and after a long pause, said somewhat hazily, "a lot of things are queer to me right now, Celia."

"Such as?"

He waved a hand in the air. "Like all this, lady, everything . . ."

"The green," she said, "all the green," and laughed, drowning nerves again. "*Everything* green."

"Sure. Jese, I was real fuzzled after that ice, Celia, you wouldn't bloody know, no, you wouldn't."

"Wish it was light," she said, "I could go home, and you could go to Plaistow."

He thumped his knee. "That's it. Calls for a drink, lady, sure thing. Lots of it around here, Celia. Love the stuff, simply love it," and directly against her ear, "Always scared of the cold, lady, and that ice's sure cold, I mean *cold* . . ."

"Poor you."

He kicked an empty bottle down the room, obtained another from the cupboard, held it up to the light, smiled, broke the neck across the table edge. "So what?"

"Another glass," she said, "you smashed yours."

"So I did," and he vanished into the next room and brought back a fresh one. "That's it, lady. A great ship."

"It's somebody's flat," she said.

She supposed he was about twenty-five or thirty, but her curiosity broke the moment he caught her eye.

"Show you something else, Celia," he said, and again vanished into what she supposed was the kitchen, and when he returned he was carrying to the table two more bottles of whisky, one rum, and three bottles of Volnay. "How's that, lady?"

She did not reply, thinking only of two lucky spinsters down in Somerset, she knew, the whole house knew how lucky they had been. She thought of the man upstairs, the smashed staircase, the hole in the wall, she thought of the sailor dreaming about the ice, the wall of darkness outside. You couldn't be surprised any more, not by anything. Her lips moved, she seemed on the threshold of a smile, then noticed the tear in the blouse, and what it exposed. So it sent her back to an old time, and she was sitting with Clem, and she was just nineteen. The geni-wenius didn't half like her bust. And a smile came. The sailor hummed a tune, and she was still miles away, didn't hear the fresh pop of a cork.

"Bloody fine ship," he said, "lots of stuff, a good ship, lady. Gettin' it out of my bones."

"What?"

"Ice," he said, "ice."

"Christ!" she exclaimed, "not that again?"

He wasn't difficult, just awkward, clumsy, she wasn't afraid, he couldn't be dangerous, only simple. Lost his way. People did lose their way, especially on nights like this. Lived in Plaistow. And she lived in Bermondsey, and sometimes forgot. She had never been good at geography.

"Wonder what time it is?" she asked, was suddenly fidgety in the chair. Was she dreaming? Sitting drinking with a sailor, a complete stranger in a green room. She hadn't noticed, but she had finished her drink. "Please," she said, and he awarded her another ration.

"Like you fine, Celia," he said, drew in his chair, was close again. She made him think of bright colours, something soft, like velvet, after a hardness, the dark places, after granite, the rocks, the seas, and the ice on your nose, the scalp freezing. He hugged her hard. "Jese! You're great," he said.

Warmth was in her, going out to him, she felt the words on her tongue, but did not speak. Just stared and stared at the eyes.

"He has a horror."

He felt as he held, the softness there, and no sea smell. When he opened his mouth she closed it again with her fingers, said quietly, "No, don't speak. Ssh!" brushing the thick, lost lips.

He forced back her head, kissed her throat, her hair, and he kept pressing her back, and she was slowly slipping from the chair. Staring up at a white ceiling, she thought that this, too, should be green. He staggered, began to pull, and then was over her, on a green carpet.

"You're fine, Celia, you're fine."

"Let me *go*."

"Jese! You're not afraid of me, lady," he stammered, began to laugh. He was feeling his way out of cross-currents, he looked at the things that were green, but did not see them her way.

"Bit like the jungle, Celia. Only wants a tiger, a few

leaves. I like you, tell me . . . I mean I heard you say something, didn't catch, what was it, Celia, tell me."

He was closer still, but she did not feel his weight. For the first time she noticed a small star tattooed on his right thumb. She felt herself cradled, gently rocked.

"Tell me something," he said.

When she laughed, he laughed, a green dream gone, Clem gone, the rain ceased, and the wind had died down. The last bus was quiet in a garage and men were washing it down. There was silence everywhere, sudden, unbelievable. And she was calm.

"What'll I tell?"

He liked her when she giggled, it meant something to him, and he grabbed at a sudden change of mood.

"What'll I tell?" she asked again.

"Don't," he said, "don't," put fingers in his ears, smelling sea and ropes and ships, seeing ports and docks, and the women that were waiting.

"What's the matter?"

"Nothing."

"There is."

"Isn't, lady. Leave me alone," he said, suddenly covered his face with his hands. "I'm drunk."

She uncrossed her legs, pushed clear of him. "You *scare* me *proper*."

"*Me?*"

"You."

"Giggle, lady," he said, "come on, goddam it, giggle again, I *like* that." Everything had a technique, even a feeling. "Come on, Celia. I *love* you, told you, lady, *told* you," holding hands again, squeezing them, letting them go, and she felt his fingers up and down her arms, and thought of snakes. He held her face between his hands, kissed her again, said, "How about it, lady, how about it?"

She wanted to laugh; it was funny. She wanted to cry; it was sad. Loved her, he loved her. Here, in this room. They swayed again, then were still. And suddenly it was out, spoken, over, done with.

"You have a horror, sailor," she said, "a horror."

He didn't answer, wasn't thinking, thoughts not mattering now, only the softness, the warmth, and something was melting, he could feel it going, riding out of him, flowing away, into a cold wilderness, and he said softly right against her ear, "It's gone, Celia, it's gone."

She sat up violently, pushed him away, saying, "Gone, what's gone?"

The tone was hushed, the voice sepulchral. "The ice," he said, and smothering her ear with yet more words, "hate it, always something moving under ice, lady."

"That's good. I'm glad," and her own normal tone of voice surprised her.

And she thought, "That's the only thing he remembers."

He was moving, she was moving, he was pushing again, pushing her back so that she felt the hard wood of table behind her. "Come on, Celia." Her hands reached out, gripped the green cloth, which swished to the floor, and the bottles with it.

"Christ?" he said. "It's you, lady, it's you that's drunk, not me."

She did not speak, and she couldn't move. She smelt the whisky in his breath.

"Say something, Celia, Jese! Say something," he said, and she said nothing. After the cold, warmth, after the ice, the fire. She couldn't think of it in any way but this. Life seemed like that, patches of light, then dark, the silvery bay, the barren reef, a man as lonely as a whale. The words falling out of his mouth, the light shining down on her closed eyes, which yet saw the big mouth, the lost lips, and blood on a chin. She felt the tremble in him. "We're *both* drunk."

"You said they'd been over, and I said who are they? You said they might be over again, who's *they*?" The words wet at her ear, "you tell me *that*, and I'll tell you about the ice."

She felt cold all over. "The bombers," she said, feeling coldness, cosmic, mysterious, terrifying.

"Oh! Those bastards," he said, and began to laugh, and went on laughing. She could see right inside his mouth, saw the green teeth, one shining gold. "Civilized on the inside."

"I never worry about those bastards," he said.

"*Tell* me," she said, in the instant that she felt heaviness of hand inside her blouse, an instant fear, and the shout. "God almighty, *tell* me."

"Not scared?"

"Not of you. Tell me about it, go *on*."

And another whisper in the ear. "How about another drink, Celia?"

"That's fine."

"What say about that fizzy stuff, makes you belch, lady."

"I like whisky," she said.

"There! Water?"

"No, I *don't*," shouted in his face.

"Okay, no need to shout."

After which they touched glasses, drank, and she smiled, liking it, it was good.

"First today, lady."

"What time is it?"

"Don't know."

"Doesn't matter."

"Sure. By Jesus, but you're swell, you really are bloody trumps, miracle how you fell over me, been staggering London, yes, after the ship hit a quay, the walking I done, the bloody walking, lady. Ah! I'm glad you're not scared of me, Celia, God I'm glad," feeling her hand being stroked, watched the other shakily rise in the air, the glass dither. "Skin off your nose," and his right arm came round her shoulder, something soft to paw, pretty to look at, after the long crawl over ice.

"*Tell* me."

His manner changed, she didn't recognize him. "I won't, I bloody *won't*."

"Then *don't*."

"Jese, lady. I'm happy, *happy*," and dragging the words after him, "and you leave me alone, Celia, stop bothering me. I'm okay, I'm fine. You're fine. Yes, I *was* on a goddam ship—ah! bugger me Jack, I won't, no, I won't," pulled himself up, got himself another drink, drained the glass, refilled it, spilt whisky on his chin, which made her laugh.

She hadn't heard such swearing, like a new language.

"The way them things shake when you laugh, Celia," he said, and stroked them, one by one. "Jese! You're fine, then Christ, lady, why don't you come on then, come *on*."

"Go on," she said, "tell me. Told me you would. Get it off your chest, sailorman," and she was laughing again.

"Ah! Forget it, told you, don't wanna talk about it, Celia."

She was quick to note the apology in his voice, as though it were something he shouldn't have mentioned, not important, didn't matter.

A great wave of the hand embraced the room. "The ship with a fo'c's'le like *this* hasn't yet been launched, lady. I wonder if it's still raining. Listen!"

They both listened.

"I got to get to Plaistow," he said.

"Where's that?"

"Some goddam place," he said, and then he was pouring whisky into her glass, into his own, spilling it down his trousers. "Lovely stuff." He pushed the bottle at her. "Smell! *Real*. Ah! what's a bloody horror, anyhow?"

Her speech was thickening, she stammered it out. "What about it, the ice? Tell me all about it, get it out, sailor, *out*."

"Careful," he shouted, but the glass flew from her hand, smashed into fragments against the door. "Stubborn bastard," she said.

He got up, walked slowly down the room, stood, stared stupidly at the glass at his feet. "Bloody waste," he shouted, "waste, lady, *waste*."

"D'you . . . you . . . d' . . . know . . ."

He turned, stared at her. "Get it all up, lady, all of it, every little bit," and came slowly down the room and stood over her. She lay full length on the floor. He knelt over her. "You okay, Celia, you okay?" She shivered when he touched her. "You got the heebie jeebies or something, lady? Come on, sit up, let's have a drink, Celia, come on."

She struggled to her knees, "Tell me about the ice," she said, and he caught her as she fell.

"Bugger the ice."

"Bugger *you*."

"Ah! It was nothing, lady, nothing. Just cold, colder than cold. Tha's all. Drink it," he said, "I said *drink* it."

She drank, and she lay heavily across him, suddenly wanted to be sick.

"Easy there . . . ee . . ." and then he felt her teeth at his ear, "Jese, you getting something bad, Celia, real bad, sure, go and be sick, I said . . ." himself slobbering.

"We're both drunk, sailor, *drunk* . . . I . . ."

"Sure," he said, "sure. What I said, it's real, real stuff, lady, ah, it's wonderful, I mean being here, looking at you, I mean *looking*."

Her voice smashed into him. "Tell me about that bloody ice," she said.

They lay stretched on the floor, facing each other.

"Tell you," he said.

"Listening."

She waited, watched, the lips moved. "Go on."

"Ah! . . . nothin' really, nothin' . . . I mean . . . cold, said it was, hard, like iron, we were just pushing along there, two thousand tonner, lady, Neptune's bastard, shoving her along in a real nor'easter, freeze your guts. Spike was way up top, his name was Spike, good skipper, always know that at the beginning, too late the other bloody way, just doin' his job, shoving her over, and when the horn blew we knew what the horn meant, sure thing . . ."

"Go *on*," and he felt his hand squeezed; she would squeeze it all out.

He looked at her, white-faced under the light. "Ah!" he said, "ah! To hell with it," looking again, seeing her dead still, scarcely breathing. "Listening," he said, "she's listening."

A strange sound very close to her ear, and the words following.

"Told you, lady. We were up, out, slithering, falling,

getting up again, and all the time Spike was there, still push-ing, still watching her move towards a bay whiter than any snow is, and some kind of a shout came out of the bloody air then, sure, I remember that, lady, and then Spike bawled it out of a megaphone, hit everybody like bullets. 'See it,' he shouted, and we saw him, sure we saw him. 'A black sod,' my mate shouted, spitting ice bits, not breath. 'Up there! *See*'."

The mouth wet and warm at her ear, and the eyes closed.

"Sure we knew, lady, sure we saw the sod, blacker than hell, circling over, circling round and round, going higher and higher, then lower and lower, coming down, down fast, and the bloody darkness flying after him, almost *feel* it that time, that dark, and then, whup!"

The word like a whip. She felt it, suddenly smelt the ice behind it.

"Go on."

"Smashed the wireless, Celia, that's what the bastard did, *smashed* it. Then he flew away, left the darkness with us, we got lost in it. Lost. 'Got to get her fixed,' Spike shouted, 'got to bloody fix her.' Sure it had to be fixed, getting near the bay, where the white was, lady, I mean white. 'Get a man up there,' he shouted, and we knew what he meant," and after a long pause, the whispers. "I was leaning on a port rail remember that, sure, exact minute bosun heaved his way up. 'Up you go,' he said, fixed a man with his finger, up he went, up, up, right up to the bloody top, and still we were shoving her over and over, pushing like hell, tons of darkness, feel it sitting on your shoulder, in your eyes. Spike knew . . . we . . . knew."

She was yet still, and he slobbering at her ear. "Hours up there, Celia, *hours*," dragged the word to its fullest length, "maybe four, maybe five, we stopped counting, couldn't, ice everywhere, cold, guts full, freeze what you thought, sure, colder than bloody cold, lady, like steel, rock, like that, *you* know, *that* hard. You try counting again, ice bits in your skull, you stop counting, not seeing, not knowing, nothing, nothing. Where is a man got to, lady, yes, where is a bloody man got to? And then suddenly I'm in, Celia, like I am now, in, I mean *in*. Unfreezing at a bogie I was when the bosun came in. Sure, he just *came*. Grabbed me, chap whistled whenever he spoke to you, teeth he said it was, teeth, used to call him the whistler. His hand was made of ice, didn't stop it gripping mine. He spoke fast then.

" 'That man ain't come down, Johns,' he said, quiet-like, no fuss, really, very quiet, considering everything. 'Get on up,' he said, 'I mean *you*.' So I went on up, had to, my job. 'Sure, bos',' I said, 'sure I'll go up.' Had to relieve him, might forget he was *there*, hidden away, way up. So I was thinking about up there as I climbed, wished for a hot bogie on my backside. I just went out, and just as I was opening the door I threw at him the words out of my mouth.

" 'Ought to have had him down,' I said.

" 'A Heinkel makes you forget a lot of things, shipmate,' he said, so I just closed the fo'c's'le door quiet behind me. That's all, lady. I was going up that rigging, and Spike was still shoving her along. 'This buggering cold,' I said, all I could say then, inside myself. Sure, that goddam cold. And then I was up there, where he was, where he should be, so I shouted then, 'Aye aye there!' No answer, so I give it him louder then, 'Aye aye, Brown, where in hell are you, *are* you?' Stuck out my fist, lost it in the dark, went on climbing. Roared between my hands, 'Brown, where are you, *Brown*?' Couldn't hang on, I couldn't, flung my arms round wire, pressed, pressed, Christ I was pressing myself to that rigging. And then . . . and then . . ."

Was she listening, wasn't she? Where is she? *Feel.* He felt. "Jese," he muttered, "Jese! You're there, now, you're *in*, lady, like me."

He paused, watched her take out her handkerchief, wipe her ear.

"Saw him then, I *saw* him. Knew he wouldn't say aye aye, wouldn't spit any more. I was truck top then, saw his legs, then it slipped out again, 'Aye aye, Brown,' I said, and then I wondered why. He was near *and* far, Celia, sure, legs froze, face froze, arms froze, stretching up and up like he was

170

reaching for something, ends, picking up ends, what the black sod smashed. Said nothing, just looked at him. No answers. 'This bloody, *bloody* war,' I said, and I slid down then, slow and careful by God, yes. Whole thing give me the jimmys. I got to the fo'c's'le, got there."

They stared at each other, she motionless, he shaking a little, still remembering. Slowly he lowered his head, felt for her hand again, held it, "That's it." Her eyes slowly opened, her lips moved.

"Tell me about the ice," she said.

"Jese! I told you, just *told* you, Celia."

"Tell me about the—" saying this, and then was sick.

"Oh God! You're absolutely bloody tight, lady, absolutely."

She felt his breath, he was leaning on her again, the hands moving up and down her arms, the snakes again, and then he slobbered.

"Couldn't say anything twice, kiddo," he said, "that's the bloody way I am."

She felt something splash on her face. Was it the rain? Was it still raining out there? And then she was smothered.

"God, lady, but you're warm, *warm*," and she was sick again. He held her head. "There, Celia," and he was gently rocking again, she cradled.

"Don't be scared of me, Celia, don't be, I'm just a gutful of swears. The warm's lovely," hugging himself in, feeling coldness again, thinking of ice, seeing it rise, white, then bluish, towering, great sheets and walls of it, blue, white, shining, cold, silent. The head sank lower, and the words came after.

"Was no man there, lady, no man."

She, fast asleep, did not hear his first drunken snores.

9

"I'll go this way," she thought, not moving, and remained motionless, breathing night air. Darkness reeled about her, but she was still, stood to her full height, a still column, as it rose and fell, like waves, swept forward, engulfed what you could touch, what the eye saw, a wall's shape behind her. As when one moves seawards to bathe, apprehending the sea's touch, so adding conscious weight to prisoning clothes, so she had come down to night's shore, took the touch of air, the feel of it. As one strips for the sea, the unsure foot testing an extreme edge, so she was now stripped, and things were falling away from her, stood motionless in a black desert, the extreme edge of a reeling sea. She felt a weight move, feeling it go, falling, feeling it fall, the rust of days, bric-à-brac of hours.

"How good the night air, I'll go *this* way," beginning to move, slowly, uncertainly, apprehending voids where no voids were. She put a hasty hand to her hat, wondered if it was straight. There was now no sound and no movement, save that of her own footsteps, and the echo of them, on a road that yet might be endless. Words came up, and, parrot-like she spoke them. "I hope he sleeps," and was again sure that Dr Beecham's pills were good. Saying which he was now risen in her mind, life size, he was with her, he was where she went, stopping at a street's end, turning, walking on another road. And darker than dark, and yet she could see. Instinct turned her left, she felt this road, knew it, a long, quiet road, always had been quiet, in a noisy world. She had always liked what she would not now name. Darkness obliterated shape, but she had the feel of it; often in the old times they had tramped it together, had sometimes sat in a quiet garden, under elms. Road of the Elms. That was total, would do. Suddenly the light of a passing car dazzled her, though this itself was dim, the new ordination of night itself, and the air seemed to shake long after it had passed her. And then she stopped abruptly, uncertain, was undecided, and then her mind said, "This far, and no further," crushed the words, went on, and on, it seemed the thing to do. "I'll go on," and if *only* he would *do* something, move, *walk*, and the fairy whisper to her own ear, "He used to, we often went out at night."

A footfall was thunderous, an outstretched hand a white blob, trembled as leaves under wind.

"I know the place exactly, *know* it. I'll sit down," and somewhere behind, like an echo of her own footsteps, Clem's.

She moved inwards now, knowing where railings were, where a wall was, she found this seat. Fingers stroked the wood, felt the film of damp. This was it, *their* seat. She could see no elm, nor shape nor shadow of elm, yet she felt it there, upthrusting from winter ground, lost in a black, rolling sea. A friend, and he had once painted it, and she watching. It was there to touch. He was there, too, by her side, she could touch him with her hand; so she saw the face, the small face, and the grey hair at twenty-six. The snub nose, and the mouth that always seemed to hold an expression of wilfulness. Clem was his mouth. She saw the light brown eyes, the small hands, feminine, yet powerful. She saw him, real.

"The road gets narrower as one moves on," she said, as though he were there, listening, so remembering how suddenly the roads in their lives had forked, they had had to slacken their step, had to go slow. Four floors up in a grey house, that's where he was, an eyrie, somewhere where you could work.

"I know it'll be good, I *know* that," looking at it, at him, lifting it down, carrying it out, and then descending, down and down, and after that, up and up and up. So she was with him four floors up, hand clasping hand, stood together at an easel. "If it wasn't good, I would have told him."

She turned quickly, imagined she had heard a voice, and looked back by the way she had come, back through dark columns that now fell, a darkness obliterated, so she could see that house. See the hingeless front door, stood against a wall, and behind it the long stairway with fissures that gaped, remembered a going away morning for two spinsters that liked green things, and the green car that tooted its way towards Somerset air. And on another floor, the laughter, the music, the crying child that one never thought about, never even knew existed until the music went off the air. Robinson the name, and he was in blue, machine-faced, and how he could laugh. Laughing, and laughing, they would never stop; she knew this who was so often drenched by it. Clem and she in the cellar's dark corner, and the laughter there, filling a whole house with it, right up to the top floor where he was, working, cursing a rationed daylight, battling with colour. Strange, and always would be different from Euston. Thoughts raised her up, she started to walk again, a sudden hurrying, as if she now wished to reach its end, and all the time thinking of the laughter in the house, not giggles, not guffaws, just outright laughter, cascades, showers, roulades, floods, an endlessness, a kind of wrecking power in this so often abrupt smashing of silence. Perhaps it would go on for ever. Her pace slackened, and the laughter was gone. She was on the next floor, thinking of two that were old. Fraser the name was, you could hang a label round their necks, *Lost*. Behind the screen of fear they remembered a world where doors would close, a magic touch. The striking of a clock made her jump, she counted the strokes. Now she turned right, not faltering, knowing the world, these streets, these roads. The black sea, and how cool it was. A quiet sea, and you could think. You had to think when the road narrowed, you thought of him, of you and him together, you had to think of an end.

"The world is drunk with shouts," you heard the word "future", and you thought, "How heavy the mortgage on this."

"Oh!" she cried, her heart leaping, "oh! . . ."

"Excuse," the man said, "this infernal blackout, madam."

"It's all right," she said, moved on, her body still feeling the jolt, his footsteps died away.

"If I turned right here I know I could cross the park," and she was turning right, moving for the park, drawing strength as she walked, and she felt she could yet walk miles and no tiredness reach her.

"Wonder if the pills worked, wonder if Flo will turn up. Cancer of the heart. Poor, silly Clem," so she for the first time laughed into night air, then was struck by the sudden pain in her chest. "Only hurting *now*," she said.

Perhaps the pressure felt was of a kind Dr Beecham could not diagnose. Perhaps Clem was right, a new disease, an elusive germ, and the slide waiting for it, it could not be filed. When she touched the kerb she jolted alive a woman that had called to see her husband, whose name was Celia. "And I don't have to bloody know that she used to sit for him." And that sailor, poor drunken fool, to whom everything was jungle unless it smelt of sea, was water, salt. Together in that room, drinking. "Bitch."

Crossing the short street, she again turned right, and into another known road. Somebody crossed behind her, walked level with her, but she heard no sound, felt nothing, looking ahead, beginning to sense a new feeling, a damp breath, and knew she was not far from the river. She knew the river, loved it. Hands lightly clasped in front of her, a loose hold on the coat, feeling neither cold nor the air's damp, until of a sudden it was thick in her nostrils, the river smell. Ghosts walked by, not touching, but footsteps often rang clear on the dark road.

"I know this will do me no end of good."

If only he had come, dropped everything, just *come*. But he hadn't, and there it was. She would take back to that room a freshness, carry home a river smell, remember an hour's walk, and she would talk about that, and of a coolness their room would never know. She would mention the roads walked, and the streets crossed, the bench she sat on, and the elms behind. She stopped suddenly, threw her hands into the air, made a quick, staggering movement, as though she had reached precipice edge. No precipice, only light, a mass of light falling, and darkness rolling back, a white flood, and shapes looming up. The moon had emerged from behind heavy laden cloud. She stood quite still, she was like a swimmer, who, diving from a great height, surfaces with some confusion of mind. She was like that in the instant. The light had come, and waves of darkness receded to an unseeable horizon. It was all too sudden, this drenching light, those patterns of street, hole, corner and road. An unwanted revelation, too sudden, and too much. The dark sea had seemed more secure, but this was only brazen, cold, struck at the eye, burrowed in a mind's fastness, resurrected hours, time striking, a handless clock grinding out time, because a cloud moved, because a moon shone. She raised her head and looked all about her, then continued on her way.

Past and around shapes she walked. If the moon vanished, it would obliterate these shapes, and the dark sea cover the phantasmagoric, the galvanic nightmare frozen by light. If? But the moon was full, and clouds were sailing fast to the west. The eye could rest or sleep in a dark sea, but here it was fish-open, and could not close against the forest of shapes, towering and tottering, turning and twisting, the frantic reel that forced eye's total power. Shapes and emanations of shapes, a widening horizon. It could not be shut out. The pavement suddenly widened, she saw railings, she leaned against them.

"I don't want to walk any further."

She drew up the collar of her coat, pushed her hands up the sleeves of it, and remained hunched there, and not a sound nor a step heard. Behind her the wall that appeared to stagger, beyond which the small church she knew, remembered the red brick of it. She was dwarfed by shapes, a drab brick pile, an eyeless window, a demented stone pillar holding up nothing. She had felt more secure under the darkness. She made a sudden move forward, then stepped back again.

"Shall I go on, shall I go back?"

How much a face would count now, someone turning a corner, emerging from house, hole, or window, a single face to break the welter and frenzy of the shapes about her. Rooted in these moments, her own footsteps startled her, so in the end she passed by the red church fallen, and to her left a grey stone building that was not standing, it could not stand as buildings stood, but hung in air, as draperies hang, and the next building grey, and another of bathstone, and these hanging, all draping sky. In a world of suspended motion, a sudden movement, unexpected, strange. She had to stop, she had to look upwards. And then she saw it, a balloon coming down, with slow, isolated, elephantine movements in a city that seemed now so very still. It was like something out of another time, you thought of an un-discovered sphere, a new kind of mammal. And lower and lower it came, at the end of this street, to rooftop level, and so at last to barren ground. The eye was fixed steadily on it, noticed a giant shudder, something enormously swollen, watching it shiver, settle, and be still. A bugaboo. This mammal had gigantic rubber ears, and she thought of it high, and thought of it anchored, and the ropes that trailed everywhere.

"Oh God!" she exclaimed, turned on her heel, and saw it, the first face.

"Sorry, mam," the man said, close to her, in moonlight, a face violently red under the helmet, and the teeth now showing. Was it a smile?

A moment ago she would have warmed to this face, but now her whole attention was concentrated on the balloon. A prodigious white louse.

"Dangerous to be *out*, madam," he said, the eye glittered, the teeth shone. He heaved out the remaining words, "better to be *in*. Yes. In." And watched her move, and watched her suddenly run.

"Silly woman," he thought, turned sharply, began to attend to the first of many practical matters.

"Like a nightmare," she cried to herself, still running, and then, "I'm here. At last." The surprise and the relief of it,

177

this was known country. Water flowing by, lapping against walls, and standing very still, regaining her breath, and thinking how glad she was that she had at last done it. Softly lapping water wafted away her own confusions, and in a clear moment she thought only of swans as white as the moon above.

"Once upon a time we were very very close to it, Clem and I."

So a small house grew where she stood, and they were in it, Clem and she. And they had watched together. She felt herself river full, and watched it flow by, through streets and roads, round buildings, round walls and people and children, round those working and those asleep, and round them together as they watched, the girdling strength of an old time, those beginning days.

"Poor Clem," she thought, involuntarily, the words jerked out, a jack-in-the-box movement, like the quick, electric flutter of a swan's wing she had seen in her mind's eye, as though this bird had dreamed, a tossing fragment whirling by. Words had been like that. Leaning over the low wall she devoured the river, sucked in the smells. So the small house had come by, was clear, she saw and touched it, the bright future, the buoyant hours. "The river," she was saying to herself, "the river," like a child's hurrah, a sudden smile, somebody saying, "I'm glad." After which the footsteps were ringing in her ears.

He went up three steps, and opened the little door, the sun following him in, his shadow danced, a house flooded with it. He shut the door and hurried down the short, narrow corridor, came to a white door, was instantly cautious, silently turning the knob, pushing in noiselessly, peeping. He saw Lena. She was putting bluebells in a stone vase, and he followed the hand's movements, studied her in profile. He enjoyed this; it was not often he caught her like that, disarmed, poiseless. What a strong face hers was, and seeming more masculine than ever looked at in this way, something earnest there, a belief. And then she turned, looked towards the door, knowing him there, feeling for thoughts. He held his breath, wondered if she had seen him. He had a horror of being caught like this, and was yet entranced by the expression upon her face. He knew he would never get it in any other way but this, and no miracle or magic would hold it. Never get it on canvas, never. And then he pushed violently at the door, entered.

"Hello, darling," and as she jumped, "sorry, dear, afraid I frightened you, didn't realize you'd be here this time of the morning, expected you'd be shopping. Anybody ring?"

She dropped her hands at once, her lips moved, nothing came out, she shook her head, and this said, "Telephones do not ring."

"Post gone?"

A heavy falling word, lead, "Gone."

"Oh Christ!" he exclaimed, and she knew the anger, no longer thought of bluebells in a vase, and an anger stronger than his own forced the words out.

"Something will, Clem, I'm sure it will, darling, I feel it," eager, earnest, half smiling, and then the sudden laugh. "Those words are ten years old."

His hands rested on her shoulders, he held her close, his eyes smiled.

"You see, I *have* to tell myself this, have to believe it, to drive myself. It's not as you think, 'tisn't short, life—I *mean* that—there is time, something will happen. I saw Rupert this morning."

Jerky words in the air could not hold down bluebells in a vase. She was moving from him, hurrying out of the room.

"Wait, Lena, do sit *down*," caught the arm, drew her in close. "I have to explain. Do *wait*. Something *will* happen."

He forced her to sit down.

"What did he say?" she asked, her fingers stroking the chair's arm.

"Who?"

And she screamed back in his face, "*Rupert*," trying to relax, knowing she could not. She couldn't do it. The words were old, the sounds the same. She watched, waited, and her fingers were still on the chair's arm.

"Well now," he began, expansively, "well now . . ." staring at her, staring hard, hoping she would understand. He was sure she would. Ten years was nothing, really.

"Yes, dear?"

"I told him he could take the two paintings Burt has, that I didn't object in any way to his sense of values, in cash terms, *not* this morning."

She drew back, from the words, the fierceness in his voice, supposed he had been drinking, and was almost on the point of saying, "I do wish you wouldn't drink when you've not eaten, darling. I'm always asking you."

He slumped into the opposite chair. "I can't value a bloody thing this morning. For Christ's sake, don't go looking at me like that," seeing the now ashen face, the plain face, wondered if it would ever light up, suffuse to life. "Don't you under*stand*? It's all I can do *now*." Now was a long word, dragged the tongue's length, a big word out of a small mouth. "I can't do anything . . . *now*."

She rose. He thought she would embrace him, but she did not, but stood very still, and looked at him, and said slowly, "I don't want to stay here. It's no good," was suddenly crying.

"Oh hell, Lena," hugging her. "Perhaps it's best not to talk about it. Let's forget it, shall we. This very bloody minute. God! Let's go out," and dragged her after him to the door.

"Wait, Clem . . . wait a minute," and then he wiped her eyes with his handkerchief.

"There there!"

Her look remained, penetrated, there was no other way she could look, felt suspicious of his words, again wondered if he had been drinking.

He took her hand, "Come on, Lena, for God's sake, let's get *out*."

She half turned, looked back at flowers in a vase, flowers strewn on a table.

"Damn them," he said, "come," dragged her after him, and she did not resist. They were at the front door.

Sun was on them, they felt warmth. He opened the door, and they went quickly down the steps. They were suddenly silent, as though by some prearranged plan. They crossed the road, leaned close together, and watched. Looked up the river, and looked down, And then he was looking one way, she another. His words struck the air, shot over his shoulder.

"I saw that bloody hopeless fool, Gorton, too," but she didn't hear, was thinking of swans, her head was full of a whiteness. "Said my exhibition was now out of the question. Said there would be plenty of work very soon, dragon painting, the new 'thing'. Though dragons are any time fierce, they pay good money. I told Gorton to go to hell," blurting it all out, and not moving, and she too was still, not questioning, not seeming to hear.

"Angry," she thought, "he's *damned* angry," remembering the words hitting the air as bullets, but there was no target.

"You all right, darling?" he asked.

She didn't hear, she didn't move.

He sensed a pressure behind him, and turning saw that there were many people on the embankment, all of whom seemed to be moving in only one direction. Perhaps some fated ordination at work. Looked at Lena who was already lost in a world of ships, barges, tugs, rowing boats, swimmers, seagulls, gliding by swans, but he saw nothing of the sprawling life about him.

"Lena!"

No answer.

"*Lena!*"

And silence. And he was unaware of the distance, the desert suddenly between them. She was not with Clem. She was in a room, lost in a big, broken-springed armchair, she was stroking a cat, and unconscious of it, in a room that was cold. He had left her, on this, their first day together. But the room was word-choked, the atmosphere electrified by them, a chaotic mess of words that now began to fall into some kind of order. She hoped for a meaning to a situation, it might come clear eventually. And now he was there, in the room, stood over her, relaxed, and almost idly listening.

"You might have told me, Clem."

"Told you what?" he drawled.

"About this," Lena said.

"About *what*?"

"This," she shouted, her hand sweeping the air, her hand in one big encircling movement, embracing coldness, and cat, and the decaying grandeur of another day, the dilapidation, the things that looked mean. "All *this*."

"D'you suppose I like it. You knew what to expect."

"I don't know."

"It's just one long bloody struggle," he said, and the moment he said it she was sorry, reached out her hands, took his, smiled up at him.

"It's all right, I'm not afraid, darling, and I believe in you. I mean that. I'll stand by you."

He was laughing. "You are a darling, Lena, you see if you went away on me *now*, I'd be done. I have to lean on you, have to know you are there."

He glanced idly round the room.

"This rotten façade, this rubbish, it's all mixed up with the crazy machinery of struggling along," and he bent down, looked steadily at her. "Doesn't bother me, not *really*, and soon it won't bother you, either. Soon, you'll scarcely notice it."

So they were one again, embraced, resolved, and nothing mattered except this, being together, holding, determined, and involuntarily he exclaimed passionately, "Hold on, Lena."

"Yes."

"I'll see Rupert again if you wish . . ."

"Then please don't be long," and quickly, "Couldn't I come?"

"No. Don't come. I shan't be long."

The moment the door closed on him she threw down the cat, and a sudden recklessness sent her bursting into his room. She sat down. This was the room where he worked, her eye wandering. Paintings heaped against a wall, an untidy pile that might have been disgustingly abandoned, and a shy glance at a painting on the easel, budding hope. The smell of paint, and the general disarray, the tubes, the brushes, the torn letters, the cigarette ash filming everything she saw, knots and infinitesimal fragments of paper, the half burned cigarettes, and one isolated splendour of an unsmoked cigar, and how often she had asked him to either smoke or crush it. Sitting here made her think of prison and cage, a sleeping energy beneath the stale air, then endless wishing. Crossing the room she began to look at canvas after canvas, noticing the signature in the bottom left hand corner of each, something fierce about it, a thumbnail insanely scratching C.

"God! He works."

She went to the window, stood looking at the fragmented sky, the burdensome shadow of bricks and slate. Yes, you could stand here and you could work, you could say something, you could see where to climb, to fix what you said, see a clear flight of steps, upwards. You worked from root, from the very bottom, so suddenly when you looked again, this staircase had become spiral, had no end. You worked on because you were sure that somewhere there was an end to these stairs. There would be some place you could stand, keep a foothold, *stay*. Silence would be long, have a leaden weight, so you felt this as you worked slowly, from bottom upwards, you felt there was somebody about, someone in a forest of rounding stairs, watching, listening. You worked on, blindly, then, almost before you realized it, somebody was there. When he spoke, you laughed, the silence broken. You had met one that understood your language.

"That was . . . how long ago, how many years, one, two, five . . .?" it didn't matter.

10

When the first shiver enveloped her she knew where she was, and immediately drew away from the wall. Darkness and coldness still surrounded. She rubbed vigorously at her hands.

"I just came out for a walk, and *look* where I am."

Cloud passed, moon shone, she saw, and she laughed at what stared back. A wooden bridge, one of a congregation of shapes.

"Heavens! It's only half a bridge." A clock struck, and she counted strokes, still staring, the shock of surprise still with her. A bridge that began on stone foundations and ended in the air, in the middle of the river, not a bridge, a gesture, an attitude, a sense of its desperate striving to reach the other side.

"What on earth happened there?"

The rack again, worrying about Clem; suppose he woke suddenly, found she wasn't there, suppose those pills had been useless.

"I hate him worrying about anything, *now*."

She turned, walked quickly away. "How long have I been out? An hour?" Increasing her pace, forgetting a bridge that yet reached out frantically to reach the other side. "Fancy not noticing *that*," she thought, crossing another road, standing on an island. "It is late," she said. "I've only been thinking of myself," was shivering again, it had come right home.

A car flashed by, a bell rang, and she did not notice it. "The walk has done me good."

"If only just the once he'd say 'yes'," go out with her of an evening, even a little shopping one morning. "No. He'll never do it now. Something has happened to Clem."

Seeing him again, five floors up, refusing to move. Suppose he *never* left the house any more.

"I stood there in the darkness, the air was beautiful, but something wasn't right. I know now, I can't shut my eyes to it. He *has* changed. Each time I have to *find* him. Lord! How my mind wandered as I walked, suddenly vanished, and returned."

It made her think of pressures. "Yes, that's it. Pressures."

Against this a pressure on her chest seemed a mere itch.

Walking and walking, eating up roads, finding a way back, a way in.

"What he's doing now is good, I know it is. Yes, I believe in Clem. Once I didn't understand a thing, never even understood what strength *was*. Couldn't fathom what he meant, what he wanted," then, after a long pause, and tentatively, "I think I know."

The name Rupert darted into her mind, Clem's brainchild, never even existed. And how he had laughed when he knew she sensed it, when she had read out the obituary, supposedly from *The Times*. "Died, privately, at 18 Holmes Place." It made her laugh again.

The moon vanished, darkness again, a black sea coming up, filling street and house, hole, corner, and road. This was signals down, and a sudden blindness, a loss of direction, but soon, very soon, she would have the feel of her own street, the house, the room at the very top. And then she heard it. A sound coming up river, chasing as hound.

"Yes, there it is, it *is*, they're back again, my God, three times this night," a sure foot faltering, beginning to grope. A sound could do this.

"He'll wake, he'll say, Christ, not *again*?" talking aloud, as if she were addressing an audience, "well, it's not far now," trying to hurry, not hurrying, feeling frantically for the torch in her pocket, the torch she had forgotten about, why on earth hadn't she remembered it? And then the shout. "Here it is. *Got* it."

She would run, she would squeeze her way in, she would hurry upstairs, the sound behind her, and this sound would swell. Imagined herself home, bumping about in a dark hall, his name on her lips, climbing stairs, and the drunken light from the torch showing her the way.

The sound paralysed her where she stood. A long, deep sound, you could measure the length and depth of it. You knew it would come, but there was no music, nor any bird's cry. You listened, were not surprised, you couldn't be any more. You gripped the ground you stood on, you waited. This sound would rise and fall, spread as wings, make ever widening circles, and you knew this mentor of your time, of a city's time. It had no root but here. You tried to imagine some far off region whence it came, its substance spinning there, the dementia region. You hated it, yet unheard you would feel insecure, lost. It was your day, your time, your watching hour, your third hand. You would know this as you climbed and climbed.

There was no place this rolling sound could not reach, and she felt it behind her, pushing her up, up, to where he waited.

You thought of the loneliness of a city. Could it be that cry? You said no, loneliness having no voice. You said, "This is an emanation," pouring in, rising and falling, far spreading, it might have no end. A cry from stone, those strangled shapes, pride sucked from the bone. All the sounds in hell sung, all the sounds known, yet you could not name this. A lawless sound, outside all music. And the drunken light in her hand flung shadow to walls, and she was still mounting stairs, and the sound following. She began groping in her pocket for the key, found it, muttered "Christ! I think he's awake, those bloody pills were no good, no *good*," and the words drowned in that other sound. She put the key in the lock, but as she turned it, the door opened of itself. "That's odd," going in, calling aloud, "you there, Clem, you all right?" No answer.

And then she saw him. Her calmness amazed her, as she asked in a quiet voice, "Did you sleep, dear?"

And he said, casually, even more quietly, "No. I did not. I was wide awake after a few minutes."

He was stood with his back to her, and she saw that he had a soaked handkerchief around his forehead.

"Your head again, Clem. Oh God! I shouldn't have gone," putting an arm around him, feeling a moist bandage, smelling the vinegar. He did not move. She stared into his back, wished he would turn round, look at her. There was something about staring into a person's back. She longed for him to turn, now, face her, say "Hello. Glad you're back, Lena". And then a silly question. "Have you been working, dear?" knowing he would never work without daylight.

"They'll be back, Lena," he said, bumped into the easel he was now covering.

"I know. I heard the sound," and wondered if he had, or standing there, staring at his work, were his ears plugged, shutting everything out.

"I'll have to get it down, Lena," he said, at last turned, looked at her. "Wondered where you'd gone, thought you might never come back."

It shocked, wounded her. "*Never?*" she asked.

"The way things were," he said, "it was the way things were."

"I had to go out, I had to get some *air*."

"Of course. I know that, dear."

"*Do* you?" and the nerve edge showing in a moment. "You *are* all right?"

"I'm all right," he said, stood back from the easel, reached for her hands, took and pressed them. "I *must* get it down."

"Yes, darling, you *said* that."

"Did I?" suddenly hazy, wondering.

The silence was sudden, fell as clean as a blade, they looked at each other, and the sound was greater now, and the clock appeared to have died.

The ultimatum. "Who's been *here*?" she asked.

"I didn't notice anybody here," he replied.

"But somebody has been *in*," she said.

She waited a long time for the answer. "Never saw

anybody," he said. On which she clapped hands to her head. "What is the *matter* with him?"

"You don't mind helping me down with it, Lena. I saw that man Jones. A nice man, his wife's nice, too. He said he'd see I got it down all right. Suggested I put it between the two dustbins back of the cellar."

So she laughed, something was free. "Dustbins," she said, "*dust*bins?"

She saw him excited, a wild waving of the hands, the handkerchief falling from his head. "Look. Come and look," he said, dragged her to the easel, flung away the covering. "Got it! What I wanted. Depth, got it, Lena."

And she heaved it out, "I'm glad," she said, the sigh of relief.

"Who came, dear?"

Holding him there, firmly, waiting for an answer. "I said who came?"

He turned his back on her, leisurely covered the canvas, muttering, "Got to get it down, each time the bastards come over I've got to get it *down*."

"You've told me that three times already."

"Did I?"

So she shouted "Yes".

She wondered who had called, what had awakened him, and as she stared at the huge covered canvas she got the echoes and feeling and stress of other journeys. Extraordinary. He would go no place without this. An aberration, and once she would have laughed at it, and now she could not, thinking of roads, mountains climbed through the years, falls, obstacles. Yet he had said nothing, and perhaps would not, locked in his own resolve, knowing the way he would go, doing what he believed in. So he believed in this, part of him, so together they would go down to darkness and damp of cellar. She would help him, who had shown her each strand of his own strength.

"Come and sit down," he said, pointing, "*here*," and she sat.

Taking her hands, and at last a smile. "Hello, dear," he

said, "hello. You went out, out, on a bloody awful night like this. If you go out without telling me, I always wake up," then anxiously, "you *are* all right, darling?"

"Yes," she said, "yes," then stressed it, "I *am* all right, Clem."

"Warmth," he thought, saying this "Clem".

"Who came?"

He was nonplussed, caught out, staring at her, the robot words ready.

"Somebody came in. I think. Never really noticed," and then he was looking beyond her, at the door, and at the man in the helmet stood there.

"Better get down again," the warden said, "they're on the way . . ."

"*Again?*"

"Again," he said, and was gone, and his hurrying steps down to the hall sounded thunderous at the top of the house.

"Come, dear," Lena said, "we'd better go. I knew it would come, felt it all the way home," gave him a great hug, kissed him, "I was glad to be back," and he said nothing, the head fallen, the hands clasped, the nervous fingers pulling at the cloth of coat, not noticing she had gone into the other room to collect his overcoat, the tweed cap; he would never wear anything but a cap, his mask.

She got the thermos, the handy sandwiches wrapped in newspaper; vigil might reach as far as hunger, a great thirst, you never knew.

Jerky words, fitting the moment. "Here! Put it on, dear."

"Lena," he said, soft in her ear.

"What?" she said, sharply.

"You think it's all right," he stammered, "I mean now, as you looked at it, as you look at it again," and he rushed to the easel and flung clear the covering. "Yes?"

Something screamed past her as she looked, as they both looked, and she said, "Yes, you've got it," moments before the explosion came.

"Everybody *down*."

"There," he said, "let's go."

"You have such patience," she said, "you've got it, Clem, you really have," almost enveloped him with her smile, and getting the strong gritty smell in her nostrils at the same time, and the thunder up the stairs for the third time.

"Everybody *down*."

"We're coming," she said. "Don't fuss."

They lifted the canvas clear, covered it, slowly dragged it across the room.

"Right. Come along now," she said, pulling hard, and the sudden commanding tone, a quite changed voice, a shielding one, the tool of a long apprenticeship used on others, when the going was hard, the hard side of her that he did not know, the raised screen whilst he worked, whilst he waited for the telephone to ring, the post to come, whilst he waited for the light, the *right* light. Suddenly, she wanted to cry, knew what was wrong, knew it now.

"I wonder who came?" she asked herself for the hundredth time.

"Lift," Clem cried, "*Li*——"

"I am lifting, dear, I *am*," the easel creaking, her mind suddenly full of pills, "I do wonder who came, somebody did. 'Somebody,' he said, he hadn't noticed . . . No. There are quite a number of things that he doesn't appear to notice these days," the canvas fully free, the full weight between them, moving slowly down, in a half darkness, moving slowly along, the twilight of a new time, remembering her long walk, remembering how glad she was to be back.

"You all right, Lena?"

"I'm all right. Go *on*."

Moving bat-like, slowly, carefully down, counting each stair, how soon would they reach the cellar?

And the thought pursuing. "*Who* came?"

Not Dr Beecham, not sister Flo, Essex grass pulled too hard, she would never be certain of Flo . . .

"Wait a minute," stopping dead, pulling backwards, and that pain in the chest again, back. Clem's "cancer of the heart", and she shouted her loudest, "Stop!"

"All right, but hurry up, I must get it *down*."

"Christ yes. I haven't forgotten, dear."

"Poor Lena," he thought, "poor Lena," he said.

"My God! Of course. That one might have called whilst I was out. That bitch. The Bermondsey morsel. *That* one!"

"What?" he asked, "what's that, Lena, say it again."

"Nothing."

"Come on, dear," he said, "come *on*," the words like fists behind her.

And she moved, saying nothing.

"All right now. Carry on," he said, so she again took the weight, her thoughts miles from a cellar, her eyes closed to what you could hear in the darkness, forgetting people, one after the other, even the waiting dustbins. She thought only of one that had called, said her name was Celia.

"Careful, Lena, *care*ful," he called, and her sudden, angry exclamation quite escaped him, though he heard the final shout.

"Oh God! All *right*. I *am* being careful."

Down and down. Where did it end?

Her head throbbing, the words circling again.

"Said her name was Celia," involuntarily, aloud, at the top of her voice.

"What's that?"

His voice was as keen as a razor blade.

"I said nothing, I mean nothing, will that *do*?"

And the new voice, splitting them in two.

"Everybody out, everybody down, and hurry up, I mean *hurry*," Richard cried, who thought only of a waiting Gwyn, in the usual place, the cellar. "Blast the bastards. Something told me they'd be back."

Something bumped into him, and he called out, "Hello there. That you, Gwyn?"

A giggle followed, and the voice said, "Only me."

"Who the hell are you? What d'you want, how'd you get in *here*?"

The flash of his torch struck her in the eye, which she closed, and she looked up at him, said, "Just walked in, dear. Anything wrong?" She then offered him another giggle.

"Somebody broke into the ground floor flat. Have you seen that damned drunken sailor?" he asked, tense, sharp, and she felt the grip on her arm.

"You're hurting me," she said.

"Somebody broke into—"

And louder than loud, gulped out. "Eh! Wha's that, mister?"

He waited till her sudden bout of hiccoughing ended.

"Into the cellar with you, you silly drunken bitch, and don't you giggle at me. If something hit you, your giggle'd be bloody cheap. *Go* on, get *down*," pushing her, catching her as she staggered, after which he said in a low voice, "Oh Christ," heard her being sick, "I'll *carry* you down. You were in there with that sailor, weren't you? As drunk as you are now, damned fool. I could report this. Perhaps it was *you* that broke into the Benson flat."

"Tha's it," she said, and he hated her burst of laughter, thinking only of slobber, and ended up by talking through his teeth.

"You're going to be into one load of trouble, Miss, who-ever you are."

"Tha's music, listen," Celia said, started to hum a tune.

"Come on, and don't be *stupid*. Where'd he go?"

She was heavier on his shoulder, and he counted the steps to the cellar. "Come on, where is that *sailor*?"

She made no reply, pressed her head against him, he smelt her breath.

"*Bugger* you."

He heard the voices, pushed his way through, called, "You there, Gwyn?"

"Here," she said.

"Good," and he dropped his load to the floor, bent over it, shouting, "There! And keep *quiet*, and stay bloody put."

He groped towards the lighted candle. "You comfy, Gwyn?"

"Yes."

"Ah!" he said, "ah!" sat down beside her, found himself wildly stuttering in a dropped voice. "I mean you're not scared or anything, dear, I mean . . . I'll *have* to go now, hope everybody's down, think they are, hope so. Done my stint."

They clung to each other. "Chin up," Richard said.

"Who's that?"

And he whispered in her ear, "A drunk, some young woman, just been horribly sick, don't know who in hell she is, been in the Benson flat with that sailor, another drunk, talk about who's lucky, he's vanished." His hand tightened in her own.

"I was going to say, Richard," she began, but he was on his feet in a flash, saying, "So long, darling," rushing away, was gone, and only then was she aware of the heavy breathing at her feet.

"You all right?"

"Eh!" a belch, and then, "wha's that?"

Only the falling bomb drowned out another loud giggle.

Cis didn't know whether she was all right, and she cared less, her mind in this moment was swamped by Clem. The first sight of him had made her laugh, it was funny, after which she had been sick again. She remembered this the moment she began to move out of the green dream, moving with Johns, out of heat and into fresh air, his wet mouth close to her ear.

"You'll be okay, kiddo," Johns said, "sure, you're fine," getting her out into the cold hall, feeling the blaze of light from an upper landing, waves of music coming through the half open door.

"Somebody enjoying themselves, Cis, let's go on up."

They went up, and he felt a heavy drag on his arm, bent to her, "What?"

"Never told me about the bloody *ice*," Cis said, "you said you—"

"'Struth! Told you, lady, *told* you. Sure I did. Come on, let's get up there, I like that kind of music, don't you?"

Laughing, pulling her back, kissing her, pushing her

forward, so the ascent of stairs was slow, staggering, so the light seemed it would never be reached.

"Jese, hear that, Cis, that's fine, sure. Heard that song once, in Peru it was, sure, lovely stuff, lovely . . ."

Robinson was at the door, and he was in his blue.

"Come on in, sailor, have a drink," Robinson said, extended a hand.

"Sure," Johns said, and turned to Cis. "Well so long, kiddo," kissing her, "you're dandy, ah, I wouldn't hurt a hair of your head, lady, mean it, love you, listen to *that*. Makes you feel sort of sad."

Robinson gripped his arm, pulled, and Johns hung on to Cis, looked longingly at her, who was "fine". "So long, see you in the cellar, yes, sure," and the smacking kiss loud enough to carry its own echo.

"Sink her, man, she's just a *tart*," and Robinson pulled him in, closed the door. So for the first time Johns saw Ducksie.

"Here's a chap likes my music, Ducksie," and Johns was under a bright light, looking down at a young woman in a chair, a child in her arms.

"Here's my wife, sailor, Ducksie to you."

"Hello there, why, hell*o*," and Johns stumbled forward, took her hand, "hell bloody lo, lady."

"What you drinking?" the blue man said.

"Goddam, that sounds great to me. Anything, sir, any-*thing*."

He flopped into the chair, took the child's hand in his own where it promptly got lost, stroked velvet fingers, "Yours, lady?"

"Christ man! Course it's hers. Here we go," and the glasses tinkled.

"Up the bastards," the blue man said, and Johns laughed, bellowed his own observation.

"Sure, up them," he said, and they both drank.

Robinson hovered over Ducksie. "Drinking, darling?"

But Ducksie shook her head, concentrated on the child, began a sudden frantic rocking in the chair.

Cis, prone at Gwyn's feet, gave off an occasional belch, but was otherwise still, in a damp cellar. Gwyn sensed her powerfully there, but was as motionless as she, her hands clasped behind her, leaning against brick wall, the eyes closed, and thinking only of Richard, and second following second she wished him back again, right back, close, safe, in uncertain moments. But the figure at her feet was again clutched in green dream, moving away from the feet that had so often touched her face, half on her feet now, and staggering towards the door. This banged behind her, but no one heard, none moved. After which she started to clamber up the steps, arms out, hands spread, feeling for where stone steps would end, then suddenly into air, feeling dizzy, leaning on the wall, confused, wondering what time it was, dreading sounds, the cosmic feel, would they . . . were they . . . and at last clear, and standing in the deserted hall, staring upwards. She climbed, groped for a top landing, reached it. She walked along, knew where the door was, knew it blind, was there, leaning, listening. No sound. He was in there, alone, and she knew he was, Clem, the "little geeny-wenius". She knocked once, twice, swore loudly, hiccoughed, and finally kicked in the door that would have opened at a touch. He was there, she saw him, and she laughed.

"Hello, Clem!"

"Hello," he said, automatic, not moving, never turning round, immediately forgot her, walked up to the easel, stood, a hand waving wildly in its area.

She went deep into the room, stood, saw him clearer, stone still in front of an easel.

"After all them bloody years," she cried, slobbering, wiping her mouth with the back of her hand, again felt a dizziness, looked round, seeking a chair, found it and slumped down, wanting to vomit again, and not vomiting, hand pressed hard to mouth.

"Hello there!" she cried again, this time louder, the words shaky, fragmenting in silence.

"Hell—o, Clem!"

He did not hear, did not speak, he was very busy, she saw the hand moving, as she sprawled, was heavier in the chair.

"Bugger me, don't you remember me, you *pig*, used to sit for you, used to si' . . . oh yes, dearie, I did, didn't half like my bust, you bastard, so you don't know anybody these days. Well, bloody well."

She leaned forward, opened wide her eyes, and there he was, *real*. He was moving, he was painting, he was jigging in her focus, she thought he had a bun on his head, this moved in her vision, danced, this was bandage, she wondered what made it smell.

"Cle' . . ." staggering to her feet, down the room, coming right behind him, "hello, dear."

He was yet unhearing, there seemed no time, and one hand held up the bandage round his forehead, the other hand gripped a brush, and it might never let go.

"Are you . . ." bumping into him, throwing him off balance, "are you *sick*, Clem Stevens, are you . . ." and slobbered and gripped one arm, but no word came over his shoulder, and he did not turn to look at her.

He had got it now, he was sure he had, and he suddenly dropped the brush, clapped hands, shouted, "Got it!"

"You're a stuck up bastard, Clem Stevens," she said, "stuck *up*," started to laugh, began making slow circles round him, felt dizzy again, turned and staggered back towards the chair, twice stumbled, arms threshing air, then stepped on to something that was soft, which later hissed, spat.

"Ugh!"

She had always hated cats. You didn't at first notice it, merely an ornament rigid in front of an electric fire, until it moved, sprang. For the first time she seemed to be aware of the heat in the room, a blaze of light flooding a red carpet, and a live cat in a room that Lena had always thought was cold. Cis aimed a kick at the cat and fell flat on her back.

"Christ! Where am I?"

She sat up, stared up the room and down the room, and

yes, he was still there, jigging in front of an easel, and something white had fallen from his head.

"Bloody swine," she shouted, "you do remember me, you pig, turn round I say, turn bloody round, look at me. Sat for you when you counted the breadcrumbs, parted my legs when you couldn't pay the rent. Sod, that's what you are, sod."

He stood at the easel, motionless, and he would not turn round.

"Knew you'd bloody end up in front of the dustbins, stuck up swine."

She shut her eyes, opened them. Yes, he was still there. Working again, after all that time. She moved slowly across the room, found the wall, leaned there, then slid slowly to the floor, and then her hand touched something, and she knew what this was.

"God yes, that's it," touching canvas after canvas stood against the wall. "Course, *course.*"

She picked one up, stood it on her knee, peered cross-eyed at the man staring up from the canvas. "Oh lor!"

And another, and this one had a grey look, which she immediately put down, disliking it, and then examined a third, a fat woman in yellow and green, "Good heavens," muttering to herself, and Clem would never hear it. No more gabbling against his sealed up ears, she thought, staring closely at the woman, then dropping it like a stone, taking up another, and suddenly a loud exclamation, and she closed her eyes, unbelieving, against what she saw.

"Christy! It's *me.*"

And it was.

"Well I never," she said, gave a great gasp, "here's me, fancy that, fan—" she had quite forgotten a momentary fame, "really me," holding it close, then distant, high above her head, low at her feet, her mouth wide open, *her.* "It *is* me," she cooed, then shouted wildly down the room. "Me, Clem. *Me.*"

Yes, there she was, smiling and not drunk, "Oh lor," seeing herself nude, stuttering again, "yes, he did like that

. . . rem—ember now, ye' . . ." and she ran the tip of her finger across the painting, traced her own anatomy, "can't believe it, really, fancy *finding* the thing . . . bloody me," and emitted another sigh, then relaxed where she sat.

"The col—that's it, the *col*our. Course . . . that *day*," and staggered to her feet, fell to her knees, rising again, running the room's length with the canvas over her head, standing right behind the man at the easel, shouted, "It's me, Clem, I *found* it."

He was too absorbed to move, too deaf to hear, being at this moment lost in distance; that was important to him, *now*. And a sense of relief that he had found it, *got* it, and there was nothing in this room, nothing except himself, and the distance he had got. And then she heard him shout, "It's *there*!"

The silence enraged her. "Clem! You *bastard*, you know I'm . . . I'm," and resting the canvas on one shoulder, peeping from behind it, cried, "I spy. You can't see me, Clemmy, you *pig*, I'm *here*, behind you, are you drunk, too?"

The silence, his motionless, further enraged her, "Stuck up *swine*."

"God! It's there," he shouted, suddenly raised hands in the air, clapped them, cried, "Lena!"

The canvas in her hand was suddenly pressing against his back, but he felt no pressure, as he said, "Ah!" and a name leaping out, "*Lena!*"

"You *know* who I bloody am," shouting, wiping slobber from her chin, and her voice climbing.

He made a quick, jerky movement backwards, trod on her toe.

"Ow! You *pig*."

He did not hear, he just said quietly, "*Mind*. See it. Yes. *Got* it," and an arm was thrust backwards, but she had drawn away, and not before she had spat at him, then turned and reeled down the room. The excellence of Miss Benson's whisky, the warm of the arm of a lost sailor was still with her, and she had quite forgotten the night before, the horror, the icy cosmic feel. She sat heavily on the floor, leaned against the wall. And there, to right and left of her, canvas after canvas.

"Well! *Really*. Fancy that. Never stopped working, *never*."

There seemed so many of them and she couldn't count. She got slowly to her feet, moved along the wall, fingering them, one after the other.

"The pig," she thought, "the pig," she muttered, wiped slobber from her chin. "Poor old Clem!" Inspecting them one by one, returning them to their rightful place. She looked up, looked back down the room.

"The . . ." and her mouth wide open, but the words had died, and it remained open, too heavy to shut, dead fish-head, flopping to the floor again, renewing the moment, staring at herself. He did it. He had always liked that particular one, refusing to sell, and she remembered that, a clear moment out of the haze, and the inward smile that followed. Yes, and here it was now, in her hand, and she pressed lips against it, hugging it. "Ah! Me." All of her, the whole body, real. She leaned back to the wall, still holding it, trying to think, thinking. In a sort of way it *was* yours, you were on the canvas, in it, and this would dance in your eye every time you looked at it.

"And all *these*," she thought, her eye enveloping the canvas pile, yes, there they were, all lying with their faces to the wall. Perhaps he'd already forgotten them, killing an old one when he got excited about a new one. No, she just couldn't count them.

"Must've worked, must've," and a sudden laugh, low in her throat, seeing Clem now, remembering him the day before yesterday, before a lost sailor heaved his way over her horizon. Her fingers moved slowly down the back of the canvas, she got the feel again, knew the answer. Yes. It was real. Was her. And he was good.

"Always knew he was . . . was . . ."

When you were like that, like Clem, you just piled them up. And then you pushed one away under pressure from another one. The way it was, then, that *other* time. "Something just pressed it out of him. Yes." Clem Stevens was like that, not counting, not even thinking, just working, riots of energy, it had always been like that. So for an instant she was back in Bermondsey, on a cool morning, walking her long way to that other world, Chelsea. She kissed herself for the third time, wanted to shout and did not, and the man at the other end was moving, yet made no sound. So here was one that she liked, from this dust pile, yesterday's ghosts. He would not miss this, miss *one*; besides it was really hers, her head and shoulders, her arms and her breasts, part of a belly, it *was* her.

And she had not forgotten what she saw when he moved, another woman on canvas, and the shout behind him "Who's *she*?" and low in her throat, "This is *me. Mine.*"

He was unhearing, inwardly laughing at the depth he had got, the colour *bled*, and that was right, what he wanted, what he had, and happy now. He had forgotten a particular picture he had done, a girl, eighteen and a half, a beauty from Bermondsey litter; this could sometimes happen. He had liked it, too, had had offers, six times had, and he was deaf to these, so he would never sell, who had now forgotten it, forgotten her, lost her in a heap, against the wall. And he looked at the wall, on which he so often flung his dream pictures.

And a forgotten model knelt on the floor, mused, hugged herself tight. He'd never know, never miss it, the days were so uncertain now, the nights more so. Celia would be safest with Celia. So, thinking in this way, there slowly grew a moral right of sorts, and she clutched at it. She'd go now, leave this room, a room miserable in its very length, and look and shape, leave a wilderness, and the puppet in it, jigging in front of an easel, forget the vinegar smell and a cat's arched back. At any moment it might spring again. It seemed gigantic effort that got her to her feet, and the actual feel of what was under her arm drew her upright. Lena, and who Lena was would never matter now. She had that for which she had so often longed, against his hard core of determination, and a refusal to sell, but she did not know this. No effort required; you simply tucked it under your arm and walked away, staggered to the door holding it tight, being sure.

"He'll never see this again, *never*."

She wondered if "they" would be back. "One bloody bomb and it's gone for good."

She crept out into darkness, left the door wide behind her, sensed darkness of stairway, and went slowly down, an inward smile of satisfaction sustaining, stair by stair. She would take it home, hang it up, so brightening the air of a Bermondsey attic, she could stand and stare at it, admire herself, forget the "little geeny-wenius" that had done it. It was at this moment that she heard the great shout, felt a trickle of ice at the back of her neck, cried to herself, "Oh, my *God*. They're back, they're . . ." hunching herself, clinging to the banister, wanting to rush down, not daring, stiffening where she stood. She sat down on the stair, aware only of flying feet and continued shouts.

"Damn them. Where'll I put it? Must hide it, *hide* . . ." and at the bottom of the stairway found what she wanted. Though the cupboard was full of old newspapers she soon had them out, and her painting safely in, and the door shut. She'd collect it later, go home. After which she staggered into the hall, into the torchlight.

"God! You again," Richard said. "Who the hell are you anyhow. Come on, down you get, into the bloody cellar, and *quick*," grabbing her, running her to the short flight of steps, pushing her down. He caught her as she fell, inwardly cursed her, "Drunken bitch," carried her down.

You were carried down, you felt this man's strength, you felt the horror that was back, and you knew what lay safe below the stairs. You would get this when the light came. You would get money for what he had left against a dusty wall. She felt the hot breath against her ear, the words exploding.

"And when the all clear sounds, *beat* it," Richard said.

II

In a dark corner.

"You all right, Gwyn, dear?" Richard said, feeling the warmth of her. "Sure you won't have a light? Just say."

How the warmth got at you, sucked at you. He wondered how he could ever get away from it, the warmth of Gwyn. But he must. He *had* to go. When the whistle blew, go he must. Over-anxiety pressed, pushed at him. "I'm sure you'd be better off with a light, dear. How about a candle, *really*."

"Listen to them," Gwyn said, "just listen," the voice quaking, listening to the drones.

"My God!" he thought, "how in hell can I go out and leave her *now*? She's scared stiff," and the moment uprooted for him when she laughed, sudden, right out of the blue.

"Listen to that," she said, "she's got a snore like an elephant," still laughing.

"Yes dear," he said, sensing the nerve's sharp edge, squeezing tight her hands, "ye—s, she's still tight, she and that damned sailor chap, I . . . he . . ."

"*What* sailor?"

"Oh . . ." and after the irritable sigh, "fell over him coming in a few hours ago, flat on his back in the hall, dear, and singing, think of that, *singing*, all through that damned roar up above, and that's another thing. I'm still trying to work out how he got in here . . . sure you'll be okay, darling, sure? I must go soon, Gwyn, *got* to."

"Pray you don't have to, Richard," Gwyn said, began stroking a long arm, "do pray you won't have to . . ."

"Catchword," he thought, "and how easily it reaches your tongue, how easy," and then he was hating himself for the thought. "Gwyn!"

"What, dear?"

"The Benson flat's a nice mess, broken glass everywhere. They pinched her drink, empties all over the place, had a *hell* of a time, they did." And savagely, "No wonder that thing down there snores her head off. There'll be a row about this, you see, you know what Miss Benson and Miss Cleate are like. Suppose they decided to come back from Somerset. That sailor and this one *here*," his foot nudging, "they left the flat door wide to the world, all the lights on, fire burning away. I switched everything off, shut the door, it's all right now . . . all right now . . . sure you're okay, Gwyn?"

"Yes, really. Honest, darling. Don't *worry* about me. Hadn't you better do something about the Frasers, Richard, and Mrs Robinson, what about her coming down, that *child* . . ."

"Of *course*. Hell, one gets sick of the whole thing at times. I don't much mind what's coming down now, it's what may come after, fire—oh damn, just listen to me, darling, Job's comforter. Listen. I got a plan for tomorrow afternoon, off then, thought we might go and see that new Gable job at the Plaza. Say it's good. Sure you're okay?"

He got up, covered his mouth just in case a repetition might leap out, like a clever trick, the new technique, "You all right, dear?", when you could only be all right in polar regions these days.

"Better go up," he said.

"Wait. Oh God, wait, Richard," she cried, so he held her, against an avalanche of noise that was coming down, held her cruelly tight, thinking, "Bloody near, that."

"*Richard!*"

"I *must* go," shouting it, breaking away from the warmth. "Won't be long, must get them down, stupid people they are. Should have been down twenty minutes ago. One of these days somebody will be too casual," and moved violently for the exit, called over his shoulder, "Chin up, Gwyn," and was gone, and she sat very still, listened to drunken snores.

He was in the hall, the torchlight struck darkness. He shouted.

"Everybody down, everybody *out*. Come along now," the cone of light creeping upwards, as into voids. "Down to the cellar. *Everybody*," thinking of the Frasers, Mrs Robinson. "What kind of bastard is Robinson, with his bloody music, and her there, and that poor little kid? Silly swine. I call it mad."

Hurrying up, and up, the light leaping, then suddenly thoughtless, deaf, hurrying, shouting. When he reached the first landing, he stopped.

"Hello hello hello. Somebody moving on top. Ah! It's that woman, yes, and that painter chap, I'll bet they've got that picture between them, up down, up down—Christ, stop me laughing."

He was at the Frasers' door, remembered her name. "Hello there, hello, Emily," peeping in, switching off the torch, switching it on; there were times when this torch could almost speak, and a series of flashes filled the Fraser front room. "*Come on.* Let's have you. They've been over some time," and a dropped voice, a gentler tone, "*There* you are. Yes, Mrs Fraser they *are* here, heavy stuff and all that. Come along, where's Mr Fraser?"

She stood in the doorway, stared at him, blinked against the light.

"Where's Mr Fraser?" he asked.

"This door won't shut, Mr Jones," Emily said, and frightfully casual, and, like a sentinel to its post, her hand went to the doorknob. "I wish it would, Mr Jones, I wish to God it would."

Not remembering, clean forgotten. Shut!

"What shut?" he asked, "what—oh God, yes, sorry, I'll get the damned thing fixed tomorrow, Mrs Fraser, I'll ask Mr Morton to do something about it." Her stillness, her stare, riled him. "I did *say*, yesterday, *say*, Mrs Fraser, that I'd see to it, and I will, I will I will I will." He wanted to swear, bravely held back the words. "Do come. Move. Where *is* Mr *Fraser*?"

He looked at the tired, red-rimmed eyes, he lowered his torch. Her very calmness upset him.

"He's just having a cup of tea, Mr Jones, we'll be down after tea. Yes, we'll be all right, I'm sure we will. Mr Fraser thinks that any sort of hurry is useless these days."

Anger rose against slowness, against this diversion. "I'm responsible for everybody *here*. Do you under*stand*?" And against nonsense. "Damn the bloody door," he said.

"Mr Jones! Well indeed! I'm surprised, I am indeed. We are quite capable of looking after ourselves, thank you. We shall come down when my husband has finished his tea, and not before. You are very kind, you are very thoughtful of us, yes, thank you, Mr Jones. But half the evening we've been worried—that crying child upstairs—sometimes of course it doesn't cry, and then you hear that loud music. Mr Fraser hears it, too, sort of jungle music, really. My husband is an authority on jungle music."

She turned her back on him, she went inside, left him standing there. Richard mounted stairs, and the stabbing questions followed him.

"How did that bastard get in here? . . . Christ, I do hope Gwyn's all right, she hides things sometimes, even her feelings . . . why on earth Mrs Robinson didn't bring the child down as soon as it began, God knows, I don't. Hope Gwyn's okay . . . I'll kick their sodden door in, damned suicide," flung the cone of light upwards again, listened to rain, "I must get that damned hole seen to . . . the way that bastard Robinson *laughs* . . . must get that door fixed, *must*."

It was no good, you couldn't hold back what you felt. "Are you lot coming or aren't you?"

And echoes, and raging when they came back at him, and he hammered on the Robinsons' door. "They're dropping *stuff* . . . I'm responsible for everybody here, I mean *everybody*," and gave the door a mighty kick. Blast!

That door would open, music cease, that child would cry. This would be normal. He waited, rocked on his heels, switched off the torch. "Are you *coming*?"

He heard a fire engine rush past, a lorry revving

up, somebody shouting, "Jackie? Put that bloody light out."

After which, nothing but music in his ears, and then it suddenly stopped. "Hope his damned battery's run down," he thought, wanted to give the door another kick, and didn't, and waited, and wondered. How long could patience last? From patience to hope, and then to child's cry. He hung on to the cry. "Are you coming out in there?" and another kick, which, in some odd way, seemed only to increase the music's tempo. He stood there, quietly waiting, then suddenly he heard the feet above his head, moving feet. He listened.

"Wait." A frantic cry.

"Yes, I *am* waiting," the words struggling up, "yes, dear God! *Hurry*."

"It's caught, Lena, it's caught, the torch, the torch."

And the hollow sound. "I forgot it, dear," Lena said.

"It's caught somewhere, can't you *do* something . . ."

"A moment, be patient, *please* be patient, it's heavy, it's a weig—"

And Clem, on the stairs, admonishing, replied, "Careful, careful."

"I *am*," sighed out.

"Don't fall, careful there, Christ! Don't drop it, Lena."

"All right. I've got it, but the damned thing's stuck fast, these bloody banisters, I'll try and pull it clear," and the voice climbing, and louder, "Pull, pull back, yes, towards *you*, pull now, *hard*," all in a breath.

A low screech, "I am."

"Good Lord," Richard said, "I forgot all about you two at the top," and sotto voce, "Why will they drag that bloody tearing thing with them everywhere they go? I don't know, I just don't know. I don't *know*."

A lightning impulse hurled him against the Robinsons' door, and, as the knob inside had been turned, he fell inwards, flat into the room.

The radio was off, the child could not cry, it was feeding, behind a curtain, flimsy red. Robinson and the sailor were seated opposite each other, the airman with one blue arm half round his Philco, something he felt he could never leave, since he loved it. They had been talking in low voices, under the music's roar, talking a mumble-jumble in between the tots; they could not understand each other, and it never mattered. But now, when Mr Jones fell in, they were both of them suddenly laughing, and always Robinson could laugh louder than Mr Johns. One knew he could laugh, whole reservoirs of it behind his smiling face, dead white, against blue uniform. About thirty, dark-haired, and balding, two prominent teeth, very big teeth, dams to his reservoir, a small chin, and thin hands, the fingers of which danced on his knees, danced anywhere they might happen to be, never would be still.

"Hello there," Johns said.

"Hello there," Robinson cried, "you come right in and have a drinkie."

Richard got slowly to his feet, hating them both, hating himself, and the voice was dead flat.

"Better get below," he said, "and bloody quick. Get that child down, too. *And* your wife, and no damned messing about, *chummie*, one of these days you'll get that Philco smashed up for you," leaning forward, baring teeth, "when does the damned thing *stop*?"

Johns staggered to his feet, moved, hovered. "Jese, you look funny," he said, laughing at Richard. "Have a drink."

"I'll have one time enough. Where's your wife and child, Robinson?"

He stood just inside the door, one gloved hand on his hip, the other listlessly hanging, pulling away threads that weren't there, saying, near sepulchrally, "Hurry up, don't want a bomb on top of you, do you?"

He felt strong standing there, and his mind searching for words, for something better to say, more apt, an ultimatum, the *fact*. Anything to shatter the Robinson smile, choke a threatening laughter, smash the inane stare, thinking, "Drinking half the bloody night." He watched the sailor with the bottle, the glass, so close to Robinson, and he saying, "Goddam it, sailor, I *told* you, I don't drink that poison." He didn't drink, but he could laugh.

"On a leave," thought Richard, his glance falling first on Robinson, then on Johns, now sprawled in his chair; the face had a timeless, bovine expression.

Robinson rose, placed his hand on the radio switch; he could shake atmospherics from this by the shipload, and then he cried, "Ducksie! Ducksie! Gentleman to see you, darling, a Mr Jones," and to Richard, "'tis Jones then, yes?"

"Jese," Johns said, "this gen'leman's being goddam stubborn, won't have a drinkie with me," jumped to his feet, advanced with the gin. "Now Jonesy. Hell's fire, man, you *do* look excited," leaning over Jones, one paw holding aloft the green bottle.

"Look out," the blue man shouted, but it was all right, the Johns paw had a sure hold on the bottle, and the glass he held was near to Richard's mouth. "Come on, man, drink the bloody thing. Lovely stuff." Richard promptly spat in the glass. "Go to hell."

He could only think of one single thing as the radio began to shriek. "Gwyn," he thought, "Christ! Gwyn."

Robinson clapped hands, cried, "Got her at last, sailor man. Listen!"

Listening, Johns said, "Makes you sad," leaned heavily over the table, put down the green bottle.

Robinson shouted above the noise, "Ducksie, darling, what the hell, I said a chap name of Jones wants to see you. Come *on*, dear," a nervous finger playing with the switch. Could he get it any louder, this wonderful music? "Just fancy that, from Bolivia, sailorman. Bolivia. Hurry up, Ducksie, doesn't take all day to feed it, does it?" And was laughing again, watching Richard's nose being tweaked, caught between two strong sailor fingers.

"Too goddam stubborn, Jones, sure, come on now, drinky drinky," and he looked from Jones to the proffered glass, and the spit in it.

Ducksie came from behind the curtain, child half over her

shoulder. The child dangling, a hand clutching at a silk shawl, gay, golden colour.

"What, darling?" she said, and this was the blue man's wife.

"Nothing, ducks, 'cept that, and then getting down, I mean downy down, bastards hovering over us again. Yes, here he is, wants to see you," and pointed at Richard.

She looked, she laughed; this could be contagious. "Lordy, darling, do look," she said, gave the child a shake.

"I bloody am, Ducksie," Robinson said. "He looks damn funny. Mr Jones wants you to go down, to take it with you, to the cellar, Ducksie. Can you hear the pigs, dear? You can tell how high up they are. Makes my fingers itch, just thinking of those effing Nazis," a slight pause, and then the clipped question. "Fed it?"

"Yes," Ducksie said, "and I'm fine myself," out of a too red mouth, a thin line of mouth that could zip open and shut, the machine touch, just like her blue man, "the lovey-dovey."

"Splendid! Excellent."

And Johns swallowed the gin, spit and all, and cried, "Ex—e bloody lent," his fingers yet holding the Jones nose, who did not feel this, nor see them, grouped, laughing at him, did not hear them, only thinking of Gwyn, now, where the dark was. He had come up shining a torch, your voice echoed, voids loomed, tipping the polar region.

Robinson let go his Philco, walked to Ducksie, studied "it" still dangling over her shoulder, watching it make froth bubbles on a silk shawl. He gave Ducksie a quick peck, stroked her bottom, grinned, said, "You *have* fed it?"

She nodded, smiled, shook "it".

"Goody," Robinson said, rushed back to the radio, increased volume.

Richard had risen, come erect, said quietly to the sailor, "Move," and Johns didn't, and Richard just tightened a fist, knocked him on his back, turned and shouted, "Bugger you all," flung himself at the door, opened and slammed it, hurled himself down the stairs, rushing for his wife, the dark.

"A bloody madhouse," he cried, taking five stone steps at a bound. "*Gwyn!*"

The blue man was very close to Ducksie, saying, "Got it clear for the first time, let's have a dance, shall we?"

Only the grin disturbed her. "*Now?*"

An itch was working downwards, infusoria to his legs, "Come *on*, Ducksie, never mind the bastards overhead, I'm on a *leave*, don't you know?"

"Of course I *know*," Ducksie said, gave "it" another shake, "I *know*."

"Hell," Robinson barked, "hell."

"We've had enough music, darling, *enough*, and I'm going down to that cellar, they're all down now. Come on, darling, just listen to *that*, we can't *stay* here," she paused, showed pearly teeth, a thin red line of lip, "getting bloody strenuous overhead, darling."

"*Bug——*" and, "you *have* fed it?"

"Of course."

"Christy, darling, look at that," but Ducksie didn't, not knowing what his eye saw.

"I'll get the things," Robinson said, and she said nothing, since she had a sudden feeling that "it" was slipping, like a feeling her garter had loosened; raised a hand with five bloody tips to it, dug at what "it" wore, something long, something white, pulling it back, safe. "Googins," Ducksie said, and "hello, podgy wodgy," and the other hand came from behind "its" back, then both hands gripped, holding the child high, looking up at it, a round face, violently red, all blood, and two glass eyes. He *saw*.

"Blast, I say, Ducksie, you've . . . I mean . . . she's had too much, darling, got wind, that's *it*, wind," caught and held by the glass eyes, in the podgy face, "podgy" was her name by proxy christening.

"Do de dah, dah de dah, do de doo," and "it" rising, falling, in the airless room, and the light bright, and singing again, and higher and higher, increasing the tempo, "do de do de dah de doo de doo, lovey dovey." So Ducksie and child moved to Bolivian music, which was the only music his Philco would at present receive.

"Always tell a good set, Ducksie," Robinson said, laughing again.

"You are a dear," Ducksie said, whilst the child sucked air, and he wrapped a coat about her shoulders. "Bloody cold tonight, watch *her*," he stressed, suddenly getting the gender.

"Yes, darling," she said, put one arm round lovey-dovey, hung on hard to "it".

Robinson screamed, "Okay, let's go."

"Got everything?"

"Yes," he said, and added, sing-song, "we're all going to the cellar to join the mouses, *quick*."

"Can't leave him *there*," Ducksie said.

Johns was flat, and spread, sucking in hot air.

"You go on, Ducksie, I'll bring this man down with me. He's at sea at the moment, poor swine."

Ducksie said, "Do come, darling, do come. Can't you *hear*?"

"Yes yes yes," Robinson said, knelt before Johns, studied him, then mused. "And who the hell did that Welshy, Jones, think he was? Yes, who? Changed his bowler for a tin hat, yes, bowler-hatted, really, and changed by magic overnight. Come on now, shipmate, we got to join the mouses. Sorry Taffy dotted you one, old boy, come along now, we'll be okay. Sure, I got the stuff here," and he patted both pockets, river Gin still being in full flow. With some effort he managed to get Johns's fifteen stone upright, though he staggered a bit, and stared at Robinson with partly closed eyes, noting the stained neck of the white shirt, the ruby nose, the ham-like hands. Mused again. "Said he comes from Plaistow. H'm! Where the hell is *that*?" And the shout. "Come . . . *on*," so slowly he got the lost sailor clear of the flat.

Johns sprawled, sea legs unsuited to cities; the mouth opened, he wanted to say something, but the words would not come. And slowly down, stair by stair, and holding on grimly to sheer weight, and listening to the whistles and the booms, being glad Ducksie had gone down. He supposed that odd pair from the top of the house would be there, too. Odd lot, really; looked as though he had been born in a cask of malt vinegar, he mused as he went, the Johns head too heavy on his delicate shoulder, and suddenly cried into the dark. "Okay, sailor?" A grunt followed, and was accepted. He hoped Ducksie was down, safe. "Silly bitch, overfeeding 'it' like that, no wonder 'it' belched wind . . . Must get Ducksie to hell out of this city, must, dangerous— silly *cow*, begged her three times to just *go*, relatives at Henley."

"You okay, Johns?"

And Johns stuttered into the dark, "Where am I, Mr Robinson?"

"Everywhere," the blue man cried, "every bloody where," and was laughing again, and almost without noticing it. "Damned cheek of that pig coming up, spoiling our evening. Christ, *why* didn't you tweak his nose right off, sailor?" and the dropped voice, the whisper, "Nearly there, terra firma has a sweet smell, Johns, a sweet smell," then very close to the Johns ear, "I got the song you like, sailor man," pausing to give his Philco a nice pat, saying, "we'll shake the cellar tonight. Lordy! And what a change. Careful, here, *care*——" so for a moment they paused at the head of the five stone steps that would at last bury them in the dark. Then slowly down, and sing-song, "And here we are again, my dears, here we bloody are . . ."

"Oh God!" Gwyn said, "them."

"Easy," Robinson said, then cooed, "Oo Oo, you all right, Ducksie, love?"

She held "it" tight, she felt relief hearing his voice, her lovey-dovey. "Hurry, darling!"

"Sure," Robinson cried back, and Johns added, "Hello there, missus, hello."

And again Gwyn said, "Oh God! Them," after which she closed eyes, prayed for Richard. And would the noise never cease? And would *they* never go?

Sailor and airman pushed in, trod on toes, sucked in heavy breathings of others, and the dark seemed darker than dark, and they halted.

"Another all night do," Robinson said, and, "where *are* you, Ducksie?" groping, feeling a knee, a shoulder, a face, a head of hair. "Christ! Nobody got a candle, nobody got *anything*? Didn't you hear me *say* it? All night do. Move, sailor, *move*."

Johns moved, Johns fell.

"Ow!"

"Who's you?"

"Me," screeched.

"Jese!" Johns said, "Jese, you Cis, goddam that's fine," lowered himself to ground, lay on her, got the warmth, and Robinson shouted, "Look *out*!" and silence died when the bomb came down. And after the rumble, the smell. Gwyn split the air. "Richard! Oh Richard!"

The cellar drowned in the instant light from Robinson's torch, limbs stiffened, eyes closed against it.

"There you are, Ducksie, darling," he said, promptly trod on Johns and Cis without apology, and Gwyn, head down, hugged her piece of corner, prayed for Richard. Sailor hugged Cis, and Cis clung. The light went out, a word dropped into the darkness, and Ducksie heard, dropped another word into lovey-dovey's ear, "Yes, darling, *course*, darling," and immediately Robinson switched on, let the music flow. Gwyn covered her face with the flat of her hands, still praying.

12

Mr Fraser, shaved, a cut here and there, said, "Aren't you having a cup of tea, Emily?"

He was out of his dressing gown, his grey hair had a middle parting, he wore a rubber collar, slightly yellow at the edges, a pale red tie, he never bothered much about colours, the main thing was to get it tied without too much doddering. He knew he doddered, was old, all of sudden old, surprise with the ice in it.

"Aren't you . . . d'you mind, dear," looking up at his wife, "come, dear," half rising from his chair, suddenly sitting down again, seeing her move, so she was going to sit down, after all.

"I wish you wouldn't stand by that door all the time," he said.

"Mr Jones told me he was going to get it fixed, dear," she said, then joined him.

"*Did* he?" and then concentrated on tea drinking. Why talk about the door any more, it would never be fixed now. And he knew, who had lived longer than Mr Jones. It had been a blow, a fright, waking up in the night like that, finding it half open, something had got *in*, he knew, a gust of wind, someone in and out, quickly, yes, something *had* happened. He looked across at Emily.

"I just could not sleep with that awful row upstairs, dear," he said.

"I quite gave up the whole idea of repose," and he reached for the teapot, an action that always made Emily feel afraid. Once, her husband would always use his right hand to this pot, and now he used his left. Strange. And there were other things that made Mrs Fraser afraid. Mr

Fraser putting things back on shelves, drawing curtains, filling a kettle, turning on a tap. She noticed these little things. Why only the left hand *now*? He had always been a right-handed man, and most clumsy with his left. Her eyes remained riveted on her husband's right hand.

"Wish you wouldn't be so odd, dear," Emily said. "Not like you . . ." Saw yesterday, saw him shaving with his *left* hand. She would watch this, motionless, the left hand in control, the right hand somewhere behind his back, as if in hiding. She remembered, too, how, after the door had been blown in, he had tried to close it with his left hand, as though the right was useless. *Very* strange. And added to her fear was the thought of their having slept all night with the flat door wide to the world, struck by a *force*.

The right hand useless. Emily talked to Emily about this.

"An odd idea for me to have," she thought, and it wasn't funny, you couldn't laugh at it, and she watched him spill tea into the saucer.

"*Do* let *me* do it, dear," she said, took the pot from him, filled his cup, milk and sugared it. "There!"

He protested. "It was all *right*, Emily, and stop fussing," then, after a pause, and thoughtfully, "I can still hear those people overhead, Emily."

And Emily said, "Yes, dear, those people are still over-head. Mr Jones wishes us to go down to the cellar right away, dear, but I told him you were finishing your tea, and he went off in a great huff, silly Mr Jones."

She often thought of Richard in terms of direct authority, like a stationmaster, a prison warder, a policeman, and she could remember a hale and hearty Richard Jones, travelling in chemicals, before the great convulsion began, an always happy Mr Jones, and, like the Welsh will, hanging on hard to what the valleys had endowed. She used to love listening to him singing. She thought of him in his bowler hat, and his blue serge suit, the coat double-breasted, the trousers as peg-topped as could be. But now Mr Jones had changed.

"Emily?"

"Yes, dear?"

"How long would you say those people had been over?" as he got up, pushed away the chair with his left hand, and Emily noticed everything.

"You said you hadn't slept, dear," she said, "they've been over for hours, and the noise, the *noise* . . . Mr Jones told me it might be an all night affair," as though there would be dancing till three a.m., with refreshments afterwards.

"It certainly does look like it, Emily," Mr Fraser said, nodding at her, doddering away from the table. He went and sat by the fire, having quite forgotten the urge in Mr Jones's voice.

It worried her. "Do hurry, dear," Emily said, realizing that he was going to make himself comfortable, forgetting everything, including the state of the world. She hated him lighting a pipe with his left hand. "Everything's ready," she said, having remembered "those people" and dreading an immediate departure for the cellar. Those people had gone away, and now they were back again. "Do come along, dear," she said.

Hearing the drones Mr Fraser would emit a sigh, an "oh dear!" whilst for Emily the whole thing was covered by two words; "those people". They had heard them referred to as Germans, Nazis, swines and bastards, but for them everything became covered by the two words.

Moving about the room, they appeared totally unconscious of the noise and the crash of what "those people" were sending down, they seemed casual in the face of emergency, and even Mr Fraser had begun a leisurely winding of the clock. She jumped to her feet and took it from him, wound it herself, saying, "Hurry, dear, get your coat, your scarf, the sandwiches. Mr Jones will worry about what is happening to us. Somehow I have a feeling they'll soon go away. Oh, and don't forget the flask."

"No, dear," putting on an ulster, an enveloping scarf, pocketing the flask, the sandwiches, and all the time carefully watching Emily.

"*You* hurry," Mr Fraser said, but Emily ignored this, and leisurely put on her big brown coat, wrapped herself in two scarves, and dropped an extra flask into her husband's pocket, which, like a handy bag, had a habit of collecting the most unexpected things. He didn't notice it going in, and suddenly began doddering again, up and down the room. He put an empty kettle on a gas jet which Mrs Fraser at once retrieved.

"You *are* ready?"

"Course I'm ready," he replied, and added in a very shaky voice, "the same old thing, dear, all over again," remembering getting ready, the journeys down, panoramic flashes across tired eyes, that often watered. He thought of the door that would not close. *That* was the trouble, the ever present worry. They had had tea, and now they must go down. But she would pause at the door, grip the knob, suddenly dread going down to the stuffy cellar, hating it, the door dominating, overwhelming.

Mr Fraser shook violently as the swishing sound shot past their window.

"Mr Jones is shouting again, dear, can't you hear? Do *hurry*," pulling at him, and again thinking of Richard in stationmaster terms, who at this very moment might be shouting, "Last train going, definitely the last train." And then it happened. Emily was rooted at the door.

"If *only* it would close, dear," she said, and Mr Fraser said "Ah!" and "ah!" again, "we said *everything* about the damned door," he said.

Nothing you could say, nothing you could do. There it was, door of a room that held all their lives, together lived, all in this room. There had never been any other place but one, and that was jungle. All had been built here since his retirement, and monthly, as regular as clockwork, his government pension for services rendered had dropped through the letterbox, OHMS. Yes, there it was, open, *wide* open.

"*Come* along, Emily," appealing, sorry for her; how keenly she felt about this door, and thought to himself, without confusion, "So do I, really, but one has to try and be practical, try and be normal, even though I dodder everywhere these days, and she's come to hate my left hand."

"*Do* come *along*, dear," he cried, and gave a rough pull and¦ she was clear of the door at last. "I'm sure Mr Jones will get it fixed, dear," he concluded, and essayed a smile.

You had to force the words out, you had to say something. The same expression on her face, and once he thought of her as a person on the threshold of a great journey. How odd that she should think him a changed man. Women were illogical creatures, surely it was she that had changed overnight. And he thought of a journey down to a cellar, where you sat in the dark with others, where you didn't really fit in, you were old, and of a time when things were normal, and doors would close in a perfectly natural way. Sitting there with people that never stopped talking, and you didn't understand very much of it, the tempo of everything new, even the language that had been pressed into being. There seemed no key.

They doddered on the top step, and Mr Fraser said, encouragingly, "Only a few flights, Emily, a few . . ." so here he was, again appealing and trying to conserve his energy, for use in what remaining days there might be, endeavouring always towards a rhythm, an old calm.

Mr Fraser leaned in, pressed, held her tight, looked into her eyes. "He *will* fix it, Emily. *There!*"

But Emily, who might have been moving off in the direction of the Sahara desert, said quietly, as if thoughts had cooled.

"I'll never feel safe with it open, dear."

"God," he exclaimed to himself, "*how* can I loosen her hold on that *door*, the grip on the knob?"

A sudden peal of laughter hit the darkness, a present uncertainty, and then a light flashing in and out. Then he was aware of feet on the stairs, people talking, and another abrupt laugh. Richard, too, heard it.

The Frasers descent was slow, careful, holding each other's hand.

"Ah!" Mr Fraser said, and she said nothing, and after that, the cries.

"Damn, Lena, can't you move it *now*? Try *again*," the voice out of the blue.

"Oh!" and Emily jumped, and Mr Fraser said, "Careful, dear, careful."

"Who's talking, dear?" gulped out.

"I don't know, it's somebody higher up. Emily, do please *move*," and he did at once, pulling her after him.

In a cracked voice he called down to Richard, "You there, Mr Jones?" Followed by Mrs Fraser's voice, equally cracked, thready, breathless, "Oh, Mr Jones, are you there?" a stationmaster again, the last train moving.

And down, and down, and down, as though the platform at this station was long and dark, endless, a strange sight, but you had your part to play. Mr Fraser thought it was like a play without a title, and the cast there, on the stage that was bright, and all staring at each other, wishing the words would come. None knew their parts in this play, so they waited, the lights went out, the actors vanished.

"Are you there, Mr Jones?"

The sudden clutch on his arm frightened him. "Emily's strong, so *strong*."

"Hello there," Richard cried, a velvet laugh, laughing upwards, thinking of feet that were old, and of a broken stair, crying, "Careful, careful . . . So there you are," he continued, "both of you. Good. Thought you'd *never* come down, dears," so Mr and Mrs Fraser sucked in the warmth from the voice that spoke to them.

"Here we are," Mr Fraser cried, stretched out a hand, "here we are, all safe and sound, Mr Jones. Sorry we're late, I just *had* to finish my tea," and Emily's voice drowned him with an abrupt, parrot-like, "Is your wife safe, Mr Jones?"

And the barnacled words that followed after.

"You never fixed our door, Mr Jones," Emily said.

And an airy reply. "Tomorrow," Richard said, casually, and then his light caught them both, and Mr Fraser imagined he had reached the edge of abyss. "Half a minute," Richard shouted, taking her hand, taking his, leading them down the remaining steps.

"How calm he is," Emily thought, "splendid Mr Jones."

"My wife's in the cellar, Mrs Fraser, sit with her, she'll look after you. Everything will be all right . . . oh, and there's a drunken young woman lying on the floor there, be careful going past," and the laugh that so surprised the Frasers. "The drunk's fast asleep," Richard said, still calm, indifferent to outside tumult, the frantic shouts and the unending noise, indifferent to the hawk's eye hung high in sky, and what sounded like hell's engines.

"*There* we are. Now slowly, *slow*——" inching them down the stone steps, then very close to their ears, "and don't *worry*," the voice earnest, and the words hidden behind words, "Catch hold, take a strong grip on yourself, you are safe, I'm normal if you are not, hang on . . ."

A silence.

"Where are you, Mr Jones?" Emily cried.

He was there, listening to cries from streets, thinking of Gwyn's warmth, of how it fastened about you.

"*Easy.*"

"Thank you, Mr Jones," Mr Fraser said.

"Yes, indeed, Mr Jones. You are kind, thank you very much," Emily said. She reached for Richard's hand, held it tight, like it might be her own son.

"Just two more," Richard said, then a jerky shout to his wife. "You okay, darling?"

And she softly back to him, the lifebelt, "I'm all right, darling. Are *you* coming in?"

"Just Mr and Mrs Fraser, dear," Richard said, "see to them."

"Of course I will."

"Good," and a conspiratorial whisper to the Frasers, "all right, do go in, dears, careful now," and suddenly wanted to shout, "and don't fall over the drunken bitch, nor the lost sailor who has nailed her to the floor," then talked to himself. "Wooden partition here wouldn't be a bad idea," and then what seemed the ultimate roar. "Light, please, a bloody *light.*"

Gwyn cried, "I've a candle, darling, have you a match?"

"*Right,*" he replied, groped, reached out, dropped matches in Gwyn's lap. Listened to the heavy breathings, and then the silence of cellar, the movement of bodies. "Okay. Here we are," he shouted, struck a match, and it glimmered in cellar fog. And a candle was lit, and he watched the Frasers dodder. "There you are. Mind your head, Mr Fraser," and they clawed space, found Richard's wife, and she half rose, helped them settle down. "At bloody last," he thought.

Emily hesitated. "Oh dear," she exclaimed, just as the candle went out. So a darkness eight feet by six changed to endless desert in which was neither height nor depth.

"Oh dear! What's that?" she called.

"Only the young woman I told you about, Mrs Fraser," a slight titter, and, "just listen to that snore. And look at him. *Come* along, Mr Fraser, do sit down, seat's just *behind* you. Take his hand, Gwyn."

"Yes, dear."

"Ah! That's it. Thank heaven you're settled, Mrs Fraser, all nice and comfy," leaning over them, reaching to where Gwyn was, gripping her arm, thinking of warmth again.

"There we are," Gwyn cried, sing-song, and the candle spluttering on a little concrete shelf, and Richard as close to her as ever he would be, the whispers, a mouth warm to her cold ear, and the words, a sort of language the Frasers would never comprehend, as he whispered fiercely, "Yes. Three. Outside. Good Christ! You *heard*, didn't you? Must have heard the last one, *must*. Don't guess what's gone, dear, don't. Reilly's place blazing—*sure* you're okay, darling?" flinging it, meaning it, as a cellar shook, giants amok, vibrations, lifting up cellar, dropping it down. He gripped both her hands. And he must sit down. Hold her. The terror language, the cosmic answer without the question. Think of her, your wife, Gwyn, think of *her* now, think of her, not the Frasers, their labels said, "Lost!"

"Hold on to me, darling," Richard said, "Jesus, cling, just *cling*," feeling it there, the emanation, the weight coming downwards with the speed of light, frenzy's vomit, out of an iron mouth. And crushing her to himself, and suddenly stammering in her ear, "Yes, dear, pray, that's it, pray if you like . . ."

What the hell does it matter about a drunken bitch, about two that were lost. She felt the sweat on his forehead, she prayed with closed eyes, travelled back years, she and he together, crying Jesus, in children's dresses, at Capel Penuel, the Jerusalem wonder in her room, in his, at a school desk, and her mind cried, "Wait, wait," as though this man were there, now. "Richard," she whispered, "Richard," felt herself crushed, lost in his arms, his face smothered in her hair, his half laughing, half crying face.

A threadlike voice, a fairy breath, and Emily saying, "Pray, dear, pray now."

"Yes, pray, son," Mr Fraser said, "do pray."

No more was said, the drunken snores lost, and Gwyn falling somewhere.

"All right, darling, I'm *here*," Richard said.

"Keep close, dear," Emily said, and Mr Fraser held her hand, saying, "Oh," and gibberish following, and then, "yes," his heart heaving, it might leap into his throat. Something had fallen near, exploded, yes, those people were still over. They clung, and he thought of wilderness. "Pray for Mr Jones," he said.

"I am."

A loud ahem, and Richard's word leaped out, "Gwy—n?"

"What, dear?"

"Oh! Something's happened, *happened* . . ."

"I know," Gwyn said, "seemed so near. How hot you are, darling."

"Am I?" lifting himself up. "Heavens! We're on the floor," he said, nervously laughed.

And she laughed, too. "So we are, darling," feeling cold stone, touch of grey mould, near a mouse smell, "so we are," laughed softly, as though this laughter was secret, severely rationed, holding Richard tight, who cut it off with a kiss.

"You all right, son?" asked Mr Fraser, quietly, calmly, as

if through this hour he had been sailing on a calm sea, "are you all right?" for Richard was now son, flesh and blood to him.

"I'm fine," Richard said, out of a dry mouth.

"We're all right, too, Mr Jones," Emily chimed in, just returned from the same calm sea.

"That's good," Richard said, not noticing a quake in his voice. "Damn! Must find those bloody *matches*."

"I think it's begun to rain again," Emily said.

"Is it really?"

"Oh yes."

This was glass raining, this was raining glass.

"Listen!" Gwyn said, and Richard listened, jumped to his feet, cried, "Won't be long," rushed from the cellar, bumped into the dustbins on the way out, he knew what to do. Gwyn was safe, the Frasers were, but the others, the others, where they hell were they? They must be got down at once, this was a night stretched out, night stretched ultimate, it might never end, "those people" might never go.

"The worst yet," he thought, then loudly as if addressing multitudes, "Bastards!" the torch out and the torch on. Then he was stone still, saying, "*Damn* them," and a soft call, "hey there!"

"What the stinking merry hell," Robinson cried, "what's this, what's all bloody this? Come to do the decorating?"

And Richard's torch shone in Clem's face, in Lena's.

"Shush," Ducksie cried, "you'll wake her," just as Johns broke wind somewhere below.

The blue man screamed. "I say, what's going *on* here?"

The light spread, the sailor half sat up, looked out, laughed, cried, "They're moving house by God."

And Ducksie said again, at the top of her voice, "Shush."

Lena was sat on a stair, Clem was. They were resting. The canvas was stuck again. He would not move, and she would not leave him, so she sat watching over him as together they rested, after labour of two flights. They had heard the bomb, had not cried out, had spoken no word. Nothing to say.

When you understood you said nothing. The cone of light was cruel in her eyes, in his.

"Take that light off my eyes," she said, and Richard deflected it. So, for the *n*th time he said, "*Again?* Do you have to drag that thing down every time there's an alert?"

"We have to," she said, leaden, turned to where her husband sat. "You all right, Clem?"

"Thought it was my head again," Clem said, "yes, I'm all right. Are you?"

"Then dammit, get a move on," Richard shouted, "can't stay there all stinking night. Suppose they dropped one here *now*, just suppose, evacuating queer street, without even a dividend," and then Robinson was right behind him, and he hadn't noticed this until the blue man spoke.

"Listen, missus," Robinson said, "you do as Mr Jones says. Get right down to that cellar *now*. Your husband and I will manage this thing of yours," and the bright ring of confidence, "*you'll* be all right, my wife's there."

"Thank you," Lena said, "then help me get it free."

So they pulled and the canvas was free.

"What is it?" asked Robinson.

"A picture," she said.

"Oh! And what's he going to do with it, your husband, I mean . . ." and Richard threw the light directly upon it, and this made Robinson laugh, adding, "oh! I *see*."

And Lena thought, "He . . . what was *he* going to do with it?" looked up at Robinson, noticed his twitching features, said quietly, "Ask my husband."

Robinson seemed only to see Clem for the first time, sat on the stairs with his head in his hands.

"Hang it, of *course*," addressed him directly. "Where you taking it, Mr . . . er . . ."

"The name is Stevens," Lena said.

"Into the cellar," Clem said.

"The cellar? But the place is full already, of *pee*—people," and then he heard the sound, an old sound, grabbed Lena's arm, cried, "down you go, Mrs Stevens, down you *go*. Take her down, Jones, you're the boss here."

And Richard led her down, and Robinson moved up two stairs and leaned over Clem, sniffed loudly, and thought, "Too bloody close, that was *too* stinking close," then a hand on Clem's shoulder, and continuing, "Now is there any reason on earth, on this bloody old earth, I *ask* you, any reason *why* you have to shift this thing every time the siren sounds?"

In the darkness he saw only the painter's eyes.

"Can't tell anything in the bloody dark, can you, thought it was a piece of furniture, and it isn't, damn the dark, damn the sods up there, damn it, thing's too big, too big, leave it there, get down into the *cellar*. Hell's bells," he cried, as a shower of dust came down. "Good God!"

He rushed cellarwards crying, "Coming, Ducksie, love, coming," moved at speed, and Richard was there again, the cone of light stabbing at Robinson.

"Hurry," Richard said, "*hurry*."

He felt the touch on his arm, it was Lena.

"For God's sake, Mrs Stevens," but she went past him, climbed stairs, took Clem's hand. "Do come, dear, *come*."

"For Christ's sake, go," Richard shouted, pulled him down the stairs, "go on," pushed them both, then grabbed the canvas and dragged it downwards.

"My head, Lena," Clem said, as she pushed him into the cellar.

"Okay," Richard said, "it's safe now."

"Where is it?" she asked, and he said casually, "Between the dustbins, it's okay there, never be any room in here for *that* . . ."

He grabbed Lena's arm, "And where the hell are you going?"

"Upstairs," she said, "for the pills, must get them, my husband suffers from pains in his head," thinking of his head, of how lately the pains had increased, and believing in the pills Dr Beecham had given her, and at the same time doubting them.

"Go *down*, woman," Richard said, "I'll get them. Just tell me where they are."

Pushing past Jones, she said, "You couldn't get anything,

Mr Jones," and she hurried upstairs, cursing her forgetfulness, admiring Clem, he had said nothing, just accepted the fact. *Why* hadn't she brought them with her, and even the vinegar bandage would have helped. How foolish. So little he asked for, and always patient, good at hiding things. She stopped dead, cried "Oh! Not again," her hand to her chest, looking up, looking back. She took the remaining flight at a bound. How dark up here, after the torch's brilliance. But she knew where to go, and she would not stumble. She kicked open the door, switched on the light, searched about, found what she wanted, reached the door, then turned and went into the kitchen.

"I've never felt so dry, never," she said, and turned on the tap, filled a glass and drank it, then hurried back to where her husband was waiting. The light again, and Richard stood in her path, staring at her, thinking her mad.

"Get them?"

"I got them. Thank you," Lena said.

"Glad!"

"So'm I."

"Then for Christ's sake get down, get in," he cried, just as Robinson came into view, so slowly up the five stone steps, he having assured himself that Ducksie *was* safe, *was* warm, and even better, "it" was, strangely enough, sleeping. He leaned away, let Mrs Stevens pass.

"I say, that was a real stinker," Robinson said, "you heard it, I'm sure," and a cold word from Richard that rolled all the way down the stairs.

"Heard."

"Everybody down now?"

And the sepulchral reply, "*Down.*"

"Goody," and he offered Richard a smile. "We all appreciate what you're doing, Jones," Robinson said, but Richard was at the moment beyond the reach of words. "So I'll just get back to the mouses. Wonder how long this is going on—damn it, man, hear *that*?"

Richard watched him go, counted his steps, then called after Robinson, "I think it'll go on forever."

And Robinson screamed back at him. "You *are* a clever bugger," and then vanished from sight. The loud banging of a door seemed to shake the whole house.

Robinson reached depth, it was final, this was it, you could get no further; suddenly covered his face with his hands, thinking of Ducksie. "Poor little dear, wish to God she'd get out of this damned city, but she won't, she *won't*," sent a call into the hinterland where "the mouses" lived, "Oo—ee, you okay there, Ducksie, duck?"

And from the depths heard a man talking, and he knew who it was.

"Is that drunken devil still lying on his tart?"

And he was, so he climbed over them, wished them both to hell, stumbled his way to Ducksie, and she, seeing him at last, cried, "Oh lovey-dovey," pulled him down beside her, so now this cellar was packed, *packed*.

The candle spluttered, and Gwyn fingered a fresh one in her wide pocket, ready the moment the other went out. And the Frasers crouched and were silent, save for Mr Fraser's quite heavy breathing, audible to all. Robinson wasn't comfortable, and, inch by inch, squeezed in the balance of his bulk, felt Ducksie so close to him, hugged her, talked in whispers. "It's *asleep*. Think of that, through all *that*, thank God for *something*," and then a salvo, his voice shaky, feeling for her hands, holding them, speeding with the news, nonstop. "Last one was bloody near, love, bloody near, you must get to hell out of here, I just can't go up after those sods tomorrow knowing you're still stuck here, and look what we're surrounded by. Christy! Talk about a rave. Sorry for that old lot over there, should have been evacuated long ago, poor devils, don't know where they are half the time, and they're forever crying because their door won't shut, as if theirs was the only damned door that wouldn't shut on this crazy night, thought last night, night before was bad, but this stinks, you got to say yes, Ducksie, you *got* to," whispering in her ear, battering on, you had to, and all he got for an answer after the breathy bombardment was a low crooning from Ducksie, now leaning low over the

227

bundle on her knee, silently praying that "it" would go on sleeping, through the whistles and the shouts and the shuddering and that sound, the sound of that rain from time to time, a strange sound and nobody getting wet. It was at this moment that Johns, still hugging Cis, began to sing.

"For God's sake," Robinson said, "*shut* it," and silence struck like a knife. "Ducksie!"

"What, lovey?"

"You will, won't you, you will *go*? Be sensible, get out of this. Simple. Your mother's there, your sister, *go*."

Ducksie cried softly, the words were whips, and she put her head on "lovey-dovey's" shoulders, continued crying, and she was loaded with dread, thinking, "Tomorrow he'll be up *again*, and I can't. I can't, and I won't."

"Darling?"

"What, Ducksie, love?"

"I *won't* go. My place is here, with you," a short pause, and then the ultimatum. "And that's *enough*."

So the blue man, climbing skywards tomorrow, sucked back his anger.

Gwyn lit a fresh candle, all watched, like this was sacred ritual, whilst Cis snored, and Johns hummed to himself, caught now between two dimensions, a white sea, and a scent of flesh. He rubbed his face in her hair, had forgotten the time, the day, the meaning, and it didn't matter.

"You all right, dear?" Gwyn asked, leaned to Emily.

"Yes, Mrs Jones, and thank God, my husband's having forty winks. Ah! The relief," and slowly, very casual, "did I ever tell you that my husband and I lived in the jungle for years?"

"No, dear, and you can tell me all about it if you want to, pass the time."

Emily coughed delicately. "And Mr Jones *will* mend our door?"

"Oh no!" Gwyn thought, "not *again*," stabbed it out. "*Said* he will."

"Thank you, Mrs Jones."

"You were saying . . ."

And Emily stuttered back, "Oh yes, of course, *well* now . . ." driving back to jungle, darkness, endless Bornean drumbeats.

Gwyn listened with one ear, the other alert for Richard, wondered where he was, clasped hands, prayed again, waited on.

Richard was back, *in*, and the torch smashed, dropping it as he reeled drunkenly towards the door, breathing heavily, the cordite smell strong in his nostrils. He pressed his forehead to the wall, felt the coolness of it, pressed the flat of his hands likewise, sighed, said "Ah! That was near," Gwyn large in his mind, and behind her many confusing patterns, and now he was back, weaving beyond them, trying to think, thinking, "That crazy bloody journey up and down, that silent man, his damned canvas, and that long-suffering wife of his—"bloody noble." How close he had been to her, so very close, seeing again the white face, the strong, hard, almost masculine features, the austere look, rooted. Assuring and assuring and assuring, seeing he and she together, hovering over his work, thinking of them as possessed children, and he talking to them with the warmth of a father, all authority behind it, and the words climbing up the wall.

"I'll see that nothing happens to your painting, Mr Stevens, I mean that, *nothing*," the children again, lost, the dark room too near. Saw her closer still, but now in shadow, how quiet she was, and what a contrast to that drunken piece nailed to the floor under a drunken sailor, seeing her clear, and then all too sudden, Gwyn, hovering behind, waiting. Remembering the canvas, big, heavy, and wondering why on one corner of it a child's slobber should be writ so large, hearing her words, so soft, and so low a voice, "Thank you, you are very kind," a voice that might have emerged from mist itself. Sealing it all up with the simple explanation.

"My husband won't lose sight of it, won't *leave* it, there's a reason, but you wouldn't understand."

Richard spat. "Understand," he told himself, "understand

—what a word in my ear *then*, what does she think I am, plain stupid? H'm!" And the single smile, remembering his own "thank you", long and loud, loaded with surprise, shaking the stairs. Feeling the canvas again, the weight worming its way down, and the abrupt halt, and the shout.

"Warden! Out! *Out!*"

"Hear that?"

"I can hear," Lena had said.

Richard turned round, lay back to the wall. "Am . . . I . . . *tired*?" Then slouched away, stumbled towards five stone steps, gave a tiny little cry.

"I'm back, Gwyn. Coming, dear."

13

Lena was still, in still air. Mercy was around. They listened to the silence. Clem was sat in his chair at the window, unbelieving, in spite of the silence. And Lena was stood behind him, at this small high window, beyond which they saw the same view, the view at which they had so often stared. They were back, and the door closed, another voyage ended.

"The silence," Clem said.

But she heard nothing save the echoes of her own footsteps as they climbed stairs, so slowly upwards, and the words crowding her as she ascended. "Thought it would never end. It has," and then aloud, confusing him. "The most beautiful sound of all," she said, and he turned to her, saying, "What, dear?"

"The silence," Lena said. "Beautiful."

"You haven't got your breath back yet," he said, "why don't you sit down?"

"I like standing here," she said, then mused. "I don't really know how I got to the top of the house, I really don't," remembering her own short, sharp sigh as she reached the door, her hand tentative at the knob, as though this might never turn. The very opening and shutting of the door moved her. He spoke, and she didn't hear, and he spoke again.

"I was really afraid, Lena, I really was."

"So was I."

"The quiet," he said, "the *qui* . . ." the voice fading out, and she watching the hands that gripped so tightly to the arms of the chair.

"I'll see Beecham this afternoon," Lena said, bringing him

back to earth, and his own somewhat curt reply that she must do that. "The smell down there," she said.

"Yes."

"And that drunken little bitch, actually making love on the floor."

"Drunk."

"So was he."

"Yes."

A monosyllabic session.

"What time is it?"

"Three fifteen."

"Seven hours of it," Lena said, and he said nothing.

Words trailed her as hounds, as she stood, motionless, and he still, and staring, staring.

"Do take off your coat and *hat*, Lena."

"Yes, dear," taking it off, and the thick gloves that kept out the cold. "It's hot in here, I'm glad you opened that window."

"Yes."

"I think the world owes us something," Lena said, as she dropped coat and gloves on the couch.

"What?" he asked, without moving, and she said, "A *drink*," hurrying for it, getting it, pouring into two glasses, handing him one, "There. Drink it, dear, do you good."

So he at last turned, offered her a smile, a whispered "Thanks"; they touched glasses.

"One more night," he said.

"Yes. One more. Come and sit beside me, dear," she said, making herself comfortable on the couch, and he came, sat close beside her, looked at her with a sudden admiration.

"Lena!"

"What?"

"I would never know what to do without you," he said.

"Tut tut! Are you happy with what you're doing, that's far more important to me, dear."

"Groping."

"You're very good at that," she said, giving him an instant kiss, so now he grabbed her hand, pressed it to him, saying, "I mean it, *mean* it."

"Of course. I'm glad you're happy, Clem."

And a silence in the small, the tight room, and the air tighter.

"I was wondering, dear . . ."

"Yes?"

"Why don't you go down to Barntley, surprise your mother, you'd like that, and she'd simply love it. Why don't you, dear, I'd be all right."

"No go."

"Why?"

"They loaded the area last night, heard it on the radio, didn't you?"

"No. Oh God. That far now."

"That far."

"How awful. I do think you should go, dear. I'll be all right. Just for the night."

He made no reply, but got up and went to the easel, flung away the covering, leaned in, stared and stared, and she watched him.

"Clem!"

No answer.

"*Clem!*" louder.

Silence. She got up and joined him, stared at what he stared.

"It's good."

"Not good enough," leaning further in, his face almost touching the canvas. "Still not right," turning violently, confronting, as if in this moment *she* had the answer.

"It'll come right, do come and sit down," taking his arm, pulling him back to couch again, and again seated, adding, consolingly, "how is your head, dear?"

"Not bad."

"You won't go to Barntley, then?"

The surprising shout. "*No.*"

"All right. No need to shout my head off. It *is* your head, it is, isn't it? Christ! I begged you to take the damned pills . . ."

"No *good.*"

"There's nothing else, dear."

"When it comes right, I'll be right, Lena," he said, "and don't *worry*."

"No."

"Good."

She filled his glass again, and he said, "Much left?"

"Enough till tomorrow, dear."

"Glad."

She strained for a feeling of distance, thought of pulling him after her, anywhere, out of this, away from the easel; there were times when it seemed to her to have claws, clutched him, would never let go, and she thought to herself, "Let go, *now*."

"That Mr Jones was most helpful, a nice young man."

"Yes."

"Such a nice girl, the wife, Gwyn, I think."

"Yes."

"Have you thought of trying to contact Latimer again, dear?"

"No."

"Cruickshank then?"

"*No*."

"As you say, as you must," she said, then cried out, "Lord! How odd."

"Odd! *What?*"

And the rapier thrust, "Nothing."

She saw his hand shake, the whisky spill. "Must be something," he said, blindly groping for meaning, root, message.

"Yes," very pronounced. "It's like passing through voids."

"Indeed!"

"Working slowly," she thought, "from bottom upwards," reaching the top, the heights, and it was hollow, shell. "Shell," she said, "hollow," she said.

"What the hell are you *talking* about, Lena?"

"Just thinking."

"Listen!"

They listened. Lena got up and went to the door, opened it, peeped out.

"He's got Bolivia again," Lena said, laughed outright, she couldn't do anything else.

"Mad bastard."

"That poor child," Lena said.

He put an arm round her, saying, "Come closer, Lena, *closer*."

"I worry about you, Clem."

"So do I," he replied, gave a slight titter. "Last night I was thinking, oh, a way ago, a long time, came all of a sudden, that first evening, when we met . . ."

"Dreaming," she said, gave a curious little laugh, "dreaming, dear."

"Real," Clem said, "I remembered it all, the whole lot of it."

So she warmed to the words, so she whispered in his ear, "Do tell me," and he told.

"Last night, lying there, not sleeping, not really wanting to, I was travelling backwards in a moment, yes, and you wouldn't believe it, but I found myself standing in the Euston Road again . . ."

"Really?"

"A more uncertain time than this, but peaceful, I can see the whole evening again as I'm talking to you, and what a road, and hooded in fog, drowned in it. And before I knew it I was walking slowly along towards a dingy café, in a dingy road. What a road. Seemed endless, straggled, it might never have been *planned*, a mess of a road, and all the splashes of light out of dark buildings . . ."

"So real to him," she thought, and noted a sudden brightness of eye, a sudden pressure from his fingers.

"I went into the café, even remembered the table at which I sat, drinking lukewarm tea, eating a stale scone. I even remember the awful slattern of a waitress . . ."

"Fancy your remembering that, dear. A long time ago. The café's gone now."

"Lots of things have gone."

"They have indeed," she said.

"And the sad thing is they'll never come back."

"Never," Lena said. "I was wondering the other day just how long we've been in Chilton Place . . ."

"Years."

"Those awful rooms you had behind the station, Clem, I expect you remember *that*."

"Pity about that flat Renton let us have, the one on the embankment . . ."

"I loved that," Lena said.

"Been a bit of a struggle, dear, but we'll pull out of it."

"Of course. God! How I've come to dread the evenings here, dread them."

"There's nowhere else."

"I *know* that."

She lay her head back on the couch, closed her eyes, was suddenly silent.

"What are you thinking of, Lena?" he asked.

"Nothing at all," she said, and was. She knew he wouldn't go to Barntley, knew he wouldn't move anywhere from here, as though in the wide world there was no place to go, and only one place to stay, *here*, at the top of the house, beyond the mountain of stairs, huddling there in two tight rooms, and a mean little kitchen that might have been designed for dwarfs. In her imagination she stretched out arms towards the embankment, the big rooms, the high ceilings, "those curtains, beautiful", and repeated the word, "beautiful", knowing they were gone, and rooms, and root, demolished, and the river not half so friendly now, even smiles seemed to be rationed these days, after reflecting on which she quietly fell asleep, gently snored. He heard it and sat upright.

"Are you asleep, Lena? Damn! You are tired, dear, you bloody *are*. I hate myself for this . . ."

She opened her eyes, offered a single smile, said quietly, "Like you, dear, I was just having a little dream."

He sighed. "Ah well! It can't go on forever, that's dead certain."

And she only thought, "What a lifebelt, *now*."

"Would you like some tea, dear?"

"Would be nice."

"Right," and she was gone, and the kitchen door closing immediately opened one in Barntley. He thought of Mum, heard her laughing, thought of a load on Barntley, cried out in his mind, "Horrible, horrible," just as Lena came in with the tea. Handing him a cup, she also handed out an ultimatum.

"Should you finish that—" she said, pointing, and he flung back the reply, wouldn't allow her to finish, crying, "*Course* I'll finish it," then louder, as though suddenly bereft, "I *always* finish my work."

"Should you finish it, dear, I wondered if you had any particular agent in mind," spoke calmly, as though she had never heard the abrupt, the aggressive interruption. She watched him sip tea.

"Ollensen's," he said.

It rang a bell with her, brought the hollow reply. "I see," she said.

"Who else is there, *now*?"

"True enough."

"How are we fixed, Lena?"

"You *know* how," she concluded.

"Something'll happen," Clem said.

"How? You never go out."

"I went out last week," he said.

"And you were back in five minutes. Lunch at the Garrick with people that are loaded sets no horizons for us."

"Cruickshank served his turn, he did his best. What else could I do in the circumstances, be discourteous to him?"

"Sorry."

"What time is it now?"

"Another day is trotting slowly along," she said.

He got up, flung out his arms, embraced the room, said, "This, Lena, this is *total*." But she made no reply.

"And there isn't anything else," he concluded.

"Tomorrow again," she thought, "tomorrow," heard

herself talking, hours ago, remembering her own involuntary sigh, his words crowning a situation, a situation suddenly manifest as physical weight, skin close to a problem, theirs, about tomorrow and tomorrow.

"God almighty, have we to have it all over again, dear? I do *know*. I'm not *blind*," yet pregnant with the moment itself, realizing in an instant that a root had begun to shudder.

"You worked, Clem, and I solved the problems. It's like that now, will be, on and on," and hearing somewhere behind her a whole litany of negations, their very echoes following, the root and the fact and the meaning coming clear. She half turned her head, the eye began an exploration of the room. It lingered on known things, the familiar things that suddenly seemed less substantial, less real. The future was a distant, unanswered question.

"I'm going to lie down, dear," Clem said.

Her reply was dragged, lazily the words fell from her mouth. "Then do that."

She watched him go, heard the door close, covered her face, quietly cried. "We must plan," she said to herself, "must", and immediately felt a surge of action, rushed to the bureau and sat down, stared at the indescribable mess, mess of papers, letters, and began a violent opening and shutting of the drawers, negations choralling in her head. No result. No meaning. No end. No plan. No children. Nothing, and she began sorting out the mess of papers.

Bills and bills and bills. "Damn," she said, "damn!" putting on her glasses, inspecting every shred of paper beneath her hand, then tearing and tearing, the fragments flung to the basket, "And these receipts," tearing and tearing, "and these *letters*," idly dangling some of them in her hand, trying to remember, wondering about them. And fingering one after another the cards that indicated more than one unfulfilled invitation, a fugitive recalling of "occasions", and suddenly unable to remember a single person involved in them.

"I must plan," she said.

From the bottom drawer she took out a photograph, so surprising herself. It had lain there how long? She didn't know, and somehow it didn't matter. She held it up to the light, exclaiming, "Good Lord! Out of the ark," studied Clem. Not a tall man, and yet not small, stiffly stood, his hand in her own, but no smile. Just the quiet, determined expression on his face, and looking out, and out, as though the distance he saw was itself endless. "Hard to believe. But oh, that lovely Renton flat, dream days, hope burgeoning, and Clem at it, always *at* it, shut away, unapproachable, no questions asked and none answered." She then looked at herself. Taller than he, and wearing the plainest dress in the world, and hatless. "The sun shone that day," thinking of it, feeling the warmth, wishing the photographer gone and well gone, and then a leaping expression of, "The river. How I loved the river." Clem's mother, known as Mum, she had never met. She put back the photograph, saying to herself, "He'll never reach Barntley, never," knew he would never go, who didn't want to go anywhere, might never . . ." and inwardly shuddered at the thought, old drones already echoing in her mind. It prompted the same old question. How much more, for how long, smelt the cellar, and the people in it, a convulsed household, skin close to fear and a continuous bewilderment. Flinging words wildly round the room, "How the hell can anybody keep calm these days?" And when suddenly he called from the bedroom, "Are you coming to bed, Lena?" the words were barnacled, belonged to yesterday. It made her think of the old couple, the Frasers, who in these long, devastating nights no longer lay, but sat close together, clutching at each other, not daring to undress, she demented about the door, and he wondered if the whole of the Civil Service had gone off its head. No pension, and a whole month of waiting. "Poor dears," and who *can* sleep *now*?

"Lena!"

"I'm coming. You all right?"

And the silence told her that he was. "Thank God for something," she thought, as slowly she pushed in one drawer after another, paused for a moment just to lift up and drop down a sheaf of papers, and then just one more surprise. "Good heavens!" It made her laugh, and she picked up the drawing and took it to the light, studied it, "Very early stuff," and "God! it's made me remember that swine Dolan," words creeping back, "I think it's good, Mr Dolan," and Dolan's, "Quite good," and then the final judgement, "as good as some others I know."

She carried it back, pushed it in the bottom drawer, under everything, and then forgot it, and almost dreamily, hanging on to the words, "I wonder where that pig is now."

"*Lena!*"

"All *right*, dear."

A final walk round the room, a halt at the window, looking at blackness of curtain, not daring, not wanting to touch, the unnameable just beyond. Suddenly she knelt down. "Oh God! Leave us with it, leave it with us," feeling, loving, clutching at the unbelievable, merciful silence. And the final hope. "If they never came back, *never*," thinking of the things that would rise, people, hopes . . . she paused a moment at the door.

"He's right, this, *this* is the root."

She found him lying on his back, very still, in the darkness, and he had not heard her enter. She tiptoed to the bed, eased herself on to it, lay.

"You asleep?"

"No."

She wanted to fall asleep this very instant, wanted to sleep for days; instead she lay as still as he, listened to his breathing, prayed that he would fall asleep. A hand tentatively put out told her that he had not undressed. Nobody did, everybody suddenly wise. "How's your head, dear?" "Going off now," he said, and she was quick to note a slight hurt in the tone of his voice, and then he turned towards her, put an arm across her shoulder, saying, "Can't understand it, Lena, just can't."

"What?"

And a hushed voice replied, "This *si*lence."

"We're not exclusive," she said, longing to fall asleep.

He sharpened his tone and replied, "Aren't some people lucky?"

"You took the pills, dear?"

"Yes. When d'you have to see Beecham again?"

"Some time tomorrow, and he can't always oblige me, I might have to go to his surgery," adding quickly, as life-belts, the old reassuring words, "but I won't be long, dear, and I'm sure you'll be all right till I get back."

When he said that he *would* be all right, she made no comment whatever, and closed her eyes, covered her face with her hands. And then the whisper.

"Lena!"

"*Yes?*" and a whisper tautened her.

"I was thinking of Ollensen's."

"What about them?"

"If I can finish that painting I might go along with it, I still know one of the partners quite well."

She begged to fall asleep, and words seemed unimportant now. She snapped back at him, "Closed."

"Closed?" he asked, and he sat up in the bed, "closed?"

"Gone, *left*, over a week ago, off to the war—it's every-body's, didn't you know?"

"What the hell are you angry about, Lena?"

"Nothing."

"Sorry I spoke."

"I'm tired, Clem, *tired*."

He came in close, took her hands, squeezed them, "I'm a forgetful swine, yes, I do forget, sorry, Lena dear, I know how splendid you've been, *always, everywhere* . . ."

"Don't," she said, "don't."

"Don't cry, I am sorry, bloody nuisance, really, forget it, dear, my nerves, and this pain, tired of my head, sick of the bloody thing, wish it would fall off—"

"*Christ!*"

His voice broke, it suddenly shattered her, his words crawled. "Poor Lena."

"You *mean* that?"

"Lena! What is this? What the hell have I done? Half an hour ago we were so different," the voice dropped, "yes, dear, we were, and I felt happy, and if I can only *finish* that work, I'll be happier still. I *mean* that. Please don't cry," he concluded, put his lips to her cheek, stroked it.

"I'm *not*," she cried out, "I'm *not*," and was.

He felt disarmed, helpless, he felt miserable, he felt decrepit, wanted to shout, "I'm sorry, let's forget it," instead shut his mouth, tight, turned over, stiffened where he lay, his hands making curious movements over his forehead, his head. He listened, he waited. The silence was still there, and it had now become mystery. What had happened? The house cradled in the same silence, nothing moving; perhaps everybody lay flat, sleeping, deeply, tremendously, after the five nights that nobody wished to remember. And she was still close, still with him, her name trembled on his lips, but the name would not come, and he felt suddenly afraid of the silence. The faintest whisper, his restless fingers clawing at his mouth, wanting to say, "Lena! Lena!"

Lena slept. Realizing this with some relief, he pulled the blanket over his head, closed his eyes, and the moment he did so the words were again free, tumbling, and frantic in his mind. "Sleep, try and sleep, she sleeps, she prays, I don't, shall I, shall—"

The whistling sound was cosmic, and the shout was old.

"They're back," Clem shouted, "they're back, Lena, wake up, wake *up*," shaking her, shaking her violently, suddenly lying on her, as if he must cover her, totally, protectively, and he shook and shook and cried, "God! Wake up. I said they are back, I mean back," and shook and shook one already drowned in sleep.

14

"Everybody out, everybody down," Richard cried, "and hurry, hurr—*ee*."

And Robinson heard the shout, knew, smiled his knowledgeable smile, cried up the stairs, "We are. And we've been listening to the mouses for hours and bloody hours. We're all down, Mr Jones, and it's only the mice three floors up that haven't arrived. Three steps at a time, old son, and remember to hold your breath, and then you're there, at the very door of that mysterious chamber, where he lives, where he goes cracked over what he's working on, I know bloody all about that now, Jones, sure I do. You okay, Ducksie?"

And Ducksie was.

"Get those carpet-slippered mouses down here, Mr Jones, and forget what's lying between the dustbins, their problem, their showery, and when *are* you going to get us that hurricane lamp? I say when, said you would, like you said you'd fix the oldsters' door, one of these days, man, they'll just never come down. Job for you then, Jones, the final stuff. Sure you're okay, Ducksie?"

And Ducksie again said she was, then pressed her lips to child's hair, said her little prayer, "If only 'it' sleeps, goes on forever . . ."

"Four times in one bloody night, Ducksie," Robinson said.

"Shush."

"I'll shush."

Robinson vanished in an instant, ran up into the hall, stood, listened, heard the drones, began some cosmic calculation, wondered if Jones had really warned the mouses.

"You all right, Mr Jones? Want any help?" he cried, through cupped hands.

But Richard was already outside the Stevens' door, listening to other words.

"No."

"Yes."

"*When?*"

"I just couldn't leave it there," Clem said, "and I just went down and brought it up again. Had to."

"God!" she said.

And Jones hammering, and Jones shouting, "Come on, for Christ's sake, and *hurry*."

Lena opened the door. "Don't worry, Mr Jones, it's all right, we'll manage."

"You didn't last time, did you?" flung.

"Somebody calling you," she said, but Richard was already half way down the stairs, the noise he did not like now louder in his ears. "It'll never end," hammering on doors as he ran down, that would only echo in empty rooms, and when he reached the hall was fiercely clasped by a small man in a raincoat and wearing a helmet that had descended over his ears.

"Quick," he said, and Richard and he flew through the door. A bomb fell.

The candle went out, and they listened to Gwyn's movements, waiting for the light again, and nobody spoke.

"There!" Gwyn cried, almost gaily, like a hurrah.

"Good show," the blue man said. "You're the only person that remembered candles. And by the way, your husband is still trying to get us that hurricane lamp . . . he . . ."

"I know," she said.

Robinson looked round, then blurted out, "Something's happened, Ducksie?"

"Something's happened—what?"

"Tart's gone."

"Good heavens! So she has, and he's gone, too, the sailor, I never heard a sound, did you?"

"Too busy listening for others, dear," Robinson said, "thought the whole damned thing phony, silence I mean . . ."

He saw Gwyn cover her face, speak through her fingers, "Don't *talk* about it."

She watched Robinson hover, over Ducksie, over the child, still sleeping, and thought, "Sleeping, miracles of miracles."

Emily cried, "That was near," and nobody seemed to hear, and nobody made comment. She turned to Gwyn. "Awful for your husband, Mrs Jones, Mr Fraser and I think he's splendid," but there was still no response from Gwyn, who, looking up suddenly, met the blue man's gaze, and then she got up, shoved her way along, bent over Ducksie, the child, fingered a silk shawl, said quietly, "Poor little thing," and Ducksie looked at her, and smiled, but had nothing to say, and she returned to her place alongside the Frasers.

"Carpet-slippered lot not down yet," Robinson said.

This cellar was oblong in shape, and alongside each damp, shining wall stretched a wooden bench. A candle stood in a tin, clumsily fastened to the wall. It spluttered continuously, always fighting the damp, cast shadows on the concrete floor where Celia had lain, in deep sleep, and was now far beyond green jungle, floating in a calmer sea. She had lain prone, very still, wholly unaware that her sailor friend had removed his weight, had sort of slipped to starboard, and hadn't noticed the difference between body temperature and that of damp concrete. He, too, was becalmed, and now lay just outside the entrance to this cellar, his backside to the world.

"I'll be damned," Robinson shouted, "there he is, look!" and those that wanted to, looked, and nobody spoke.

"Hear that," Emily shouted, threadily, words bouncing off her lips, "hear it," and Robinson didn't, he having noticed for the first time that Ducksie was actually sitting on the damp floor, having slipped quietly down from the bench. "Good God! I *say*, Ducksie, you're on the bloody floor. Up you get," heaving wife and child, seeing them safe again on the wooden bench. "Wouldn't surprise me to see that chap Johns sitting in the dustbin," he said, giving a quick, nervous laugh, having heard another whistle, having waited for the result, having said to himself, "Another dud, good show." He shook his head, rested chin on breast, took another look at the child, flat across Ducksie's lap, listening to it suck in its sleep, loudly, taking in damp air. And on Robinson's knee was his little Philco, ready to do its duty at the word go, and always his fingers appeared to be drumming on it, perhaps waiting for the moment that would fill this cellar with gay music. From time to time he got up, dashed to the entrance, leaned over the sleeping sailor, and then would return with a report, and he was generous with these. He would cry, "Lull," or "They're high tonight," or, "Flying westwards now, Ducksie duck," each report dramatic in its utterance, but to those sat there, silent, hugging themselves to themselves, it all seemed to them like the bits and ends of some crazy geography.

He leaned across to Richard's wife, lightly touched her knee, "Mrs Jones?"

She jumped, saying, "Oh," and he laughed, saying, "Like a cup of tea, dear?" "Lovely," and profuse thanks, and then leaning to him, whispering, "Shush, the old people are asleep, Mr Robinson."

"Are they?" he asked, not looking, and it seemed to him unbelievable that at this moment in time anybody could sleep. "Ducksie."

Ducksie's head seemed to him so heavy, it came up slowly, and she said in a flat voice, "What, darling?"

"Drop of tea for Mrs Jones, she looks all in, lovey— won't let on, never does, there are people you have to admire."

"Must be very worrying for the poor dear," Ducksie said, handed him the flask, "there! Hope it's hot enough."

"Right," pouring out tea, and, "There, dear, still hot, do you good," and a final pat on the knee, "Can't last forever. Chin up."

She looked at this airman, who tomorrow would be racing across skies, was deeply sorry for him, admired him, hated his radio, and thought Ducksie a rather pretty, though silly little bitch.

"Lovely, thank you, Mr Robinson," and sipped slowly, and leaning a little to her right caught the deep breathings of Mr Fraser. "A shame," she thought, "poor old dears, should be miles away from here, *miles* . . ."

"There they go," cried Robinson, and it woke everybody, made Gwyn jump.

"What is it?"

"Them coming down, dear, at last," he said, winding the lid on the flask.

The carpet-slippered were at last under way.

Gwyn felt a clutching hand, said automatically, "It's all right, dear."

"That last one gave me such a fright, Mrs Jones, it really did," Emily said. It touched her seeing Mrs Jones holding her husband's hand, who thought she held a wild, fluttering bird.

"You all right?"

And Mr Fraser surprised them by growling back, in a gruff voice, that he was, and that he had told Emily five times in one hour that he *was*, and meant it, his hand, all tremble, now covered by Gwyn's other hand.

There were moments when all three would lean close together, talk in low voices, trying to help, helping, encouraging, but nobody appeared to understand a word of the mumble-jumble language.

"Comfortable?" Gwyn would ask, and Emily would nod, and once she had to shock Mrs Fraser all the way back from Brazil, giving her time to stuff her ears with her fingers when the next "thing" whistled down. And there were no smiles. The Fraser nod would send Gwyn right back into herself, so she thought of Richard again, worried for him, prayed for him. It was total. It was all. She felt a sudden weight on her shoulder, and realized that the old man's head had come to rest on it. It was at that moment that the candle went out.

"'Nother candle, Mrs Jones."

"Coming."

"Goodo."

Robinson found himself kneeling at Ducksie's feet, suddenly realized that she was fast asleep. "Poor Ducksie." And how long were they going to be stuck in this damned cellar? "I must get her *out* of London, must."

"Matches, Mr Robinson," Gwyn called.

"Damn! Of course, now where the hell are they," frantically searching, scraping the floor, pawing the bench, and hands violent at every pocket. "Blast!"

"Oh dear."

"Got it," he cried, struck it, leaned to the bench, lit the candle, this fell, they were in darkness again.

Robinson cursed himself, "Bugger it. Last match," shouted, "half a minute," then crawled out to the sailor, still lost to the world, "he'll have some," groped from pocket to pocket, even tentatively, afraid to wake the man, and half expecting to find, not matches, but a few live mice. "Got them."

"Hurrah!" Gwyn said, who, in this last hour, had been so glad, so relieved that Mr Robinson had at last turned off his radio, the music sickening her. Much pleading had silenced it, "that awful music".

Mr Fraser gently snored, and Emily, too, had fallen asleep. Robinson struck a match, held it high, surveyed cellar and contents, then burnt his fingers, "Blast," and struck another one. "Here we are."

"There's half a packet of candles somewhere on the floor," Gwyn said, not thinking of candles, but only of Richard.

Ducksie woke suddenly, cried, "Where's my little podgy-wodgy," bent low, kissed the child, and it opened its glass eyes, stared up at her.

"Darling!"

"What?"

"I wish—" but Robinson closed Ducksie's mouth with a kiss, then began fishing about for the sandwiches. "Bring them?"

"Of course I brought them. There," and she gave the bag a slight kick, and he removed the sandwiches, offered her one, and she said, "Not now, dear."

He wolfed at them, "Mutton, lovely," bent very close to the child, a look of concern. "Poor devil," he said, stroked its cheek, "ah," he said, as if he was going to offer the child a mutton sandwich.

She couldn't help it, she said it again, "I wish, lovey, I do wish . . ."

He gave her the news of the world in whispers, concluded, "War, Ducksie, we're at *war*."

"But you were up there only yesterday—oh God!" Ducksie exclaimed.

"And I'll be up *tomorrow*," Robinson said, still munching. And the shout, too sudden, that stiffened everybody, "Hello hello hello, here we are again, Ducksie, hear them coming, the mouses, dear, the mouses," just as Clem, pushed forward by Lena, made his way to a corner of the cellar.

"House full!" Robinson cried, then quietened, munched on, enjoying it. "Tea, Ducksie?"

"*No!*" and almost a cry of despair.

"That sailor," Lena said, and Robinson said, "Yes, that sailor, poor devil, John bloody Johns or something, just look at him, been snoring for hours."

"She's gone," Gwyn said.

"Had a sea of drink tonight," Robinson said, aggressively.

"Don't know how they *take* the stuff," Lena said.

"Wish the bastards up there would go, I mean bloody *go*," Robinson said, and then looked from one to the other, saying, "Yes, I wonder where that piece got to. Never heard a sound, she just slipped away, like that," flicking finger and thumb.

"Darling!"

"What now, ducks?"

"Let's go up," she said.

"*Now?*"

"Now."

"What is the damned time, anyhow?"

The blue man was irritable again, couldn't relax, not even eating mutton sandwiches, couldn't even hear the mice, and they had been an occasional distraction. It astonished him when Ducksie rose, lay the child across her shoulder, moved.

"Merry *hell*," he said. "Don't know what you're doing, Ducksie, you can't go up now. Bloody raid on," turned to all, "well, isn't there, ladies and gentlemen, the fifth jolly old call of the night."

He listened to the snores, thinking, "When I'm up top tomorrow, they'll just look like insects to me.—It could be funny," he whispered to Ducksie. "A mile up, and you'd be small, dear, I mean *small* . . . insect."

"And podgy-wodgy, lovey, what about her?"

"Baby insect."

They both laughed softly, leaned in to each other, their laughs embraced.

A fierce whisper in her ear, "Move up, darling, *up*," and she moved.

He clasped hands, thought of a tune, his feet tapped out a rhythm.

"You keep nodding off, Ducksie, spoke to you three times in the last half hour. Ah! Damn everything. Did you hear those two arriving? They *are* here, again, yes, and his big canvas locked behind the dustbins, calls it *Daylight* or something, so I hear. Wonder sometimes how she can take it, wife, I mean," and the increasing tempo as the whispers grew, "Jones thinks he's nuts. She's *ice*. You can tell, face'd crack if she ever laughed, ha ha. Offered to help them down just after tenno when that third siren went, but no go."

"Heard he's ill, can't sleep nights."

"And that's not exclusive *these* days, Ducksie."

He watched her begin to rock the child, which began to cry, then all of a sudden stopped, opened its eyes, after which it gave great sucks at nothing.

"Jones says Stevens used to travel in vinegar, things you hear, could be, of course, say their flat stinks of it."

Irritation overtook Ducksie, and she asked, "Who are *they*?"

"Ah!"

She smiled when her blue man took the child's hand, as though he had just remembered it was *there*, watched him swing it to and fro, and he felt a petal softness against his own, hard, dry skin.

"God! If only it would stop," Ducksie cried.

Robinson played with the tiny hand, said nothing, but a sudden low tapping filtered into the temporary silence, and Ducksie was the first to hear it, leaned to him, grabbed his fingers, saying, "No, lovey, *no*."

Emily heard it too, and immediately got up.

"Oh dear!"

"Anything the matter, Mrs Fraser?" Gwyn asked, but Emily made no reply, began tugging Mr Fraser's sleeve.

Gwyn jumped to her feet. "You can't, you really can't, dears," she said.

Emily was resolute, and sealed it by her silence, as Mr Fraser stumbled to his feet, dragged slowly after his wife.

And Gwyn frantic, "Where are you *going*?"

"*Out*."

"But you can't, no all clear, dear."

"I'm going out," repeated Emily, and Mr Fraser stuttered, "Er er . . . what's that, Emily?"

"I'm *here*, but I'm not staying here," she announced to all, dragged her husband to the entrance, who doddered, stumbled, but she quickly caught him.

Gwyn rushed to them. "*Please*."

But Emily could not wait. There was no time, and she was resolved, she would not stay a moment longer. She had been dozing, peacefully, until the low drumming of Robinson's fingers reached her ears, and she woke. In her dozy mind the first thing she thought of was South America, the great forests there, her mind fumbling back through years, through clouds of fog, haze, backwards to when they were younger, Mr Fraser and she, sleeping behind mosquito nets, listening to the distant drumming. It was like that to her, and she knew what drumming meant, danger. She *must* go.

"Good Lord," Robinson said, got up, stared at the departing occupants. "What's happening, what? I say Ducksie, there's a general retreat, all pulling out. It's crazy," and shouted at the top of his voice, "I say, it's crazy."

Emily felt the tug on her arm, Gwyn saying, "Wait, dear, wait. It's still *on*."

"Podgy-wodgy," woke up, cried.

And a tug on Emily's other arm, and Mr Fraser stuttering, "Please don't go, dear, hear what they say, they know, dear, they *know*. Those people are still overhead somewhere, *listen*, wait, dear, *wait*," mind doddering, feet doddering, what was all this about?

He, too, had been quietly dozing, and now in an instant all had changed. Everything violent, urgent, people pushing each other around, a baby crying, somebody shouting, "Ow!" It bewildered. What had happened? And then he knew, shouted, "No, no," threw his weight against his wife, held her. And Robinson's screech drowning all. "Christy! You can't do *that*. Mad." But the Frasers were clear, and Emily had nicely manœuvred past the sailor, heaped, she was clear.

"Oh heavens."

Richard was now pressing hard in Gwyn's mind. She hoped he was all right. He had been away so long. What was happening outside, in the world?

"I wish you were back, darling, I wish . . ." and, "for God's sake, keep that child *quiet*."

"Give her me," Ducksie's blue man said, "give her *me*."

She gave, and Robinson swung the child, up and down, and up and down, crying "Shush," and "there now, yum

yum yum," holding it tight to him, and suddenly bent over it, kissing it, as though for the first time he had realized that podgy-wodgy was *his* child.

"That's enough, darling," Ducksie said, tore the child from his arms, sat down again, hunched, rocked it, sang to it, "Do de doo de doo de dah," and "dah de dee and do dee doo," determined to drown its cries, and "luvums duvems," and "de doo de dah."

She sang fiercely, like battle cries, and the child's face leaped in and out of the candlelight, which sometimes gave a spasmodic leap, as the draught fanned; it would soon burn out.

"You'll make her *ill*, Ducksie," Robinson said, and whispered very close, "I'll switch on, ducks, might stop it crying," and Ducksie shouted in his face, "I'll scream in a minute, for God's sake shut *up*."

Mr Fraser's well-known cough reached them from a distance, and some stair creaks became too audible.

Robinson and Ducksie were suddenly quiet, huddled close, hand in hand, and she continued to rock the child, and might rock it forever.

Gwyn sat silent, she couldn't think of another thing to say. All the words had died. In spite of a distant whistling sound of responsive gunfire, she sat mute. She watched Robinson open his flask, guzzle, offer it to Ducksie, who, momentary blind from events, saw nothing. Gwyn moved, and words moved, round and round and round, and she caught them, made a cradle of them. "It can't go on very much longer, Richard must be back soon, *must*," assuring herself, trying to believe, believing, so sat still, held on to this single thought. And at the top of the stairs Mrs Fraser suddenly knelt down outside her door, an action that frightened her husband. "Don't kneel, dear, get up, get in, let's get *in*."

"I *will* kneel," Emily said, and she spoke in a loud, clear voice, said, "Thank God," rose, pushed her husband in, paused only a moment at the mad door, the infernal, the irritating predicament, knew it would never again close.

They clutched each other in the dark room, were close together, and always listening.

"Everything's mad, dear," Emily said, "mad!"

"Yes, Emily, I know," Mr Fraser said, after which they knelt together, but only for a moment, then lay down fully dressed on the bed, closed eyes, were at last silent.

15

Some people were walking in Chesil Place, and Richard and his friend and colleague were at this moment crouched at a too small table, in a steamy café, over the weak tea, and the bread that was far too fresh. Only the brick and mortar of Chesil Place crouched, after the visitation of the night before. The small man in the raincoat, wearing the helmet that was still too large, talked to Richard, who would always dominate him by some six inches. And he had not forgotten the lost sailor whom he had rescued from the sea of ice. Looking across at Mr Jones, Rawlins thought a wash would do him good, but refrained from mentioning this owing to the fact that the times were no longer normal.

"Bad do last night, Dick."

"Bad."

"Bread's horrible."

"So is the tea."

"Number fifteen and twenty-three are now left to the mice," Rawlins said.

"Know."

"Four thirty when those bastards decided to get back to their beer halls."

"Aye. Sod them."

"How's Gwyn?"

"So so."

"Ditto, Marge," Rawlins said, and so the first laugh. "Heard about the adventures of the chap from Plaistow?"

"Wasn't in *The Times*," Richard said, showing off white teeth as he smiled. "How is Marge making out, and where's Lucy?"

"Henley way, and lucky they are, her mother was damned glad to see them."

"Good . . . Wish to God my wife would get out of London, but no, won't budge, ah! . . ."

"But you admire her?"

"*Course* I admire her, what the hell difference does *that* make?"

"We're both tired," Rawlins said.

"Buggered," Richard said.

"Ah!"

Richard sent the message echoing down the room. "Tea, please."

"That's the fourth cup," Rawlins said.

"And the next will be the fifth, got a fag with you?"

"Sure."

They both lit, they both puffed wildly, almost savagely, and both sighed.

"Ah! Nice."

The tea came.

"Thought last night would never end," Rawlins said, "five and a half bloody hours of it."

Supping tea, Richard said, casually, "Talking is dangerous, don't you read the papers, listen to the news?"

"Ha ha."

"How many in your place?"

"Seven."

"Our landlord's solicitor came to see me yesterday morning, looked over the house, then us, asked how things were, and I said pronto, 'Which things?' after which he smiled, waved his hands in the air, sat down, sat back, inquired about everybody's health."

"Sounds a decent chap," Rawlins said, lit another cigarette, tried to relax, couldn't. "Hear about the row in the Ring o' Bells last night?"

"Only heard one sound last night," Richard replied, supped remainder of his tea. "D'you know that people are beginning to amaze me, *amaze*."

"A real ding dong, and the bar crowded out . . ."

Richard looked up, dropped one word, "Important?"

"Was to some. Some fellow called Chamberlain a shit."

"Isn't he?"

"Suppose he is."

"Shall we?"

"Let's."

Richards and Rawlins settled at the counter, were finally glad to escape the smell, the fumes, the steam, slammed the door behind them, stood at the corner of the street. Rawlins looked east and Richard looked west, then they turned sharply, looked at each other.

"My pillow's positively crying out for me," Rawlins said, "ready to skip in a split second," caught Richard's arm, and asked solemnly, "Hesitating again? You surely don't want *another* cup of tea?"

"If you get your orbs on that nice A V S lady today, would you ask her to look in, two oldsters still worrying me, should be got out, nuisance to themselves, everybody else, you *will*?"

"Sure."

They walked slowly up the street, halted abruptly, and both spoke at the same moment, like a duty to do, the same thought striking sparks in two heads.

"*What* a mess!"

"Ah!"

"I've fallen in love with daylight," Richard said.

"So've I."

They patted each other's shoulders, parted.

"See you."

"Sure."

"Bye."

"Ta ta."

Richard stood, stared at the front door. Still there, hingeless. "Must do something about the bloody thing," dragged himself in, surveyed a silent hall, a damp feel in the air, checked up on the locked door of Flat 1, began climbing stairs, sometimes hesitating, was careful with the fifth stair up, saw a closed door on the first landing, dreaded the next.

"Wish to God they'd get out, too old, useless, nothing they can do, nothing." Reached the next landing, then, feeling a sudden shame, removed boots, and crept past the useless door that could no longer shelter the Frasers, so up and up, and a most satisfying sigh. The door opened, like magic, and Gwyn was there, smiling again, getting the whiff of a new London morning, throwing herself into her husband's arms.

"Darling."

"Gwyn."

She wanted to say, "You're late," didn't, time having been cut to shreds.

Richard collapsed into the chair.

"The relief," Gwyn said, "oh, the relief, I thought it—"

"Drink, dear," he said, as his head fell, as his chin scraped roughness of coat, as his hands sank heavily to his lap.

"You're all in, darling."

"Ssh!" he said, "ssh!"

"There, drink it, drink it," and he drank the whisky neat.

"Don't know what we'll do when it runs out," he said.

"We'll be all right."

"Will we?"

"Come along, darling, up you get," helping him up, shepherding him to their room, helping him undress, then rushing out for cloth and towel, washing his face, stroking his hair, kissing him, admiring him, behind the solid screen of her own fear.

"There!"

"Thanks, darling, you remember everything," holding her hands, pulling her down to him, whispering in her ear, "Love you, love you," and holding, and pressing, and suddenly silent.

She did not move, didn't want to, held, she felt safe, assured, fortified herself, she mused, "Won't go, won't leave him, not here, never."

It was only when she heard the deep snores of Richard that she at last freed herself from his tight hold, came slowly erect, covered him with the blanket, noticed his teeth as his mouth came partly open.

"Poor dear," and gave a final look round the room, tip-toed out, drew the door to, and went off into the tiny kitchen and sat down. She was glad, knew she was, was safe, for another day, was thankful for the daylight that had come, and in the offing, the same endless, agonizing thought, "When will it end?"

Then buried herself in the things that were still normal, peeling potatoes, slicing swede, chopping onions, making quick journeys to the stove, checking on the gas meter, hoping Richard would sleep, and making up her mind to get out, *out*, anywhere, for a walk, along the river, into the park. "And I must go down and tidy up that cellar."

"There!"

And it was finished, and now she was free, perhaps an hour, perhaps less, but more and more determined now that she must go, get into the air, breathe it all in, after the smoke, and the shouts, and the smell. She went back to the tiny sitting-room, put on her hat and coat and gloves, opened the door, closed it silently behind her, went slowly downstairs. She paused on the next landing, stood outside the wrecked door, thought of them inside, should she go in, say hello, ask them how they were? No. And she went on down. Her footsteps echoed in the hall, and she stood for a moment outside the locked ground floor flat, thought of the sailor, wondered where the girl had got to, then partly ran to the front door, got out, stood for a moment on the pavement edge, sucked in the air, looked up at the sky, warmed to daylight.

"Lovely."

Slowly walking, past the holes, a tottering house, a skirmishing cat on the rubbish heap, not listening, and not wanting to, and always eyes to the ground, a fixed rhythm to her gait, thinking of yesterday, the days before, her mind reaching out to the time when she was glad, Richard and she together, remembering it, warming to it, holding it all tight inside her.

"Sorry," the man said, as she bumped into him, head down, drowned in the day before yesterday, and she did not hear the voice, or see the man, but went on walking, as though this road was new, was endless, and no black question mark at its end. Once she halted, but only to take a swift, fugitive look up at the sky, seeing one monstrous balloon, hating it, shutting her eyes to it, standing quite still, not realizing that other people, too, were so standing, and all looking upwards at what to them was not monstrous, but spelt saviour, for the time being. Voices and movement all about her, and suddenly she was leaning on the low wall, the river there, yet not quite seeing it. So she was surrounded, so they had come up from cellars, out of holes, from rooms, and shelters, saluting the light, another morning. Clouds rolled westwards, they watched these go, far into the distance, vanish. Gwyn stood quite still, her gloved hands pressed to the wall, and the news of the world came to her, from many mouths. Suddenly she was glad she was there, with them, heard a man speak to her, answered him.

"Lovely morning, miss."

"Yes," she said, "it is lovely."

"What a night," he said.

"What a beautiful morning," Gwyn said, and he seemed closer now, studying her, a smile in his eyes, a man from nowhere, anywhere, hiding his night, loving his morning, and the river there, still there, and the ships, and the shouts, and then caught his faint whisper, returned the smile.

"*Some* things are good, miss," he said.

"Yes," Gwyn said, expanded, responded, "how right you are. And nice to hear somebody actually laughing . . ." herself laughing, feeling suddenly free of the weight she had carried from the house.

"Well, good morning," the man said, and set off at a sharp pace, as though the world's business now awaited him, and she watched him go, further and further into the distance.

"What a nice man," she thought, thankful that he had spoken, broken the web that had meshed itself about her, and she turned sharply and began the walk home. "If only Richard could have come, too," she thought, as she crossed the road, and carefully checked the time on the clock with the watch in her hand. Turning a corner she came on three men stood close together, heard a single hurrah from one of them, and wondered what he might be hurrahing about. And into Chesil Place, and back to the house and the stairs, and the momentary pause outside her door, and listening acutely as she put the key into the lock. Closed the door, listened again. Silence.

"At last. Poor Richard. Still asleep," and then aloud into the room as she removed her outdoor things. "Glad I went out, glad."

"That you, darling?" Richard called, and she cried shrilly, "Yes, dear, it's me. I'm back. Went for a little walk. Whole world seemed to be out walking this morning," opening the door, and there he was, sat bolt upright in the armchair, a glass in his hand. He held aloft the bottle.

"Do remind me, darling," he said.

"You really did get a good sleep, Richard."

"Fine. Feel much better. You having one?"

"Not now. Must do the lunch, dear."

"Had a visitor," he said.

"Oh! Who?"

"Do sit *down*, Gwyn," Richard said. "Mrs Stevens."

"No."

"What's mysterious about it?" he asked, "she only called to thank me for helping them. Both hard up, you could tell, and she's cagey about why, wonders, thinks the sun shines out of her husband's bottom. I gave her a drink, made her sit down, far from well herself, staring you in the face. She hates the Robinsons. And apparently that drunken little tart used to be a model at one time, and do you know what?"

"What?"

Richard leaned forward in his chair. "She got away with a couple of his canvases, fact, vanished, left her drunken sailor flat. Bloody mean, I thought."

"What a shame," Gwyn said. "Glad she's gone, she was sick all over the place, she—"

"Don't tell me. Come over here, sit down, darling. Want to talk *real*."

She sat by him, listened to what he said, then slowly shook her head.

"It's real, Gwyn, real, I *mean* it. Everybody's getting out, and why not. Rawlins got his wife and daughter out, mother lives Henley way."

She put a finger across his mouth, said, "Please, Richard, *please*."

"She wants me to go up some time, have a look at his pictures . . ."

"Who?"

"Steady," he said, "steady, dear. Why, Mrs Stevens, of course. Who else could it be? Apparently he had two chances of work with the MOI, turned both down, said he won't paint dragons for anybody, whatever the hell that meant. Surprised me, since they are hard up. Two of the galleries where he used to show stuff have closed down. But he just goes on—"

"And on, I suppose," Gwyn cried, and he cried back, "All right, all right."

A silence followed, and she saw him get up, begin a wild pacing of the room, where, at the window, he paused, stared out, saw nothing, but feeling everything, getting the answer, knowing it was no use. She would not go, would never leave him. He returned to the chair, stood over her, a hand light on her shoulder, the fingers of the other running through her hair. He kissed her, said gently, "I understand. I won't mention it again, darling. You want to stay, stay, to be with me, good, I mean *good*, and something else, dear," stroking her cheek with his own, "I'll always remember this. *There!*"

"You won't mention it again?"

"No."

"Whatever happens?"

"Whatever happens," he replied, and wished and wished, and killed the words that might have followed.

"They'll be back," he told himself, "back tonight, and tomorrow, and—"

"I brought you the paper," Gwyn said, and he noticed her

calmness, and hidden somewhere beyond it, her own triumph.

"Wish to Christ it was all over, darling."

"I'll go and make the lunch," she said, and he followed her to the door.

"And you won't go down and clean up that filthy cellar. I've *done* it."

"I can't get that child out of my mind," she said, and closed the door on him.

"A real brick," he thought, and went slowly back to the window, stood there, idly staring out at London. "I won't ask her again. Never."

He then left the room. He could hear her busy in the kitchen, then suddenly called out, "I'm going out, darling, shan't be long, around ten minutes," but she didn't hear him, and he didn't wait for the answer. He went to the top of the stairs, was suddenly hesitant.

"What the hell am I going out *for*?"

He laughed loudly, and that was the answer. But standing there he was now acutely aware of a silence that was not normal. He leaned on the banister, felt it shaky, pulled back, and went on listening. "Strange," he thought. "No music this morning, no crying child."

He turned and took the stairs at a run, bounced into the kitchen.

"You weren't long, dear," Gwyn said.

So she had heard him call. "I got half way down stairs, and then I was suddenly aware of the Robinsons, and their flat. So quiet. Not a sound."

"Perhaps his radio's broken down, darling."

"Bloody good job, I'd say. But not even the child crying."

She was busy at the tiny stove, moving pans here and there, and stirring, and wondering why the gas power was so low.

"They went out," she said.

"Oh!"

"It's ready," she said, and he sat down to the table.

"They were on their way to the park," she said, began serving his lunch.

They had the Robinson family with their lunch.

"About twenty-five," Richard said, "can't be more. Must have joined up pre-war, very young, don't you think?"

"I hated myself last night," she said, and he jumped in with a staccato "That's silly."

"Well I did," she said.

"The man's living on his nerves, and his wife sounds absolutely stupid to me. I haven't heard either of them address the child by name. He's got the world on his back all the time, and where the hell does he get the drink from? Been tight for the last week."

"It's not just the drink, darling."

"Oh!"

"It's the benzedrine," Gwyn said, "he eats it . . ."

"*Eats* it?"

"I saw him open a tube the other night, got a niff. It's an inhalant, but, of course, you know."

"Good Lord! Eating the stuff, no wonder he's sometimes high, thought it was just the gin straight."

"No, dear, it isn't. Sometimes it's so quiet in that cellar you can hear every word spoken, and I know he's pressing her to take herself and the kid off. There are relatives somewhere out of London."

"Where's he fixed up then?"

"Biggin."

"Oh Christ! *There.*"

"There," Gwyn said, and added quickly, "do get on with your *lunch*, Richard."

And he stuttered, "Yes," concentrating on his meal.

"Gwyn!"

"What, dear?" the voice lazy, dragging.

"Somebody's coming in to see to the Frasers' door," Richard said.

She covered her face with her hands, and he said quickly, "Anything wrong?"

"Nothing at all," speaking through her fingers, and

feeling utterly sick and tired of the door. It dominated everybody in the house, the house itself. "Richard!" and she drew down his head.

"Well?"

"Never mention that damned door again."

"Course not."

"Nothing whatever is exclusive these days," she said.

"I was talking to Rawlins this morning about the Frasers. He's sending along an AVS lady to have a talk with them, might persuade them to get out. Get worse before it gets better."

"Wonder if he ever got his overdue pension, Richard."

"Haven't seen a postman in days. He'll be lucky if one turns up."

"Finished?"

"Thanks. Nice. You certainly haven't forgotten how to cook."

She threw off the reply in the most casual way. "Nice to know."

They returned to the sitting room where she immediately relaxed on the couch. He crossed to the window to check on the blackout curtain, and he saw that the light was beginning to go. Gwyn quite involuntarily addressed the ceiling with a loud, abrupt, "How strange life's become this last few days. I've been thinking such an awful lot about it."

"Wish you didn't."

"The drill," she thought, "the drill all over again."

He joined her on the couch, and the moment he took her hand, she closed her eyes. He hated the action, it seemed like a dismissal.

"When that bloody siren goes I've got to get out, *do* things, understand?"

"Know."

"Not our bloody war, you know, others happen to be involved, dear."

"Know."

He caught her hands, pulled her to her feet, and eagerly, almost enthusiastically exclaimed, "How about a quick walk round the block, darling? I could pick up a bottle on the way back before the pub shuts."

She freed herself, lay down the couch. "You go, dear."

"I wish . . ."

Her voice was steady, the tone measured, it took him by surprise.

"Just leave me alone, Richard. I like being where I am *now*, I'm enjoying where I am. *You* go."

She felt his lips at her ear, the hot breath, and one more assurance.

"You still think I want you to go, don't you?"

"Leave me *alone*, Richard."

"I'll leave you alone," he said, and immediately left the room.

She heard the slam of the door, his heavy footsteps echoing on the stairs.

"Doesn't understand, even now," she thought, and in an instant she was back in the cellar, close to the Frasers, listening to the Robinson music, a crying child that appeared to suffer from an eternal bout of wind, and listening to the stutterings, low voiced, exchanged observations of the Frasers. She thought of their friends. So strange, not a single friend had looked in on them for a whole week. How positively *nice* if somebody turned up, right out of the blue. A ring of the bell, a voice crying "Hello", and she savoured the moment. She got up and went to the window, hesitated a moment, then pulled back the curtains, so she, too, watched the light begin to go. "I don't want to change, I don't want to change ever, I don't. Sometimes I'm afraid that I might. Poor Richard, he doesn't even understand that," and as she drew the curtains to, and left the window she heard the well-known steps on the stairs, felt a lift of the spirit, he was back, he was here, and then the door burst open, and there he was. She rushed at him with relief. "Glad you're back, darling."

"What's wrong?"

"Nothing," she said, "nothing now."

*

Low, shuffling sounds, as from a sly, slinking river, after the roar of seas. And then the silence, sudden, total. He stood on the bridge, watched the traffic go by. He was angry, with Gwyn, with himself.

"Bloody nerves, that's all," and then he heard it, an old sound, far down the river. "Here we are again," he told himself, and hurried off the bridge. In the short walk back to the house he stopped three times, each time to listen, to make sure. Yes, it *was*. "It is. The bastards are back." He glanced at his watch. Five fifty-five. Dead on. He began to run. One moment people were everywhere, and the next, vanished. He stood outside the door, summoning up, remembering, being careful, "Forget nothing," and with some effort he eased aside the big black door. Inside, no sound, and no movement, as though exactly at five fifty-five the house had rocked itself to sleep. He took the stairs at a bound, and she heard it, opened the door, and he knew she was ready. Overcoated, gloved, a gas mask over one shoulder, and in the bag over the other one all the things that were necessary. The sandwiches, the matches, the tea, the candles. After which they were both in the Bradshaw area, calm, collected, a pattern fixed, and words at a premium.

"They're early," Gwyn said.

"Dead on time, darling, same as last night and the night before. Got everything?"

"Everything," still calm, as if she knew the exact second the train would depart, feeling the powerful grip of Richard's hand, the message he gave her, the warning and the hope. "Don't wait, darling, now, get down, there's a dear, come along," leading her out, slowly down the stairs, aware of the wail coming up river, and stronger and stronger, reaching the foot of the stairs, and the fiercest whisper, "Any minute now, Gwyn. Pray for me like you always do," echoing footsteps, and then a short, sharp thud. "Blast!"

He picked himself up, took her down the five steps to the cellar, saw her to her usual place, "Good, good, *that's* done," heaving it out, staring at her, loving her, agonizing with the moment he stood in. "All right?"

"Hurry, Richard," she said, "hurry, you must call the others."

"Christ, yes, of course, what's wrong with me, first time I ever forgot."

Watching him go, hearing his steps up, closing her eyes, praying again.

The wailing sound was full, final, it drowned the house. The drill began.

"Everybody out, everybody down," he roared, running up the stairs, hammering on doors, then headlong down again, standing on a bottom stair, waiting for the response, the cries that were now monotonous in his ears.

"Coming."

And louder still. "Okay, Jones, we *are* awake."

"Is that you, Mr Jones?" a faint cry, a desperate cry, as though it wasn't.

"Hurry up, Mrs Fraser, shall I come *up*?"

"It's all right, Mr Jones, thank you. Those horrible people are over again."

Not answering, not listening, but waiting for another sound.

"Robinson!"

A door burst open, a thin, emasculated voice calling, "Hello there, okay this area, I heard the sods," and Richard straining for a louder response, hearing Ducksie called, and then a tumbling out of husband, wife, and child, a clatter down the stairs, and his final gruff, "God almighty, do get a move on, will you?"

The trio passing him, and then Robinson's most casual, "Where's that Johns guy?"

"Find out."

"Temper, temper," Robinson said. "You okay, Ducksie?"

She was, the child half across her shoulder, and Ducksie's sudden cry. "Oh no, darling, not *again*?"

Crowded in the hall, at the top of five stone steps, smelling the damp, the cold.

"What the hell, something wrong, Ducksie?"

"That bloody radio," she said.

"My music cheers everybody up," he said, turned sharply, flung an observation at Richard, "Don't forget the carpet-slippered, Jones, not a sound from their flat."

Richard was behind them. "Get down," he said, "and damn your bloody radio."

"Sour puss. Come on, Ducksie, get in, the little mouses are waiting, dear."

Gwyn huddled in the same corner, silent, hidden, and the candle beginning to splutter. The Robinsons coming in.

"Hello, hello, here we are again. Ah!—" he exclaimed, "hear that?"

And they heard nothing save the faintest cry from the child, now flat across its mother's lap. He talked, had to, liked it, liked hearing himself.

"Comfy, Ducksie?"

"You all right, lovey?"

"Course. Hope she sleeps," he said, recalling at the right moment his daughter's correct gender. A change in the voice, soft, gentle, "I never look at it, Ducksie, without wishing, know what I mean, course you bloody do, still, won't budge, got everything with you?"

"Ssh!" she said, "ssh."

"Where are the Frasers?" asked Gwyn.

"Your husband's just gone up to collect, Mrs Jones," Robinson replied.

"Thank heavens."

"Really sorry for that old pair, you know, damned bad luck, really. Say he's an old Civil Servant cove. Seem to have no friends, never hear a sound their way, do we, Ducksie?"

"They are quiet most of the time," Ducksie said, leaned over "podgy-wodgy", smiled at it, bent very low, lips stroking its hair, and murmurings, "Um, yum, yum, de do de doo," and back to the rocking movement, fixing her eye on the candle, praying it would lie still, sleep, and sleep, and sleep.

"Ducksie?"

"What?"

"Oh nothing, nothing at all," Robinson said, dropped his voice, "wonder how long the pigs will be over this time?"

"Take my hand," she said, hearing a distant sound that she knew would grow, and he took it, then pulled her very close, "There there, darling, there *there*," crushing her to himself as the first loud, whistling sound descended.

Gwyn exploded, too. "Pray, dears," she cried, "pray," and then the explosion, and then the silence.

"The *stink*!"

"Awful."

"Another *candle*."

"Coming," Gwyn said, "coming . . ."

"And some are not," Robinson said, "better have a look see, hope your husband's okay, Mrs Jones. Back in a tick, Ducksie, must have a look see—"

"Don't," she cried, "don't, darling."

But he was out, up the steps, calling through cupped hands, "Okay up there?"

After which a mumble of voices, and feet on the stairs.

"That's okay," he said, and hurried back to the cellar. "It's all right."

But nobody answered.

He had cursed the Frasers, he had hated them.

Emily was adamant, "My husband says he will not come down, Mr Jones, and he will *not . . . come . . . down*."

And the Jones reply was sepulchral, weary, dragged, "*Very* well, Mrs Fraser. Here. Take my hand. All right? Good. Easy now, and careful, dear, careful."

So stair by stair, down and down, a moment's pause, and the words jumping into the air. "I'm sorry, Mr Jones, if Mr Fraser says no, he means no."

"I'll pull him out," replied Richard, and mused, furiously. "Silly old bugger, absolutely senseless."

Down and down. "Easy, ee——"

"Don't let go my hand, Mr Jones."

"I'm not, dear, but God, do hurry, hurry—"

"I am doing my best, Mr Jones," and then, unhurried, almost casual, "That man that paints, Mr Jones, his wife, where are they?"

"*Come along*, I said."

And a tiny screech as they reached the echoing hall. "I am, Mr Jones. I *am*."

"*Wait!*" he shouted, embraced her, pressed her to the wall, "wait, wait."

The same sound, same message, but louder in his ears.

"There!" he said, "come now, it's all right, Mrs Fraser, nearly there."

"Mr Jones?"

"What, dear?"

A conspiratorial whisper, "D'you think it'll be an all night affair, like yesterday?"

There were some questions that you could not answer, and he could not answer that one. "We'll see," he said, and, "easy, dear, *easy*."

"Thank you."

"My wife's there. Are you quite sure your husband won't come down?"

"I am certain," Emily said.

"There we are. Here we are, dear, look after Mrs Fraser."

Back, to the same place, hunched against the wall, getting the smell, the *feel* of it, all over again.

"My husband has positively refused to come down, Mrs Jones."

"Oh dear! Comfy?"

"A silly man," Emily said, "it's the stairs, I think, so many of them."

"Richard!"

"Your husband's gone, dear," Emily said, "I expect it's to help those other people down."

"He's always *gone*," Gwyn said.

"What's that, Mrs Jones?"

"Noth—*ing*," Gwyn said.

"The guns are just as bad," Emily said, and turned to Gwyn, gave her a wan smile.

"What's that, dear?"

"The *noise*."

Emily was suddenly on her feet.

"Do sit down, dear. You're safe here, it's all right. And don't *worry*."

"What has happened to that poor man outside?" she asked.

"Still there. He hasn't moved."

"He's not . . ." and Gwyn said, "No, Mrs Fraser, he isn't. If he wakes, he'll be here quick enough."

"When he *wakes*?"

"Do sit down, Mrs Fraser."

Emily put a hand to her mouth, exclaimed loudly, "Oh dear! God, what have I done, I—"

"Where are you *going*?"

She caught Emily's skirt, held on, but Emily tore herself free, and cried into the cellar, "*Out!*"

She moved, and Gwyn moved faster. "But you can't. There's a raid on, dear."

"See to yourself, Mrs Jones. The smell here, it's *awful* . . ."

The candle flame grew bigger, and then the child cried.

"Please," Gwyn shouted, "*please*."

But Emily had gone.

"Let her go, Mrs Jones. It's her right if she wants to. Leave her alone."

"Don't," Ducksie said, "don't, darling, *please*."

"She once fell fast asleep to the music," Robinson said. "There!"

"Look *out*," Robinson cried, "hold tight, wait . . ."

The house shook, they heard the shouts, the glass, the masonry. He covered wife and child, pressed them to the wall.

"Twenty-one steps, I know it's twenty-one," Emily muttered to herself. At last, she was out, and groping hall-wards, and glass there, and the light gone. "Twen——" her mind full of stairs, "one . . . two . . . *three*," the gloved

hand clawed at the banister, "four . . . fi . . ." the hand pawing at damp wall, feeling the tang of night air on her cheeks,
but she saw nothing, neither sky, nor building's shape,
counting, "seven . . ." pausing, moving again, "nine . . .
oh dear . . . I should have stayed with him, I should . . .
eleven . . . twelve . . . where am I?" Her mind cried, "Up,
up," knowing that she never should have sat there, alone.
And carried with her the drift of words she had left behind.
"Don't *go*, it's dangerous, the stairs . . . the *stairs*, wait,
wait." Which was the very thing she could not do. She had
to go. "I hope he's all right, I do, I do," remembering fifty
years of utter loyalty that stood behind her. "Seventeen . . .
eighteen . . ." and the faintest cry, the pathetic signal,
"coming, dear, it's all right, I'm here, I'm . . ." and then a
panic word, "Oh!"

"It's all right, Mrs Stevens said, "it's only me."

"Oh dear. What's that?"

"Only me, Mrs Fraser. Where on earth are you going,
just listen to *that*."

"So dark," Emily cried, and called out, "where are you,
dear?"

Mrs. Stevens switched on the torch. "You," she said,
"you."

"Mind out of my way, please," Emily said, but Lena was
not in her way, the path was clear, and Lena held to the wall.

"Go if you are *going*, dear."

It was at this moment that Emily saw the man sitting on
the stairs.

"Oh, it's you, Mr Stevens," she said, "fancy. You have
those awful headaches, I hope you're better now. Mr Jones
told me all about you last night, so sorry about your head.
You should take Aspros, they are very good. We always
take them whenever those people are over. Where are you
going?"

The torch went out, came on again.

"There's only one place to go, my dear," Lena said.

"The smell," exclaimed Emily, "the awful smell down
there. That airman said the whole house was full of mice, in

273

all the rooms, everywhere. You better hurry, Mrs Stevens, those horns have gone long ago," she always referred to the sirens as horns. "My husband said they'd be over quite a time. Nearly four hours last night, I believe. Isn't everything awful?"

"Ready, dear," Lena said, and then with the child's surprise Mrs Fraser exclaimed, "What is that?"

"A picture," Lena said.

"Oh! Fancy."

"We always take it down with us," Lena said.

"I used to like pictures, Mrs Stevens, very fond of them, but my eyes . . . I used to paint myself, once, when my husband and I were in South America. The most beautiful sunsets."

"That was nice."

"My word. It is big," Emily said, and moved on, past it, past the man, the woman, and another call, "Coming, dear, coming."

When she turned, she received the full force of the torch in her face.

"All right, Mrs Fraser, you're safe now. Just one more stair, dear."

"Thank you. That Mr Jones has changed, such a nice man he used to be, so helpful, but now . . . and the shouting . . . the . . ."

"I *am* sorry," Lena said.

"I just couldn't stay, neither of us can sleep any more . . . I mean—"

"Do go up, dear," Lena said, and she gave Emily a slight push in the right direction, and then she paused again, put a tentative hand on the back of the canvas.

"It is big, isn't it?"

"Go on, dear. Can't you *hear* what's happening around you?"

"Those dreadful people," Emily said, at last moved, and called again, "I'm here, dear."

Above, something gave a loud creak, after which Lena said, almost casually, "You've forgotten the cloth, Clem."

"What?" And he came to life.

"The *cloth*."

And he couldn't hear, and it seemed too late. They held each other on the stairs. They heard the sudden thud far below.

"Wait," she shouted, "wait here," and she ran up the stairs. He waited.

She was back in seconds. "There. Put the damned thing on, and don't forget it next time."

"Damn!" he said, and covered the painting. "Ready?"

"I'm always ready. Let's move," a slight pause, and an extreme change of tone. "The next one might hit the house."

"The torch!"

She flung the light downwards. "Mrs Fraser is silly as well as old," she said.

"The what?"

"*Nothing*," a low screech, and moving again, and thinking of one that was silly as well as old. "Extraordinary," she thought, remembering the cellar, the chatter, and the unexpected. "Something has happened to my husband, Mrs Jones, he does everything the wrong way round now." It forced a smile from Lena, in spite of everything.

"A minute," Clem cried, and they stopped, *again*.

"God! What *now*?"

"All right, dear," he said, "keep going," and they kept going.

She didn't reply, just lifted her end, they started down again.

"Watch that stinking light," Robinson shouted, hearing the voices in the distance, and a whisper for Ducksie, "those loonies are back, listen to them, him and his bloody masterpiece. Move up."

"I am moved up."

"Goodo."

The dustbin lids rattled. "Here we are again," he shouted, as Clem and Lena pushed their way into the cellar. "Standing room only." He rose, faced Lena, "Back again," he said, he ignored the man behind her. "Room over there," he said.

She did not answer, and taking her husband's hand, drew him after her.

"Evening," Gwyn said, "good evening," like it *was* a good evening, and the thing to say.

"I've never heard so many alerts in so short a time," Lena said.

And everybody had forgotten the candle, that now went out for the fifth time.

"Light!"

"It's all right," Gwyn replied, and lit another one.

"There's a dead man out there," Clem said, breaking a silence.

Robinson leapt to his feet, cried, "You *what*?"

"Just outside," Clem said, "just noticed as I came in."

Robinson flung himself to the entrance. "Rubbish. Damned rubbish. *I* know who you mean. It's that sailor friend of mine, been sleeping it off for hours, poor swine, still doesn't know where the hell he is, I guess."

And Gwyn cried into damp air, "Oh Lord! We forgot all about him."

Robinson had vanished.

"He's been dead drunk since we arrived," Lena said.

"Poor man," Gwyn said.

Robinson found Johns, still flat on his back, bent over him, felt his pulse, exclaimed excitedly, "Ridiculous. *Dead*, silly bastard, what made him think my friend was dead*o*. *Ass*. Astonished me to hear Stevens talking at all, wonder what wound him up," then inserted his toe under the sailor's backside, who now opened his eyes, stared up at night sky.

"Here! Come on, sailor, what you doing here anyhow, thought you'd got lost again. Wake up there, man. Shift your carcass. Wake *up*. There's a bloody raid on."

Johns broke wind, sat up. "Bugger me," he said, and stared hard at the man standing over him.

"Come on, out of the bloody way," Robinson shouted,

caught his arms, began to pull, "sitting *there*, blinking like an owl."

Johns staggered, got to his feet, swayed a little, and Robinson spat it into his ear, "Can't you move, man, d'you *want* to be killed?"

Mr Johns went on blinking, he liked being an owl.

"Where is she?"

"Where's *who*?"

"My girl, Jese, she was great, where she gone?"

"Just gone, come on, come bloody on," Robinson said, and pulled the sailor into the cellar, put a foot behind him, then let him fall. "Okay. Stay right where you are, sailor, this cellar is full already."

Johns stretched, flanked by feet, did not see them, turned over on his face. "I wish . . ."

"We all wish, sailor," Robinson said.

Gwyn hugged the corner, and Lena and Clem held close, sat next to the Robinsons. The Frasers had not come down, nobody had noticed it, and nobody seemed to have remembered.

"Down," Robinson shouted, "*down*."

And were heaped in a moment, and Johns smothered, lost to view.

"I feel like a damned rat stuck here," Robinson said, "those swine."

"You never seem to stop talking," Lena said, righting herself, pulling Clem with her, seated again, trying to relax.

Robinson drew away from her, she seemed far too close, and he could not escape the surprising observation.

"When you go up tomorrow, Mr Robinson, I should try shooting out a star or two, it might help."

"You bitch."

Clem struck him in the face. Clem had wakened up, for the first time, exploded. "Bastard," and turned to Lena, "you all right, dear?"

Gwyn was silent, heard nothing, felt nothing, saw only in her mind's eye the husband she prayed for, and he was near, and he was far.

277

"Here! Sit here, Mrs Stevens," she said.

"Thank you," and they sat.

Gwyn talked to Clem, quietly. Would he like a drink of tea, a sandwich? Was he comfortable, and how was his head, she was so sorry to hear about his sleeplessness. Lena sat quiet and still, said nothing, saw nothing, didn't feel a thing, and not a thought stirred. The guns started talking.

"There they go again," Gwyn said, afraid again, "if only Richard didn't have to go out like this," but he had.

The man beside her accepted some tea, his mumbled thanks unheard. And a final cry, "God! Why don't they *go*."

It roused Mr Robinson. "Ssh! You'll wake her *up*."

He sat at Ducksie's feet, knees drawn up, arms clasped about them, and the whispers began to flow to her in a steady stream.

"Bloody funny, really, Ducksie," arms suddenly round her, "I mean, well, I'll be up myself Monday, and actually looking down here, at myself, curled up, scared rat. I'll be high Monday, sure thing. Hell! The stink here, wish I was up there *now*, can't relax, just thinking and rocking with the whole damned thing, so helpless here, like *this*," viciously, an arm swinging violently, "like that little mouse over there, makes you hate yourself, ah! . . ." stroking her knee, "you wouldn't understand, Ducksie, I mean about being up, high, I mean high . . ."

"*Please*," pleaded Ducksie, covered his mouth with a finger, "*please*," so he was silent, kissed the finger, "O—kay!"

She dreaded Monday, hated it. The whole thing made her feel sick again, and she was unaware that all this time Mrs Stevens had been staring at her husband, and with some fascination, some Robinson words having slipped quietly away from the main stream. And it was then that she saw him bring the small radio set round to his front, and press the switch, so music that was soft, slow, gradually climbed into and filled this cellar. Nobody spoke, nobody moved except Mr Johns, as if the music's rhythm had strongly affected him, for he turned over on his back and began to sing.

"Oh! when I was a sailor, a bloody old sailor, sailing on the good old sea, when I was a sailor sailing on the good old, bloody old sea."

"Shut it *off*."

"*Listen!*"

"There!"

Gwyn felt them low, knew them low, and as she jumped to her feet she felt a coldness in her, as though a trickle of ice had slipped down her neck. She buried her head in her arms, cursed the monotonous drones.

"Blast them," shouted Robinson, then louder, "Down, down, for Christ's sake. Hang on to me, Ducksie, and keep to the wall, the *wall*," hearing it come, shielding wife and child, pressing them to the wall. He had quite forgotten the music that had got mixed up with the downrushing, screaming sound.

"Jesus!" Lena shouted, and Gwyn cried, "Richard!"

Sounds deafened them, and they were heaped, Robinson and wife and child, Lena and Clem, tight and close and heavy now upon a sprawled sailor. Lena forced herself free, clawed for the wall, and then the door blew open, and Johns's sudden endeavour of bone useless in the moment, as he was flung into the air, the reeking air. The noise of the explosion had barely cleared away when Clem struggled madly to free himself, and in doing so, tramped upon all, dived for the opening, let go of Lena's hand, and the warmth and trust that lay within it, tore himself free, and shouted wildly, "I must see it, I *must* see this, I must—"

"Clem! Wait for me, wait. Wait, I'm coming, Clem— I'm—"

Robinson stuttered in a dark corner, "You okay, Ducksie?" smothering her, "is she—"

Gwyn flung herself at Clem, hung on to him, "You can't go now, you can't—your wife—" fell as he pushed her clear. "Let *go*, I want to *see* it," stood for a moment in the great gap made by the explosion, watched a river of light flowing past, and then his eye caught the figure of the sailor lying outside, and he looked at him for a split second, then stepped over his great, shuddering arse.

Lena screamed. "Don't *go*."

The child sucked horror home. Clem ran out. Was clear.

16

Every level of air hurling as he ran, and wherever he ran he still saw the shuddering Mr Johns, and Johns was dark against this river of light into which he ran, and swiftly past a reeling wall, yet Johns was still there before him, a shuddering sailor. He stopped dead, to look up, look round, and saw light scattering light, a steeple half way through space, and vastly before him a river in tumult, flowing wild. Engines tore past him, followed by faces and faces and faces. He clambered up steps, reached a roof, leaned against stout iron railings, and now looked down, felt a tremble beneath him, a whole city rocking with outrageous power. And a life lived to see this, a great wall collapsing, a door hurling into the air, a falling girder, and a wind beginning to rise. He sensed the pressure of the earth beneath him. He let go the railings and ran across the flat roof, clung with one hand to a small iron gate, which collapsed as he held it. And always the light sweeping past as though the wind was behind it. A life lived to see this, a city rocking. Not what you felt, and he couldn't even think, the mind closed in. It was what he saw. And stared entranced at a blazing sky. All that light, a sea of it, from what reservoir had this flooded up, this drenching light, blazing red, and to his left a falling green, cataracts of light, red and yellow and green. The riot of colour shouted at him.

"God!" he said, "it's magnificent, it's . . ."

He ran back to the ladder, went headlong down, ran on through the streets. He sensed wind behind him, felt the pressure of flying feet. Turning a corner he knocked down a man, did not wait, ran on. Somewhere there was a high place, higher than that roof, a calm oasis, a place to stand still and watch it all. And then a forest of writhing snakes, silver under the light.

"You goddam fool, where you running to?"

He didn't hear, didn't feel, he only *saw*. Suddenly he was drenched to the skin. "Christ," he said, and began shaking himself like a dog. He came to a tall building, watched it sway, and it seemed higher than any building he had ever seen. He passed through a gate, groped along until he at last found what he wanted, the iron staircase that spiralled to rooftop. He ascended carefully, and every few steps he took he turned to look down, and now he saw a blackness below. The staircase throbbed as he climbed, life had come to iron, steel, and stone. He went on, and did not once look back, keeping a firm hold on the rail. He stood on the roof, he stared up at the light. He heard a grinding of brakes far below, loud hissing noises, but it was the sky that reeled that most attracted him. Bright colours reeling, like an overflow from revelries. He leaned against the low stone wall, looked down again. Roads opened, streets collapsed, and heard hollow sounds where once old giants had stood, great gaps, fissures, a river in tumult, showering glass, saw it from the heights, an orgy of movement, in one direction, moving under the light. An ocean of floating trash. He put his fingers in his ears, and the moment he withdrew them he was conscious of a distant, battering sound. He walked the length of the wall and back again, leaned over, looked down. Something white threshing about below, he saw it clearly, and he continued to watch it, and in doing so experienced a strange excitement, and he could not fathom it. He walked back to the spiral staircase, and began to descend. The sounds seemed more distinct, and he suddenly exclaimed, "It's something *alive*," and began to run. Clattering sound came to his ears, and he ran faster. And then he saw it, the white threshing thing. "A horse!" and threw out a hand, and something seemed to explode beneath it when it found flesh. A mad beast threshing, he knew now, and he felt electric waves moving across its broad back. He made to grab at the head, caught the leathers, was jerked into the air, and the beast dragged him after it, they were clear of a mews, they were in a widening street.

"Whoa! Steady! Steady."

The powerful forelegs rose up, threshed empty air, then a mad plunge and it was careering down the street, and dragging him after it. Against the light he saw it real. A big, white stallion, a maddened animal that had smashed down its stable door, had seen flames, had been lost in smoke. He held on, he could not let go. He felt himself dragged, and did not resist. When the strong smell reached his nostrils, he glanced ahead, then pulled on the leathers with all his might, realizing that this beast was pulling him towards a fire, and heat and smell were strong to him, as he held on, and would never let go. He pulled with all his strength, felt he was pulling against tides. The enormous power terrified him, he felt humbled by this plunging animal. The sweat began to drip from his forehead. When it reared again he lost his footing, felt himself torn along, as though he were now one with this rushing sea. It began to canter, and he cried out again, "Whoa! Whoa!" and held grimly on, as though all his life had been but a single movement towards this, to hold fast with a hoofed creature, in a rocking city. His body hung heavily, and under the horse's thunder the world itself seemed upside down. When suddenly the beast stopped, and was still, he scarcely realized it. He drew himself up slowly, and at first he refused to believe, but this beast was suddenly still, as though calmness had enveloped it, and it touched the man that dwarfed beneath its height. For the first time he found himself staring into its huge eyes, and in a flash he was delighting in their liquid light. Fear had gone. He put a hand on its shoulder, felt sweat there, began slowly stroking it, patting its neck. Its head stood over his shoulder and he delighted in the calm now come to this once plunging Clydesdale. He felt the flesh quiver under his hand, and he leaned against it, felt its warmth, knew it was calm, was safe, and he continued to stroke it. He talked to it, he smiled.

"Good old boy," patting it again, and suddenly relieved

at his own calm. He picked up the leathers, began to walk, and it followed after him, huge, shy, and shambling. How obediently it followed him.

If you walked far enough you came to something green, older than steel or stone, where this beast belonged. He kept on patting, and he loved it, feeling for the first time a trust between them. First demented and now quietened, he knew it would go where he went. He did not look back, but walked on, and the great hooves clattered behind him.

"Listen!" Gwyn cried, and they listened. "Yes, it is," she said excitedly, "it really is, how marvellous. Thank God."

She looked at Lena sat on the bench, her hands clasping its edge. Her head lay low on her breast, and she had not moved.

"Mrs *Stevens*!"

"My husband must have been quite mad," she replied.

But looking down at the woman Gwyn could only think of one thing; *her* husband would be coming back. She sat down beside Mrs Stevens, waited.

"Come on, Ducksie," Robinson said, "it's all over till next time. Come on. Let's *get*."

He helped her up, took the child, told her to collect the things, and slowly made his way past the two women, paused for a moment, bent down, and whispered in Gwyn's ear. "The Frasers never came down."

"No, they didn't, did they?"

"You all right, Mrs Stevens?"

"I'm all right."

"Come on, Mrs Robinson," he shouted, and in the same moment "podgy-wodgy" decided to wake up, and immediately he cried. "Damn! Shush, shush! Got everything?"

"Your radio, darling," Ducksie said, a kind of half frightened whisper.

"I'll manage, get on up," he said, and went back and picked up the Philco.

The Robinsons vanished with a loud clatter, and it was

then that he noticed the sailor, still lying there, far beyond the cellar. He had not moved. "I'll be damned, that fellow could sleep through anything, Ducksie. You go on," and he walked up to the prone figure, thought, "poor devil," and joined Ducksie at the foot of the stairs, suddenly shouted, "Wait." She waited, and he went back to have another look at Mr Johns.

"Oh no!" he said, staring down, at the wide open eyes, the long nose, the half open mouth, the thick, lost lips. Spoke. "Are you . . . oh no! Poor devil. You'll never reach Plaistow now," and stood there slowly shaking his head. The child's cry on the stairs broke the momentary sensation, and he joined Ducksie as she reached the first flight.

"Ducksie?"

"What, dear?"

"The sailor's had it."

"The poor man."

"Give her to me," Robinson said, took the child, and they went on up. "Trust that Jones chap not to be there when he's wanted."

Ducksie paused, subjected her husband to a long, cold look, and said, "He could be dead, too, darling. It's been the most awful bloody night."

"Don't *cry*."

"I'm not," she said, and he helped her to the door, and opened it. "In, dear, *in*," he said irritably, and pushed her before him, and now there was just one more thing that he had to do, and he did it with great satisfaction. He gave the door a violent kick, and turned his back on the world.

"I'm so sorry about your husband," Gwyn said, "I'm sure he'll be back."

Lena was quietly crying and only now did she notice it. "Poor thing," and the hand shyly reached out, took the other, and with an almost loaded assurance she said, "I'm sure your husband will be back, Mrs Stevens. Please don't worry. I'll wait here with you. I'm sure he won't be long." After which the words refused to come. She gave the woman's hand a sudden squeeze. "There, dear," she said, "there."

Lena looked up, stammered, "I must have been dreaming, it's nothing, don't worry. I know he'll be back."

"What a night," Gwyn said. She felt there must be something else she could say, but the words refused to come.

"I know he'll be back, I've always known that," Lena said. "It wasn't that. It was something else."

"What, dear?"

And Mrs Stevens with some effort, dropped the single word. "Nothing."

When the footsteps rang out she cried, "There! It's him, it's all right, Mrs Stevens—"

"Gwyn!"

Lena did not hear, she had travelled back twenty years, to the bright days. And then the megaphone voice, the rush down steps. "Gwyn! You all right, I—" and then she saw him in the doorway, cried, "Richard!" She ran to him, clung.

"All right, darling, I'm okay," Richard said, out of a blackened mouth, looking at her from red-rimmed eyes, "Everything's fine. Bad outside, bad, I mean bad. Rawlins had it, dear, you remember Rawlins . . ."

"Oh God!"

She buried her head in his tunic. "Don't tell me," she said.

And he did not tell her of five houses down, and of people that were down forever. He crossed to Lena. "Where's your husband, Mrs Stevens? He all right?"

"He ran out, darling," Gwyn said, "right into the middle of everything. The poor dear, she's so brave, she says he must have been mad."

A silence fell between them, and then Mrs Stevens made to rise, but at once sat down again. "He would have loved the colours," she said. "I'm so glad you're safe, Mr Jones. Your wife has been wonderful. Wonderful."

And there, a short distance away was Mr Johns, like a great dividing sea.

"It's Mr Johns," Gwyn said, so for the first time Richard noticed the man lying on his back.

"Oh hell," and he rushed forward and knelt down. "The devil," he said, "the bloody devil," felt the pulse, opened the vest, the shirt. "Oh Lord!"

Gwyn came up, she stared. "Poor chap," Richard said.

"It fell just outside, the dustbins made the most awful row, and that Mr Stevens' painting has gone, too."

"Ssh!" he said, an arm round her, crushing her to him, glad she was there. He knelt again and stared at the sailor. "It's too late, darling, too late." The position of the sailor's hands held his eye, the palms upwards, the fingers stretched as though reaching out for something, a kind of gesture. He put a finger on the lips, pressed them close.

"Let's go," he said.

"We can't leave her there, dear," Gwyn said.

"What happened?"

"She told you. Just after the bomb fell her husband ran out, I've never seen anything like it, shouting at the top of his voice that he must see it."

"How stupid can you get. You go up, dear, I'll talk to her."

"Richard?"

"Yes?"

She drew him close, whispered into his ear.

"The Frasers never came down, Richard, I mean Emily did, but he wouldn't, and she didn't stay long, so nervy, she just got up and went out. We tried to stop her but it wasn't any use, dear."

He stared at Gwyn for some time before he answered her.

"I know," he said, his voice suddenly flat, hollow, and Gwyn made an abrupt attempt to speak, but nothing came out.

"I've just come down," Richard said, his voice strangely calm. "I found them both standing close together against the bed that had never been disturbed. I spoke and there was no reply. When I touched them they just fell down together."

"Oh God!" exclaimed Gwyn, "the poor old dears. He won't get his pension after all."

He put an arm round her as he said in a hushed voice, "The whole bloody house trembled as I came down . . ."

"It won't *fall*?"

"It *might*," he said, serious, and then gave a curious little laugh. "And then again it might not."

"Your teeth, darling," Gwyn said.

"I *know*. Shall we go up then?"

"Come on. You have had a time of it, darling, you really have," she said.

"Fancy Stevens running out like that, right in the middle of it. I used to think he was dotty, and now I'm sure. Silly b—"

"Come *on*," she said, pulling at him.

The sudden slamming of a door made them jump.

"What was that?"

He didn't know, he didn't care. "Let's *go*," he shouted, and pulled her after him. They stood together on the bottom stair, hesitating, listening.

It was Celia, now safely returned from Bermondsey, and under her arm the canvas she had hidden under the stairs. She was walking quickly down the street, knowing the way to go, as she always did.

"Are you *coming*, darling?"

"Go on up. I shan't be a tick," said Richard, "go on, up you go, dear, and make some tea," and he turned and ran towards the cellar. He stood for a moment looking in.

A fresh candle was still burning in its holder, directly over Lena's head, fanned by a light draught. She sat upright, and still, stone to this stone. She was waiting for Clem. He would come back, he would never leave her. She knew he was safe, that he was on his way *now*. She felt it, she *knew* it, she must wait. After which they would again ascend to their shell, the hollowness in the room, the pain in the chest, and the pills that were not really any good, after all. He was quite right, he nearly always was. Useless bloody pills. She had a fugitive thought of Flo, lost in all that Essex green.

"I wish he'd *come*," in a loud voice, addressing the wall,

the damp, the smell. She heard voices in the distance, and then the approaching feet, but she did not even turn her head to look. The hands, unclasped, were suddenly pulling at the skirt. "God! I wish you'd *hurry*," loud into the hollowness. "He *will* come, and we'll go up together as we always do."

When the voices grew louder, she turned sharply, and saw two men standing a few yards beyond the entrance, and then the known voice, and the man suddenly standing before her, saying quietly, "It's all over, you know, I mean for the present," and wondered if she even knew.

"Is it?" she asked, confused, wondering what was over. What on earth was the man talking about?

When she looked up, Richard had gone, and now she saw him join the other man she did not recognize, saw them bend over Mr Johns, lift him up, heard him shout, "And you go on right up, darling, I thought you *had*," as they made their way to the hall.

And Lena sat on, as still, and always listening.

"And let's have that tea really *boiling*, Gwyn," and after a pause, what came to her like an echo, "All right, Harry, can you manage your end?"

And Harry could. And Lena sat on, waiting, and was sure.

"This poor devil came in here only hours ago," Richard said, "he and some tart he'd picked up. Rawlins found him wandering about in the street, and flung him into the hall. After which he appears to have broken into the landlord's flat, got really drunk on free whisky, and then brought in the tart. They were both drunk. He's been drunk ever since, poor bastard, and she's scooted."

"Probably never felt a thing," Harry said, as though trying to soften a cold fact.

The words floated down to Lena's ears, after which the slow, clumsy footsteps were lost in street sounds.

"Poor Mr Johns," she thought, "the poor shouter."

Staring round this cellar she saw it full, and saw it empty, saw Mrs Jones kneel down and pray, heard the child scream, the radio die.

"I could **pray, too**," she told herself, the hands clasping and unclasping; made to move and did not, and went on waiting. A movement did not disturb, and she closed her eyes. It was at this moment that Clem came in, was stood before her, a hand reaching out, and what sounded like a ghost voice saying quietly, "Lena!"

She did not open her eyes, and did not speak, and he looking down at her, muttered, "Poor Lena," and touched her with his finger, "Lena."

She fell to the floor. She did not yet realize that he had returned.

He knelt down, took her hands, "It's all right, Lena," he said, "it was always all right, I knew I'd come back, and so did you," and he lifted her up and sat her down again, himself beside her, and she did not feel any pain in the frantically squeezed hands. The voice in her ear awakened her.

"Clem!" she said, and "Christ! You're here."

He put a finger under her chin, lifted her head, smiled at her, was calm, as though he had just returned from a morning walk. "I'm here, Lena. Safe. Let's go up."

The hands running up and down his arms, feeling him, holding on to the unbelievable. He was here, safe, it was over. He helped her to her feet. And then the torrent in his face, the heat of the words, it shocked him.

"You ran out, I thought you were mad, *mad*, in all that, leaving me here, *here*," the voice rising and falling, the hot breath at his ear, "I cursed you, just thinking about it, mad, mad."

"I just wanted to see it all," he said, "and I did, and that's *all*."

"To see *what*?" And shook him, and continued shaking him, "Well?"

"I'm sorry, Lena," he said, his hands coming alive and the words under them. "I had to *see* it all," and after a pause, "I might never have seen it again, *never*."

"You must have been mad . . . *mad*," she said.

His calm astonished her. "Everything, Lena, everything,

and it was wonderful . . . *won* . . . the *colours* . . . the . . ."
the voice climbing, "I even wished you were with me."

And then she embraced him, saying quietly, "You'd never understand, never, and it doesn't matter."

"Understand what, dear?"

"*Me.* Being here, *here*, waiting, waiting."

And his calmness stayed as he said, "I freed it, the poor demented thing, I *freed* it," his hands on her arms, clutching, pressing, staring at her, living it all again, sparks in his eyes and hooves in his ears.

"Freed it?"

"Yes."

"What?"

"The horse. Beautiful it was, marvellous, and the strength, the *stren* . . . I took it to the nearest park, left it there. It's home now, Lena, really home."

"God! You're shaking all over, dear, let's—"

He took her hands, pulled, and she pulled against him.

"Sit *down*," and she forced him down, held him, thought quickly, "My God! Yes, he has to know . . . *know* . . ."

"Imagine running out like that, the people here thought you *were* mad."

"Let's get out of this bloody hole," he said, and turned, stared through the door, "I want to—" and the moment he said it she pressed him against the wall. "What's *wrong*?"

He saw her slowly close her eyes, as she thought, "What's *right*?"

"The whole bloody house was laughing at us," she said, the voice hollow.

"Come *on*," he said, began pulling her clear of the bench, but she still held back.

He felt her hands on his shoulders, felt them pressing and pressing, was suddenly bewildered by the strange expression on her face. The voice was hollower still as the words came, like a litany.

"There are no dustbins here any more."

His mouth opened, remained so.

"It's gone," she said, and she saw the now slack mouth,

the trembling lips. "There's nothing out there, Clem, save one dead man. One drunken sailor. The poor devil."

She remembered the slack mouth, the hands falling away from her as he quietly slid to the floor, covered his face with his hands. She watched him gently rock there, to and fro.

"It's terrible, and I'm sorry, dear, *sorry* . . ."

He leapt clear of the cellar, sped to open ground, and she followed, saw him kneel, stare at the emptiness, a wall, and nothing but a wall.

She knelt with him, held his hand, said quietly, "Let's go up, dear."

"Christ!" he said, as a hand turned fist hammered the paving stone. Kneeling, he gave a sudden low, guttural screech. "What'll I *do*?"

She bent over him, and then he felt moist lips at his ear, the sepulchral whispers that came, unable to get the sense of the words she spoke, but only their sound in his ear.

"You can do another one, dear, you can, I know you can. That sailor is *dead*, Clem, and he'll never shout again, but you can, I know you can, I feel it, do come along, please, *come . . . along.*"

He staggered a little as she helped him up, and they slowly climbed five steps into an echoing cold hall, and slowly across it, halting at the foot of the stairs.

"That poor sailor," Lena said.

And he said nothing. She leaned heavily against the banister, a message spelt out in a bent head, in the slumped shoulders. They moved, climbed the first few stairs, and halted again.

"You are all right, dear?" she said.

"Move," he shouted, "*move*," and the echo of his words rolled down behind him.

"Up again," she thought, as she moved aside and let him pass her. A sudden wrench within her forced out the single word. "We . . . we . . ."

He turned round, suddenly stuttered it out, "I . . . he . . . I mean, he was all right when I ran out, I remember stepping over him."

She didn't look, and she didn't answer, and they reached the next landing. And he never quite registered the explosion that followed.

"That drunken bitch has gone, too," Lena said, so he turned again, and this time saw her teeth.

"Christ, come *on*," he said.

She had forgotten the lost sailor, lost the spoken words, could think only in terms of stairs, counting them in her brain. He took her hand, "Come along, Lena," he said, and they started up the next flight.

"Clem!"

"*Well?*"

"I know."

"And so do I," he said. "And say when you're ready."

"I *am* ready," she replied, still climbing.

"I don't feel angry now, Lena," he said.

They went up and up, in silence.

"*Clem!*"

"Don't *talk*."

"I won't talk," Lena said.

And they went up, and up, and up.

"I thought you'd *never* stop talking," Clem said.

"Strange how it all came back in a flash, just staring out of that window."

An open newspaper lay on his knee; he had been trying to catch up with the news of the world. He looked up as she came to him. And no movement, and no sound. She put a hand on his head, ran her fingers through his hair.

"Clem?"

"What?"

"Smile, dear," Lena said, and he smiled, and she sat down beside him.

"Nearly two hours," he said, caught her sudden glance, and answered it.

"Talking," he said, "just *talking*."

"We're two trees leaning on one another, dear."

"What the hell does that mean?"

"Nothing."

They listened to a clock striking through the open window.

"I worry about you, Lena."

"You still think the whole damned thing a bad dream," she said.

"*Yes.*"

He rolled the newspaper into a ball, flung it across the kitchen.

"A cheap kick for history."

"I thought you'd never stop talking," he said.

"Ah well!"

"All that damned stuff about the day before yesterday," he said, made to rise, but instantly sat down again.

"It was real to me," she said, rose abruptly and made for the door.

"What's the hurry?"

"I've something to do," Lena said, paused at the door, turned, and with some emphasis concluded, "and I'm sure I don't have to tell you what *that* is."

He jumped to his feet, rushed to the door.

"Going out?"

"I generally do, dear, on certain days of the week," closed the door in his face.

He was still stood there when she returned, he saw the basket, noted the coat, the headscarf.

"I know what you'll do," she said, "and I know what I'll do. Is there anything you want?"

"Nothing."

And she left the house.

Not Tomorrow

17

Questions and answers, and Renten listened.

"Well now, Mrs Grimpen," Hughes said.

"I was out at the time," she said.

"I know that. Can you tell me anything about these people, Mrs Grimpen?"

"Such as . . ."

"*Anything*," he said.

"Been here a long time," she said.

"How long?"

"Think they came here just before the war, anyhow they were here when we came."

"Mr Grimpen and yourself."

"That's right. My husband was away in the war, and when he came back here he carried on just as usual."

"Caretaking?"

"That's right. Looked after this house and three others further down Chesil Place. Used to belong to an old lady named Benson, dead now. She and her companion, a Miss Cleate, cleared out the moment the first bomb fell. Mr Grimpen's father did the same job when Miss Benson's father was alive."

"I see."

"The only nephew, Miss Benson had copped it in the last raid," Mrs Grimpen said.

"Who owns the property now then?"

"Mystery. In an agent's hands now, have to ask him, a Mr Jensen. Anything else?"

"Can you tell me anything else about the Stevens couple?"

"Nothing."

"*Nothing?*"

"Lived a sort of secret, private life up top there for years. There's only her now, and us in the basement. Heard they're planning to sell and then demolish, soon's they can get a good offer for the land."

"But you must have met them, Mrs Grimpen."

"Sometimes, and even that was rare. Used to see her going out, about once a week, used to bus it to Euston for her shopping, think they used to live that way one time. They used to go out quite a lot, together I mean, but in the last few years neither of them seemed to bother overmuch, except as I say for the necessaries. Always seemed to me a long bus ride just to bring back the few things she returned with, though there was always a bottle in the basket, hook or crook."

"They drank?"

"He did, I think, perhaps they both did. But I couldn't tell you anything much about them, neither could Grimpy. Lived very quietly, minded their own business . . ."

"What I'm trying to find out, Mrs Grimpen," Hughes said, "is whether they had any friends. All I've been able to get from Mrs Stevens is that her sister went off to America a few years after the war, but tracing her is difficult, we don't even know her married name."

"A pity."

"It is indeed. Apparently he was a painter, Mrs Grimpen."

"So they say. But all the time we've been here we never saw anybody call on them. Often talked about it, Grimpy and me, I don't think I ever saw a postman carry a single letter upstairs."

"Your husband says they had the telephone taken out some months ago."

"That's right. They weren't very well off, I think, besides seemed no sense having one if nobody rang them ever."

"Very odd, Mrs Grimpen."

"Very."

"A sad business," he said.

" 'Tis sad, poor woman. I wonder what she'll do now."

"Ah! There's your husband now, Mrs Grimpen. That'll be all, thank you."

"Right," Mrs Grimpen said.

"Now, Mr Grimpen."

"Not more questions, surely?" Grimpen said.

"I shan't keep you long, Mr Grimpen."

"Right."

"Carry on," said Hughes.

"The gentleman did say that when he ran in he called out all the way up the stairs, said he heard nothing. Well, he wouldn't, would he? There's only them up top, and us below. Makes me sad sometimes, just going up and down them stairs, used to be a lovely house one time," Grimpen said.

"And you were doing some chopping in the cellar, Mr Grimpen."

"Said so. All over when I come up. Poor devil. Tell you something, last week, and for the first time in weeks and weeks, I saw Mr Stevens go out. Seemed strange to me, used to say to myself sometimes that man Stevens will die if he ever jumps out into the world, just from the fresh air."

"Continue."

"Before old Miss Benson died I used to collect the rents here, take it round to the solicitors, all finished now, agent's got everything under his thumb. Sorry for Mrs Stevens, poor woman, missus and me've been wondering what on earth she'll do. Don't think they had much money."

"She's badly shocked," Hughes said.

"Understood. Wish we could do something to help."

"Rather pokey little set-up, don't you think? You could throw those three rooms together, and include the jigs and it still wouldn't be a large room."

"They managed, anyhow."

"It's only an arm's length from where he worked into the kitchen."

"That's right."

"Oddly enough," continued Hughes, "I had a good look round up there, and I even wondered whether Stevens had been trying to set fire to the pictures there, a few of them ruined . . ."

"Could've been the oil splashing over them when the stove exploded."

"Could be. It was damned lucky the gentleman upstairs was passing the house when it happened. Whole place might have gone up," and Hughes paused, and then added with some emphasis, "By the way, Mr Grimpen, do you always leave the front door wide open on a windy day like this?"

"Doesn't shut properly now," Grimpen said, "and I've lived long enough in London to know that any door's better shut than open. The people going about these days, pinch the bloody dust off the floor if they thought it was worth it."

It brought forth Hughes's first smile.

"Your wife tells me that they hardly had any visitors at all."

"I never opened the door to any," Grimpen said.

"And the telephone, Mr Grimpen, they had it taken out, I hear."

"Never rang, sir. Would've heard it if it had, hear anything from where I am."

"Where's that?"

"Basement, of course," Grimpen said, and put the single question to himself. "Is this chap talking just for the sake of talking?"

"My wife would like to see Mrs Stevens if that's all right?"

"Not yet. Later."

"Where is Mr Stevens?"

"He's gone, Mr Grimpen, surprised you didn't hear."

"Poor woman," Grimpen said.

Hughes sat swinging his legs on the box, studied the

caretaker. A tall, heavily built man, in his middle forties, with thinning sandy hair, and features as big and heavy as his own feet. He was dressed in an old pullover, and wore denims and carpet slippers that were much worn. "Could do with a wash," Hughes thought, "and he hasn't combed his hair today."

"Mr Grimpen."

"What?"

"Seems odd to me that you never heard a sound at half past eleven in the morning. Where was Mrs Grimpen?"

"Out."

"Out where?"

"That's her business."

"The name *is* Stevens?" Hughes asked.

"Course it is. Awful when you think about it, be on her own now." He took out a cigarette, and added, "All right, I suppose, free country and all that?"

He took in the Grimpen man, twiddled his fingers, said, "Okay."

"Can't you think of *something*, Mr Grimpen?"

Grimpen stood at his full height, took a great puff at his cigarette.

"Well now, let me see . . . yes, one time as I think the wife told you, I used to collect the rents, got it once a month from the Stevens. They'd barely open the door when I called. Remember once it was night time when I went up to get it, and standing outside their door I thought they were saying their prayers, but I gather they used to read to each other quite a lot. I've seen Mrs Stevens coming back from the library on occasion with a basketful of books. Once or twice I heard their radio on. Music. But as I say, they kept to themselves, like they just didn't care, or want to know anybody. I've seen a few lodgers in my time, but nothing like them. Talk about mice. There's a barmaid over at the Granby, used to have rooms opposite here during the war, and she said she often saw them going out late at night for a walk, during the war, I mean, and the raids on and all. She said they got the nickname of the 'midnight folk'."

"How very interesting."

"Always paid their rent prompt enough," Grimpen said, "and that's something these days."

"I gather from your wife that your father originally did the caretaking on the properties."

"That's right. I looked after it in Miss Benson's father's time. A real old skinflint if ever there was, sort of chap as would spit on his hands for luck if you give him a tanner. Rich they were, very. The daughter was a bit lightheaded I always thought, but nice, spite of it. My father used to be a licensee, in a small way . . ."

"Doesn't help much, does it?"

"Not much, I'm afraid."

"Did Mrs Stevens's sister ever call here, Mr Grimpen?"

"Not to my knowledge. Didn't know much about her 'cept she went off with some American officer to the States. All I know."

Hughes yawned, saying, "And that's a great help, isn't it?"

"Sorry."

Hughes got off the box, led Grimpen from the kitchen.

"Hang around, may want to see you again," he said. "What seems odd to me is their never having any callers, so Mrs Grimpen says."

"That's right. Might have been years ago, I don't recall any myself." The Grimpen brows puckered. "Half a minute though, constable, there was one chap called a long time ago, can't remember his name, little man with a goatee beard. Probably dead by now. No, sorry, can't remember the name."

"We'll think about it."

"Course. Sure. Sorry I can't help much," Grimpen said.

"You did your best. Hang around."

"Will do. When can my wife see Mrs Stevens?"

"I'll let you know about that," Hughes replied, watched Grimpen depart. After which he returned to the kitchen, sat down on the box, took out his notebook, murmured his notes.

"I was on my way home after visiting some friends, I suppose it would be nearly noon. I remember there wasn't a soul about in Chesil Place. I live a few doors down from this house. Something made me look up as I went by, and then I heard what sounded like a small explosion, and when I looked up again I saw curtains on fire at the attic window, and I ran across; the front door was wide open at the time, and I rushed upstairs, calling all the way, but there didn't seem to be anybody in the house at all. However I managed to break down the door. The place was thick with smoke, and there was a strong smell of oil everywhere. I tore down the curtains, and I don't even remember *what* happened after that, except that I managed to smother the oilstove. A few buckets of water did the rest. The door from the kitchen to his workroom was wide open, the floor covered in oil. I presumed he'd dropped the stove as he carried it between the two rooms. It might have exploded in his hands, I don't know. I closed all the windows. I left the stove in the sink. In the other room an easel had been knocked over, and a half finished canvas underneath it. Back in the kitchen I then noticed for the first time what looked like a bundle of old clothes lying under the window. Something made me give it a kick, and then I found there was a man underneath, dressed in an old dressing gown. It was Mr Stevens, as I now know him. He was dead. He had one badly burned hand, and his hair was terribly scorched."

Hughes shut the book, put it back in his pocket, his mind now occupied with the conversation that had followed the taking of the notes.

"Lucky you were passing, sir."

"It was," Renten said. "One hell of a mess, constable. So's this house. I used to visit here before the war, different now though. This used to be a quite elegant little street."

"Wouldn't remember, sir."

"I live at Number 27, constable."

"Yes sir. I've made a note of it."

"Glad I was able to help."

"Much obliged, sir," said Hughes. "Did you happen to know the Stevens, sir?"

"No. I knew Mrs Stevens by sight, in a sort of fugitive way. I'd see her passing down the street on occasions, generally with a basketful of books."

"I see."

"Well now," Renten said, and Hughes quickly interrupted, said quickly, "I hope you won't mind sitting with her a little longer, there'll be somebody along in a minute. Won't be long. Doctor'll be here any second."

"I'll wait, certainly."

"Good."

He watched Renten return to the room where the woman lay.

"And that's him now," Hughes exclaimed, and took the stairs three at a time.

"This way, doctor," and he preceded him up the stairs.

The doctor was precise, clipped his words, it was just another day.

"Where?" he said.

"In here, sir," and stood aside to let him enter the kitchen.

"Right," and the door slammed on the constable.

Hughes remembered quietly pacing the corridor outside, the doctor returning, abrupt as ever, as if there was no more time, and he was chasing madly after the minutes that were left.

"Heart, constable, shock. You've sent for the —"

"On its way, sir."

"Good, where is the woman?"

"This way, sir. She's in deep shock."

"Right," the doctor said, threw open the door, and Renten rising abruptly, leaving the room.

"A Mr Renten, doctor, from lower down the street. Was passing at the time, he put out the fire."

"Good show," and again the door closed on Hughes, and

Renten. They paced up and down outside, looking at each other, saying nothing. The door opening.

"I've given her something, constable, she'll be all right later. Somebody should stay with her."

"Yes, doctor."

"Goodbye," and the man chasing the minutes was already half way down the stairs, and Hughes heard the banging of the front door, the echoes in the hall.

"Well! That was quick, wasn't it, sir?"

"I'd say it was. I'll go back now, constable, wait till somebody turns up."

"Greatly obliged to you, Mr Renten, expecting a young woman any minute now. And thank you again."

"Forget it," Renten said.

She lay on the small iron bed, and Renten sat down, watched her. The sheet had slipped down, and now he got a clearer view of her face, the eyes were closed, and then he noticed the limp hands, leaned forward, studied them, and thought, "More like the hands of a man," recalling those of the man under the kitchen window. "Not a wrinkle in them, almost hairless," as if they had actually changed hands. It made him think of the bundle beneath the window, kicking it. It upset him. He sat back in the chair, asked himself questions.

"Why was there nobody in the house? Odd. I hammered on a number of doors, no response whatever," so, musing, he found himself back in the moment, heard again the woman's voice, so close to his ear. "Clem! Oh Christ!"

"Awful," he thought, "she was quite demented, the poor creature. The way she tore up those stairs, saw me standing at the top, something near savage the way she flung herself on to the landing. But what could I do? Nothing. I reached out my arms to her, I said, 'It's all right, my dear'," and then aggressively under his breath, "but it bloody wasn't. God! I did feel a fool. The whole thing so hopeless. How utterly useless one is in the extreme moment, turns one into a cipher. I carried her into this room, lay her down, held on to her, it was just like having a throbbing engine in one's arms."

Renten closed his own eyes as he remembered. The things he had tried to say, and hadn't, unaware of the mad moments on the stairs, his own shock, the shouts.

"The shouts," he said to himself, and heard them afresh out of the woman's mouth, back in the scene.

"If I hadn't gone *out*, if I hadn't gone to Euston this morning, if only I'd shouted to that man yesterday, 'No, no oil today, no oil, no oil, no *oil*'."

The words struck his ears like hail, and when he opened his eyes she was still there, flat inert. Would somebody come soon? How soon? He got up and opened the door, looked out and down, heard nothing.

"I wonder how long she'll be?" he asked himself, closed the door, resumed his vigil by the bed, thinking of the door opening, somebody arriving, freeing him, and he, going back to his own life. He leaned over the bed, stared at the woman, wondering if she might suddenly open those tightly closed eyes, look at him, so once more he was back at the beginning.

"She was so *strong*, the way she broke away from me, burst into that kitchen, slammed the door in my face. Yes, and the way I stood there, feeling helpless, not moving, bewildered as I waited. Then something made me open that door and go in. Terrible. She was on her knees, holding up the man, dead weight, eyeless, pressing him to her, then letting him fall from her grasp. The way she wrung her hands, see them now, at floor level, she on her knees, like she was crawling to him, crawling for his life."

He came erect suddenly, hearing heavy steps on the stairs.

"Her *hair*. Those heaving shoulders, what a scene to walk into, like a kind of play, yes, and I remember saying to her, forcing it out, feeling stupid and helpless at the same time. 'Don't cry,' I said, 'don't cry, madam,' and she shouted back in my face, 'I'm not crying,' and cried." Renten spoke aloud, as though he were now alone in this room.

"I wiped her face with the handkerchief, I carried her here, wished somebody would come. Just sat there, and waited, and waited."

The door opened suddenly, and Hughes said, "What's that, sir?"

Renten looked up, shyly, said, "Sorry, talking to myself, I'm afraid."

"It's been and gone, sir."

And after a long pause, Renten said, as though it hadn't, "Has it, really?"

"How is she?"

"Deado."

"Good of you to wait, sir, shan't be long now, some delay somewhere, could be traffic, way it is these days. She should sleep now."

"Hope so," Renten replied.

"All I've been able to gather is that the name is Stevens," Hughes said.

"You have my address?"

"Yes, sir. Thank you. I'll take another look round," and he shut the door, and Renten sat on, wondering on when that "somebody" would turn up.

Hughes dallied in the kitchen, the bathroom, the workroom. "Shabby." Back to the kitchen, and standing stock still he got the smell, the feel of the whole thing. Hearing steps outside he went out again, and walked into Mrs Grimpen.

"Yes?"

"Is she very ill?"

"Deep shock."

She wanted to throw off the hand that lay on her arm.

"You can't see her now, Mrs Grimpen," he said, "come in here," and she followed him back to the kitchen. She was appalled.

"*What* a mess."

"Would you say it was rather unusual for a married couple to be without friends?"

He motioned her to a chair, she sat down.

305

"Perhaps they didn't want any," Mrs Grimpen said, "there are people like that."

"As simple as that," replied Hughes, smiling now. "Damn good job the gentleman across the way was passing at the time. D'you know him?"

"No, I don't."

"Lives lower down Chesil Place," Hughes said.

"I still don't know him," she said.

"No reason on earth why you should then, is there?"

"Hope she'll be all right."

"Looks a strong woman to me," he said.

"He was on the delicate side, I think, used to suffer from headaches a lot."

"Just a moment," he said, and left her sitting there.

The opening door made Renten jump. Hughes leaned over the bed, studied the woman, said, "She'll sleep now, sir, sure of it. You can go now, and thanks again. The caretaker's wife's outside, and I think it would be better if she came in for a while. They at least know each other."

"Yes," and Renten got up, and he felt he wasn't as certain about things as was the young constable at the door. "Right."

Hughes followed him out, called out, "This way, Mrs Grimpen," and when she appeared pointed to the open door, then followed Renten half way down the stairs.

"I'll be seeing you again, Mr Renten. Thanks again."

A wave of the hand, a closing front door. He wondered where the hell Miss Fairfax had got to, entered the room, saw Mrs Grimpen seated at the bed, and whispered, "Call me if she wakes up, Mrs Grimpen, won't you?"

She stood up, said, "Certainly," and waited for the man to leave the room.

Hughes went downstairs at an even greater speed, then stood at the front door, looking anxiously up and down. "What the hell!" he exclaimed.

"Oh Lord!" said Mrs Grimpen, stood at the foot of the bed, then suddenly looking up. "That awful light, shining down on the poor creature like that," and she went off to the kitchen, searched for candles, found some, went back to the room, lighted one, and stood it on the low mantelpiece.

"Fancy them not noticing that," and she stared up at the naked bulb. "How stupid some people are." She saw the hands on the sheet, the near ashen face of the woman. "Looks years older, poor dear," and then bending over her, asked in a tentative whisper, "Are you awake, dear?"

It shocked her when the words came, even more when Mrs Stevens slowly opened her eyes, stared up at the ceiling. One hand moved, the fingers picking at the sheet hem.

"Who's that?"

"Only me, dear. How are you, what a terrible thing to have happened. I *am* sorry, really I am, Grimpy is, too, awful, shock for us both," all in a single breath, covering a hand, holding it in her own.

"Must be something we can do, Mrs Stevens, anything you want, *anything*, just say, would've come sooner, but only just got back from shopping myself. Couldn't believe it when I heard, dear, *couldn't*."

The eyes closed, and she stood back a little from the bed, fingers to her mouth, wondering what to say, and then another stuttered whisper in the woman's ear.

"Are you awake, dear, are you all right?"

But Mrs Stevens seemed wholly unaware of the other's presence.

Mrs Grimpen gave a little sigh, "What a change, she looks awful, really . . . Yes, don't worry, Mrs Stevens, it's me, Cis Grimpen from the basement. I'm here," smoothing down the sheet, feeling for the hand once more.

"I am awake," and the eyes wide.

"Thank God."

"I had such a strange dream," Mrs Stevens said, addressed the ceiling. "I was hanging head downwards . . . I . . ."

"Oh no! How dreadful, but you are all right now, dear?"

She stroked a limp hand gone suddenly cold. "You mustn't . . . I mean . . . the dreams one can have sometimes.

All right now. Just try and rest. I'll stay with you, I'll be here," and she saw the woman shiver in a warm bed.

"I'm lost."

"What's that, Mrs Stevens?"

"Where is he?"

"Where's *who*, dear?"

"The *man*."

"What man?"

"The *man*."

"He's not here now, Mrs Stevens, I told you, it's all right, dear, forget it. I'm here, Mrs *Grimpen*," and she lowered her voice, spoke more slowly, "I've brought you something, Grimpy gave it me for you, dear, always has something handy does Grimpy, I mean when the odds are the other way round, as you might say," and she took a small flask from her pocket. "Drink this, dear, do you good," and she put an arm round the woman, raised her up, put the flask to her lips. "Now you just take a sip of this. You *have* had a time of it."

And Mrs Stevens sipped, spluttered, broke into a bout of coughing.

"There now! And don't go worrying about a single thing, dear, just leave tomorrow until it comes," and more sipping, renewed coughing. "That's it. Lie down now, Mrs Stevens."

Mrs Stevens turned her face to the wall, and it seemed like a gesture of despair to Mrs Grimpen.

"You must think of yourself now, dear. That's it."

"What?"

"You must think of *yourself*, Mrs Stevens."

The woman talked to the wall. "He left the question behind him," she said.

"Not herself at all, poor dear, God, the way things happen to people."

She saw the woman turn again, raise one arm as though to signal, then watched it fall flat to the sheet. Then she looked directly at the woman in the chair. Mrs Grimpen's returning glance carried the answer.

"All right. Yes, they've taken him away, dear, best thing. Poor man. Everything'll be all right soon. Yes, I *do* understand, dear."

And the shout that frightened her as she studied the partly open mouth, the trembling lips.

"Christ!"

"There, Mrs Stevens, *there*."

And the louder shouts, "No . . . No . . . *No*."

"Try and settle, Mrs Stevens, that's right, lie back now," and she lay back.

Mrs Grimpen began fidgeting with the bedclothes, began tidying the woman's straggling hair, then the head turned away, and she was glad of that.

"All in pieces, poor thing. This room's got a cold look about it, somehow I never imagined it to be like this, *such* a surprise, all so sudden, and that *kitchen*, oh dear, copper's right when he said the whole place looks shabby, neglected."

Mrs Grimpen remembered yesterday, the other days.

"They were so happy, sure they were, so quiet, peaceful like."

A violent movement in the bed, trying to sit up, trying to say something.

"You were saying something, Mrs Stevens?"

"Nothing," and the shout upset the woman in the chair, and she wished that Grimpy was there. The hand torn from her own, and Mrs Grimpen on her feet, and another shout, "Clem! Clem!"

She took both the woman's hands and squeezed them, wished that by some miracle she would fall asleep again.

"What the hell did he give her then, half the time it's just aspirins, h'm! Got her real, *real*."

She thought of the departed Hughes, a promise of somebody to come. She thought of Grimpy waiting downstairs, and certainly wondering. "Feel I'd best stay here, not decent to leave her like this, fancy going off like that, the things people do, really . . ." and she had the sudden feeling that everything was wrong, the room, the furniture, the bed, and the woman in it.

"Sad day this," she thought, looking round the room, and quite involuntarily, "disgusting."

She expected her husband any minute now. "Bit of a worrier, he'll be up to see what's going on," and then the voice that made her jump.

"He said a strange thing to me the other day," Mrs Stevens said, the flat of one hand covering her eyes.

"What day, dear?"

"The *other* day."

The door blew open, the candle spluttered. She watched the woman move again, face to the wall, and one arm raised, touching it, and then coming slowly down, and muttering, and another frantic shout, as though she were alone in this room, and Mrs Grimpen hoping that her husband would come.

"What can one *do*?"

"Where is he?"

"Who, dear?"

"The *man*," the words dribbled through her fingers. "Carried me here, I'd just got back from shopping, I remember now, I think I do—yes, I ran up the stairs and he was standing there, waiting for me, and he said something, and then I fell, and he caught me, carried me *here* . . . what time is it?"

"The clock's stopped, Mrs Stevens, I don't know, I expect it's turned four. How d'you feel, dear?" ministering again, worrying, being sorry, "Wish he'd come up," then moving in the chair, and a hand out, the words leapt at her. "Don't *go*."

"No, dear, of course not. It's all right. I'm still here, I'm Mrs Grimpen from downstairs, you know *me*, Mrs Stevens."

She stiffened when the knock came, and she opened the door to find her husband standing outside.

"It is you," she said.

"Course it is," Grimpen said.

"Ssh! Ssh!"

"Oh!"

"Come in, Grimpy, that's it," and she quietly closed the

door. They stood at the foot of the bed, watched the woman turn over and over.

"Thought they'd given her something," he said.

"Ssh! So did I. Expect anything from the health lot these days. I can't leave her, Grimpy, state she's in, somehow I don't think she really *knows* yet. Nothing's happened, nobody's turned up," she said.

"See what you mean."

"That awful light shining down on her all that time, Grimpy, it hasn't even got a shade to it. Candle's much nicer, don't you think?"

"Yes, Cis. Want any more?"

"Some in the kitchen."

"Would you like me to stay?" he asked.

"No, no, you'd only be in the way, 'sides, it's a woman, isn't it?"

And the whispering continued as Grimpy turned for the door.

"Having a sort of nightmare when I came in," she said. "I explained and explained who I was."

"What'll we do?"

"Where's that copper?"

"Outside last time I saw him, said he was waiting for a woman constable, thinks it's a traffic hold-up."

"What a business, Grimpy."

"Ah!"

"You'd better go, Grimpy," she said gently, "perhaps you'd bring up a tray of tea, 'case she wakes sudden, might help. Can't do much in that kitchen."

"Course."

She patted his arm, saying, "You are good, Grimpy."

"Real sorry about the whole thing, Cis."

"She's got nothing now, nothing."

They stood close in the open doorway, and he whispered to her. "Got *some*thing, dear, got his work, hasn't she, that's *something*. Sure you wouldn't like me to stay?"

"I don't think he ever sold anything after the war, Grimpy, used to make me wonder how they managed."

"Ah! But anything's better than nothing these days," he said.

"Suppose it is."

"Listen!"

They listened, and Mrs Grimpen approached the bed, bent over the woman.

"Grimpy," she said, the voice hushed, and he came over. "Think she's actually gone off, what a relief if she has, the dope stuff might have worked."

"Thank the Lord for that."

"Might sleep heavy now."

"I'm off," he said.

"Remember the tea."

She heard his heavy steps on the stairs, closed the door, returned to the chair and sat down. "If Grimpy and me hadn't been here, *well* . . ."

"He would have loved the flames."

"Dreaming, poor thing, she does look real exhausted to me."

"Colour always got him," Mrs Stevens said.

"Wish he'd hurry with that tea." Mrs Grimpen listened again, watched the door.

"Let the stove go out, asked him not to that day, said he was sorry, always saying he was sorry," and the gibberish dying on the tongue.

"*Mrs* Stevens. It's me, dear," bent over, whispering in the woman's ear, "my husband's bringing up some tea, that'll be nice, do you good. Let me settle that pillow for you," she said, again fussing, "think you had a nice little sleep, how d'you feel, come along, sit up, dear," striving again, "what an awful dream you had," and it suddenly made Mrs Grimpen feel very alone, sat still and silent, and somebody was out of reach, in another dimension. She sat back, suddenly afraid to touch her.

"He meant well, but he could manage nothing, just the one thing, good at that . . ."

"Still dreaming. God! The shock for her when she really wakes up."

A voice breaking, the words shaky, "Why did I order that *oil*, why did I . . ."

Mrs Grimpen's head slumped forward, and she stood up, stretched, suppressed a yawn, gave a little run to the door, looked out, down, "Where on earth is Grimpy, what's he doing?" shut it again, returned to a fresh stream. "Like a nightmare, 'tis a nightmare," she thought.

"Asked him not to go on with it that day, *asked* him, told him to rest, leave the bloody thing *alone*, but he didn't. Christ! I said, isn't there anything you can remember?"

The sudden harsh laugh frightened Mrs Grimpen.

"Coming up the stairs knew he hadn't taken the damned pills, knew it." The hands raised again, falling heavily to the bed, and two words splitting the air.

"Oh!" Mrs Grimpen said, and "Ah!"

A thud outside, and a shy tapping on the door, and Mrs Grimpen exclaimed, "Thank God for that, he's here."

"Here you are, dear, anything else I can do?"

She took the tray, looked steadily at him, and replied, "Nothing, just go down and get to bed. I'll be all right here, Grimpy."

"Ta then."

"*Qui*—etly, Grimpy," she said, as the door closed, and she put down the tray.

And then she surprised herself by calling loudly, "Would you like a nice cup of tea, Mrs Stevens?"

Incoherent mumbling from the bed. She poured out tea, sugared and stirred it. "A nice cup of tea, dear," endeavouring to make her voice sound as normal as possible, still disturbed, still worried and a little frightened of what she saw.

"Wish I'd known today, I'd have done your shopping for you," she said. The cup in her hand, hovering over the woman, "Mrs *Stevens*." Sitting her up, saying, "Drink this," and watching her take a sip or two, a sudden spluttering, pushing the cup away, falling back on the bed.

"Leave me *alone*."

"Oh God!" and she put the cup back on the tray, and

stood there, uncertain about the next move, caught up in a situation she had never before experienced. "Where is that damned copper, that other one he said was coming."

She closed her own eyes on the scene, wished Grimpy had stayed, felt tiredness begin to creep upon her eyelids, and completely unaware that at this very moment Mrs Stevens had begun quietly snoring.

"Well! . . . Are you asleep, dear?" hovering again, waiting for the answer. "She is."

She poured herself a cup of tea, and took the flask from her pocket, and thought only of how sensible, how practical Grimpy was in such emergencies.

"Ah! Lovely. Think she really has gone off this time. Wonder what the dope was," finishing her tea, giving the woman a final inspection, then leaving the room, breasting the dark and dampness of outside, walking slowly to the kitchen, switching on the light, looking round.

"*What* a mess. Strange really, first time we ever had a fire in this house. The poor man. Surprised Grimpy the other evening, he really did, creeping out of the house like that," moving about, examining everything, looking into cupboards, switching off the light, going into the smaller room.

"Oh dear! Oh dear dear," confronting the chaos. "I'd best get back, yes, she might wake up sudden, yes, I'd better."

Mrs Grimpen's imagination expanded as she went from room to room. She stood in the doorway of his workroom, saw the easel spread across the floor, the canvases against the wall, and something made her go in, gingerly approach, and then she turned round a canvas which was just one big area of white paint. She turned it back again, and walked to the door.

"Almost too quiet, really, both of them, perhaps they were a bit queer, Grimpy always thought he was, seemed scared of people, you'd have to heave a 'good morning' out of him," hearing the creaks in the floorboards as she made her way back to the sleeping woman. She sensed the snores even before she heard them, and then saw that Mrs Stevens had again drawn the sheet over her head, that one hand dangled beyond the bed. "Thank heavens for that."

The hammering on the front door made her jump, and she hurried to the top of the stairs. Who could it be at this time of the day? When another door banged she knew her husband was still awake, and then saw him cross the hall in his pyjamas, open the door.

"Mr Grimpen?"

"Who are you?"

"Switch on the light and see," and he thought, "A woman," and did so.

"Oh! You have turned up then. Wife's with her now, know what time it is?"

"I do. How is Mrs Stevens? Said anything?"

"Says nothing, and then everything, confused, took some tea up to the missus, she said she'd been dreaming, talking to herself in her sleep."

"Which room?"

"Show you. Follow me."

"I gather your wife was out at the time, and that you were chopping wood in the cellar."

"That's right—no, next flight, Miss," and she followed after him.

"In there," he said, and he called softly, as he tapped, "Somebody here, Cis," and the door opened.

"You can go now," the young woman said.

"She's fast asleep," Mrs Grimpen said, "and a good thing, too."

"I said you could get along now," the constable said, addressing Grimpen directly.

"You don't tell us to do *anything*, miss, supposed to have been here over an hour ago. Come on, Cis," and he pulled his wife after him. He raised his voice as he departed, "And that's the thanks you get."

The young woman stood watching them go down, then went in and shut the door. Being practical at all levels she noticed the candle, the wick of which had lengthened, and she nipped it, looked around for a fresh one. She found these in the kitchen, later. She leaned over the bed, slowly drew down the sheet. She listened to the snores.

"Poor creature."

She switched on the light, fully inspected the room, went to the kitchen, explored the two cupboards, examined the stove, took candles back with her. She decided to make herself some tea. How long had she been asleep? After which she examined the other rooms. "The smell," she said.

"Are you awake, Mrs Stevens, can you hear me?"

There was no answer, and she did what she had to do, sat down, waited.

Half way down the stairs the Grimpens paused, looked at each other.

"Thought she was never coming, Grimpy."

"She has now. Police are short staffed these days."

"Will you wait up for him?"

"Have to."

"What a nuisance, Grimpy."

"Come on," leading her down. "I couldn't settle thinking of you up there."

"Thoughtful of you."

She trailed him down the basement steps.

"How did she seem, Cis?"

He pushed her into the kitchen, sat himself down, glanced at the clock, glowered.

"She's very confused, Grimpy, a terrible upset woman, should've heard some of the things she said in her sleep, seemed deado one minute and wide awake the next. She'd nod off, start wandering. Only took a sip of the tea, gave her a drop of brandy, spilt that. Began to doze off myself, then all of a sudden I realized she was staring at me. Asked me if I was Mrs Grimpen."

"*No!*"

"Yes."

"The dope stuff they give her, I expect."

"Wouldn't mind a nip of this myself, Grimpy," she said, and handed him the flask. "The most tiring day. Been thinking about her just now, wondered if our Nellie would sit with her for a while, she *has* been a nurse."

"Why not. Nobody's turned up, have they, save the coppers."

Mrs Grimpen said "Ta", and after a drink, "nice and warming, Grimpy."

He took a swig himself, made himself comfortable in the chair, lit his pipe. "Think the day's really ended?" he asked.

"Be tomorrow soon," she said. "If only you hadn't been in the cellar."

"Ah!"

"I was quite struck by the calm way Mrs Stevens took the news yesterday."

"What news?"

"Ours as well as hers. Ah, if only that Rainbow caretaker job turns up."

"I'll be glad to leave here," Grimpen said.

"There now!" she exclaimed, and Grimpen went up and opened the door to Hughes.

"Glad you're back. She's upstairs, and my missus has just come down, she's all in, sergeant. Good job you turned up, we're thinking of bed."

"How is she?"

"Twice I made certain she was asleep, and then she wasn't, and she was staring at me for nearly a minute before I realized it. Scared me stiff."

"I shan't keep you up. And thanks for your help. Way things are in the force today we don't know whether we're coming or going half the time."

"Understood," and Grimpen showed him to the door, and then followed his wife into the bedroom. He watched his wife slowly undress.

"Try and settle down, Cis," he said, and himself undressed.

She registered his sigh as she lay down and made herself comfortable.

"Night," and he switched off the light.

"Glad when it's all over," he said, and she said nothing.

18

Seated at the bedside, the young woman constable smiled inwardly, and congratulated herself on having been able to make the date with her new boy friend, though she hadn't bargained for the traffic block that had made her so late. Now, realizing that Mrs Stevens was deep asleep, she got up and began to explore the room. She was conscious of an isolation, of an emptiness, aware of an end. Seeing a mirror on the wall she stood in front of it, admired and smiled at herself, gave her helmet, anchored in auburn curls, a slight tilt, and then stood back a pace. "Nice," she said, and continued her examination of the silent room. Seeing a great pile of books stood against the wall, she thought, "Fancy having to read all those." Stood at the mantelpiece she was quick to notice the empty pill bottles, fingered a tall green case, picked up and examined three photographs, came to the bureau and promptly sat down. The four small drawers she pulled out one after the other, and then replaced them. They were empty. She sat back in the chair, ran her hands across the desk, saw ink bottles, pens, blotting paper. She opened the two large lower drawers, bent down, looked inside. Empty. She made her way to the long green settee, sat down, and took out her cigarettes, lit one, and lay back, puffing contentedly, and an instant smile that came followed a distant vision of her new boy friend. "He's *it*." She glanced across at the iron bed, the inert form. "Poor old dear," she muttered, and then forgot her. "Wonder what the sergeant found out?"

He himself was outside the door, and she hadn't heard him arrive, but got the message, a hushed voice beyond the door.

"You there, Downs?"

She opened the door. "Here I am."

"Still asleep?"

"Yes."

"Let's go into the kitchen, Downs," he said, and she followed after him, knowing that he would immediately ask her to make him tea, and she went instinctively to the stove and put the kettle on, and then sat down opposite him.

"Good job you got here, Downs, just seen the people downstairs, all in, been up and down the stairs most of the day. And *you* were late," he said.

"Sorry. I've already told you."

"And it's accepted, make the tea."

She knew he would never call her Millie, Hughes being most sparing with warmth, and never familiar with his crew. He said "thank you" for the tea.

"Anything happen, sergeant?" she asked.

"What about you?" he said.

"I've had tea."

"Good. Has Mrs Stevens said anything yet?"

"Nothing."

He put down the cup, said, "Come and have a look at this, Downs," and she followed him into the small room containing the Stevens canvases. "See! And you can smell it strong, spoiled a few of them I must say, have any ideas?"

"You don't mean the man tried to set them on fire?"

"I do mean," Hughes said.

Millie only laughed, saying, "Why'd he destroy his own work?"

"People are very strange betimes," said Hughes.

And Miss Downs said nothing, only listening. Hughes helped himself to more tea.

"A shabby dump," he said.

"I had a look round, sergeant," Millie said, "but found nothing at all. The desk there's quite empty, not a thing in it."

"I noticed two wastepaper baskets outside, and they're

empty, too. Mrs Grimpen says they've been here for dog's ages, hardly ever went out . . ."

"Perhaps they didn't want to, sarge."

"Could be. But fancy having no friends, everybody has friends, relatives, these people were right in the desert if you ask me . . ."

"Perhaps they liked it that way."

"Still odd."

"More tea?"

"No. Go and take a peep," Hughes said.

Millie went off, after which Hughes did some reflecting.

"Inquest, Monday. Doctor said it was heart, shock. I've got my own ideas."

"It's a sad case, sergeant," Millie said, returning, helping herself to a cup of tea.

" 'Tis, really. Two a penny to me. Sentiment never paid dividends, not in our line of business, Downs."

"No sergeant."

"Still odd to me," Hughes said.

"Everything's odd," Millie replied.

"Then you're an odd girl," he said, extended a stiff smile. "By the way, I've run out of fags."

She tossed him a packet. "Thinking of making my own in future," she said.

"Thanks. I'll just slip along and see if anything's happening, Downs."

This required no reply, and it gave Millie another chance to muse on her good fortune, and "he" was still "it".

Hughes gently opened the door, peeped in, switched on the light. Nothing happening, switched it off, stood hesitant, then again switched on the light, stepped into the room. He approached the bed. She had again turned her face to the wall, and one hand still hung over the side of the bed. "Well away," he thought. The still woman, and the mystery and silence around her gave Hughes's curiosity a gentle push, and, like Downs he began a slow walk around the room, noting everything. He went to the window and looked out. A slight breeze coming in, a distant hum of the city, light scattering light on a main road, a dog barking distantly. What a quiet, hidden life the pair of them must have lived all those years. It seemed incredible to him that two married people hardly ever crossed the door, and were apparently quite indifferent about any possible crossing of their own.

"Perhaps they didn't like the world at all," he thought, and told himself that there were people like that. Like Millie he took a glance at himself in the mirror, crossed the room and bent down to examine the pile of books, then took a chair and sat down to work his way through titles and authors. He had never heard of Stendhal, and he had certainly never heard of Plato. He dropped the book, and continued his slow pacing, looked at the photographs on the bureau, examined the small radio set, and in a far corner saw a small red bucket full of empty cigarette packets. He had another look at Mrs Stevens, and then walked across to the cupboard, opened it, and raised his eyebrows at the sight he beheld.

"Well! H'm! That Grimpen chap did say they drank, but he never said how much," and he leaned in to examine the countless bottles on two shelves. Very carefully he lifted up two or three to the light, read the labels.

"Whisky!"

He took a quick nip from a quarter bottle. "Some people are lucky."

He quietly closed the cupboard doors, made his way silently to the bed, suddenly decided to sit down. He sensed a sudden discomfort in the sleeper when she turned over on her back. The eyes remained tightly closed, and Hughes studied her. "She's an old woman," he thought. "Yes, and he's years younger, *was*, wonder if they ever had children?" He got up, stood over her. "I'll hate the questions when she comes to," he thought, but knew he would love the answers, just a part of the whole business.

"Better get back to the kitchen," he thought, changed his mind, sat on. Echoes of Mr Renten's observations came back to him. "So he used to come to parties at this house one time."

He leaned back, looked up at the badly stained ceiling. "Where the skivvies worked it all out," he thought. "These were quite elegant houses one time, sergeant, but everything's changed now, a very nice place altogether, Chesil Place."

"In his very uncommon day, I daresay," and Hughes continued his reflections. "And this was now anybody's house, everybody's. H'm! Before my time, and I told him so."

He took another look at Mrs Stevens, took in her whole anatomy of feature, the high, lined forehead, the cheekbones, the nose, the lips that trembled, and were pale. It made him feel uncomfortable, and in a moment he thought of chair and bed and woman and room as a kind of trap, and got up, and stole silently to the door. She might wake this very instant, see him there, get the message that was *real*, something spelling *end*.

And at the door Hughes telegraphed to Hughes. "She better get in there, and I'll wait in the kitchen. Woman to woman. Downs can take the first load, and I'll take the second." He quietly shut the door and hurried to the kitchen, where he found Constable Downs bent over yet another cup, this time empty, and studiously working out her fortune in the tea leaves.

"There you are, Downs," and Miss Downs replied, without looking up, "Yes, I'm still here, sergeant, anything happen?"

"No. But I think you should now go in and sit with her," he said. "She might wake up any minute, and it's better for you to be sitting there than me, woman to woman, okay? And take off that helmet when you go in."

He took the cup out of her hand, saying, "Have another try tomorrow, Downs, the future might be even brighter," then as she rose did an unusual thing, he gave a glancing slap at her rear as she left the table.

Millie fumed, "And that's a bloody 'nough, sergeant," she said. It angered her. If only her new boy friend was here, he'd knock the sarge for something.

"I'll call you if she wakes."

"Do just that," he said, following her to the door. "I counted over sixty empty whisky bottles in that big cupboard they got."

"Oh yes," Millie replied, banged the door in his face and returned to her duty at the bedside. She glanced at her watch, carried on with the waiting game. But at this moment, sitting quite relaxed, her hands in her lap, she saw no woman and no bed, was in no room, but miles away, the roads in her own life purely imaginary, a boy friend beckoning at the end of every one.

"Was I *too* loyal?"

The words washed away Millie's thoughts, and she sat up instantly, and watched as the eyes opened, as the woman tried to sit up, then lay back again.

"Are you awake, Mrs Stevens?"

The eyes wide, and the glance fixed. "Who are you?"

Miss Downs leaned across the bed, said, "You are awake, Mrs Stevens?"

And it was real, and Lena knew, and Millie knew she knew.

"How are you, Mrs Stevens?"

She was on her feet, glancing at the door, wishing Hughes would come, he was used to this, and she wasn't, and then she said, "Excuse me," and hurried from the room leaving the door wide, calling softly as she hurried to the kitchen. "She's awake, sarge."

Hughes appeared at the door like magic, dragged her into the kitchen.

"Unload."

"I was just sitting there, then all of a sudden I heard her say, 'Was I too loyal?' and the next minute her eyes were wide open and she was staring at me. 'Who are you?' she said."

"And then?"

"I called you, sarge."

"Right. Stay where you are," Hughes said, and hurried to the room. Lena was sitting up. He stood at the foot of the bed, hesitant, studying her.

"How are you, Mrs Stevens?" he asked.

"I wondered where I was," Lena said.

Tentatively Hughes approached the chair, sat down. He then called, "Downs," and Downs came, stood at the door.

"Would you like a nice cup of tea, Mrs Stevens?" he asked.

"Thank you," Lena said, looked anxiously from one to the other, then said, "what time is it?"

"You've had a nice long sleep," Hughes said, "and I'm sure you'd like that tea," and to Downs, "Weave."

He helped the woman sit up, fixed the pillows behind her. "There!" thinking, "and she's not looking me straight in the eye, she's not really here yet."

"Won't keep you long, madam," he said. "And you'll feel better after that cup of tea. Just a few questions, madam, and I'm sure you'll understand."

A grave nod of the head in reply, and then Miss Downs appeared with the tea.

"Right. There, madam. Drink that. And let me say I'm very sorry about it, very sorry."

"Thank you," Lena said, gradually surfacing, getting a feel of the moment, of the room, of a ticking clock, and never taking her eyes off the man in the chair.

"Yes?" she said.

On which Hughes took out the notebook, placed it flat on his knee, licked the pencil.

"Your husband was a painter, madam?"

"Yes."

"Clement Stevens, and you're Lena Stevens?"

"Yes."

"We've been trying to trace your sister in New York," he said.

"Died four years ago."

"Oh! How old was Mr Stevens, madam?"

"Fifty-six."

"You've been here a long time, so I understand."

"Just before the war."

"Had your husband any relations, madam? *Please* drink the tea," he said.

"None. A floating mine removed them all, 1940 or '41, I forget which," Lena said.

"Oh! I see."

"Had he any friends, madam?"

"The best friend we ever had died privately in 1941, sergeant."

"*Privately?*"

"That's right. We were never married," she said, and the quietness, the casualness of her utterance surprised him. "Not here *yet*," he thought.

"Is there anybody we could send for, Mrs Stevens, at a time like this, we're anxious to help, madam. You were out at the time."

"I was out, and when I got back I found a man standing outside that door and I don't remember very much after that."

She pulled away the pillow, then lay flat again. "If I'd hurried back, if I hadn't *gone*, Christ, if I'd forgotten the oil, the *oil*."

The tea spilt on the sheet, the cup fell to the floor, and Hughes stuttered, "Is there *anything*, madam?" and drawing back at the explosion.

"Yes. Go away. Leave me *alone*."

Her sudden sobs shook him, he turned his head away, thought of Downs.

"She's the answer," he thought, then said, "Excuse me, madam," and rushed from the room, "Downs! Downs! Come here, will you," and they met half way. He put a hand on her shoulder, saying in a low voice, "It *has* happened. She is wide awake, she knows. Still shocked, I couldn't watch. You go in, dear, better than me. Don't ask questions, just let her say what she wants to say."

The expression on Hughes's face quite touched Millie, and she remembered it was the first time he had ever called her "dear".

"The doctor should look at her tomorrow," he said, and

as she went off his whispers followed. "Remember, Downs, ask no questions. Let her talk. And you know where I'll be. Any tea left?"

Millie half turned, cried into the air, "*Tea!*"

Hughes heard the door close. "The poor woman," he said, and cleared the pot of the remaining tea. "Could never stand a woman crying, really," he told himself, "in a real daze, does she know it's happened, is *fact*?"

He supped cold tea, then by a sudden endeavour of will reached beyond the frontier of the situation he was in, and thought of two important dates for tomorrow that must be kept.

"Reman job Wednesday, *Wednesday*, yes, wife's sister tomorrow afternoon, Lendon station around sixish. That's it."

And Millie called, "*Sarge!*"

19

A knock, and after a pause a "come in", and she went in. The man at the table did not look up, but said, automatically, "Yes?"

"Coffee, sir," the girl said, and stood hesitant, and he still did not look up, being concentrated at the time.

"Yes yes, put it down, thank you, Nellie—it is Nellie?"

"Yes, sir," Nellie said, gravely. "There's a lady downstairs, Mr Cruickshank."

"What kind of a lady?" he asked, still concentrated, and he hadn't even seen the coffee, though he smelt it.

"Just a lady, sir, elderly, very stout," Nellie said, and she watched the tiny hand moving about on the table.

"What does she want? Did she say?"

"Said it was important, sir."

"Indeed!"

And only then did he look up, the coffee held out to him, taking it, saying, "Thank you, Nellie," and Nellie, always dutiful replied, "Yes, sir, hope it's all right, Mr Cruickshank."

The first smile. "It's always nice, Nellie. But don't stand there. Hadn't you better send the lady up, if as you say, it's important. How important?"

"I don't know, sir. I'll send her up."

Cruickshank, sipped, savoured, put down the cup, said, "*Do* that," and became once more concentrated. It was some time before he realized that somebody was knocking at the door.

"Yes?"

Silence.

"Who is that?"

"Me, Mr Cruickshank—you are Mr Cruickshank—a Mrs Grimpen, from Chelsea."

"Indeed," and for a moment he entirely forgot the lady, his eye once more fixed on the pattern in front of him, and then he remembered, said, "Come in," and when she didn't called in a loud voice, "Do come *in*, madam."

The door opened and she came in, stiffened where she stood, the sight being unusual, for Mr Cruickshank was entirely surrounded by matchboxes.

"Oh!" she said, quite inadvertently, though it suited the occasion.

After which he looked up, resumed sipping the coffee.

"Yes? You wish to see me, madam. What is it you want? As you can see I'm rather busy."

He looked up at her, and she looked down. He did not ask her to sit, but flung the question in a casual way, "Something important?"

And she still stood, staring, and the first thought in the Grimpen head was, "I've seen somebody once like him, in a pantomime."

"Do sit down."

"Thank you."

"Well now?"

"You are Mr Cruickshank?"

"I am."

"Well, Mr Cruickshank, I hope you don't mind my calling on you like this, we're perfect strangers, but actually it was on a particular matter, sir."

Cruickshank, who had been heavily concentrated on Portugal, took a final glance at a row of boxes, labelled "Oporto". He sat back from the table, folded his arms, studied her. "What can I do for you, Mrs . . ."

"Grimpen," she said promptly.

"All *right*, Mrs Grimpen. What *is* it?"

He eyed her over the cup, speculated, wondered what might come.

"I think you once knew a Mr Stevens, Mr Cruickshank."

"I've known so many people, madam, Stevens, Stevens . . . let me see. *Ste*—"

"Painted pictures, Mr Cruickshank."

"Did he now?"

"Yes, he did," and he took due note of the prompt, very direct reply.

"Stevens Stevens . . . oh no! Is he still painting then, I think I did once know a Mr Stevens, yes, oh quite a time ago. A Clement Stevens?"

"That's right," Mrs Grimpen said, watching him sip so delicately at his coffee, more certain in her own mind that she had once seen somebody like Cruickshank at a pantomime. The cup banged down on the table.

"Surely he's not still at it, Mrs er . . . er—"

"No, sir. He's dead."

Cruickshank sat up at once. "Oh dear! Dear dear dear! I *am* sorry. Wasn't he married?"

"That's right, Mr Cruickshank, it's account of the lady that I came over from Chelsea, should have rung, really, should have written, and I hope you'll excuse me, sir, bouncing in on you like this, and you so busy," as her quick eye took in the full pattern, if not the importance, of a collection of the world's matchboxes, and also noticed a row of three miniatures hanging in green oval frames.

"I am sorry," he said. "Perhaps you would tell me more about this. The girl said it was important."

"May I sit down, Mr Cruickshank," she asked, and he was fussy in a moment, and she got a rather fuller view of the man so busy with his matchboxes.

"So sorry, madam. Would you like some coffee?"

"No, thank you, I must get back, I've a husband to look after, and a good many other things to do."

He noted how uncertain, how flustered she was, and eased the situation by saying, "It's all right, there's no hurry."

"Thank you. Well, sir, the position's like this. Mrs Stevens is quite on her own now. They've been living in the house so long they're almost a part of the building. My husband and I have lived in the basement, he caretakes, and he'd tell you what I'm telling you now, that Mrs Stevens knows nobody, and nobody knows her. They hardly ever left the house. 'Sides that nobody ever called on them, nobody rang up, and it's years since I saw a postman go up their stairs."

"How strange."

"After the funeral my husband was cleaning up the flat. There'd been a fire, Mr Stevens was carrying a lighted paraffin heater when it exploded, set half the room on fire, some of his pictures are fair splashed with oil. Anyhow my husband came across a postcard that he found behind the bottom drawer of the bureau, and I brought it with me."

Cruickshank was intrigued, and he now stood up, saying, "What about it?"

"It's one that you wrote them years ago, sir, well I mean to the late Mr Stevens. I have it here," and she took it from her bag and handed it to him.

Slowly he put on his pince-nez, an action that across the years had become a kind of ritual, and it was some time before he finally felt them safe, and then carried the card to the desk lamp, and slowly read aloud:

"15 Cawnpore Mansions, Wayley Road, Putney," then stopped. "Good Lord! This card's years old, madam. Imagine it," and then read on. " 'So sorry, unable to make date with you, but perhaps you would contact me after the 17th, as you know I'm a busy man. Sincerely, Ivor Cruickshank'."

And then he sat down. "Well!" he exclaimed, and he pored over the card on the desk.

Mrs Grimpen waited, studied the whole room and its contents. "Got money, tell just by looking, but what a funny man," and noted his red dressing gown, the big signet ring bright on a little finger, glimpsed a blue silk shirt beneath the gown, and a paler blue tie. "Smallest man I ever saw *in my life*."

Cruickshank looked over, leaned forward, and said quietly, "Tell me, Mrs . . . er . . . what is it you wish me to do?"

She bent at once.

"Well, sir, I came all this way over to see you for one reason only. Mrs Stevens is a very lonely woman now, and she hasn't got over the shock either, a terrible thing it was to have happened. The flat went on fire, accident it was, though the police sergeant that hung around the house three whole days thought Mr Stevens had been trying to set fire to his own paintings, on purpose he said, but it was quite different at the inquest, doctor said he'd died of a heart attack, shock. Fifty-six he was, and she's an old woman now."

Cruickshank drew back, slowly drew a hand across his face, looked at her.

"Dreadful, madam, and it was good of you to come over. I didn't know them very well, a few fugitive meetings. I'd a small gallery at the time, and Mr Stevens showed a few things there, but they weren't very good, no. And you think I should see her?"

"Be a charity, Mr Cruickshank, and nice too, considering she's so on her own, knows nobody as I said. If you dropped in on her my husband and I would be grateful."

She was restless in the chair, wanting to go, she had done her duty, she had tried to help, and it was now up to the gentleman sitting there. And Cruickshank sensed this at the moment of decision.

"What is the address, madam?" and Mrs Grimpen, now sick of being addressed in this way, said, rather sharply, "The name's *Grimpen*, sir, Mrs Cis Grimpen. We're grateful for what you say, be a godsend to the poor creature to contact somebody she once knew."

"The *address*!"

"19 Chesil Place, corner Chesil Road, sw3."

"Thank you. I'll see what can be done, Mrs Grimpen," he replied.

"We did what we could, and of course she's just like us now, with this 'ere notice to quit at the end of the year, whole street's going to be demolished, sir."

"Indeed!"

And Cruickshank stared and stared, endeavouring to work out another kind of pattern altogether.

"I'll write it down. One moment please."

And whilst he wrote, the Grimpen narrative continued. "The last few days she's been sitting in front of the mirror, just talking to herself, and only last evening, sir, my husband went upstairs to see what the shouting was about, and he knocked, and the door was ajar, and he peeped in, and she was talking very loud into the mirror."

"How extraordinary," he said, and again a hand across his face, and speaking from between fingers, "I *am* sorry."

"Yes, sir," and Mrs Grimpen rose, and he followed.

She experienced a sense of triumph at having tracked this man down. She made for the door, Cruickshank behind her. When she turned the difference was total, he looking up, and she looking far down. She noted the small hand fiddling with the knob, then in a moment it had got lost in her own.

"I'll certainly call and see Mrs Stevens," he said, "yes, and I remember now, isn't it a Lena Stevens?"

"That's right. She will be pleased, seeing a friend after all that time."

And Cruickshank liked Mrs Grimpen, "A thoughtful, simple soul."

"Goodbye, Mrs Grimpen."

"Goodbye, Mr Cruickshank."

She felt relieved the moment she got through to the landing, then went slowly, thoughtfully, down the long flight of stairs richly covered in red carpet. Cruickshank was still vivid in her mind as she hurried for the bus stop, and memories of a pantomime long ago remained with her. "Just been like an adventure," she told herself, and boarded the bus that hurled her back to Chelsea.

Grimpen had done the dutiful things, the pot handy, the tea ready, and then he heard her heavy tread on the steps, ran and threw open the door.

"There you are! What happened? Managed to find the gentleman?"

She brushed past him and removed her coat and hat, sat heavily to the table. "I saw him, Grimpy."

"Good. Good. Made a cuppa, thinking you'd be handy for

it after that long journey on the bus. Good of you to go, Cis."

" 'Tis a fairish distance, road's very long, too, Wayley Road, never heard of it, lovely mansion flats, Grimpy, very nice."

"Not everyone would have bothered," Grimpen said.

"She's a soul, Grimpy."

"Course she is. Tell me about it," he said.

"D'you remember, Grimpy, years ago now, but I was thinking about it all the way home . . ."

"About what?"

"The name of a pantomime we once saw at the Palladium, damned if I can remember the name of it. You remember, I think there was a little man in it." The question came right out of the blue, confused him.

"What is all this, Cis?"

"He's a little man, Grimpy," she said.

"A little . . . *man?*"

"That's right. Soon's I copped eyes on Mr Cruickshank I knew, made me think of the one in the panto. You would scarcely believe this, Grimpy, but when I got there he was actually playing with matchboxes, he—"

"He *what?*"

"Playing with them, dear, hundreds of matchboxes, spread all over the table. It's a lovely flat, and he has lots of little pictures hanging on the walls, all the frames the same colour, green. He's rich, I shouldn't wonder, and he has a young maid there, apronful and all, just like the old days, dear. Offered me coffee, and though it smelt really lovely I felt too nervous to say yes, probably would have spilt it on his nice carpet. He seemed rather shy at first, and he certainly was surprised, too, kept me standing there nearly five minutes whilst he arranged a long row of matchboxes, muttering to himself all the time. But he did at last separate himself from his toys. But he was nice, Grimpy, and that's what counts every time."

"Course it does."

"He's going to come," she said.

"That is good, Cis. Worth all the trouble."

"D'you have a look in, Grimpy?"

"I did. And she was sitting there reading a book, seemed sort of peaceful, so I just glimpsed for a second and then come away. I didn't quite like the idea of her door being ajar, Cis."

"Yes, it should be shut, considering some of the swine going about these days. Thinking about yesterday all the way home in the bus, Grimpy, seemed like a kind of mad dream. And I never, *never* expected her to come. Really astonished me."

"Ah! A brave lady," Grimpen said, "though I thought she was going to faint once, good job we had her between us."

"Yes, and I thought that Mr Renten down the street was most obliging, complete stranger, really, and yet he called round to see how she was, said he'd come when I asked him."

"Some good folk still around, Cis," Grimpen said, refilled his cup, "gives one a bit of cheer."

"I do hope something happens for her, Grimpy."

"Aye. I do myself. Surprised in a way how cool she was when you give her the news of the notice, Cis."

She got up, walked round the table, bent over him, a hand on his head, and exclaimed intensely, "Can't tell you how happy I am you landed that job at the Rainbow, dear."

"Yes. Think the wheel's beginning to turn the right way now, Cis."

"And I'd better get on," she said, and she collected the cups and went off to the kitchen, leaving her husband to reflect on the events of the past few days.

"Rich," she said, "rich and old, makes the difference all the same. You'd have thought he would have kept contact with the Stevens. Odd world."

He heard his wife busy in the kitchen.

"Very obliging Cis is, and not many like her round about today."

He drew his chair to the fire, filled his pipe, relaxed and

334

made himself comfortable, then speculated about the life in the new flat, and felt so relieved about it that he shot an arm in the air as though in salute to the good friend that had landed him in such a splendid job.

"Ah!" he said, "some things do make you think."

He sent clouds of smoke to the ceiling, lay further back in his chair, felt relief about Mrs Stevens, collected an appetizing smell from the kitchen. "Interesting to see this Cruickshank chap, wonder when he'll call," and then his wife called from the kitchen, "Lay the table, Grimpy."

"Righto."

As she came in with the meal, he seemed to note his wife's height as if for the first time. He thought any small man would be dwarf to her.

"I've left something out there for Mrs Stevens, Grimpy. D'you think we should ask her to join us?"

He hesitated, not being quite certain about it.

"It was a bit awkward when we had her down yesterday," he said, "she just sat there, saying nothing, though she ate her dinner."

"She enjoyed it," Mrs Grimpen said, "she told me on her way up."

"Perhaps it's best if you took it up to her, Cis. Sure she'd rather have it on her own. She give me the impression she's a person that would like anything on her own."

"Would you like to be on your own?"

"No, I wouldn't."

"Well then."

"D'you want me to take it up?"

"Don't bother," she said, and went out, saying, "get on with it, Grimpy," and Grimpy got on with it, and she made up the tray and carried it to the top of the house, knocked.

"Who is that?"

"Only me, dear," Mrs Grimpen replied, and opened the door, saying, "I've brought you a bite of lunch, Mrs Stevens."

"It's very good of you, Mrs Grimpen."

"Tut tut!"

She laid out the meal on the small table, saying, "Come along now, it's all ready."

Lena, standing at the window, turned and came down the room.

"Would've asked you down, Mrs Stevens, but Grimpy thought you'd like to be on your own at this time. How are you feeling, dear? I'll be doing a bit of shopping this afternoon, anything I can get you, you must be out of the necessaries?"

She hovered over Mrs Stevens. "That all right?"

"It's very nice, Mrs Grimpen," who then adjusted the table. "Thank you."

Mrs Grimpen still hovered.

"I was thinking that it was strange your own doctor never called in to see how you were, dear, bound to have seen it in the papers."

"He's a very busy man, Mrs Grimpen, probably never even glanced at the paper."

"Well, I'll leave you now. It is a pity you're such a long way up, and we're a long way down."

Lena smiled, rose as Mrs Grimpen made for the door. "Thank you again."

"If you like to make a little list of what you want, dear, I'll collect it when I come for the tray."

"Thank you."

She looked at the meal before her, began to eat, heard Mrs Grimpen's echoing steps on the stairs. The Grimpens meant well. "How on earth would I have managed without them? The whole thing's like a nightmare." Not feeling hungry, toying with the food, thinking of what must be got, leaving the table, checking up in the kitchen, coming back, eating again, not enjoying it, pushing it away, getting up, going out, standing outside the door of that other room. Her hand on the knob, turning it. Locked. She leaned heavily against this door, where he worked, where it all began, where it ended, feeling in a moment the terrible isolation, a pattern, a meaning gone, and crying inside herself, "Yes, yes—yes, he's gone, *gone*," giving way, crying, then sinking slowly down until she was now sat outside, feeling a draught at her feet, registering once again the unusual silence, and in between sobs muttering, "Yes, and the last few weeks he actually locked me out, *out*." A torrent of questions, as she rose slowly to her feet, again leaning against the door. Who destroyed who? Was it a waste? What did it mean *now*? Seeing him leave the room without a word, hearing him in the passage, knob fumbling, hearing the door open, close, hearing the key. Locked. "I hated that, hated it. Shut out." What did I do for Clem. What didn't I? We were both locked in, too *close*, and the silence, that bloody silence. Watching the clock, trying to read, trying to think, and remembering, remembering. "Once we ate and slept and sat through a whole week of it, not a word spoken, afraid to look at each other, the grinding days. And wanting to shout, 'Say something, *say* something'."

She turned away, dragged herself back to the living room, went to the cupboard, threw wide the doors, stared into the history of two whole years, "The drink, the *drink*."

Wallowing in it, drowning in it, because something wouldn't move, wouldn't work, the shy, darting glances from chair to settee, and she, reading, pretending to, waiting for the word, just one, longing for him to say it, something, anything, to break the spell. What did he do? What did he think? What did he *want*? Lying in the dark, wide awake, listening to each other breathing, and always the tick of the clock in her ears, in his, and waiting, waiting. Did I do *too* much, too *little*? The arms stretched to extreme, a firm grip on the doors, staring in, the pile yawning in its own emptiness, and just as she was closing the cupboard Mrs Grimpen slipped in, saw her, stood still, half inclined to leave, until she suddenly sensed there was somebody in the room.

"Oh! Mrs Grimpen. There you are," forcing back the fact, the normal. "I did enjoy that meal, and thank you again," flinging shut both doors, tearing down the room for the tray. "Sorry. I forgot all about that list, I shan't be a second. Do sit down, Mrs Grimpen, won't be a moment."

Mrs Grimpen watching her at the bureau, tearing a sheet

of paper, grabbing a pencil, watching the shaky hand write out what was wanted, rushing to her, saying, "Here, and thank you. You *are* good."

Wanting her to go, to be alone again, feeling safe, "Close the door as you go, dear," and hearing Mrs Grimpen reply, as if from a distance, "I always close the door, Mrs Stevens, but whenever I come up it's always open."

"I sometimes forget, dear," Lena said, following her, and an expression that seemed to be saying, "Go then, *go*, Mrs Grimpen."

Mrs Grimpen paused, faced her resolutely as she thought quickly, "Perhaps I ought to tell her about that Mr Cruickshank, yes, I better had," but the now hardening expression stayed, and she knew that in this very moment, she, Mrs Grimpen was *not* wanted.

"There was something, Mrs Stevens," she began, and then turned quickly away. "No," she thought, "if I don't go this very minute, I think she'll *push* me out."

Going, pausing on the stairs, hearing a door locked, going on down. "Looks quite beside herself, poor dear, but I'm glad she liked the lunch," and feeling greatly relieved as she went down the basement steps.

"All right?" asked Grimpen.

"She enjoyed it, Grimpy, ate the lot."

"Goodo."

"Been crying, Grimpy."

"Oh dear!"

"I was going to tell her I'd been to see this Cruickshank man, and then I decided not to, it was the way she looked at me, awful expression on her face, like she wanted me to get out of her *sight*, had a kind of feeling she might even push me out to the landing if I didn't go at once."

Grimpen took the tray, said, almost with a snarl, "I hope she realizes how bloody lucky she is, Cis, the way you go about doing things for people. They're an odd lot, the whole screaming lot of them. Come and sit down."

He knew his wife was upset, wondered what had really happened. "Perhaps I'd better go up next time. *Beside* herself? There are limits even to that," and he went off to the kitchen with the tray.

"Was really glad to get down them stairs," Mrs Grimpen told herself. "She looked to me just now like she was a woman that had had a storm inside herself. But I could only feel sorry for her. God knows where she'll end up," and her train of thought died immediately Grimpen came back.

"Thought that tomorrow, or maybe Thursday, Cis, we might hook it from here to the Rainbow job, have a look at what's what, and what's for tomorrow?"

"Yes, I'd like to see the new flat, Grimpy, sure, it's very nice. How lucky we are, dear."

"Lucky?"

"Yes, Grimpy, a bus ride to have a look at our future."

"That's good, well said, Cis," taking the opposite arm-chair, making himself comfortable.

They looked at each other, exchanged smiles. It made the top flat seem many miles away, and Mrs Lena Stevens quite lost in the distance.

"Grimpy!"

He yawned, sat up, "What?"

"Oh nothing, dear, nothing at all," she said, closing her eyes, against the fire, the warmth.

"Yes indeed, we are lucky, very lucky. Some are not."

"Cis!"

"What?"

"Shopping," Grimpen said, "shopping. You get her list?"

"Got it, Grimpy. Wake me in half an hour."

"Will do."

Through the window she could see the light was beginning to go.

"Sooner that Mr Cruickshank comes to see her, the better. He *is* a funny looking gentleman."

They drowsed, and the warmth grew.

"Grimpy!"

"Now what?"

"Perhaps I shouldn't have interfered, just been thinking

about it. She may not *want* to see him, and then think of the date on that postcard, might have had a row with the man, we don't know, do we, I wonder, really."

"It's the thought that counts. And she isn't a mouse, and if she doesn't want to see him I'm sure she'll tell him to go, dear. Stop worrying."

"I'd better not settle in, Grimpy," she said, and left him abruptly, his head making the occasional nod. The door closed and he didn't hear it, and five minutes later she had left the house, and Grimpen jerking erect, suddenly housing the uncomfortable thought that perhaps his wife was right, could be interfering. "Wish I'd never found the bloody card," he told himself. "But it's done now," and emitting a yawn he then got up and went into the kitchen for a quick douse under the tap, and a few minutes later he, too, had left the house.

She didn't hear the steps in the hall, the banging of the doors as she wandered about the flat in a kind of daze, and she was grateful to the Grimpens. But now she must pull herself together, and though she had for a long time avoided it, she took the plunge and began to examine his things. She flung the clothes in a heap on the settee, sat down and began going slowly through them. The first thing she found was the broker's receipt for a block of shares, and with it there seemed to emerge a measure of practicality. She put on her glasses, and carefully read the document, and wondered what their present value might be. She felt as if she had discovered a gold mine, and only three days ago had she heard of their existence.

"I want to get out of this house as quickly as I can." She must start looking, planning. Certain articles of clothing she held tightly to, as if she never wanted to let them go, then let them fall to the floor. After which she made a pile for the ragman. She went to the kitchen and examined everything in it, and later to the bathroom.

"One room will do."

She gathered the photographs from the top of the bureau

and tore them to shreds, again ransacked the drawers, just in case.

"Burn the lot."

She carried the books to the window, set a chair, then went carefully through them, idled her way through pages and pages, into which she had so often sunk, vanished, "gone away". She would take them all, leave nothing.

"The best friends I ever had."

She examined the radio set, half turned the switch, then set it back again. Another friend. "A great pity he had no ear for music," she thought.

This slow exploring of her "things" had brought about a calm. *Doing* something fortified, made her face the facts. Soon perhaps, those "other" days would recede into the distance. On several occasions she had paused outside the room where he had worked, key in hand, wanting to open the door, go in, look at it all, but each time the key dangled limp in her fingers, and the locked door just stared at her.

"I'll have to go in, see it all, I'll just have to," and hated the very thought of it.

The one that had asked her so many questions now sent words echoing through her ears.

"At first, madam, I thought your husband had been trying to set fire to them."

"Set *fire* to them?"

"A few of them smell strongly of oil, madam. Don't take it as read, just a passing thought."

And she had repeated parrot-like, "Set *fire* to them."

The question challenged her now. Had he? "No, surely not, it's quite mad, the whole bloody idea's mad."

So she was there again, trying to make up her mind.

"The rows we had lately, and that awful night, that . . ." and she was in the room again, his hand holding her by the back of the neck, forcing her to look, and she had *looked*. "God! It was horrible. I think I started to be sick then, yes, I'm sure I was sick. And drunk as he. The bottles, those bloody bottles must *go*."

Glaring at this locked door, entrance to the dream room,

the cell, the confessional, the escape hole, the dead end. Suddenly she thrust the key in the lock, then threw the door wide, looked in. A lump came into her throat, she turned and ran back to the living room, rushed to the window, put her head out.

"It must have been the very first time I ever got drunk. And afterwards . . . afterwards . . . my head, and waking up, and him there, snoring in the other bed, God, I felt so ashamed about it all. Poor Clem, and he was so understanding about it, so . . ."

Sitting on his bed, getting up again, picking photo fragments out of the wastepaper basket, piecing them together again, letting them drop back in the basket.

"I suppose this little bureau must be quite valuable now." And how useless it had been, neither of them had ever sat down to write a letter for years. She wondered how valuable it was, and she was glad she had kept it.

"It's going to be very strange for me, *very* strange," she thought, as if tomorrow's shadows were already in the room. And one as quick as light. "Perhaps I might find a room somewhere in the Euston area."

Where it all began, where she surprised herself, where she did the unthinkable, putting a foot to a road that had seemed so long, so endless. "I always got pleasure from the simplest things," a bus roaring in her ears all the way from Chelsea. Simple things. They had been her best, her deepest, safest anchor.

"Yesterday was a nightmare. Only those Grimpens either side of me made it real. And that nice man who was *there*, when it all happened. He came, too, just fancy that. But I was glad when it was over. Heavens! The times I've cursed those damned stairs, yet yesterday afternoon I might have been climbing as for the first time. Even opening the door and coming in, sitting down, being quiet, alone, yes, even that was good. I just sat there, all the way into the evening, into the night, I never even bothered to switch on the light, just sat on, and the only pleasant thing in this room was the ticking of the clock. And then, somehow, I even managed to undress, crawl into bed. Was I glad of the silence, the utter darkness?"

"You were."

"I've never been so close to a man, he was a real *person* to me, *real*. I'd have done anything for Clem, anything. And I think he knew I would, yes yes yes *yes*, I'm sure of it. None but us could ever have lived one whole week in silence, eating at table, and never a word between us. We spoke with our eyes, we understood each other. And I was sometimes a bloody *coward*. Yes, I was. He knew it, and said nothing. And he was, too, and *I* said nothing. No man ever depended so much on me as he did, no one. I feel anger, feel shame, things done, the mad things, the stupid things, the blind moments, the hideous waiting, and waiting, and waiting. God! Unless he himself was mad, he had the patience of Job. The patience of Job." The journey round the room going on and on, getting lost on the voyage. "Who is *that*?" and the shock from a sharp rap on the door.

"Only me, dear, Mrs Grimpen. I got your few things. Hope everything's all right, can I come in?"

"Of course, Mrs Grimpen. Sorry, didn't hear you coming. There you are," the tall heavily built woman stood there with the basket on her arm. "I am grateful," Lena said.

The basket on the table. "And I hope everything's right, Mrs Stevens." Following her to the kitchen, sitting waiting whilst Lena put away the few groceries she had brought, studying this tall, thin, nervous old woman.

"All right, dear?"

"Yes, how much do I owe you, Mrs Grimpen? Come along into the other room, warmer there."

Finding her purse, paying her.

"Let me make you a cup of tea," Lena said, even smiled, adding, "you seem to have been making all the cups of tea. Make yourself comfortable. I thought I heard your husband going out a short time ago," being normal again, shutting out, forgetting, slipping quietly from the room, leaving Mrs Grimpen seated, her folded arms glad to be free of the heavy basket that she had carried all the way from Fulham.

And Mrs Grimpen thought Mrs Stevens looked much better today, and accepted the tea, and they drank together.

"If at any time, Mrs Stevens, there's anything at all I can do, you only have to ask me. And Grimpy hopes you *will* have dinner with us coming Sunday."

"Can I think about it?"

"Of course."

"More tea?"

"No thanks. It was lovely, and now, if you'll excuse me, I must go, Grimpy will be back any minute now, and he always likes me to be *there* when he gets back from a job."

Mrs Stevens rose with her, accompanied her to the door, saying, "My husband was just like that, Mrs Grimpen. Always glad when I got back from my shopping. Couldn't bear me out of his sight."

"*Fancy.*"

"Yes, dear. I've just been sitting there thinking about it all."

"But try not to, dear, try not to. You must think of tomorrow now."

Opening the door, seeing her out, continuing the conversation until Mrs Grimpen finally passed from sight, and a final call before she shut the door.

"I *have* been thinking of tomorrow, dear, most of this day."

Echoes in the hall, a closed door.

"Strange to think that this house will be torn to the ground before the spring," a sudden thought of this, and it always reminded her of the tiny cottage off the embankment, and such a change after those three basement rooms, "Somewhere behind Warren Street, think it was."

Thinking of the surprising shares, of going out, but coming back would be worst, nobody there. "Just imagine belonging to nobody," she thought. Seeing him everywhere, sitting in his favourite chair, sitting under the window, pacing the room, listening to her reading, watching her as she sewed, the eternal cigarettes and the smoke-laden room. "The Grimpens will go, too, together," it made some things different. "The strangest morning I ever lived through," waking up, shutting one's eyes, refusing to look. But it *was* there, and it was empty. "I'd like to fly from this bloody room."

The mirror again, seeing it there, stood on the open desk, the thing pulling, forcing her to go, sit, look in at what looked out.

"Christ! I look terrible."

Another knock, registering it, not moving, but waiting. Would it come again?

A tapping sound, and then the voice, "Are you there, Mrs Stevens?"

"Come in," she said, pushed the mirror into a drawer, got up, closed the desk, hurried to the door, and her first thought, "Oh no. Her *again*."

"Yes, what is it, Mrs Grimpen?" flustered and showing it, and Mrs Grimpen not coming in, but with hands hidden behind an apron saying, "There's a gentleman down below, dear, called to see you."

"A gentleman. What gentleman?"

"Says his name is Cruickshank, Mrs Stevens, and I think I've got the name right. Says he came from Putney."

"Putney? Cruickshank, Cruickshank, Cruick—" and then the shout, "Don't stand *here*, Mrs Grimpen, come *in*," pulling her in, facing her, "what is this?"

"It's all right, dear, it's only a man, and a little man at that. An old man."

"Well?"

"Wants to see you, dear."

"What *about*?"

"I don't know, Mrs Stevens, he's waiting downstairs with Grimpy. Shall I tell him to come up?"

But Lena was looking in an opposite direction, remembering. "Then crawl to him if you want."

When she once more faced the woman in the room her mouth was half open, and nothing came out.

"What's the matter with the creature?" Mrs Grimpen asked herself. And then, "He's waiting, dear."

"Is he?"

"Yes. Shall I tell him to come *up*?"

"Yes, Mrs Grimpen, do that, of course, send him up, I never expected this, I don't even understand, Cruickshank, Cruickshank . . ."

The Grimpen utterance was leaden. "I said that, dear, Mr Cruickshank. I'll tell him to come up right away."

"Yes, yes, you do that, Mrs Grimpen. Thank you . . ." seeing her out again, watching her descend, and muttering to herself, "How odd, how very *odd*. Him. It's twenty years ago, what on earth, I . . ." rushing to the bathroom, tidying herself up, repeating aloud "What is this, what is this?"

And then the steps on the stairs.

20

Cruickshank stood at the top of the stairs, watched Nellie
precede his visitor down to the hall, then turned quickly and
shut the door. The moment he sat down he was hit by mis-
giving. He sat erect directly facing three miniatures, and
they were pretty, one after the other. His gaze then shifted
to the chef d'œuvre just under his hand. And he had been so
concentrated on his task. The wrong kind of surprise, he
told himself as he looked down the serried ranks of the best
matchboxes Portugal could boast. It was more than a task, it
was a mission. Cruickshank mused. Why should he go?
Simple goodness had trapped him, and in this moment he
couldn't find the answer, even as he seemed to hear the tall
woman speaking to him all over again, the operative words
predominant.

"So on her own now, sir, it would be nice for her to see
somebody."

The card on the table, staring at it, twenty years old. The
musing continued.

"Hardly knew them, seen them on three fugitive
occasions, years ago, years and years. I do remember, but
why *me*? Do I have to go?"

How embarrassing simple goodness could be? Under this
swift realization Cruickshank knew he couldn't settle down,
and got up and paced the room. And he threw out the words
that became the immediate lifebelt.

"I'll think about it."

Matchboxes apart, he had his duty to do. After which there
was the further diversion from a fixed rhythm. He *had* to
think of Aunt Beth. Suppose he did go off to Chelsea, and in

his absence she rang up, a distinct possibility since Aunt Beth was renowned for her strange moments, uprooting fixed positions by quirk of character.

Cruickshank sat down again, Aunt Beth now securely fixed in his mind. "Yes. I'll have to think about it. I've been caught out by her so often." The ritual of lighting up another cheroot, another adjustment of the pince-nez, a very fixed glance at the assembly of bright colours, devouring the table, the air itself, the whole room. He sat back with folded arms. A pity he hadn't asked the tall lady if the Stevens had a telephone in the house. Yes, he would have to give the thing a serious think.

Cruickshank had never done a stroke of work in his whole life, and at seventy looked well on it, thanks to the devotion of his two aged aunts. Aunt Tabitha had gone, but Aunt Beth had remained. They had their differences, one of which Cruickshank always remembered. Whilst his Aunt Tabitha had sometimes raised questions as to where the money came from, Aunt Beth for her part was quite content, asked no questions, raised no issues, her sole contentment and satisfaction lying in the one clear fact that the Cruickshank money was actually *there*. It had worried Cruickshank at one time, but now, with her sudden departure to East Sheen cemetery, no trace of a Cruickshank conscience now remained. He lived his life quietly, privately, nobody worried him, and there never seemed an occasion for him to worry anybody. And this fact had its own consolations. He was still lust borne, and amply satisfied. Nellie had been obliging, submissively so, since her shrewd side had scented the smell of lucre, even at its great distance, and, like Aunt Beth, she knew it was *there*. He had his club, his friends, he moved around, he kept abreast of the whole scene, often went to exhibitions, liking to be seen on such sociable occasions. He had at one time owned a small gallery, it provided a status of a kind, and, metaphorically speaking, he often rubbed his hands together with the satisfaction that the Ronda had so often provided. Lost in contemplation, one hand moving about the table, and caress after caress for each fragment of colour that made up the whole, his mind was still full of his recent visitor, carrying that s o s in the shape of a twenty-year-old postcard, posted from this very flat. And on the spur of the moment he pressed the bell on his desk, and moments later heard Nellie charging upstairs, and finally pushing in the door.

"Yes, Mr Cruickshank?" she asked, offering him a pretty smile, and she had wrapped so many of them round this little man with the cash.

"That woman that called, Nellie."

"Yes, Mr Cruickshank," Nellie said, and no Christian name terms as yet, a hard fact that sometimes depressed Cruickshank. He got up, held her hand, the smile stayed, and he felt her sudden squeeze of it, and in it the beautiful glow of sudden assurance, as she said again, "Yes, Mr Cruickshank. What is it, sir?"

"I've been put in a rather invidious position, Nellie. I met some people many years ago, chap painted a bit, I showed a few of his pictures, not very good, really, but now the man has died, a sad business, and his widow is very much on her own, and to quote the lady, *very* much on her own, really alone. I said I'd go over there and see her. What should I do?"

Nellie positively beamed, said, "Then go, Mr Cruickshank."

"You know what my aunt's like, Nellie."

Nellie's lips slowly parted and came together again, her brow puckered, for Nellie was actually thinking. "Fancy asking *me*."

And Cruickshank standing over her, as she leaned down to admire the bright arrangement on the table, "Well?"

"If the lady would be very glad if you did, you should go, Mr Cruickshank."

"Thank you, Nellie," he said, and dismissed her with a wave of the hand, whilst she supplied the final smile, shut the door, and hurried back to daily routine.

At least twice weekly Cruickshank linked arms with his

Aunt Beth, and she staggered about Knightsbridge, wielding a stout stick, and looking nothing like her ninety-odd years. Cruickshank considered this an important duty to be done, for he never looked her in the eye without a quick glance beyond it, which always landed him at the end of a road where the money bounced.

"I'd better go. Get it over, done with. But I am sorry about it, of course."

Promptly at half past twelve o'clock, he had lunch downstairs with Nellie. He liked Nellie very much, he liked looking at her, there, right under his eyes. What a miracle the whole thing had been. He studied her. She had improved, she was learning fast. How delicately she ate.

"Nellie?"

Knife and fork down at once, and Nellie sitting back, saying, "Yes?"

"You're happy here, dear?"

"Course," she said, and there were occasions when her utter promptness provided a shock.

"Good. I'm glad."

"You've remembered the date, Mr Cruickshank?"

Cruickshank clapped hands and said he did, it was right at the tip-top of his mind. How on earth would he forget a thing so important?

"I am glad."

"My aunt's going to Cornwall for the week, on the 12th, I believe, so I thought we might do Brighton, dear."

She loved the "dear" and pouted her lips, and then cried, "Lovely." And then they went on with their lunch. Nellie was even learning to cook.

"So much for an East End stray," he thought, "lost in the West End."

"I've decided to go over and see that unfortunate lady, Nellie."

"Glad, sir. You'll be glad, too, I mean after you've been."

At eighteen Nellie was competent, diplomatic, dutiful, and always willing.

"If my aunt *should* ring, Nellie, you know what to do."

Bowing her head abruptly, half her hair fell on to her plate, and even Mr Cruickshank smiled.

"Right," he said.

"And Mr Dowden will be here Thursday evening for dinner, Nellie. Canasta."

"I do know," she said. "Finished, Mr Cruickshank," on which he got up and left the dining room, and his wife-to-be to her own resources. "*Right*." He saw her clearing the table, glanced at his watch, went to his room and changed. "Damned extraordinary thing to have happened," and as he fixed a bright tie to the collar of a trendy shirt, thought, "Wonder if it's about money?"

So many things seemed to be about money these days. Putting on his trousers he suddenly wondered if Stevens had gone on painting, a particular effort clear in his eye, all of a sudden remembered. And muttering whilst he carefully brushed his hair. "Small still life, I think. Didn't even have ground," and wondering yet again about Stevens.

"I'm off, Nellie dear," he said, and he took the first stair, and Nellie popped out from her ground floor room, and waited for him to reach the bottom.

"You know the gen," he said, as he reached the door, and Nellie said yes she did, and rather admired Mr Cruickshank in her shy, secretive way, so in on the scene. At his age. The rest could be a big laugh. Easy.

He hailed a taxi in the road, settled himself in, "Chesil Place, *nineteen*."

"Right, guv."

Cruickshank threw his head back, fingers reached his pocket, and out came the inevitable.

"Nice smell, guv."

But his passenger hadn't registered the compliment. The car pulled up with a jerk.

"Chesil Place, guv."

Cruickshank got up, searched for his purse, paid the correct fare, added a small tip, didn't look at the driver, then turned away and approached the tall, rather dilapidated-looking house. He made a slight grimace as he reached the front steps, his sensitive eye noting the almost paint-stripped door. Cruickshank not only had a quick, sensitive eye, but a dog's nostrils. There was no bell, and there didn't even appear to be a knob on the door. He looked up, and his eye came slowly down, he got the whole house and the feel of it in a split second. And then he rapped on the door.

"Odd that I should be standing here," he thought, just as Mrs Grimpen opened the door, and she didn't think it odd at all, but was glad.

"You, sir," she said, as he stepped into the hall. "I am glad, Mr Cruickshank, do her good to see somebody, poor dear."

But Cruickshank, standing there facing the long staircase, noting a general shabbiness of approach to the upper part of the house, the broken, carpetless stairs, the great crack in the wall, the now faded paint and distemper, could only think of impermanence, an end.

"This way, sir," Mrs Grimpen said, warmly inviting, and he followed her down the basement steps. "Just a word or two, Mr Cruickshank, shan't keep you more than a tick," and he followed her inside, on which Grimpen himself rose from his chair as his wife introduced him.

"My husband, sir," and to Grimpy, "this is the gentleman from Putney, Grimpy."

"Glad you managed it, sir," Grimpen said, on which Cruickshank waved a hand, dismissing the observation, saying, "Top of the house, isn't it?"

"That's right, sir. And my husband will show you the way. Grimpy!"

"This way," Grimpen said, leading the way up to the hall, and a running commentary on the way, "Have to excuse the place, Mr Cruickshank, but I'm sure you understand," studying Cruickshank as he preceded him up the stairs. "House going to pot, sir, but a lot of things are going to the dogs these days," to which Cruickshank made no reply, merely nodding, and finally they reached the top landing.

He put a gentle hand on the visitor's arm, was suddenly confidential. "She's been going up and down these stairs for the past hour, sir, never did see such going up and down, carrying down empty bottles. 'Spect she's a bit tired now, though I feel she'll be glad of a visitor any time, Mr Cruickshank."

"Here?" asked Cruickshank, pointing, and Grimpen said emphatically, "Yes," low in his throat.

"I'll be off," and he left the visitor standing outside the door.

21

She was seated in the armchair when the first light tap came to the door, resting after the effort, the resolution carried out, tactically, quietly and wholly unaware that the Grimpens had heard it all. Her head was bent forward, and she studied the hands in her lap. And was still preoccupied when the second tap came, a little louder this time, on which she came erect at once, sitting forward, listening, and finally a loud knock.

She was on her feet at once. "Who is that?"

"Ivor Cruickshank."

"Who?"

"Mr *Cruick*shank."

"Cruickshank. What do you want?" stiffening, staring at the door, feeling confused, and when the second loud rap came she hurried to open it.

To be kept standing in semi-darkness, in a very draughty house, and one that he felt was giving out the first smell of utter decay, seemed even more odd. When the door opened he was unable to speak, and hardly able to conceal his surprise at what he saw. So, after twenty years, old man and old woman confronted each other. He then wondered if he would be asked in, as for a moment they confronted each other, and was relieved when finally she opened it wide, saying, "You had better come in."

"Thank you," and Cruickshank stepped into the room.

"You're the last person I expected," she said, showing him to the settee she had swiftly cleared of the things scattering it. "Do sit down."

"What is this?" she asked herself, as Cruickshank sat down.

He was quiet, casual, saying, "Happened to be passing this way, heard about it. I'm sorry."

"Are you?" she asked abruptly, groping, uncertain, quite bewildered by this unexpected visit by someone from the past. She sat opposite him in the chair. "Who told you?"

"Shall we say a bird?" he replied, and followed up with, "d'you mind?" a hand to his pocket, and she didn't, and it made him feel more relaxed, though the message circled his mind, "What the hell am I doing here?"

She got up. "I'm sorry, do let me have your coat," Lena said, and helped him off with it, making a quick note of his apparel, this small man with the white hair cut close to the bone, the bright silk shirt, the brighter tie. She looked at the cheroot in his hand. "Hardly know what to say, Mr Cruickshank, such a surprise, it all happened years ago, I simply don't know what to say," lay his coat over the iron bed, his hat behind the door.

"You've changed," he said, as she sat down.

"We've both *changed*," Lena said, and in a voice more positive than his own, "for a moment or two I didn't even recognize you. How are things with you?" groping again, trying to find a way in, a reason for his call, trying to be normal in a most surprising moment.

"Much water under the bridge."

"Great waves," she said.

"I have thought of you on occasion," he said, "wondered how you were getting on."

She hated this, sensed the lie, and she tried not to show it, but he was quick to realize an atmosphere.

"Very sad," and then stuttering it, "Lena, isn't it?"

"It's a long time since the morning you asked me to call you Ivor."

When he smiled, she did her duty and smiled back at him, feeling an immense relief when she saw him glance at his watch, hoping that he would get up, go. She hadn't asked him to come, and didn't really want him, felt suspicious about it, never a friendship, a mere passing acquaintanceship. She studied the old man before her, a rather pinched

355

expression on his face, the lips tight in tight features. An old man in trendy clothes. And she still registered his close scrutiny of her as she had taken his hat and coat.

"You've rather caught me out," she said, lowering her head, "please excuse the room."

"Perhaps I should have written you, Mrs Stevens. My apologies. But I didn't call to see the room you are sitting in, but to see you."

She felt relief from this, got a hold on an unasked-for situation, but knew him as restless and uncertain as she, then surprised herself.

"Would you like some coffee, Mr Cruickshank?"

"Thank you," and she left him sitting there. "As tall and lean as ever," and he watched her go out. Rather haggard-looking. It seemed inconceivable to him that they had once sat together in his small gallery, that first adventure with Cruickshank money, a spurt of vanity, "the costly toy".

"We actually were on Christian name terms. She hasn't mentioned him at all," and he speculated on that score, and then she returned with the coffee.

"Black or white, Mr Cruickshank?"

"Black. No sugar, thank you." He drank his coffee, thinking, "Shall I? No, perhaps not," and then it leaped out, in spite of. "Tell me about him."

The words nailed something close to the ground, something ended and done with, something that was real, and now she was facing it all again, sat close to this man.

He handed her his cup. "Very nice, thanks."

He leaned forward, fingers drumming on his knees, "Seemed odd to me, Mrs Stevens, standing on your door-step, leaping across those years. I'm sure you'll be sorry to leave here."

The words shocked her, and her expression asked questions.

"The lady downstairs was telling me about it," he continued. "How very unfortunate. Let's hope something turns up for you, somehow it nearly always does, in the end."

Her own clipped words were, "It does indeed."

She hated this room, herself, being caught out like this, trying to avoid the occasional searching glance from the man on the settee.

"What happened?"

"A pure accident, Mr Cruickshank, it's all over, finished, and I don't want to talk about it," and now she leaned close, and stressed with, "I'm still trying to tell myself that it was *real*."

And again he exclaimed, though this time automatically, that he was sorry, and fixed his eye on her, waited.

It was time to be calm outside, explode inside, an unwanted resurrection.

"I would have to be out shopping the day it happened," she began. "Seems it was all over in a matter of minutes, so I'm told. When I got back from my usual weekly shopping my husband was lying dead in the kitchen. A newly filled paraffin stove he was carrying from the kitchen exploded. Only a miracle the house didn't go up. Some of the things down the passage are *ruined*," and flung the final word.

"How awful," he said, and getting to the root, the bone, "still working then?"

The shout surprised him. "He never stopped working," she replied.

"What determination, what patience you had," Cruickshank said.

She felt quite unable to answer that, and her head went back, her hands fell heavily to her lap, and her expression hardened. She felt furious, and he would never know the questions that hammered inside her. "Bloody curiosity, no more than that." And savagely under her breath, "Still *working*," then echoing it, imitating a small man's voice. As though he shouldn't be working. "What the hell's he doing here, who told him, what for, *why*?"

He saw her stiff and angry, and shifted his glance, looked towards the window. Who would speak first?

"Still got that little picture," Cruickshank said, "remember, time ago."

"Have you?" she asked, sitting up, "I'm glad."

357

She glanced at the clock, hoped he would have another look at his watch.

Cruickshank *was* sorry, but the gesture died under the barrage, the rage stayed.

"Caught out like *this*," she told herself, "of all days, the damned mess of the place, wish to God he'd *go*."

"Did he ever exhibit after I closed down?" he asked.

"Once only. Nothing happened," she said, each word ice-wrapped.

And Cruickshank musing. "Shall I go? Perhaps I ought to, why the hell did I come at all?"

The whole embarrassing situation arising out of a gesture of simple goodness, the feeling of one woman for another. But he sat on, he felt that eventually she would give, melt a little, even against the knowledge, the hard fact. "Extraordinary, must confess I never saw anything actually exciting about what he did. It was only a whisper, but the signal seemed real enough," and the musing was over.

"I'll go if you want me to, Mrs Stevens," Cruickshank said, looking into her eyes, saw that she had been crying, understood, and he thought it would do her good to open out, let it all go. "Wonder what she'll do now, collect the pension, the final touch, vanish."

He was restless again, he looked towards the door, and he did not expect what followed.

"Please," Lena said, "please."

"Understood," he replied. "It is Lena, isn't it?"

Her name loud in the room perplexed her, and he was even more surprised when she put a hand on his arm, saying, "I'm sorry, Mr Cruickshank, I didn't expect you, you should have warned me, I feel caught out. How did you know?"

"Just a bird," he said, "it's not all that important. I came, and that's it."

He seemed to see Mrs Grimpen tall in the room, back in Putney. He gently refused her offer of another cup of coffee.

"It's terrible in a way," she said, "knowing."

He sat up, "Knowing what?"

"Just knowing," Lena replied.

"Nothing will ever be the same again, don't you feel that yourself?"

"Were you in London during the war?" she asked.

"No. I'd two aged aunts to look after, and we were in Cornwall for most of the time."

"Nice."

And Cruickshank remembered how, years ago, they had sat together on the morning of his first adventure. "Even on Christian name terms, too. Odd, she hasn't mentioned him at all," and he again speculated on that score.

"Tell me about him," he said.

The words nailed something to the ground.

"Seemed so odd to me, standing on your doorstep, I'm sure you'll be sorry to leave here, Mrs Stevens."

The words choked her, her sudden expression asked questions.

"The lady down below was telling me about it," he continued. "Very unfortunate, and I'm sorry. Ah well. Somehow, something always turns up in the end," he concluded, and she hated the platitude.

"It does indeed."

And again she was hating the room and hating herself, caught out like this.

"You gave up the little gallery?" Lena said.

"I did indeed," he replied, and sighed a little, remembering the occasion, a sensible decision.

"I wasn't surprised when it happened," she said, "just shocked. Still am."

"It's always sad when the root goes," he said.

"Nothing was ever the same after the Eldon washout," Lena said, adding rather sharply, "I didn't see you there."

And he had the answer pat. "In Cornwall at the time, I should think."

"Not that it matters. One learns to adapt to situations, and we did. We were well drilled. Accepting's the thing, it often lightens the load. The times I've sat here waiting for him to come in, it was like somebody emerging from the confessional box."

And Cruickshank thought, "And I'm sitting here, listening," and sat on. "Do her good, if she talks her head off."

In a shaky voice, she said, "I just *felt* something was wrong, *felt* it would happen. And only a few days ago we had a terrible row. We were both drunk, I'm afraid. The last three years it's been nothing but drink. And in the end I gave in and started on it myself. Sometimes we took it in turns, it helped, blotted out the fact that the other was there, close, it made a change. It was a relief to get out once a week, and though I dreaded returning, knowing what I'd find, I just couldn't resist bringing back a bottle, a really wilful act on my part, but it served its purpose, it blotted out things one didn't want to think about. I knew that nothing was happening in that bloody room, nothing, sitting there moping, it disgusted me. There were occasions when he literally crawled back here. I wouldn't have minded so much if he had found other interests, but he was so limited, and when finally he stopped going out altogether I gave it up. I've talked my head off on occasions, and I still think he didn't even see me, know I was *there*. In the end I gave up asking what he was doing. The vanishing act morning after morning just ceased to register with me."

"What patience," Cruickshank said.

"Bled to death in the end. Sometimes I've gone out, not wanting to come back, dreaming about it, a whole night thinking of it, and then in the end I gave in. My iron resolutions broke the moment I came in through the door. And the relief when I closed it was back again, the look he gave me, and that *smile*. I could never have refused him."

Cruickshank, suffering a temporary embarrassment, stood up, looked directly at Lena, sent the message. It amused her, and she followed him to the door.

"Next the kitchen, Mr Cruickshank," she said.

"Thank you," and he went out, and on his short journey took everything in, and in the tiny bathroom noted the sparsity of furnishing, a worn look about things. And leaving it he noticed two other doors, and one with its key in the lock. The language of shabbiness was new to him. He returned to the sitting room and at once sat down.

"All right?"

"Yes, thank you."

When for the second time he glanced at his watch she felt he would go, and he watched her watch.

"Warwickshire man, wasn't he?" asked Cruickshank.

"A pity he didn't remain one. Should never have hit London. The only occasion that he went back there was for some memorial service, his people were builders in a small way. I often asked him to get away from all this, but he remained stubborn," and she told him the reason why. "A terrible blow to him," she continued, "to lose your whole family, a mine, they say . . ."

"Dear dear. Dear dear dear. So much happening then, one just couldn't take it all in."

"It did end, and that's what mattered," Lena said, "and when it did it was so surprising that people were almost unaware of the calm that followed. It left gaps in people's minds," and when she looked up he had turned his head, was looking towards the window.

"I'm not keeping you?" she said.

"No no no," nervously, "not at all, Mrs Stevens," unduly fussy in a moment. "I ought to go," he told himself, "no purpose can be served here, none. Yes, I must get off." Suddenly he asked the question, and then regretted it.

"No family?" he said, quietly, catching her eye.

Her searching, almost angry look upset him, and he hated himself for it. He gave a slight cough.

"No. Lying down and standing up for a person has different meanings for different people. We had contrary views about it. It's not the end."

And Cruickshank stuttered, "The end?"

"*Flesh.*"

"Oh."

"Tell me, Mr Cruickshank, what was the name of the bird?"

"Name of the bird, the bird . . . oh, I see. I'd rather not say," he said.

"I'd rather you did," she replied. "You're the last person I expected to see today. Who?"

"The lady downstairs, a Mrs Grimpen."

"Oh God!"

"A well-intentioned lady," he went on, "and I'm rather afraid I've broken her confidence. I just did what she asked me to do."

"I shan't pursue it."

"I'm glad," he replied.

"My husband wrote you on two or three occasions," Lena said, "but there was no reply. It got like that towards the close. But I expect you were away, you do get about a lot."

"It's years ago," he said.

"Letters became less and less, I never understood why, and I certainly don't want to *now*. But it burrowed deep, and Clem was never very good at hiding things. I think he only once mentioned it. 'It's like being left out,' he said, 'like finding yourself on the wrong road.' It broke something in me, and I began to feel like he did, left out. Strangely enough, we never again went out together, and the most pleasant memories I still have are of the times when we did, like our nightly walks along the embankment, we often thought of the river as friend. Even went out during the bombings," and then the utter surprise, he heard her laugh for the first time. "Often to the extreme annoyance of vigilant wardens. The remoteness of former friends only drew us closer to each other. *Things* began to interest us, and after a while a certain regret faded into the air. Sometimes I just went off on my own, left him with the bottle. But I always worried about it. We fed on each other's weaknesses. Christ! The times I've held him up, literally so. His very dependence on me gave me a certain pleasure, but in the end it palled. It was almost a relief when he started to drink, it made a change. First it was good, cheered him up, and later it became necessity, and finally the lifebelt. It took him on journeys away from himself. We both had our due ration of cowardice. A sudden clapping of hands in this room would have sounded like thunder."

"I wonder if the echo of a laugh ever sounded here," thought Cruickshank.

"The room would get tighter and tighter, and even the things in it seemed to have their own sessions, staring us back as we stared at them. Then something happened, I started to read to him, a tenseness would go, and he even became very interested, and in the end used to read to me, often at night. Frustration melted away, we had become absorbed in other people's lives. And what a respite, it drowned our own."

"Verging on self-pity," thought Cruickshank, and gave a quick glance at the clock.

"I never lay down at night without listening to the parrot in me asking the same questions, deep within myself. 'Will something happen? When? Will he do something that *pleases* him?'"

Cruickshank's hand came up, the watch spoke. "I ought to go, Mrs Stevens," he said, in a kind of urgent way, as though he had heard Nellie signalling all the way from Putney, or heard his aunt, irritable at the telephone, asking why, and just waiting.

"You've been talking to yourself for far too long," he said.

"Have I?"

"What will you do now?" he asked.

And she echoed it, "What will I do now?" and it drove home to her the purposelessness of this journey. "Fatuous," she told herself. "You could ask the same question of somebody standing on the scaffold."

And the thin thread of vanity at last leapt out, and she half rose from the chair.

"Two doors down the passage," she said, "the key's in the lock."

"May I? Thank you," Cruickshank said, and got up and left the room.

She heard his steps, the key turning in the lock, the opening door, he was moving about in the room.

"What will I do now? What the *hell* does he think I'll do?"

He had left the door wide open behind him, was now half bent, studying the work along the wall. And she never expected his sudden call.

"I've *seen* these," Cruickshank said.

"So've *I*."

He hadn't expected this, and it hit the room like a gunshot. After which a silence, and only the chair creaked when he sat down. And he passed from one canvas to another. Meanwhile she watched the clock, and now regretted her impromptu hint to one who would soon go.

"Damn Mrs Grimpen. Why didn't she mind her own business?" she thought.

He remained for a full half hour in the workroom, and she had almost forgotten he was there. And then she heard him moving about the room again. The Cruickshank she was thinking of now was years away, indulging in his first adventure with the "expensive toy", and so very conscious of this that he tended on occasion to be as demonstrative as a street guide. She remembered the things he had discussed. Thirty years younger, and full of it, the man who knew the answers, the lot, and she supposed he could roll them off even in his sleep. She was lost in this contemplation when he walked into the room, a leisurely pace, as though the clock, and the watch on his wrist, had assumed a secondary importance. She wanted to say "Well?" but refrained, hoped he would *not* light yet another cheroot, the air was already somewhat dense with the results of them. He clasped hands, leaned forward on the settee, and he hoped she would say something. She did.

"You needn't tell me," Lena said.

"*The sketches of the old woman with the basket are good, but there's nothing after that, nothing. No growth. Just a series of false starts.*"

"Did she ever sit for him?" he asked, and the abruptness of question momentarily bewildered her.

"Who sat for *who*?"

"*The nudes are positively ugly.*"

"The old lady with the loaded basket," Cruickshank said.

"What a silly question, Mr Cruickshank. Why should she? He wasn't as insensitive as all *that*."

"I like the preliminary sketches, but not the nudes," Cruickshank said.

"So do I."

"He seemed to have a thing about roads, hardly a landscape without one."

"I did myself," Lena said.

"*Repetitive, sometimes even derivative, where the hell was he travelling? One or two smaller canvases I found interesting, but I saw them ages ago. She's not without a degree of imagination herself, didn't she* know?"

"He certainly *tried*," Cruickshank said.

"I'm glad you think that," Lena said.

"*When did aimlessness reach in, I wonder?*"

As if she had sensed in an instant what he was thinking, she announced casually that some of the work had been thrown into the Thames, and it made Cruickshank sit up.

"Not really, Mrs Stevens, *surely . . .*"

"I didn't realize it at first—no, that's not right, perhaps I did, and I refused to look it in the face. It's not everything, anyhow, and Clem was always a *person* to me. I only started to learn myself when I was turned forty. I'd lived a simple, wholly ineffective life until then. I felt another person the moment I hit London. Nor had I ever actually seen a man working as I did that morning, when he was stood on the embankment. It opened a door for me. I stood watching him for nearly half an hour before he noticed I was there. *And* I liked what I saw," and then passionately, desperately, "and I liked him, and that was the beginning and the end."

"I admire your loyalty to him," Cruickshank said.

And Cruickshank was suddenly back in the room, staring at it all again.

"*Loyalty almost to the limits of stupidity.*"

"In the end one gets the answer," she said, "one may wait

ages for it, nevertheless it comes, it's there, and you can't dodge it. It saddens one."

"*Excellent colour sense, but where the hell's the rest?*"

"He did nothing at all in the past two years, I mean *nothing*, and then I knew, and I knew he knew," Lena said.

Cruickshank was sat right forward, almost off the settee, and he became absorbed in what she was saying, absorbed in how she *looked*, in this very moment.

"*A bloody lifetime, a lifetime. Incredible to me.*"

"Just as sad for him," Cruickshank said, and received the responsive bullet.

"Are you telling me something?" she asked aggressively.

"Perhaps I ought to go," he said.

"Perhaps you ought," but the moment he moved she exclaimed, "Wait." And he waited.

"You didn't really like what you saw," Lena said.

He came half way, said, "I liked some of them."

"*A little feeling, a little imagination might have made the difference.*"

It had to come out, and he knew it would.

"It was agonizing sometimes, seeing the whole thing, watching it, and being dumb, bloody dumb about it. I didn't even mind the waste, the drink, and the money that went on it. It's terrible when you know what a disappointed man is feeling, and you can't find the right words, nothing—there never was at times like that, just a squeeze of the hand, a fact accepted, and then the usual withdrawal, and then feeding on the damned fact. How could I ask a man to give it up, how could I?"

"You're an imaginative and intelligent woman," was all Cruickshank could say.

She seemed far away, and he was quick to notice the sudden softening of her features, the changed expression.

"One of the nice things I will always remember about Clem is the morning he first took me to see a Rembrandt, and I've never forgotten that. 'The colour,' he said, 'the *colour*.' An impact, those faces, the power of it all, the iron will, the discipline."

And Cruickshank responded to this outburst, the warmth in it, the sheer eagerness as the memory reached out to it.

"There's a great deal of sheer competence about," he said, "only a few can make such grand gestures."

"*Yes.*"

Cruickshank stared about this room, looked at this woman, sat there so quiet, relaxed, and he knew he would never fathom the feeling that lay behind it all. In the wasteland he saw a curious mixture of loyalty and stupidity.

"*How long has she known, when did she find out? What happened then?*"

"When he slipped away from this house a few nights ago, I begin to think he went out to ask himself the questions he could never have asked in this room, could never have looked me directly in the face. Perhaps he got the answer. But I'll never know, never."

It was time to go, and he knew it was, and got up and crossed the room.

"I'm glad I came," he said.

"Are you?"

And he couldn't answer that, nor the observation that followed it.

"You were right," Lena said, but the words broke free only after a great effort.

He faltered, "I don't understand," Cruickshank said.

"You've been telling yourself you were right ever since you returned to this room. Perhaps telling yourself how stupid I've been. He had his big dream, and I admired him for it. People don't so easily escape from their own illusions, you just live with them. I don't regret anything I've done, nor I'm certain did he. I knew my husband was a failure three long years ago, but you don't just walk out on a person just because they turn out to be second rate, and those are the two words that were written on your face the moment I opened the door to you. There's more to a man than that. You were quite right, wondering why on earth you ever came here, and I suppose I've been thinking the very same thing. It would be mean of me not to say thank you," she said, and got up and followed him slowly to the door. "Mrs Grimpen's kind thought isn't lost on me."

Looking at her as she opened the door for him, Cruickshank could only think of two lives, and longed to say how much he admired her loyalty through all that time. "Something beautiful about it," he thought, shutting out of sight the wreck of the room he stood in. He then extended a hand, which she took and held, and looked at him, and knew she would not see him again.

"Goodbye, Mrs Stevens," and after a momentary pause, "I'll try and drop in again some time," gave the hand a slight squeeze, and pushed wide the door.

"Goodbye, Mr Cruickshank," Lena said, knowing he wouldn't, and in the final moment even managed to force a smile. They went outside, stood for a moment at the top of the stairs, looked at each other, but said nothing, and then he turned away and went slowly down the stairs, and she stood there, watching him go, listening to echoing footsteps in the hall, the banging of the front door, then came in again, put a hand on the knob, hesitated a second before she finally closed it. She thought it the most final thing she had ever done, and stood there, hesitant, as though unwilling to turn round, to discover that there was nobody there, and never would be, that she was at last alone. Unlike Cruickshank she could only think of another kind of wreck.

"I'll never know, never."

And she didn't want the answer.